MAELSTROM

THE INFINITY ENGINES BOOK II

ANDREW HASTIE

D1738550

To my beautiful wife and daughters, thank you for everything.

To my father, may you rest in peace.

A x

Other books in the Infinity Engines universe.

The Infinity Engines

1. Anachronist

2. Maelstrom

3. Eschaton

4. Aeons

5. Tesseract

6. Contagion

Infinity Engines Origins

Chimæra

Changeling

Infinity Engines Missions

1776

1888

1

ALONE

[Boju, Chu. Date: 9.494]

Josh knelt staring at the space where Caitlin should have been, his hands still clutching at the grass. He could smell her perfume lingering in the air, feel the warmth of her body on the flattened ground.

Instinctively, he hit the rewind on his tachyon, and the world around him spun back two minutes. It made no difference; she was still gone, and there was no stable trail to follow.

He couldn't bring himself to leave that moment, even though his instincts were screaming to follow, to take action, to pursue the smallest trace of her — his heart told him to stay, to wait, just in case she came back.

The sound of Sun Tzu's cavalry came thundering across the valley. It seemed louder than before; when she'd sat there eating noodles and telling him about how the battle played out. Josh struggled to remember what she'd said; he hadn't been paying too much attention to the words, just the shape that her mouth made as she spoke them.

He waited, desperately hoping to be wrong. Seconds

turned into minutes, and still there was no sign of her. A pall of smoke rose up the side of the valley bringing with it the metallic tang of cordite and gunpowder. Josh couldn't remember if Caitlin said they used guns and right now he didn't care — she was gone and he had no idea what to do next.

He could sense there had been some kind of temporal adjustment — a 'repair' as the colonel would've called it. It felt like he'd been disconnected from reality, like he'd changed channels on the TV and was watching some foreign movie without subtitles.

Josh tried to focus on the memories of the last few hours. They were becoming hazy and vague, even his carefully thought out dishes for the picnic were proving hard to remember. He looked down to where they'd been laid out on the blanket and realised that too had disappeared.

Down by the river the battle raged on. One of the mounted warriors caught sight of Josh and turned his horse towards him. The rider was clad in gold and red, his face hidden behind a demonic mask. The sun glinted off the plates of his armour as they bounced rhythmically against the horse's flanks, his hand a blur as it whipped his mount into a charge.

Watching the horse thunder towards him through the long grass, Josh decided it was time to leave. He estimated the distance between them and began to count down under his breath.

'Ten, nine, eight, seven...'

He looked around once more, feeling the drum of the hooves tearing up the ground as the horse bore down on him.

'Six, five, four, three...'

Josh opened his tachyon and dialled the coordinates for

the colonel's house, present day — it was the only other logical place for him to go now.

'Two, one... ready or not,' he muttered, flicking his middle finger at the warrior who was levelling a bow at him.

A second later an arrow ripped through the air where Josh should have been.

[>>]

2

PRESENT

[London. Date: Present Day]

For a moment, Josh thought he'd travelled into the future; that all their talk of him being the 'Paradox' may have finally come true.

Except that the date on his tachyon told him it wasn't.

He was in the present — at the frontier.

The colonel's house was gone. The whole street, Churchill Avenue and the Gardens, had been obliterated, replaced by enormous old skyscrapers that rose up into a sickly, smog-filled sky, like rusting hulks of an abandoned civilisation.

Dirty rain stung his face, pouring down through the lattice of corroded pipes that ran between the old tower blocks. Standing in the garbage-strewn alleyway, in the semi-darkness of their permanent shadow, Josh knew that something had gone badly wrong with the continuum.

Above the decrepit towers and nicotine-coloured clouds, Josh caught tiny glimpses of blue sky. Bird-like dots circled back and forth through the lower layers of cloud where the skyscrapers punched holes through the smog. They flew erratically amongst a network of distant walkways that stretched out between the buildings. Their movements were too unnatural to be birds, but Josh had no idea what kind of flying machines could do that — he wished he was up there.

A sudden noise brought him back down to earth. It was a feral sound, like a fox scavenging through bins, and it came from behind one of the many large metal pipes that burrowed into the ground around him.

Trying not to make a sound, Josh searched for something he could use as a weapon. The pockets of his travelling robes were empty except for the condoms, which he had optimistically acquired from an Antiquarian chemist, and there was nothing remotely useful in the sea of plastic crap that flowed around his feet.

The head of a large creature surfaced from a nearby pile of rubbish and hissed.

Josh tensed, feeling the adrenalin flood into his veins. It was huge, the largest cat he'd ever seen, or at least it had been once — its features were odd, distorted like the creature had been remade. The kind of thing the Animal Liberation types would rescue from a testing facility: half its scalp had been shaved, and there were steel bolts grafted onto the bare skull. He didn't have the time to find out why. Whatever they'd done to Frankencat, it hadn't improved the creature's mood — the size of its fangs gave Josh all the motivation he needed to start looking for an escape route.

There wasn't an obvious way out. Centuries of garbage had choked the alley, and wading through it made too much noise. It was obvious that no one came down to this level anymore. Josh wondered if the Churchill Avenue had ever existed.

There were more sounds from further down the alley — Frankencats like to hunt in packs.

Josh set his tachyon to the coordinates of the Chapter House and hit the button.

Nothing happened.

Frankencat licked his lips and moved out of the trash pile.

Josh tried the tachyon again — it was dead, and so was he.

'Yo offenda! U got rads?' shouted a voice from somewhere high above him.

'No tags, on he,' came an answer from another.

'No chip. Swear tru?'

'Tru as u, bro.'

'Now double trouble. Drones be buzzin,' warned a third.

Josh felt a sense of relief: he recognised gang slang — no matter how bizarre it sounded. He still fancied his chances with humans over re-engineered cats any day.

'Any chance of some help?' he shouted up to the unseen voices, trying not to sound too desperate.

A half-whispered argument broke out among the hidden gang members, too obscure and quiet for Josh to hear what they said. A minute later, something bounced across the garbage and landed between Josh and the prowling cat. It looked a lot like a pack of batteries wrapped around a battered old tin of dog food.

'Run, no-tag, RUN!' encouraged one of the voices.

Josh didn't need to be told twice. As the cat leapt out to attack the package, he took off in the opposite direction.

He hadn't gone more than a few metres when the bomb went off and an electrical discharge hit him squarely in the back. Every nerve in his body lit up as the static arced down his spine; then his legs gave way — as though someone had simply switched them off.

When Josh hit the floor, he couldn't feel a thing — his whole body had gone numb.

The others laughed as they clambered down through the pipes.

'Ha! No-tag runs like a crip!'

3

SIMILAR

'You find him where?'

'12-240, down on the base.'

'Scan?'

'No tag. No, nothin — cep tique ticker.'

'An jonny hats,' another giggled.

'Nearly scav meat.'

Everyone laughed. Josh listened quietly: he'd identified at least five different voices since he'd woken a few minutes earlier. He still couldn't move his legs. Whatever taser-bomb they'd used had knocked out his nervous system better than a night of tequila slammers.

'He no scender,' an older voice interrupted. 'Not a shade, neither.'

The aroma of charring meat drifted into Josh's nostrils, and his stomach growled. He was hungry, which meant he'd obviously been out for some time.

'He wake,' said a girl's voice.

A boot was inserted roughly under Josh's stomach and flipped him over. His eyes were clogged with dust and grit from laying face down on the floor and they watered as he struggled to blink away the grime, blurring the figures that sat around the fire in front of him.

As the feeling returned to his arms, he realised that they'd cable-tied his hands behind his back.

Josh's head swam when he tried to sit upright. The air was heavy and filled with dust which caught in his throat and he coughed so hard it made it difficult to catch his breath.

'Deadman's rattle,' hissed one of the group.

'Oxy,' instructed the older voice.

Someone held a mask over his nose and mouth, allowing Josh to take long, deep breaths of pure, sweet air until the coughing passed.

'Two U's,' instructed the elder. 'Max.'

They took the mask off and Josh's vision cleared. He seemed to be inside some kind of abandoned tube tunnel, the walls were made of rusted metal sheets bolted together like a ship's bulkhead. Over the fire, the charred remains of Frankencat rotated slowly on a spit. From the way the flames flickered Josh assumed there must be a steady flow of air running through the tunnel, and somewhere far off he thought he could hear the faint thrum of fans.

He was surrounded by a desperate gang of street kids, dressed in rags, their faces obscured by scarves and filter masks. Each of them held a home-made weapon out in front of them, their eyes wide with fear — some of them looked no older than eight or nine.

'Why no tag?' the elder voice asked from the shadows beyond the fire.

Josh's mouth was parched, and the cough returned when he tried to speak.

'LL, juice him.'

Someone placed a straw in Josh's mouth, and he sucked down a warm, sugary liquid that reminded him of an old blackcurrant squash. It was awful, like a hundred years passed its sell-by date, but it was enough to loosen the dust in his throat.

'What year is this?' he asked hoarsely.

There was a sharp intake of breath from the gang, as though Josh had just cursed all their mothers.

'Oldspeak,' whispered some in disbelief.

One of the larger boys stepped forward, putting his blade across Josh's neck and speaking in a slow staccato as if the words were a foreign language.

'You. Tell. Us. Where. You. From. Or. I. Cut!'

The edge of the blade glowed with an electric blue halo and Josh felt the surge of current against his skin. It looked home-made, but it was deadly enough — he dropped the idea of fighting his way out.

The face of the boy holding the blade was half-covered by a filtration mask, but Josh saw enough to recognise the craziest set of eyebrows in South London.

'Benny? Benny, it's me, Josh!'

A tiny flicker of surprise flashed in the boy's hard eyes, tempered by too many years of mistrust to be thrown off-guard by a stranger knowing his name.

'How. U. Know. Me?'

The pressure of the blade on Josh's neck increased. It was obvious that this version of Benny didn't recognise him, but Josh gambled on the chance that the rest of his friends would've still hooked up in this timeline.

'I know all of you! Dennis, Lilz, Shags. I've come to help you.'

There was another collective gasp, as if Josh had just performed some incredible magic trick. Some members of the group began slowly creeping closer towards him.

'You. Help. Us.' Benny spat as he took the knife away from

Josh's neck and turned towards the others. 'No one. Help. We Shade. We help our own.'

'Shade,' intoned the rest of the group, putting their hands over their eyes.

Josh looked around, recognising the nearest ones. Dennis resembled a half-dead scarecrow, his long curly hair pulled back and threaded with all manner of ribbons, sweet wrappers and feathers. Lilz wore hardly anything at all, just a collage of plastic sheets which she'd made into a patchwork dress that only just covered her modesty, but allowed all of her many tattoos to show through.

Shags looked like he'd been in a war: his right arm was gone, and a metal device covered one side of his skull including his left eye, causing his head to tilt to one side.

'Stand him,' commanded Lilz before Josh could ask what the hell happened — she seemed to be more senior in this reality.

Josh struggled to see who the owner of the older voice was. He guessed he was watching how this played out.

Rough hands grabbed him and hauled him to his feet. His knees gave way, and he fell back against one of them as he tried to get his balance.

'Woah!' said another familiar voice. 'No touch.'

Josh turned around to see Coz, or what was left of his old friend.

'Sorry Coz.'

'How you know?'

'Magii — he of the Ministry!' hissed one of the others from behind their mask, making a slicing motion across their neck. Some others nodded and copied the gesture.

'No!' Josh shook his head, desperately trying to think what would have altered them so much. 'What year is this?'

'12.017,' Lilz said, smiling. 'U lose time?' She held up his tachyon, the dials still frozen.

Josh had no idea what the procedure would be for a busted tachyon: the colonel never mentioned that they could fail. If it was broken, then he had a bigger problem; without the watch there would be little chance of getting back to a "standard normality" — as Sim would call it. Nothing in this timeline looked like it carried any kind of history. Everything seemed to be made from discarded plastic junk, and he was trapped in this alternate until he could find something with a past.

He needed to find out where and when it had all gone wrong, but to do that he'd have to gain their trust. The fact Josh knew their names without being able to explain why just made him look like a spy or a cop and from the way they were acting it was clear his friends were just as badly treated here as they'd been in his timeline — he needed to prove that he wasn't their enemy.

'Aw, sad face,' said the semi-clad Lilz, moving closer and squatting down in front of him. Her eyes glinted with a hunger that Josh recognised only too well — desire. The old Lilz always had a soft spot for him, an unspoken attraction that neither of them would ever really acknowledge or act upon. Josh thought of her as a sister, but this version clearly had very different ideas.

'Clean,' she said, running her fingers through his hair and pulling his head towards her. 'Smells good.'

There were stifled giggles from within the crowd.

'Get plenty-plenty creds in SexBar.' Lilz's tone became more business-like as her hand ran down his chest. 'After I,' she added with a wink.

'Enough!' barked the older voice. 'Not for SexBar.'

Lilz stepped back, her hand lingering a little too long on his thigh.

A tall man walked out of the shadows. He was wearing a long leather coat, and his face was obscured by an antique gas mask. In one hand he held a chunky-looking mobile phone with wires and other parts screwed onto it — all the hallmarks of one of Dennis' creations.

'Medscan say he not Shade nor Scender. No tag or tainted. He pure — no rads.'

Lilz grudgingly moved away as the man walked around the group showing everyone the results on the small, green LCD display. They jostled each other to take a look, and when Josh saw their reactions, he knew that whatever they saw was important, and that could give him a chance.

'No kill?' asked Benny, a little disappointed.

'No kill,' replied the voice inside the mask, reaching up to unclip the straps that held it in place.

Josh immediately understood why he didn't recognise the voice: the filters distorted the tone, making him sound older.

'We go to E,' ordered Gossy, staring directly at Josh as if he were a total stranger. 'He know best.'

4

E

They cut the ties on his hands to let him eat. Josh had never tasted anything quite like spit-roasted Frankencat. It made for an unusual meal, especially when smothered in the contents of the oldest tin of baked beans he'd ever seen. He was too hungry to care.

All eyes were on him as they ate, warily shovelling food into their mouths with dirty, greasy fingers. He saw how malnourished they'd become: hollow, sunken cheeks and grey skin from lack of sun and vitamins, all of them showing signs of premature ageing and other conditions — they were a pale imitation of the friends he'd left behind.

After the meal, Lilz tied him up again. She took her time with the zip ties, and Josh felt her breath on the back of his neck, her breasts pressing into his shoulder blades.

'You pureblood,' she whispered in his ear, pulling the ties tight. 'You mine — after E.'

Josh winced as the plastic cut into the chaffed skin of his wrists.

'Yeah, sure,' he replied, wondering what exactly 'E' would have in store for him.

. . .

Gossy poured something onto the fire to put it out, and in the guttering light the gang stood as one and silently slipped out into the darkness. Lilz and Benny pulled Josh along by his arms until he kept up with the pace. They moved quickly, weaving through the pipes and tunnels in total darkness.

The route was littered with rubbish. Josh found it nearly impossible to avoid the unseen obstacles, until Benny got so frustrated with his slow progress that he put a pair of night-vision goggles over his head. Finally, Josh was able to see what they could.

The tunnel network was extensive and impossible to navigate without having grown up within it. Josh lost all sense of direction as they switched back and forth through the warren of service ducts and access tunnels. Every so often the passage would open out into larger spaces where floors had collapsed to create vast cavern-like chambers and they would have to stop while scouts were sent ahead.

While they waited, Josh had time to study the surroundings. They were made up of half-crushed old buildings, layer upon layer of collapsed construction that had been buried below the foundations of the newer superstructures. He realised that these larger areas must have once been streets and looked around for a name or a signpost, but there were none: anything useful had been stripped for salvage.

It was hard to imagine what could have caused so much destruction, so much rebuilding, and all in the streets that he'd once called his home town. As happy as he was to see the Bevin estate pulled down, it wasn't so they could build a bigger one on top of it.

Watching them carefully, Josh realised that the buildings weren't empty. The Shades, as they'd called themselves, had made their homes amongst the rubble, like a lost tribe surviving on the discarded trash of a previous civilisation. His mum watched a show about it once, about Mexico City, the kids lived on a rubbish heap.

Moving through the underworld, Josh realised there were probably hundreds, if not thousands of them, all with the same look of desperation and fear.

After a couple of hours of agonising, back-breaking tunnels, they began to climb upwards. Using old staircases and fire-escapes, they ascended through the floors of semi-collapsed buildings. Now and then Gossy would stop and check the readouts on his scanner, then hand out medicine.

Josh moved closer to Lilz as she was taking some pills. 'Are you sick?'

Lilz shrugged. 'Rad meds.'

Josh had begun to feel odd, but had assumed it was the food. 'Shouldn't I take something?'

'Got to keep you pure!' She smiled wickedly, grabbing his crotch with her hand. 'Precious cargo!'

Gossy walked towards them, and Lilz sloped away.

'Rad levels high,' he warned, giving Lilz a surly glare. He took off Josh's night vision goggles and cut his ties.

'You need this,' he said, and gave Josh his gas mask.

Josh nodded and put it on. It was hot, sweaty and smelled of old rubber, the eye lenses were fogged, and the air tasted of charcoal when he breathed. He could feel Gossy adjusting the straps to make it tighter. Sounds grew muffled and his vision blurred, but he guessed it was better than breathing in radioactive dust.

Gossy put on what looked like an emergency mask from an aeroplane over his nose and mouth, then made his way up the collapsed floor to the level above. The others followed behind, everyone wearing some kind of protective headgear.

'He like you,' Lilz chuckled as she passed him.

A long, laborious climb through the ruins of countless car parks and office buildings brought them up into an old shopping mall. Although it was still buried under thousands of tons of rubble, by some quirk of fate its structure had managed to survive intact. The interior, however, had been completely gutted, and what were once shops had been converted into a thriving shanty-town. The place was buzzing with people.

'Welcome to E. Town!' Lilz announced as she pulled off Josh's gas mask.

The centre of the mall was like a street market in Marrakech — lit with ropes of low-voltage bulbs strung across the atrium. It was the first time Josh had seen anything resembling normal since he'd arrived — the lights reminded him of the ones they used to hang around his mum's flat at Christmas, when they still bothered with Christmas decorations, though he couldn't remember the last time they'd had a tree or presents.

A few opportunists casually wandered over to check out the new arrivals. Gossy seemed to know some of them; others were just looking for news, and most drifted away when they realised there was nothing to trade.

They walked down into the main concourse. Ragged-coated merchants stood next to upturned crates selling anything they could scavenge: clothes stitched together from plastic packaging, batteries, tins of cat food, matches and scraps of old tech — nothing that had a useable past.

Lilz and Benny went off to peruse the stalls while Gossy took the rest of the gang aside and gave them orders. Each one nodded and moved off as he finished their instructions. Lilz, meanwhile, had taken a fancy to a small plastic flower and was having an argument with the seller over the price.

With them all distracted, Josh saw his first real chance to escape, but then a merchant appeared out of the crowd and took a shine to his robes — talking gibberish at him while checking for holes.

Lilz caught sight of the commotion and reluctantly pulled off one of her many bangles and threw it at the man. She came back and took hold of Josh's arm, berating the trader in a language that sounded mostly like pure swearing until he gave up and sloped off.

'Nice?' she asked, placing the flower into her hair with a pout.

'Pretty,' Josh agreed, noticing a small tattoo on her neck. It was a crude drawing of a winged serpent.

'What's that?' he asked, tapping the spot on his neck

'Dragon.' She touched the tattoo. 'For luck.'

Josh thought it looked more like a Draconian symbol, but thought it wise not to ask too many questions.

Lilz zip-tied their hands together.

'Just in case,' she winked.

Gossy motioned for them to follow.

At the far end of the mall stood an old cinema with an array of reclaimed neon signs flickering above the entrance. Josh couldn't understand any of the languages they were written in, but the sounds booming out through the doors were unmistakable. In the midst of all the post-apocalyptic gloom, somebody was rocking out some serious techno.

Gossy handed something to one of the doormen as Lilz tightened her grip on Josh's hand. The guard, who looked like he'd been jacking steroids since he was a five-year-old, took his time examining the object, turning it over in his meaty hands and talking to someone on his headset. Two others joined him, and Josh realised, as the man showed it to his friends, that it was his tachyon. They must have all received the same message at the same time, snapping to attention in unison, pocketing the watch the guard waved them inside. Lilz waltzed in on Josh's arm like she owned him, and no one took any notice of the zip ties as they entered.

They walked across the dance floor, which was packed with an eclectic ensemble of pierced, tattooed and mutated freaks. The sound system was intense — the bass was so deep it made it hard to breathe. If there was one thing about this new timeline Josh had to admire it was how the acoustics seemed to get inside his skull.

The air was full of sweet-smelling narcotics, and though everyone was high, no one was smoking. It was as if the dancers were sweating out pure dope. The decor had a retro-recycled-industrial vibe about it, built out of reclaimed parts; the lights looked like they had been ripped out of old cars and lashed to exposed pipes, the cages and platforms that some of the more daring danced upon were straight out of a breakers yard.

Lilz and Benny dragged Josh through the writhing crowd after Gossy as he struggled to get to the other side of the dance floor. Suddenly, the bass dropped on the track, and everyone went crazy, bodies crashing into one another as they became a seething, rhythmic frenzy of limbs.

Josh considered whether this would have been the perfect time to make a run for it, except he was still tied to Lilz, and the effects of the drug-infused smoke had dulled his senses, so he just let the others pull him along.

The DJ was some white-haired guy in a seriously psychedelic coat and the most unusual pair of sunglasses. Lines of code flickered across the lenses as his hands typed out commands onto keyboards mounted on the heads of two heavily tattooed albino girls — who in turn were mixing tracks on makeshift computers. It was too weird to work out how, but they were creating the most amazing sounds.

Gossy signalled to one of the guards that stood by the mixing desk and pointed at Josh. The female guard pulled down her shades to check him out then tapped something into a device strapped to her wrist.

A door slid open behind the DJ, and they were escorted through to the 'VIP' room, as the flickering red neon sign on the wall declared.

The door closed behind them and shut out the sound of the club entirely. It was a chill-out room, a sanctuary for the elite to relax, and judging by the activities that were taking place on the luxurious couches they weren't too shy about the ways in which they chose to unwind.

Lilz tutted enviously and yanked Josh's arm to get his attention.

Gossy was talking to a well-dressed man in a purple suit: they were studying the medscan device and haggling over a price.

Josh's drug-addled brain took far too long to realise who the man in the suit was — Eddy, with considerably more hair and no beard, but the nose was unmistakable, as were those large, doleful eyes.

Gossy motioned to Lilz to bring Josh over and cut the zip ties.

Eddy looked Josh up and down as if examining a piece of meat, and produced a more sophisticated scanner of his own.

'No Tag,' Gossy assured him.

Eddy played with the controls of his device and finally nodded in agreement. 'No taint either,' he added. 'Where he snatch?'

'Base. 12-240.'

Eddy stroked his chin, his fingers searching for the beard that had once grown there.

'Any scav?'

'Just the 'tique,' Gossy replied.

'Any marks? Tats. Scars?' asked Eddy, narrowing his eyes.

Gossy shrugged.

Eddy turned to Josh. 'Where scav?' he asked, holding up the tachyon.

'Oldspeak,' Gossy intervened.

Eddy's eyes widened a fraction and Josh thought his hand trembled a little as he held the tachyon.

'Inside,' he ordered, nodding towards an office at the back.

'You know what this is, don't you?' asked Eddy, holding up the tachyon to Josh.

Gossy, Lilz and Benny stood at the back of his private office trying hard not to stare at the shelves of treasures: hair dryers, jars of USB sticks, a games console with a stack of cartridges and a whole set of encyclopaedias. It looked like something from a garage sale, but Josh knew to them it was worth more than a lifetime of scavenging.

To him, it was a ticket out of this madness.

'Of course I do, Eddy,' replied Josh.

Eddy's eyes narrowed at the sound of his name. He studied Josh suspiciously, as though he was trying to decide if Josh was a threat.

'I'm guessing you're not from this timeline?'

'Nope.'

'You have the mark — the Ouroboros?'

Josh pulled back his sleeve, revealing the circular snake tattoo on his forearm.

'Tempos Fugit,' Josh quoted.

Lilz and Benny both made similar ritualistic signs with their hands and whispered 'Magii! Shield protect us,' before spitting on the floor.

Josh realised that they knew something about the Order. The colonel had told him once that the Copernicans could only predict accurately if their existence were kept secret — their algorithms failed if the population became aware of the Order's existence. Yet this timeline was using holocene dates and recognised the mark of Ouroboros — even if it was seen as a curse.

'Trap shut,' barked Eddy, switching back into their dialect. 'When did you snatch?'

'Day back,' Gossy replied.

Eddy took out a blaster from his coat and twisted a dial on it.

He pointed the weapon directly at Josh's head. Gossy was about to protest, but Eddy held up a hand to silence him.

'What's your name?' Eddy demanded.

'Joshua Jones,' Josh replied, his hands going up automatically.

'Guild and rank?'

'Watchman — fourteenth.'

Eddy looked dubious for a second. Josh could see a few different ways this could go, and none of them were good. The barrel wavered ever so slightly in front of him, and then it moved a fraction to the left, and he felt the bullets fly past his ear. The first hit Gossy, followed by two more that took out Lilz and Benny. Josh heard their bodies slump to the floor.

· · ·

'So, Jones of the Watch,' Eddy said, pointing the gun back at Josh. 'Would you mind telling me exactly what you're doing here?'

'You killed them?'

Eddy snorted. 'Their last twenty-four hours. It's a memory tranquilliser that suppresses short-term recall. They won't remember what happened here, or that they managed to catch themselves a Magii.'

'Magii?'

'Long story,' Eddy sighed, lowering the gun. 'The Order isn't held in high regard down here. Thanks to the ministry, the Shades have been taught to believe our abilities are like a dark art. It's like trying to explain an astronaut to a caveman. Which returns us to my original question. What are you doing here?'

Josh relaxed a little and dropped his hands. 'I'm looking for someone,' he replied, 'a girl: Caitlin Makepiece.'

Eddy's face hardened, and his finger stiffened on the trigger, bringing the gun back up. 'And why would you want to find her?'

'Because —' Josh wasn't sure what to say next. The way Eddy reacted was not a good sign, '— she owes me something.'

A kiss, thought Josh.

Eddy's trigger finger relaxed a little. 'You mean Caitlin Eckhart, or the "History Burner" as she's more commonly known.'

Josh shook his head. 'Doesn't sound like her. The Caitlin I know loved history — she was a Scriptorian.'

Eddy scoffed. 'Obviously, the timeline you left deviates significantly from this one. I can't say how much, and we don't have time to compare notes, but Minister Eckhart is not generally someone you want to go looking for. In fact, most of us try to avoid her and the rest of her Ministry altogether.'

Josh was relieved to hear she still existed, but he couldn't imagine how she would have ever been persuaded to marry Dalton, let alone done something so bad as to be named "History Burner". Something was very wrong if Caitlin had started burning books.

'What about the colonel? I mean Rufius Westinghouse? Do you know him?'

Eddy's expression softened at the name of the old man, and he lowered the gun.

'Rufius, he was a good friend. Resisted them for as long as he could, but in the end we all found the Determinist purges too much. Last I heard he's hiding out somewhere in the sixteenth century, before the Ostryanyn blockade.'

Josh wondered whether it would be better to go back and look for the colonel first; he could really use a little of the old man's advice right now.

'Can I have my watch back?'

'Of course,' Eddy replied, handing the tachyon to him, 'but it won't be much use to you.'

'Yeah, I think it's broken,' Josh agreed, snapping it back onto his wrist.

'More like disabled. The tachyons weren't the only thing that shut down in the blockade — the shield has some kind of dampening effect, and no one's been able to move backwards since.'

'How do they maintain the continuum?'

'They don't. The Determinists have taken total control. They obliterated or confiscated every historical artefact, killed every Copernican they could find. The past is off-limits, and access is governed under strict ministerial oversight. This timeline has had a catastrophic couple of centuries, and everyone has suffered. It's a police state up there.' Eddy rolled his eyes to the ceiling. 'Down here, amongst the discarded, we still have an element of freedom.'

'Does Caitlin have authority to go back?'

'Yes, but she won't use it.'

'Why not?'

'There's a detachment of resistance guarding the other side of the blockade. It's an impasse.'

'And that's where you think Rufius is?'

'Without a doubt,' Eddy replied, with a small amount of pride.

'I need you to get me in to see her.'

'What do you think she is going to do for you? She won't even know who you are. You'll be interrogated by her redactors until you're nothing but an empty shell.'

Josh shrugged. 'We have unfinished business.'

5

DANGEROUS MATERIALS

Gossy, Benny and Lilz were made comfortable on the couches of the lounge outside Eddy's office. Josh smiled at the thought of telling Lilz about her sex-mad alter-ego one day — assuming he managed to repair the timeline.

'What's going to happen to them?'

Eddy shrugged. 'They'll wake up with a couple of creds in their pockets and a hangover that won't shift for days.'

'But long-term?'

'The average life expectancy of a scavenger is twenty-five years, thirty if they're lucky — there's no such thing as long-term for a Shade.'

Josh stared at his friends. Eddy was right, they all looked like they were sickening for something. He knew he had to find out what went wrong, as much for them as for Caitlin.

'Is there nothing we can do?'

'Interesting thing about a world without history: no one remembers the mistakes, nothing to compare their lives to you see — people just live day-to-day, in the moment. They've no idea there was ever a better life, only the one they've been dealt.'

. . .

Eddy found a set of clothes to replace Josh's robes. They were like something from a communist state: a drab grey suit, with an insignia of a gear wheel and a lightning flash stitched in gold thread onto the mandarin collar and etched into the silver buttons.

According to Eddy, this was the kind of uniform that would help Josh blend in amongst the lower ranks of the Ascendancy — the term the Shades used for those who lived in the world above. Josh was beginning to wonder if this time-line had been based on the global expansion of North Korea.

Eddy made a call while Josh was getting changed. The phone seemed to be nothing more than a stud attached to his ear. The tone he used was very formal — Josh's Gran would have called it his 'posh voice'.

'Servitor 28491.'

Eddy paused, waiting for someone to verify his identity. 'I have an unclassified artefact violation: policy seven-beta subsection four, as well as possible breach of temporal codes 1421, 2703 and 3836a.'

There was another brief moment of silence, during which Josh imagined the person on the other end of the line thumbing through a series of thick manuals, trying to find the paragraphs to which Eddy was referring.

'Confirmed,' said Eddy looking straight at Josh, 'male, 17, Tag 10290992-H.'

Josh stopped buttoning up his jacket and held his hands up to Eddy as if to question what he was doing, but Eddy raised a finger to silence him.

'Affirmative. Credit account Delta-Five-Nine-Zero-India. Transaction ends.'

. . .

Eddy dropped the call and smiled at Josh. 'So you have your appointment with the Ministry. Although I suspect you'd have better chances in the maelstrom.'

'Do they know you're a spy for the Ministry?' Josh asked, nodding at the door to the lounge.

Eddy shook his head. 'I prefer survivor. This isn't about good and bad guys. We all have to make the best of what fate throws us.' He picked up the gun again and altered the dial. 'Even if it's mostly a crock of shit. A man's got to make a living.' He placed the gun against the side of Josh's head.

'Calm down Eddy,' Josh pleaded, putting his hands in the air. 'I'm just trying to understand what's going on.'

Eddy smiled and pulled the trigger, and Josh felt a small sting as something went into the skin behind his ear.

'That's a tag: a personal ID chip, comms device and a few other little mods I did myself. It should embed in the next couple of minutes. Congratulations, Master Jones, you're now a legitimate citizen of the Ascendancy.'

Josh winced, rubbing the spot behind his ear.

Eddy walked over to a painting and pressed his thumb against the frame. The image dissolved to reveal a safe with a lock made of intricate brass dials. He carefully rotated the numbers until there was an audible click and the door opened, revealing a small collection of old books.

'Now which one of these will she go for?' he said to himself, taking each book out and laying them on the desk. They were all meticulously wrapped in a fine white linen.

Josh was distracted by an annoying buzz of static that whispered to him, like a mosquito he couldn't quite see.

Eddy laughed at his confusion. 'The sound is bone conducted. It's trying to establish a link to the network. Should settle down in a few seconds — ah, yes, this should do nicely, I doubt you could guess what this will cost me.' He carefully unwrapped a book, a first edition of Shakespeare's sonnets, and reluctantly handed it over to Josh.

Josh could feel the history flooding through his fingers as he flicked through the yellowed pages. It felt wrong, the timeline was distorted and hazy, and there was no way to get a clear reading on where it had been. Something was interfering with his ability to read its past.

'Poetry?' asked Josh, scanning the text.

Eddy put the other books carefully back in the safe. 'Possibly one of the most dangerous subjects. It should get her attention.'

'How?'

Eddy pointed to his illicit collection. 'If we could break the dampening field, every one of these books has the ability to take you back to better times. Since virtually every historical object has been confiscated and burned or locked in the forbidden archives, these are possibly the most precious artefacts in existence. Poetry, however, constitutes another kind of threat: it has the power to inspire, to motivate the dreamer, and those kind of feelings can lead to revolution.'

The comms device suddenly kicked in, and Josh was overwhelmed by an incessant flow of information that flooded into the world around him. His vision was enhanced with multiple layers of information: maps, transit reports, news bulletins, and hundreds of pieces of data, all vying for his attention.

'Close your eyes for a second,' Eddy instructed. 'Let the channels settle, try not to focus on them, and they will drop into the background.'

Josh did as he was told, and the information streams faded away, but he could sense their subliminal activity like a background hum as he opened his eyes once more.

Eddy was staring at him.

YOU HEAR ME? THIS PRIVATE CHANNEL + ENCRYPTED = SECRET

Appeared as a text message in the lower half of his vision.

YES, he replied.

Eddy nodded.

GOOD. DON'T SPEAK OF IT. NOW USE VOICE.

'So, you're taking me in for owning a book of poems?' Josh continued to leaf through the pages, admiring the beautiful woodcut engravings that illustrated the text. He'd never really paid much attention to Shakespeare at school: the language was too strange and archaic. The most interesting thing about his plays was usually the crude remarks left by previous owners in the margins.

'Only way I could think of to get you in. You can't exactly sneak into the most heavily guarded building in the city!' Eddy put on a pair of darkly tinted glasses and tapped a series of buttons on the sleeve of his jacket — the colour of his suit turned to black.

Josh realised he had no idea where Caitlin was. He had assumed that she would be in some version of the Chapter House, a bigger one perhaps, but not one that required extra protection. Its location had always been a closely guarded secret, or at least it had used to be.

'Where exactly are we going?'

'The offices of the Ministry, of course,' Eddy responded, as if Josh was asking the dumbest question ever. 'The home of the Determinists, and their glorious leaders.' As he spoke, Eddy made a salute with one fist above his head and then brought it down to his chest.

'Caitlin is a Determinist?' Josh sputtered. This was nearly as unlikely as the idea of her marrying Dalton.

'As The Minister of Memory, she is one of the strongest advocates of Determinism.'

'The Minister of what the f —'

Eddy clamped his hand over Josh's mouth and text began to scroll across his vision.

TWO THINGS YOU NEED TO LEARN, BOY: FIRST WHEN WE'RE UP THERE, THEY HAVE EARS EVERY-WHERE. SECOND, NO ONE DISRESPECTS THE ORDER, ESPECIALLY THE MINISTRY — EVEN IF YOU DON'T BELIEVE, YOU BELIEVE. GET IT?

Josh nodded.

'Sorry. It's just that she doesn't sound like the Caitlin I know.'

'I'm sure she isn't, but if you're convinced that she can help you, this book is the only way for you to get close to her. Once we're inside the rest is up to you.'

6

ASCENDANCY

The journey up through the final few layers of forgotten streets took hours. His legs ached as Josh followed silently behind Eddy, who was nothing like the doddery old repairman that used to buy the odd piece of stolen merchandise. He picked his way expertly through the service tunnels.

They came to a precarious set of old ladders that spanned a vast sink-hole. Staring down into it was like looking down through time. Josh could see the layers of the previous cities, each one stacked precariously on the ruins of its predecessor.

Every so often, Eddy would stop and stare up towards the ceiling, taking his bearings.

Josh was still trying to come to terms with his implant, the navigation systems could display three-dimensional maps in front of his eyes, but he didn't know how to control them and had simply shut it off.

An alarm sounded in his middle ear, and a calm female voice reported: 'Current radiation levels at 500 millisieverts. Extended exposure will result in decreased blood cell count. Countermeasures recommended.'

Eddy pulled out a gas mask and threw it to Josh. It was far more advanced than the one Gossy had given him.

'Put it on. We're about to pass through a hot zone.'

He took out his blaster and twisted the dial. 'This should protect you from the worst of it,' he added, pressing the gun into Josh's thigh. The sting was like that of a giant bumblebee.

'Shit!' cursed Josh from inside his mask.

RADIATION SICKNESS HURTS A HELL OF A LOT MORE!

Eddy's words appeared on Josh's comm system.

RADIATION?

Josh replied.

BECAUSE SOMEONE LET OFF A DIRTY BOMB A CENTURY BACK. NOW MOVE BEFORE YOU RUIN YOUR CHANCES OF HAVING KIDS — NORMAL ONES AT LEAST.

Eddy shouldered his pack and set off at a fast pace. Josh limped after him.

They emerged from a service duct into the clean empty basement of a building. Eddy swiftly sprayed their exit with a kind of foam that set instantly and left no sign there had ever been a hole.

'Never go back the same way,' Eddy explained, taking the mask from Josh and stashing it in the backpack before dumping everything into a nearby bin. There was an orange flash of flame from beneath the lid.

'Burner,' warned Eddy, stopping Josh from looking inside. 'No rubbish up here.'

They marched up a level and out onto a wide walkway, which as Eddy had predicted, was immaculate. Towering buildings surrounded them, gleaming columns of steel and glass that stretched up into an infinite blue sky. The air was clean and fresh; Josh could even feel the warmth of the reflected sunlight on his face.

Eddy breathed in deeply and took off his sunglasses, letting the sun warm his face. He was interfacing with something on his implant; Josh could tell from the way his eyes were flicking from side-to-side that he was processing information.

The walkway stretched out between the buildings, and Josh could see distant figures moving about along it. Similar structures spanned the levels above them, creating a web-like lattice of connecting bridges between the buildings.

Josh went over to the rails and looked down into the swirling clouds. They were like dark, poisonous blankets smothering the planet's surface, and from above them it was impossible to know what was going on below. Josh remembered all those haunted faces he'd seen on the way up, thousands of frightened Shades trying to scratch an existence out of nothing but garbage.

Something caught his eye: a dark spot that was growing larger as it flew towards them. At first he thought it was a bird, a large one, but it was moving in strange and unnatural circles.

'Inspectorate drone,' noted Eddy, grabbing hold of Josh's arm. 'Probably best if you don't get scanned too closely just yet, your persona won't stand up to too much scrutiny.'

A glass pod floated down to their level, and Eddy pushed Josh inside the moment its doors opened.

'DETERMINISTRY' appeared on a glass screen along with a series of three-dimensional routes to choose from. Eddy tapped one, and the pod silently glided up and off along the path he selected.

'ETA 15:02:12,' displayed in small red numerals underneath the destination and began to count down in seconds.

'What's it doing?' asked Josh, studying the drone circling slowly overhead.

'Scanning your implant — making sure you're in the right part of town.'

'And am I?' Josh nervously touched the skin behind his ear. It felt warmer than usual.

'Shouldn't matter. You're currently logged as my prisoner, so as long as my security level is fine we're all good.'

The drone descended until it was level with them. It was a matte black sphere with a military-grade array of antennae and apertures spaced across its surface. As their pod continued to ascend, the drone matched it. There was nothing to signify it was scanning them except a small red light that blinked intermittently on one side.

Josh tried to hold back the rising sense of vertigo as they went higher.

'What happens if it doesn't recognise me?'

'It'll shoot us out of the sky, but don't worry, the database of citizens is vast and it will take a while to match you. The census systems are notoriously slow.'

The light winked once more and went out, and the drone accelerated away. Josh realised he'd been holding his breath and let it out slowly.

'You okay? You're looking a little pale,' asked Eddy, watching the drone disappear.

'Yeah. We don't have stuff like this in my time.'

'What, no police drones?' Eddy laughed. 'How do they keep the peace?'

'CCTV, cameras and actual coppers — policemen.'

'I heard that was how it used to be, back in 11.700.'

Josh did some mental calculations. 'You think I'm from somewhere back in the eighteenth century? I'm telling you, yesterday the present looked nothing like this.'

Eddy shrugged. 'Maybe so, but we can't change the past now, not unless you can persuade the Ministry to let you go back and break the blockade.'

The minutes counted slowly down on the digital clock, and Josh watched the vast cityscape stretch out beneath them.

'Where did all of this come from?'

Eddy looked puzzled. 'I guess you've never heard of the Fermian Shield?'

Josh shook his head.

'Science can build worlds and destroy them in a blink of an eye. What you're looking at is the last remaining cluster of humanity on the planet. The Fermi Corporation practically saved the human race. Cured everything from cancer to space travel. Ecosystem paid a heavy price though.' He sighed, looking down into the swirling clouds below. 'The surface is practically uninhabitable now.'

Josh thought about his mother, wondering whether she was down there somewhere. It had been the first time he'd had a chance to catch his breath, and it saddened him to think she might be lost among the Shades.

'Can I access the citizens database through this?' he asked, tapping his ear. 'Call other people like you would on a phone?'

'I have no idea what a phone is, but yes you can communicate with others. Who are you looking for?'

'My mother.'

'What's her derivation?'

'No idea. Her name is Juliet Martha Jones, and she used to live on the Bevin Estate, but I guess that's probably under a couple of hundred tonnes of rubble now.'

Eddy closed his eyes and Josh could see them moving rapidly under paper-thin lids.

'There are fourteen Juliet Martha Jones on record. I need something more to go on.'

Josh thought for a moment about what else he could add: *she had a son, she wasn't married* — none of those things were definite anymore. Then he had an idea.

'She has MS — Multiple Sclerosis.'

'Yes, there is one with a medical history of such a condition, but she was cured when she was ten years old.'

Josh looked at him in astonishment. 'Cured? You're sure?'

Eddy opened his eyes and smiled. 'Oh, it's your mother. I can see the resemblance. Here, take a look.'

A notification appeared in front of Josh's eyes: a holographic record of his mother with her medical history, a kind of passport style photo in 3D and maps of her last known location.

'She's a teacher,' Josh exclaimed, studying the information, 'and married.'

'Happy days.'

A small chime sounded in the cabin, and the pod began to descend. They were passing through some kind of barrier, a force shield shimmered in the air around them. The connection to the network was disrupted, and all of the data about his mother disappeared. Josh groaned, there wasn't enough time to learn how they had cured her MS.

'No comms on the inside of the forcefield I'm afraid,' Eddy apologised. 'Security measures. Seems like my clearance is still good though. We'll be landing in five.' Eddy lit a long, black cigarette. 'At least you can say you saw something of the capital before you died. What do you think of the Fifteenth City of the Ascendancy?'

'Why fifteenth?'

'Because the other fourteen are buried below it.'

Eddy blew a massive cloud of purple smoke into the air,

and for a moment Josh thought it took on the shape of an atomic mushroom cloud.

The smoke smelled like a synthetic dope, and Josh could tell from the lights on the side of the cigarette that it was some kind of machine. 'They dropped the bomb?'

'Oh, more than one.' Eddy's eyes glazed over. 'Like I said, science is a dangerous toy. It was carnage before the Fermian Shield went up and the Determinists stepped in.'

7

THE MINISTRY

The entrance hall of the Ministry was a vast, cathedral-like space that was carefully designed to make you feel small and insignificant the moment you walked in. In the centre of the atrium stood a towering bronze statue of a man dressed in the robes of the Order. In one hand he held an hourglass, in the other an almanac and abacus. A blindfold covered his eyes.

Around the base of the statue was a large circular desk with the words: THE FUTURE IS NOT WRITTEN, carved into the marble in gold letters.

There was a steady flow of people shuffling through the concourse, most of them wearing the austere, military-style uniform of the Ministry. Their faces all wore the same blank expression. No one looked at each other, and kept their eyes down on the floor. Eddy had been right to make Josh change out of his robes, as he would have stood out like a clown in the middle of an army parade.

There were guards amongst the crowds. Josh caught sight of weapons hanging from their belts, and when he looked closer, he spotted other, more lethal devices in the walls.

Eddy held Josh by the arm and strode up to the front desk.

'Name and origination,' intoned the stern-faced clerk from behind the desk.

'Eddard Van Solomon, 28491,' Eddy replied tersely, as if he were a superior officer.

His details flashed up on the transparent display, with a special symbol next to his name that instantly altered the clerk's attitude.

'Good morning Lieutenant. Your prisoner is expected.'

A large black cylinder rose up through a grate in the floor and a door opened in its side. Eddy stepped inside and dragged Josh in with him. The door cycled shut, and the elevator dropped back below the ground.

A light glowed in the ceiling above them as they picked up speed.

WHERE ARE WE GOING? Josh asked using his comms device.

Eddy nodded to the indicator counting down rapidly above the door. HERETICS, I THINK. THE POSSESSION OF BANNED BOOKS IS SEEN AS SOMETHING AKIN TO HERESY.

WHAT'S HERESY?

BLASPHEMY? APOSTASY? NON-CONFORMIST? Eddy glared at him.

Josh stared back at Eddy blankly.

A BELIEF CONTRARY TO THE ACCEPTED DOCTRINE?

BASICALLY A REBEL?

BASICALLY.

AND WHAT DO THEY DO TO REBELS?

MOSTLY THEY EXECUTE THEM. AFTER THEY'VE TORTURED THEM OF COURSE.

Josh swore under his breath.

AND THIS WAS YOUR BEST PLAN?

Eddy shrugged.

YOU WANTED TO MEET HER — THIS IS THE ONLY WAY. I DIDN'T SAY YOU WERE GOING TO SURVIVE TO TELL THE TALE. WHATEVER HAPPENS, I STILL GET PAID.

Josh thought about trying to kill Eddy before they got to wherever it was they were going, but he could feel the lift was already slowing down and he couldn't see how a dead body was going to help the situation. Instead, he thought about his mother, he still couldn't believe they'd found a cure for her MS in this timeline. If he could find out what it was then maybe he could take the knowledge back with him. Science had never been his strong point at school, but he could memorise stuff like formulas. It didn't matter if he didn't know what it meant — as long as he could write it down for someone that did.

Caitlin would know what to do. Although he was worried now that she wouldn't remember him, or anything of their old life: the cave, the strzyga or even the picnic? If Lilz and her friends were anything to go by, he guessed not, but there would be something.

He couldn't say what it was, but he just knew it.

8

INTERROGATION

It was dark, and his head hurt. Hammers pounded away behind his eyes, worse than any hangover Josh could remember, and he could taste the iron-tang of blood in his mouth.

There was a vague memory of a question, a faint recollection of men shouting at him and each other. They argued over the book. No, not the book — something on a screen that he couldn't see.

He was strapped to a weird kind of chair, one that stopped him from turning his head or moving his arms and legs. He'd thought it looked vaguely like a dentist's chair when they had dragged him into the room. Now he knew it could be so much more.

Slowly, it came back to him.

They'd started by asking him stupid questions about the damned book: where had he got it from? Didn't he know it was banned material? Who was he working for?

There was nothing he could think to say, so they prodded him with their sharp little tools and inserted electrodes into sensitive areas and turned the current up until he passed out.

When they finally realised that the machines had failed, they brought a 'redactor' down to read him. It was at that point the arguing really started. The redactor was basically a seer, but he was no master, not like Kelly or Lyra. A brute of a man, both in appearance and technique, Josh could feel the clumsy fool rummaging around in his memories until he finally reached the same conclusion as the others.

'Paradox?' they whispered to each other, like children using a forbidden word for the first time. Then the shouting began, each trying to blame the other as they traded insults for over an hour before one of them finally decided to inform their commander. Josh passed out many times during that torturous hour, but always managed to smile inanely at them whenever he was lucid enough. Someone was going to get their arse kicked for this — they were just working out who it should be.

Then she came.

In his semi-conscious state her voice was like something from a dream. It was Caitlin — there was no mistaking her dulcet tones, even if they were more hard-edged and full of implied threats.

'What exactly did you do to him?' she barked.

A mumble of excuses ensued that Josh couldn't be bothered to try and follow. They were all desperately trying to save their own necks.

'Leave. All of you. Now!' Caitlin ordered in a tone that implied they were all going to suffer for their incompetence.

Josh heard the grinding sound of the metal doors opening and the hollow echo of boots marching away down the corridor. When the door finally closed there was a blissful silence. He wondered whether this was a good time to mention he needed the bathroom. Through bleary eyes he scanned what little of the room the head restraints would allow, but he couldn't tell if anyone was left.

Caitlin stepped in front of him. Her face was thin and gaunt, and her beautiful hair had been cropped short into a severe bob.

'I can't believe you're the one. Not after all this time,' she sneered, running her gloved hand over his face.

Josh's mouth was too dry to answer, so he just stared into her eyes, wishing he could kiss her.

She held up his tachyon and waved it in front of his face. 'Can you tell me who you stole this from?'

He blinked at her. 'You gave it to me.'

Caitlin unbuckled one of his arms and lifted it up to expose the tattoo of the snake, which was the moment when he realised they'd taken his clothes.

'And this, where on earth did you get this done? Some Shade flesh carver I suppose?' she snapped. 'I've heard they call us Magii down there. Is that where you've come from? You don't look sick enough to be one of them, but your ID is a fake, and we've no record of your origination. You know that imitating a member of the Order is a capital offence? That you're a dead man?'

Her uniform was long and made of black leather, with a line of silver buttons running down the front. It reminded Josh of the Order's formal robes, but with overtones of dominatrix.

'Cat,' was all that Josh could manage before he passed out again.

A hand struck him across the face.

'Wake up.'

The voice was deep, and reminded him of someone he knew: it had an arrogant, self-assured tone.

'It's no use. Don't you think I've tried?' said Caitlin. 'Your men were over-zealous with their medication.'

Something touched the skin on his arm. It felt cold and sharp.

'So you think that he might be the Paradox?' pondered the unmistakable voice of Sim.

Josh wanted to open his eyes, but his body was still numb. He guessed they'd just given him something to counteract the sedative.

'He's not supposed to exist — a statistical impossibility.'

'And how many people died over that assumption?' Caitlin reminded them.

'Hah! Might as well be a bloody unicorn for all the difference it will make now. He's a century too late,' said the vaguely familiar voice.

Then Josh remembered — it was Dalton.

'When did he come from?'

'The last Copernican predictions that we intercepted were pointing towards a minor branch of the Westinghouse interdiction, but that was still resolving to less than a sixty-three per cent probability,' Sim said. Josh could hear him flicking through the pages of his almanac.

'From a redacted timeline?' There was a hint of disbelief in Caitlin's voice, and Josh felt tears welling in his eyes as he tried to keep them shut.

'Let's just finish him and forget it,' Dalton growled. 'We don't have time for this prophecy bullshit. The last thing we need now is another round of religious hysteria stirring up the resistance — let's not give them a martyr to sacrifice themselves to.'

Josh could feel the sensations returning in his fingertips, like a slow, creeping wave of pins and needles, as if he'd slept on them.

'We can't terminate him. We've no idea what he's here to do,' Sim protested.

'This is a matter for the High Council,' Caitlin decided. 'Leave him to me.'

As the others left, Josh passed out again.

> 'Like as the waves make towards the pebbled
>   shore, So do our minutes hasten to
>   their end;
> Each changing place with that which goes
>   before, In sequent toil all forwards do
>   contend.'

Caitlin stood over him, her eyes dark and hard as before. She'd taken off her overcoat and was wearing a long, sleeveless tunic with a high collar. In her hand, she held Eddy's book of sonnets.

'Do you know I can have you killed for this?' she asked, closing the book.

'Cat?' Josh murmured deliriously.

'Minister Eckhart,' she reminded him, putting down the book and picking up a glass of water. She held it up to his lips to let him drink.

'Thanks,' gasped Josh after he'd drained it.

'Who are you?'

The question was more painful than any electrode or needle could have been. The confirmation that everything they had experienced had been obliterated in three simple words was almost too much for him to bear.

'I was your friend, once. In another time.'

Caitlin ignored him. Instead, she lifted up his arm and examined the tattoo.

'You're of the Order?'

'Fourteenth millennial,' Josh said, nodding. 'We went back there together. It was kind of an accident.' He thought it was wiser to leave out the details for the moment.

Caitlin scoffed. 'No one has been back that far! It's impossible.'

'Not where I've come from. We watched the mammoths cross Doggerland. We started our own tribe.' He was hoping the words would trigger some kind of latent memory in her, but there was nothing but disbelief in her eyes.

'The past has been closed for over a hundred years,' she said, the anger flushing across her cheeks. 'No one can go back to yesterday, let alone fourteen thousand years — you're lying. The Paradox was supposed to come from the future.'

There was a click and Caitlin was suddenly pointing a gun at his face. 'Who sent you?'

'Cat, chill out,' Josh pleaded. 'Why would I lie?'

He held her gaze, even though the metallic scent of cordite told him that the gun had been fired recently. Josh knew better than to look away — Lenin had taught him a long time ago that people find it hard to shoot someone who's looking them straight in the eye.

'Because your followers killed my parents.' Her voice trembled a little as she spoke.

'My followers?'

'The Chaotics, they predicted you — the all-knowing Paradox. They said you would come, that you would know how to fix everything, and we didn't believe them. The world was falling apart, and they were holding out for a fairytale.'

'And so how did that end up with your parents dying?'

47

'Don't come the innocent. Everyone played their part in the Great War.'

'You went to war?'

'The Copernicans were wiped out.'

'Because of me?'

'Because people were stupid enough to believe that one man could change the future.'

Then Josh saw the scar, the fine white line on the inside of her right arm. The wound that she'd got from playing with her father's sword.

'Listen, in my timeline your parents are just missing — not dead. You told me about them, how they were the greatest nautonniers ever. You even told me how you got that scar playing with your dad's sword.'

Her expression softened for a second and he saw the faintest glimmer of hope in her eyes, but then it was gone.

'I have many scars,' she growled.

'The one on your arm, you call it a fated wound.'

The gun lowered, and Josh saw there were tears in her eyes.

'In your time they didn't die?'

'No.'

Something broke inside her, and she collapsed into a chair and sobbed. The gun hung loosely from her hand until it dropped and clattered onto the floor.

'How? How could you know that?' she said to herself. 'It doesn't make any sense.'

Josh allowed himself a breath, his heart hammering in his chest.

'I need to get to the colonel. He will know what to do.'

'Who?'

'Westinghouse. Rufius Westinghouse.'

The gun was back in her hand once more, and she was on her feet, her finger trembling over the trigger.

'And why exactly should I help you find the Butcher of Bastei Bridge?'

From the spite in her voice, it was clear she hated the old man — Josh had no idea why, but if she couldn't help him, then the colonel may be the only one who could help him repair the timeline and put the continuum back on track.

'Because, if I can get him to help me, there's a good chance you won't feel as empty as you do now?'

Caitlin's fingers flexed on the butt of the gun, and Josh closed his eyes. He couldn't bear to look into the despair any longer. She was so close to blowing his brains out, and all he could think about was the way she'd smiled at him that first time they had met in the library. Fate was a devious little bastard when it wanted to be.

'You're going to need to give me something better than that.'

'Okay.' Josh took a deep breath. 'From what I can figure out, something has gone really badly wrong with this timeline. Something has taken you down a different path. The Caitlin I know would never have married an Eckhart, and she would have rather died than become a Determinist — let alone destroy a book. You love books! You used to say that they were the closest thing to magic!'

There it was again, that slight tremble in her lip. Her resolve was weakening. Josh saw his opportunity and took it.

'Whatever crap this life has thrown at you, I know somewhere deep down you're still the same person. We were meant to meet each other, we always have been. You even showed me once on one of those chart things the Copernicans use.'

'Fatecasting? That's heresy,' she said with a hint of a smile, and Josh knew he was close.

'And after all, I am the Paradox — it's like my destiny.'

She stood with her eye sighted down the barrel of the gun, a thousand different thoughts spinning inside her head.

So much rested on what she did next, Josh could feel the lines of the continuum clustering around this moment, yet all he could do was remember the girl he fell in love with.

'Alright,' she said, sighing and putting the weapon back in its holster. 'But any smart moves and it's you I will be shooting first.'

She took out a sharp knife and sliced open the restraints on his legs and wrist.

'We need to get back to 11.558. I'm guessing you have a way to do that?' Josh asked, massaging the blood back into his left hand.

'I won't be able to go back with you.'

'Why not?'

'Because I'll be missed, and the last thing you want is a Protectorate search detail on your arse. No matter how cute it is.'

She threw him a set of robes.

Josh caught them. 'Fair enough.'

'Plus, I'm not sure I would be very welcome back there,' she added, turning to leave.

9

TYPEWRITER

'Is that it?' exclaimed Josh.

They were standing in a small vault somewhere deep underground. A single lamp shone down on the wooden desk illuminating an old-fashioned black typewriter under a glass dome.

'It's the only remaining machine from that era,' Caitlin replied.

'From 11.588? I was thinking more Shakespeare and Black Death.'

Caitlin walked to the table and lifted the glass carefully off the machine. 'We use it to communicate with the Chaos Brigade.' She pointed at the blank sheet of paper that sat loaded on the smooth black roller. 'The shield's effects are weaker down here.'

'I mean it's too modern for that era. In my timeline this is more like something from the early twentieth century.'

Caitlin typed a slow, methodical series of keys that made a satisfying clunk as she carefully picked each letter.

. . .

> Init transfer request. Ends.

She stepped quickly away from the typewriter as if it had burned her fingers.

There was an awkward silence while she watched the keys. Josh wasn't quite sure what was supposed to happen next, but knew better than to ask.

A minute later the carriage shifted down a line and a key depressed by itself, then another, until the ghost in the machine had typed out.

> Denied. Ends.

Josh looked up at Caitlin who was reading the line with a look of disbelief.

'That doesn't usually happen?' he asked quietly.

She shrugged. 'No, but then we haven't communicated for a few years.'

'Who is working the other end?'

She shrugged. 'No idea.'

Josh looked at the keys of the typewriter, which were in the same arrangement as the keyboards of the school computers. He'd never really understood why the letters were arranged in that order. As a dyslexic, they tended to move around of their own accord anyway. There was something about vowels being in certain places under your fingers, but the logic escaped him.

'Can I try?' he asked.

'By all means,' Caitlin said, swiping the return bar and

watching the carriage move down to the next line. 'The sooner I get rid of you the better.'

Josh thought about what to say. He needed to find the colonel, so he tried to think about what possible event or memory may have crossed over between the timelines.

He touched a key. It was cold, and there was only the faintest trace of a timeline, so he teased it out, letting its history drift between his fingers.

'That's not what I meant,' Caitlin said as Josh unwound the path.

He followed the line, chasing the history of the machine back into the past until he found the same typewriter sitting in a small clerk's office. An ordinary-looking man in a suit was sitting at the desk, and standing behind him was a guard dressed in a uniform from the First World War. He had a vicious looking bayonet attached to the end of his rifle.

He lifted his hands away from the keys. 'Okay. Maybe getting their permission is a good idea. Who's in charge back then?'

'We don't know for sure.'

She seemed uneasy, as if she were giving away some kind of secret. 'Their operators use codenames mostly.'

Josh had an idea.

'Does anyone ever call himself the Colonel?'

She looked puzzled. 'Yes, but how —'

'Never mind,' he said, typing out a message.

> Tell Colonel the Weatherman requests an audience. Ends.

Josh looked at the simple line of text and smiled. It was unlikely they would've had the conversation about the colonel's dislike for weathermen, but he knew him well enough to know that the old goat would still harbour the same opinions about them.

Five long minutes passed, and neither of them spoke. They stared at the inert keys waiting for some kind of response. Caitlin took off her coat and proceeded to smoke three cigarettes, one after another, and was lighting her fourth when Josh asked: 'Why Dalton?'

'He's a powerful man,' she replied, blowing out a long trail of smoke, 'and his family were good to me after my parents died. They took me in.'

'So you owe them? That's no reason to go and marry him.'

'It's none of your goddam business,' she snapped.

'In my time he was a bully. Liked to show everyone he was the boss.'

'You don't know him.' Her voice quavered a little and her arms crossed so that her hand could cover a series of bruises. They were fading, but Josh could see that they were spaced out like finger marks.

Dalton had broken her somehow, and he knew he had to put it right.

'So it's a good sign they haven't responded?' he said, changing the subject.

'Maybe.' She shrugged, wisps of smoke escaping from her red lips.

Josh found himself staring at her mouth for a little too long.

'It could mean anything. What on earth does "Weatherman" mean anyway?'

'Just a little joke he told me once. In another time.'

'And you think he has the same sense of humour?'

'Oh. I think there are certain things that never change — no matter what timeline you're from.'

The typewriter suddenly sprang to life, hammering out a message.

> Accepted. Transfer of WEATHERMAN granted. Ends.

Josh read the message twice and smiled. 'Looks like it worked then,' he said, turning towards her.

She was staring at him intensely, in the way she used to do. It took Josh's breath away, her eyes like lasers burning into him.

'How?' she asked.

'I'm the Paradox.' He smiled, pulling the sheet of paper out of the typewriter. 'This is what I was born to do, my chance to put it back the way it should be.'

There were tears in her eyes: she'd wanted to believe all along.

He waved the sheet in front of her. 'I'm going to fix this. This whole fascist Nazi thing you guys have got yourself into.'

Then, on an impulse, he grabbed her around the waist and kissed her. At first, she tried to push him away, and then slowly surrendered. Her lips parted and he felt her body soften and fold into his.

A long minute later he stepped back, then gave her his best self-assured smile and disappeared.

Caitlin stared at the space where he'd been, touching her

lips as if savouring the sensation, then shook her head and slowly put her coat back on.

'What the hell is a Nazi anyway?' she murmured to herself as she carefully placed a new blank sheet of paper in the type-writer and replaced the glass dome.

10

THE COLONEL

[London. Date: 11.588]

The bespectacled chubby man in the tweed suit was obviously unaccustomed to holding the pistol; the barrel waggled around in the air as he tried, and failed, to keep it pointed straight at Josh.

'Mainwaring, for God's sake put that down before you hurt someone.'

The sound of the colonel's unmistakable bellow was something Josh never thought he would miss. He wanted to hug the old man, but the sight of him as he came through the door made him reconsider. The colonel was wearing a stained, threadbare tunic of a General from the First World War and leaning heavily on a stick. The skin on his bald head was puckered with scars and he had a patch over one eye, but his beard was as wild as ever.

'So you're Weatherman?' he slurred, looking Josh over. 'I'd be interested to hear how a Terminist came by that little joke — never met one yet who had a decent sense of humour!' The old man slurred his words, he was obviously drunk.

Two stone-faced guards appeared behind the colonel. 'But first, I'm afraid you've an appointment with our reception committee. A formality really: just need to ask you a few questions, pry into your past — you know, the standard kind of interrogation thing.'

Josh nodded and let the guards handcuff him. They looked just as grim as Dalton's squad: their thick fingers were clumsy and twice the size of his, meant for crushing and not precision work.

He knew another round of interrogation was a small price for being here, even if the colonel hadn't given him a second look. It was just border control — all he had to do was prove he wasn't a spy.

'Give my regards to Major Kelly!' The colonel saluted as they walked Josh out of the room.

Great, thought Josh, at least this time it would be an expert tramping around in his memories.

11

TO THE PALACE

After they'd questioned him for a night and most of the next day, they let him sleep. At breakfast the following morning Edward Kelly had appeared; a much more reserved version of the one that Josh was used to, but still surrounded by an aura of madness — he was definitely 'touched', as his Gran used to say.

Fortunately for Josh's stomach, the Grand Seer had no intention of turning him upside down this time.

Kelly had taken his hand and stared at him for the longest time. Josh could hardly feel his mental presence, it was almost as if someone were talking in another room. The seer moved like a ghost through his past, until he finally came to the same conclusion as everyone else.

'Paradox?' he whispered in disbelief, as though it were a question for himself.

Josh smiled. They all reached the same conclusion in the end. He pulled back his sleeve to reveal the Ouroboros, just to show that the answer had been there the whole time.

The Grand Seer clicked his fingers and two guards

appeared. 'Guard this man with your lives,' he ordered before bowing to Josh and leaving.

The colonel sat opposite him in the Royal carriage. It was some kind of steam-driven car, which, by Josh's estimation, had a top speed of twenty miles-per-hour. The old man looked out-of-place sat on the velvet cushioned seats wearing his dress uniform, he was obviously not comfortable in enclosed spaces and reminded Josh of one of those Russian bears who'd been put into too small a cage.

'So it appears you and I may have met before,' he said, staring out of the window.

They were driving through an alternate version of London. The streets were narrow and full of soldiers and Josh caught a glimpse of barrage balloons floating above the buildings.

'Yeah, you recruited me.'

'I seriously doubt that.'

'Like I kept telling Major Kelly, and the guy before him, this timeline is seriously screwed up. Whatever you've got going on with this war thing' — he waved at the window — 'is totally out of control. My version of the sixteenth-century involves Shakespeare and sword fights — not Zeppelins and bolt-action rifles. Someone has gone back and changed the past — just like you said they would.'

The colonel scratched his beard, *another habit that had survived the time shift.* Josh thought to himself.

'Did I indeed? How insightful of me.'

The car came to a stop at the gates to the Tower of London, a beefeater in a black and red uniform opened the door and saluted the colonel.

'They're expecting you sir.'

The colonel tugged on the front of his jacket and puffed out his chest. 'Right. Come on then Mr Paradox, let's get this over with.'

12

ELIZABETH I

The Royal apartments were grand — not as extravagant as those of Louis XVI, but these had more style: the walls were lined with oak panels, and there were gold-framed portraits of the Tudor Kings lining the walls. The room was warmed by a large fire that burned in the ornately canopied fireplace.

A group of important-looking people stood around a long mahogany table debating tactics on a large map that had been spread across it. Josh spotted Lord Dee immediately. He was dressed in a three-piece suit rather than his usual sombre robes, but still had the beard and the piercing blue eyes. The other men, who were dressed like high-ranking members of the army, were collected around one elegant Lady — a beautiful redhead in a long green dress.

The colonel waited impatiently for them to finish their conversation. Josh could see that it was killing the old man to stay so quiet for so long.

From what he could overhear, they were discussing an impending attack. There was a fleet of Spanish airships currently somewhere over France that would be in British airspace within the next few hours.

'The Armada is due at 0500 hours. We can have our fighters in the air by 0200,' declared one of the gold-braided officers as he pointed to the South Coast.

'Their gunners will cut your squadron down before they get within striking distance,' said another. 'We should use our long-range artillery batteries.'

'They've not been proven to be that effective and the collateral damage to the civilian population would be too high a price to pay.'

'Gentlemen, please,' demanded the lady. 'I believe the Royal Astrologer has something to add.'

Lord Dee bowed to her. 'If I may be so bold, my Lady.'

The others did little to hide their dislike of Dee, whispering insults to each other like schoolboys.

'There is a high chance of bad weather over the coastal areas, thus, I believe the Armada will be blown off course by a factor of three and a half degrees to the West. If Commander Drake were to send his squadron to approach from here,' — he used his cane to point to a particular spot on the map — 'the sun would be rising in their eyes, blinding the gunners temporarily and giving his men the weather gage.'

The Generals' smug expressions turned sour as they considered the details of Lord Dee's plan — it sounded like a good one to Josh, and he could see from the smirk on the colonel's face that his master had put them in their place.

'So do we have a stratagem gentlemen?' the lady asked of her council.

They each nodded reluctantly.

'Good. Then I suggest you make ready. I want to teach Philip a lesson once and for all.'

The generals trooped out through a secret door in the

bookcase, leaving the lady and Lord Dee at the table. The colonel coughed, reminding them of his presence.

She turned with all the grace of a prima ballerina, and Josh was entranced.

'Majesty, may I present Joshua Jones Esquire,' the colonel began. 'Joshua, this is her Royal Britannic Majesty, Elizabeth the First, Queen of England and Ireland, Empress of the colonies and Supreme Governor of the Church,' the colonel recited with a bow.

Josh felt awkward as the Queen walked towards him. There was an inner radiance about her: her skin was so pale as to be nearly transparent, and her eyes were deep brown pools that were hard to look away from.

She put out her hand, and he bowed his head, touching his lips to her ringed fingers in the way the knights used to do in the old movies his mother watched.

'So, Lord Dee. This is the mysterious Paradox you've been telling me about? He's rather more handsome than I'd imagined.'

'I hadn't noticed Ma'am,' observed Dee.

'Quite as it should be, and how fares my favourite Colonel?' she asked without taking her eyes off Josh. There was a hunger behind the stare that made him feel quite vulnerable.

'Can't complain, my Lady,' answered the colonel gruffly.

'Good.' She pursed her lips. 'So master Jones, Lord Dee informs me that you have travelled from the future.'

Over her shoulder, Josh caught the eye of Dee and knew immediately that he was on dangerous ground — a tiny shake of the head was enough to convey the seriousness of the situation.

'Yes. Your Majesty.'

'My lady will do. And how do you find it there?'

'It's all wrong... My lady.'

She laughed, a girlish, high-pitched giggle that lightened the mood.

'Of course it is! Lord Dee is such a tease, and gives me nothing but riddles. Too worried about the end of the world.' She leant in close and whispered: 'Do they still believe in the monarchy?'

Dee's cheeks were turning purple with anger, but it was the colonel that spoke up. 'Your highness, you know we cannot divulge —'

'I know, I know. God's balls!' She held her hand up. 'If it wasn't for your damned strategies — I would've had you both hung, drawn and quartered years ago!'

Josh realised that this wasn't the first time they'd been asked these questions.

'But this is all wrong too,' Josh began, knowing that this may be his only chance. 'Something is out of place.'

The colonel looked puzzled, and Josh wondered whether he still harboured the same old conspiracy theories about the advancement of the past.

'Time is out of joint?' replied Elizabeth with a theatrical flourish. 'Where have I heard that before?'

'Hamlet, Ma'am. Shakespeare's latest.'

'Ah yes, master Shakespeare has quite a talent for memorable phrasing. So Joshua, what is it that you find so *pas à sa place*?'

Josh could feel Lord Dee's eyes burning into him, cautioning about giving too much away.

'You have guns when you should have swords. You fly airships instead of sailing in warships. Someone has given you technology that you shouldn't have!'

The Queen's features hardened as she listened to him.

'My Lady...' began Dee, but he stopped as she raised one delicate finger.

'It seems to me that we have no more or less than we deserve, Master Jones. Whether that was by happenstance or fate — these weapons are equal to those of our enemy, who are bearing down on us with all speed.'

She walked back over to the map. 'So, gentlemen, can you assure me that we shall be victorious tomorrow? Will I still be Queen of England in twenty-four hours?' There was a steeliness in her tone, one that spoke of a lifetime of threats and hard choices.

'My calculations predict —'

'No more of your damned calculus! I want him to tell me!' she shouted, pointing directly at Josh. 'If he is from the future, he should know.'

Dee bowed his head respectfully, and the colonel did the same. Josh felt the weight of the world on his shoulders. The truth was that he had no idea: his history lessons had never really involved Elizabeth I, and certainly not this version. He tried hard to think of any questions from his mother's quiz shows regarding the Spanish Armada. He wished he could ask her now, as she had such a good memory for random facts, especially historical ones.

Then it came to him: "What are Hellburners?" A tiebreaker question from University Challenge. The English Navy had set fire to their own ships in order to break the Spanish fleet's formation.

'They were turned back, my Lady.'

Elizabeth smiled gracefully.

Dee was scowling at him, and Josh remembered what Eddy had told him in the travel pod.

'But this won't be the last war. The battle tomorrow will be the first of many.'

13

COLONEL'S STUDY

Painted wooden models of bi-planes hung suspended on fishing lines from the ceiling of the colonel's war room, arranged as though they were in the middle of a great air battle.

Every spare inch of wall was covered with heavily annotated maps of England and charts of the surrounding seas. Long red lines of ribbon were pinned across them, mapping out routes of possible attacks. It reminded Josh of the attic room in the colonel's house, but these plans were different somehow — more sinister.

'So you believe me?' Josh asked, gazing around the room.

The colonel ignored him, too busy flicking through an old journal and talking to himself in the way he did when trying to solve a problem.

Josh helped himself to some whisky from a crystal decanter on the sideboard. The interview with Elizabeth had been intense, and his hand shook a little as he poured the liquor into a glass.

He closed his eyes and let the heat of the scotch warm him, feeling the tension release in his neck and shoulders. Two interrogations in two days had taken it out of him, and still he was no closer to finding out how to fix the timeline — the change went further back than he'd expected.

Josh found himself staring at an oil painting of a semi-naked woman. It reminded him of the one from the French revolution — except in this one, there was no swan, only a lady reclining on a sofa, her hands placed strategically to cover her modesty — as his Gran would say.

'Reubens,' said the colonel, 'a life study from the thir-teenth century. I studied under him for a while before the war — before I lost my good eye.' He pulled off his eye patch and showed Josh the milk-white orb beneath.

Josh coughed as he drank, the whisky catching in his throat. 'You studied art?'

The colonel stiffened a little and put down the journal. 'Don't presume to know me, boy, no matter what may have transpired in other times — you and I are not acquainted.'

Josh put the glass down and turned to face him, the alcohol giving him a little Dutch courage.

'But we used to be, and I think a part of you is still in there — a part that wants to help me sort this mess out.'

The colonel grunted and turned back to his charts. 'Kelly tells me that Mistress Eckhart sent you back herself. I'm curious to know how exactly you persuaded the History Burner to let you go. If I'd have known, I'd have had you shot myself and sent your body back to the witch.'

Josh could tell by his steely tone that he wasn't joking.

'I guess she believed in me. She and I were kind of close once — in another time.'

'Ha! You're telling me you melted the ice queen's heart? I didn't think she had one.'

'I think she knows, deep down, that something is wrong with the continuum.'

'Well, your little speech to her Majesty about something being out-of-place certainly struck a chord — Dee's beside himself.'

'It's one of your theories! You told me that someone was trying to advance the past, bringing knowledge back to make the present — what was the phrase? Technologically something?'

'Superior. Technologically superior.'

'Yeah, someone has changed this timeline. You're using weapons that you weren't supposed to have for another six-hundred years.'

The colonel went over to the whisky and poured himself a large glass, then slugged it back in one go. He stood for a moment with his eye closed, savouring the smooth liquor as it washed down his throat.

'Do you know what was written about the Paradox? Why we have spent so long fighting about it?' the colonel asked wearily, the years of constant conflict having obviously taken their toll.

'No. They asked me a whole bunch of stupid questions about it, but no one ever told me what I was meant to be.'

The colonel poured himself another drink and cleared his throat. Josh noticed that adults tended to do that when they were about to say something that made them feel uncomfortable.

'The prophecy states that the Paradox, apart from being from the future, of course, is a lodestone — a kind of compass. That he or she would instinctively know when the continuum was not on course. That they would have some inherent ability to detect deviations — when we'd strayed from the prime eventuality.'

He drained the whisky again, took Josh's glass and poured them both a very large measure.

'The ability to retain the knowledge of how things should be, no matter what changes are made to the past; to be the persistent vessel of memory, that is the true power of the Paradox.'

Josh wondered if the colonel wasn't a little drunk. The old man's eyes were red-rimmed, and there were tears in the corners of both.

'After all these years,' he muttered, slumping back into his chair. 'I'd begun to question whether you could actually exist.'

'Well, I'm here now. So, do you think you can help me fix it?' Josh asked, putting his drink down. 'Because this tastes like shit.'

14

GUNPOWDER

They'd spent many hours going back over the last five centuries. The colonel would consult one large leather volume after another, reading aloud events that bore little or no resemblance to anything that Josh could remember about his own timeline — which he admitted wasn't great. He wondered how his old history teacher, Miss Fieldhouse, would feel about the fate of mankind relying on his recollection of her lessons.

As far as Josh could make out, the past had become significantly more violent; the advances in technology had been mostly for the military, escalating the scale of their conflicts and bringing the world to the brink of total devastation more than once.

'Why didn't you just go back and fix it?' Josh asked the obvious question after they gave up on the twelfth century.

'We tried, many times,' the colonel said, sighing, 'but the Determinists were adamant that events were following the grand plan. When the Paradox debate got out of hand, they went on a witch hunt for the Copernicans and purged them. Any surviving members are in hiding, branded as Magii, with a price on their heads. They left us blind, so we have no way to calculate the best outcome, no access to the continuum.'

'And you can't go forward?'

'Nor back, but we made sure that they couldn't either,' he said with a glint of pride. 'It is a fragile truce, a stalemate.'

Josh wondered what he'd done to earn the nickname 'Butcher.' It sounded bad, but you never knew how much of it was true — war made people do things they never thought they'd have to and so he decided it was probably better not to ask.

'How did the Determinists become so powerful?'

'I assume the situation became so critical that they had no choice — it's one of the disaster scenarios that Lord Dee considered when he shut down the Infinity Engine.'

'He can stop it?'

'Yes, in a time of crisis. He had no choice but to disable it before things got any worse. I think, secretly, he was waiting for you.'

'So how come I can still travel?'

The colonel laughed. 'Time is not controlled by the engine, the continuum is merely a computational model, an observational tool. You are the Paradox, the "Strange Attractor", and aren't bound by the laws of the continuum.'

'Cool — I think.'

The colonel opened another book and leafed through the pages. 'Shall we continue? Battle of Hastings, 11.066, at which Guillaume, Duke of Normandy and his knights attempted to conquer Britain.'

'Knights? That sounds like the right kind of history. He won, right? Harold got shot through the eye with an arrow.'

'Bullet.'

'Bugger.'

'The Saxons were massacred by the French artillery.'

'Next.'

The colonel leafed back through the pages of the book, his face a mask of concentration. Josh watched as he went back and forth to the shelves, picking out other volumes and silently comparing a series of events.

'That's strange,' he murmured. 'I have cross-referenced three other reliable historians. I don't know why I missed this before.'

'What?'

'Before 11.066, there's no mention of gunpowder being used in mainland Europe. China had invented it a hundred years before, but not really used it in any tactical way until —'

'The Battle of Boju?' suggested Josh.

'Yes. How did you —'

'I was there. So how did it get out of China?'

'Someone gave the Normans the alchemical formula and taught them how to make the guns. But there are records that show that no one traded with China until Niccolò Polo met the Kublai Khan in 11.266 — two-hundred years later.'

Josh remembered something Caitlin had said about the impact of future technology on the past: 'It was like giving a five-year-old a nuclear weapon.'

The colonel's face lit up. 'I believe we've found our deviation,' he said, patting Josh on the shoulder. 'Now all we need is a way to get back there — we need to go and see the Founder!'

15

FOUNDER

When they arrived at Richmond Palace it was buzzing with the defeat of the Spanish Armada. By the time Josh and the colonel were finally allowed an audience with Lord Dee, he seemed to be in unusually high spirits.

'Rufius!' Dee smiled. 'It's good to see you, my old friend!'

Josh thought the founder sounded a little tipsy.

'My Lord,' the colonel replied with a bow, 'I hear the latest Spanish assault was well and truly routed?'

'Indeed it was,' Dee acknowledged with a wave of his hand. 'The wind changed exactly as I predicted.'

Josh had no idea how many men had just died, and guessed it didn't matter when you were protecting your country.

'My Lord, I have a special favour to ask of you,' the colonel requested more formally.

Lord Dee's eyes narrowed slightly. 'How special?'

'I need a platoon of Dreadnoughts — just for a day or two.'

'My most elite troops? Why on earth would you require their services?'

The colonel hesitated slightly. 'I believe I have located a potential... deviation.'

'A deviation?' The founder scowled. 'Not another one of your ridiculous theories about those elusive Determinist sappers by any chance?'

'No.' The colonel waved his hand. 'Not that. Jones here has helped identify a level five variance in the eleventh century. It wouldn't require a whole platoon, perhaps a fireteam: a lensman, three artificers and a nautonnier should be sufficient.'

Lord Dee raised his eyebrows and steepled his fingers in front of his face. 'A level five is it now? Perhaps I should accompany you myself.'

'By all means, Master,' the colonel lied, 'but won't the Queen be requiring your counsel on the repercussions of the Spanish assault?'

'Quite possibly,' Dee agreed, turning to Josh. 'What say you Master Jones? Does the Paradox believe I should spare such a valuable resource at this time?'

Josh didn't really know what to say. He'd never heard of the Dreadnoughts or had a clue what an artificer was, but the colonel was glaring anxiously at him. He was obviously pushing his luck — the founder was a clever man, whatever his strategy was, and it seemed to put the colonel off his game.

'I have to go, with or without your precious Dreadnoughts. It's the only way to put things right.'

'And what exactly is it that you've discovered?'

The colonel told him about the gunpowder, and the difference between the Norman conquest in Josh's time and theirs. The founder's eyes closed as he listened to the plan to find the source, his lips moving silently as if he were whispering a prayer.

'I can spare two,' Dee concluded, opening his eyes. He wrote out a note and stamped it with his personal seal. 'A lensman and an artificer. A thorough impact assessment would take weeks, but by my approximation, they should give you at least a seventy-two per cent chance of locating the variance and rectifying the deviation.'

He handed the note to the colonel.

The old man took the note and smiled at Josh like a kid who had just been given the keys to the sweet shop.

16

DREADNOUGHT

J osh had encountered the Draconians once before, when they'd rescued Caitlin and himself from a prehistoric cave in the deep, ice-bound past of the Mesolithic. Sim was always talking about them: it was hard to hide his obsession with the most adventurous guild of the Oblivion Order.

Caitlin's parents had been part of the Nautonniers, the exploration division of the guild, but he knew virtually nothing about them. Josh had always assumed they were nothing more than a bunch of cartography nerds off on some school trip into the dark ages.

None of this prepared him for his first encounter with the two members of the Draconian Defence Service, or Dreadnoughts, as they were more commonly known.

After the meeting with Lord Dee, the colonel had led Josh down through a series of interconnecting tunnels beneath Richmond Palace. He'd explained that this was all that really remained of the Order's headquarters, nothing more than a storage facility for their most precious ancient artefacts. Antiquarians in long black robes bustled along the brick-lined vaults, carefully carrying the most unusual objects as if they were made of glass. They stared suspiciously at Josh and the colonel, and he was sure he heard more than one curse muttered behind their backs as they passed.

'What are sappers?' asked Josh, as they took a right-hand turn into another tunnel.

'Hmm?'

'The founder said you had a theory about Determinist sappers?'

'Time tunnellers. Trying to dig back into the past.'

'Really? How do they do that?'

'Through the maelstrom of course! Bloody dangerous job though. Ah, here we are!'

The colonel stopped at an iron-bound door, one of many that Josh had seen along the passage. Unlike the others, there wasn't a symbol or sign to hint at what was behind it. The old man smiled, tapped his cane upon it three times, then pushed it open and stepped through.

Josh was totally unprepared for the bright sunlight that greeted him on the other side, nor the thick, humid Amazonian jungle he found himself surrounded by. He shaded his eyes, blinking as he stared back at the open door into the dark corridor of bustling academics, one of whom stopped, tutted, and slammed the door shut.

They were standing in an ancient sandstone courtyard. Vine-covered statues of Aztec gods gazed down at them with cold, pitiless eyes. A goat was bleating, tied to a stake in the middle of the sandstone floor. The heat and the ancient carvings reminded Josh of a holiday competition his mum had entered once, somewhere in Mexico. She'd banged on about it for weeks — Teotihuacan.

'Sohguerin,' the colonel called out. 'Captain Leone Sohguerin?'

A woman appeared out of thin air. She was tall, with coffee-coloured skin and long black hair adorned with feathers like a native-American. Her jacket and trousers were leather, studded with symbols. A set of bandoliers were wrapped around her upper body, on which hung her own personal collection of curiosities: charms, artefacts and some things that looked a lot like shrunken heads.

'Colonel Westinghouse,' she acknowledged, snapping to attention.

The captain scrutinised Josh with cold dark eyes. 'And this is?'

Josh stepped forward, offering a hand. 'Josh.'

She ignored it.

'I take it you have a mission for me?' she asked, bending down to take a long knife from her boot and cutting the tether to the goat. It ran off into the bush, bleating its thanks.

'Still after the Quetzalcoatl?' The colonel nodded towards the disappearing goat.

'It's a worthy prey,' she said, pulling out a multi-coloured feather that had been woven into her hair. 'The feathered serpent has powerful wisdom.'

'And not forgetting the wind jewel?'

She blushed a little. 'Who wouldn't wish to command the elements?'

They were suddenly cast into shadow as if a dragon had flown across the sun. Josh instinctively looked up to see a man in a crude parachute gliding over them before landing gracefully a few metres away.

'Sergeant Johansson?' the colonel asked the captain.

The captain put her knife away in one fluid movement. 'Base jumping off the Pyramid of the Moon. Says it helps him understand their culture. He's full of shit — he's looking for treasure.'

The canopy of the parachute collapsed, and Josh saw a young man in a similar outfit to the captain's.

As he gathered up the cords of the chute, he smiled and waved at them. He was a big man, with a dark beard that reminded Josh of a much younger version of the colonel.

'Sergeant Johansson, Artificer First Class, reporting for duty, sir!' said the young man when he reached them.

'Colonel Westinghouse, and this is Jones.' The colonel waved a thumb absent-mindedly in Josh's direction. 'He's going to be our nautonnier. This mission falls under the offices of the founder himself.' He showed them the signed orders from Lord Dee. 'It's a level five incident. We're going after an deviation back in 11.066.'

Johansson's breath hissed through his teeth. 'Man, that's a lot of sixes — hate going back to the eleventh — they didn't call it the Dark Ages for nothing.'

The captain ignored her junior officer. 'How many are going in with us?'

The colonel took a deep breath. 'We're the entire company. It's a risky venture, but the founder estimates we have over an eighty-percent chance of success.'

'Plus he couldn't spare any of the A-team. Too busy fighting the Spanish, eh?' joked Johansson.

The captain turned on Johansson and punched him square in the jaw.

'Enough! I swear one of these days I'm going to string you up instead of the goat and let the damn birds peck out your eyes.'

Josh and the colonel exchanged glances, both sharing

similar suspicions about why the founder could afford to spare these two particular officers. Josh also thought that the odds that Dee had quoted them probably weren't quite as realistic as he'd made out.

'So,' the colonel continued, 'do you have any relevant questions before we begin?'

'No sir,' Johansson replied, rubbing his jaw as he got back to his feet.

'Are the tachyons operational?' asked Sohguerin.

'No. I'm afraid there'll be no safety net on this mission.'

17

1066

[Telham Hill, Hastings. Date: 14th October, 11.066]

I t was the middle of the afternoon, and the sun was already beginning to wane. They stood in silence at the top of Telham hill looking down onto the battlefield. Carrion rows picked at the bodies of English soldiers who lay dead or dying, scattered across the ground and half-buried in the cloying mud.

It was a massacre, the English infantry wiped out by the superior firepower of the French carabiniers . Their primitive axes and wooden shields were no protection from their musket balls.

The colonel stood up in his stirrups to get a better view. 'How long does it take?' he muttered anxiously.

He was wearing the ill-fitting uniform of a dead French commander and it was irritating him. Being made to sit still like a petulant child at pony club was not making things any better. The long velvet cape kept catching on the hilt of his sword, and he was continually adjusting the dented iron breastplate that Sohguerin had insisted he put on.

'You'll get your head shot off if you keep doing that!' growled the captain, stroking the head of the colonel's horse — the gunfire was making it skittish.

'He should have found it by now!' The colonel sat down heavily into the saddle, causing the horse to whinny. 'This is worse than watching a Copernican decide what he's having for lunch.'

'He's an engineer, not a soldier. I'm assuming he's not taking any unnecessary risks,' she replied, more to the horse than its rider.

They were waiting for Johansson, who'd volunteered to go in search of the French armourer. They needed a vestige, an artefact that could be directly linked to the alchemist and the making of the gunpowder, like a page from his journal or one of his tools that made the ammunition — which the Normans seemed to be getting through at an alarming rate.

The route back to 11.066 hadn't been the easiest. The Antiquarians were incredibly protective of their meagre collection of historical artefacts, and even the signed orders from the founder was treated with derision and superstition. Josh was shocked when he saw exactly how small their stores were: pieces had been piled into storerooms like the back room of a charity shop and it took the curator of the eleventh century over an hour to find the item the colonel had requested.

He was like a grumpy shopkeeper when he finally shuffled out, carrying a small roll of material.

'Bayeux Tapestry,' he grumbled, hefting it off his shoulder and onto the counter.

The colonel unrolled it carefully, and Josh recognised the embroidered knights and horses from primary school, although it was odd to see the men carrying muskets instead of bows, and the slaughter of the English was no less horrific when woven.

'Where's the rest of it?' asked the colonel.

The Antiquarian shrugged. 'Lost. The fire in the cathedral took the rest.'

'Wasn't this made in France?' asked Josh.

'No,' said the colonel, shaking his head. 'I think you'll find it was commissioned by Bishop Odo, William's brother — it was rediscovered in Bayeux in 11.729.'

'By the Terminists,' said the curator, scowling. 'It will get you back to 11.070, but from there you're on your own.'

When they first arrived, Josh had wondered why they didn't just pick up the first weapon they found and work back through the timeline, but the captain and the colonel shook their heads as if he'd made some kind of rookie mistake and went back to their argument about the colonel wearing a breastplate.

'Too many variables,' explained Johansson. 'There's a high probability that the French have been planning this for years. We have no idea how many blacksmiths were conscripted to help make their weapons. We need to find something out on the field that comes from the source.'

Johansson was dressed in the uniform of a Gard du Corps, a French foot soldier. His bloodstained blue tabard hid the ringed leather jerkin that he'd stolen off a dead English archer. It would provide little protection from a stray bullet, but he said he preferred it. He was lighter and quicker than the heavy armour-plated Knights, who looked like mediaeval Robocops as they stomped around the battlegrounds with 'hand cannons' strapped to each arm, blasting away at the retreating English forces. Josh could still hear the screams of the men as they fell, their bodies ripped open by the crude spray of grapeshot.

'So, what exactly does an artificer do?' Josh asked, helping to strap a shield onto Johansson's back.

'I'm a specialist — an engineer. Since we can't bring anything back with us, I'm trained to fashion tools from the local era, adapt technology — make useful stuff.'

Johansson picked up a small musket and shook the barrel until a small round ball rolled out. He kept the ball and threw away the gun. 'Not that she would agree,' he added, nodding in the captain's general direction.

'What's wrong with her?'

'Not a people person, my captain. Been thrown out of every squad she's ever been assigned to.' Johansson inspected the smooth round ball closely. 'Smooth bore, lead shot. Deadly at 50 metres. Should do nicely.'

'Then how did you end up with her?'

'That, my friend, is another story entirely,' Johansson replied, shifting the shoulder straps to make the shield more comfortable. 'Right now I have to go find me an armourer.' He held up the lead shot and winked out of existence.

When Johansson reappeared, he'd taken a bullet in the shoulder. His breathing was laboured and his legs buckled under him — the captain caught him before he hit the floor.

The colonel quickly dismounted and Josh had to grab the horse's bridle to stop it from trampling the sergeant. The wounded man took out a small book from inside his jacket, wincing at the pain it caused his injured shoulder.

'Damned gunsmith had a gun, who'd have thought it?' he

said, panting through the pain. 'Not that it did him much good in the end.'

Johansson began to laugh, but it quickly turned into a rattling cough.

'Rest easy soldier,' ordered the colonel, relieving him of the book.

The captain searched through her bag until she found a small vial of white powder. She cut the straps on Johansson's armour to expose the wound, then pulled the stopper out with her teeth.

'I need some help?' she pleaded to Josh. 'Let the damn horse go and come and hold him down!'

Josh did as he was told and the horse bolted off towards the trees.

Johansson screamed as Sohguerin poured the medicine into the bubbling hole, fizzing as it mixed with the dark red blood.

Josh found himself staring in awe as the musket ball surfaced through the pink froth. The captain picked it out carefully and inspected it.

'No fragmentation. You're a lucky fool.' She kissed the now comatose artificer, confirming what Josh had begun to suspect.

'He's a bloody hero,' added the colonel and holding the book up. 'I shall see he gets a commendation for this!'

'Is it what we need?' asked Josh, impatiently snatching the book from the colonel. It was covered in Johansson's blood, but the inner pages were untainted and full of handwritten archaic chemical symbols and diagrams of guns.

The colonel tapped on a crest at the top of one of the pages. 'This is the almanac of Guillaume de Belladiere, the Duke's Armourer! Johansson must have managed to infiltrate the Royal enclosure, the very heart of their battle command.'

Josh felt the timeline begin to unravel from the pages, and

saw the moment Johansson surprised the Royal Armourer, sweating over his experiments in a tented workshop. There were glass vials and tubes full of bubbling liquids, candles and braziers boiling off all number of chemical compounds. Josh could smell the acrid fumes that gathered beneath the canvas roof. Guillaume was a small, round man with a bald, cannon-ball head. His book was the first thing he reached for when Johansson jumped him, closely followed by a newly-made gun that was lying on his workbench.

'You have the line?' asked the colonel, interrupting Josh.

Josh nodded, weaving further back through the stream of events, following the book as it made its way over the channel and into France. He felt the pen scratch across the paper as Guillaume made notes on his journey. He could smell the ink on the gunsmith's fingers as he copied out the complex chemical formulae at his desk deep within some dark castle. Someone was talking to the man as he worked, but Josh couldn't see his face: it was a blur, as though the moment had been edited, redacted somehow.

'I've got the location,' Josh said, repeating the temporal coordinates.

'Gisors. Interesting — Templar territory,' noted the colonel. 'Wake him up, we have to leave.'

The captain dumped a canteen of water over Johansson's face, and he woke with a start. The wound was nothing more than a pink bruise on his shoulder and healing quickly.

'The curative powers of time, eh?' he spluttered, wiping the water from his face.

They all placed their hands on the book — the captain trying her hardest not to touch anyone else — and the battle-field twisted away.

18

ALCHEMIST

[Château de Gisors. Date: 11.060]

They appeared in one of the lower levels of the castle: a storage space full of rusting armour, broken equipment and discarded furniture. Josh had let the colonel navigate through the timeline, as he had a knack for finding safe, out of the way places to land — 'minimum risk vectors,' or MRVs as he called them.

Sohguerin was wandering around looking at various parts of the room through a glass ball, while Johansson was inspecting random pieces of junk as if browsing for treasure at some crazy medieval jumble sale.

'Strange to think that in just over two-hundred years this castle will become the prison of Jacques De Molay, Grandmaster of the Templars,' observed the colonel, lighting a torch with a flint. 'They held him here for years before burning him at the stake. Legend says that he cursed the Pope and the King with his last breath — both were dead within a year.'

'The Templars? The Crusader Knights? Weren't they the

ones protecting the Holy Grail?' asked Josh, thinking about the pictures he used to draw in his diary.

'There were a few myths about the Grail,' the colonel corrected him. 'But many of them were spread by Philip IV of France, who happened to owe them a few million francs at the time. He had hundreds of them arrested or shot on Friday the 13th October, 11.307. The navy escaped with the majority of their treasure, but their leaders remained behind. The interrogations were brutal, according to the Vatican records.'

Josh was still finding it difficult to imagine the Templars with machine guns instead of swords.

'The aperture is close,' the captain reported, holding up the glass sphere. It was more intricately designed than the one Josh had seen Caitlin use: made out of miniature mirrored panes, each separate face catching the light and splitting it into the most unusual range of colours. It was nothing like the prisms they had used at school — light seemed to slow and dissolve as it passed through it.

'Show me,' instructed the colonel, taking the lens and wandering off with the captain in tow.

Johansson returned from his own treasure hunt and emptied a sack full of parts onto a table.

'There should be enough here to make a few diversions for our friends upstairs.' He began to sort through the assortment of glass vials and copper tubes.

The captain and the colonel walked around the room, checking the readings at various points as if trying to triangulate the location of the aperture.

'So what exactly is an aperture?' Josh asked Johansson once they were out of earshot.

Johansson looked concerned. 'You haven't had the training?'

Josh shrugged. 'Must have missed that one.'

'You're not Draconian — what guild are you from?'

Josh had never really given any thought to the other guilds, as they were all to wrapped up in their own sets of rules to appeal to him. He'd always assumed he was like the colonel, a Watchman — which wasn't really a guild as such, more a collection of misfits and rejects that had been thrown out of every other department.

'Scriptorian,' he lied. It had been Caitlin's guild, so it was the only other one he knew enough about to blag convincingly — plus no one ever seemed to care what they got up to.

Johansson grunted. 'Bookworm, not sure how much I can tell you. It's need-to-know, top-secret kind of shit.'

'Well, it looks like I'm going to find out soon enough,' said Josh, watching the captain wave the lens in front of the colonel's face.

'Yeah, I guess.' Johansson picked up a length of twisted copper pipe. 'It's a bit difficult to demonstrate in three dimensions. Imagine the air inside this tube is the continuum, that all space time flows through it, and this,' — he ran his hand along the metal — 'is the outer chronosphere, a kind of field that shields that flow.'

'Like a force field?'

'Yeah, sort of. Anyway, do you know what lies beyond that?' He waved his hand above and below the pipe.

'Nope.'

Johansson leaned in close, and his voice dropped to a secretive whisper. 'Nobody does. We call it the Maelstrom. Sohguerin believes it's the realm of the elder gods, primeval beings who have existed since time began. Whereas the reavers think that it's where you go when you die.'

Josh remembered the void that he'd glimpsed at the end of the colonel's timeline and the feeling that there had been something malevolent waiting in the darkness within.

'An aperture is a weakness in the wall.' Johansson tapped the metal with a copper nail. 'A breach is when something manages to break through.' He paused, the colour draining from his cheeks. 'Everything I've ever seen come out has looked like it fell out of hell.'

'Like a monad?'

'Monad, strzyga, plus a whole bestiary of hairy-arsed monsters that the Order won't admit to. Before the war, we had a department called Xenobiology — not that you Scriptorians would ever know that it existed.'

But he had. Josh remembered the monad the colonel had used to finish off the strzyga in the temple. Caitlin had been outraged by his misuse of the 'Xeno' department property.

'How do they break through?'

Johansson shrugged. 'No one really knows, but by the time we get there it's usually just a case of damage limitation and closure.'

He flipped the copper tube over and began to bend it carefully around a wire lattice. Josh watched him work, his hands expertly manipulating the metal, re-engineering parts from his collection of scavenged materials. Before long he'd built an unusual array of jam-jar hand grenades, modified a brace of flintlock pistols to be semi-automatic, and created what Josh could only guess was an electric shield.

There was a noise from the far end of the room, and the colonel was waving at them, calling for them to follow.

Johansson gathered up his creations into a bag and nodded to Josh to grab the rest.

'Whatever happens next, I suggest you keep your head down,' he warned. 'This isn't going to be pretty.'

19

THE BREACH

They followed the captain and her lens through a labyrinth of damp, stone corridors until they finally arrived at an ornately carved set of wooden doors.

'The breach is less than a minute away,' whispered Sohguerin, staring wide-eyed into the iridescent globe of light and glass. 'Approximately five metres inside that room.' She pointed at the door.

'Good,' declared the colonel, brandishing a sabre that Johansson had modified. 'Shall we?' He pushed open the doors and strode in as if he owned the place.

A deep French voice shouted: 'Va te faire foutre!' as Josh walked through the door. A minute later the colonel had taken out the only guard and was pinning a flustered Guillaume to the wall with the end of his sword. Johansson was busy drawing a coal dust circle on the floor around himself and the captain, who was counting down as she held the lens up in front of her.

'Three, two, one!' She dropped the lens and yanked two of the shrunken head charms off her belt.

At the far end of the room was a large, circular stained-glass window. As Josh watched, the air in front of it shimmered, and the details of the window bulged like bubbles of molten glass as the aperture broke through into their timeline. He thought he could hear distant sounds, distorted and fragmented, coming from the other side of the breach. The distortion expanded, and inside the bubble he could see a writhing mass of inky tendrils weaving their way out from its centre.

'First wave,' Johansson declared as the dark skeins formed into shapes. He was working frantically on one of his devices. 'I'm going to need another minute,' he warned, looking anxiously over to Sohguerin.

'Inside the circle,' she barked at the colonel and Josh, who stepped quickly over the coal-dust boundary. Josh noticed that the edges had already begun to crystalise into diamond.

A creature coalesced out of the seething mass. Its pale, eyeless face was still cloaked in strands of dark vapour as it took on the form of an old man. His jaw had been ripped away, revealing rows of shark-like teeth that seemed to go on forever down into his throat.

The monad broke out of the aperture and rose up in the air above them, beneath the layers of smoke, Josh caught fleeting glimpses of deformed hands and claws of many other creatures.

It was like staring at a nightmare. He could feel his heart hammering in his chest, and his mouth went dry. The monad emanated despair, feeding on his fear.

'Level three at least,' the colonel said from behind Josh, 'and there's at least two more coming. Sergeant, we need that weapon pronto!'

There was a cry from the corner and Josh turned to see Guillaume shaking, wild-eyed and still pinned to the wall. His hands were bloody where he had gripped the blade to pull the sword out.

Attracted to the sound or the blood, the monad turned towards the alchemist.

'Stop it!' shouted the colonel. 'Captain, we cannot afford to lose him.'

The captain whispered to one of her shrunken-head charms and lifted it up like an offering to the monad. The creature's misshapen head turned, the half-eaten nose seeming to wrinkle as if sniffing it out. Sohguerin was chanting in a language that Josh couldn't understand. When the monad drew closer, an outline of a Hindu god projected out from the charm, an elephant-headed being with six arms that took hold of the monster and held it fast.

'Hold it steady,' said Johansson, opening one side of a small metal cage and offering it to her. The captain dropped the charm into the box, and Johansson pushed it across the floor and out of the circle. The monad, unable to free itself from the grip of the effigy, was pulled inside.

'What the hell was that?' Josh asked, while Johansson pulled a glass jar wrapped in wire out of his bag and began to wind up the clockwork device that was attached to the side of it.

'Godheads — she's a mystic,' Johansson replied as if it were the most normal thing in the world.

Josh didn't have time to ask what that was before another wave of monads solidified before them.

'Make yourself useful.' Johansson handed Josh a couple more jars.

'What are they?'

'Timetraps. Faraday cages of sorts.' He showed Josh how they opened. 'Mousetraps for monads!'

The first two were followed by five more. The traps were running out, and there seemed to be no end to the flood of monsters.

'Are we going to have enough?' Josh wondered aloud, counting the next wave as they began to take shape. There would be at least ten more in the next few minutes.

'Not unless she can seal the breach!' Johansson nodded towards Sohguerin, who was using two deities against a posse of monads.

They were surrounded, though the colonel was holding his own against three grotesquely mutated creatures, each individually horrific in their reimagining of a human body.

'Time for a little exorcism,' Johansson cried out, stepping forward and swinging a mace-like incense burner above his head — he ploughed into the newest arrivals.

Josh's eye caught sight of the dark gaping hole at the middle of the aperture and was captivated by the feeling that there was something else within it. Concentrating on the swirling centre, he began to catch glimpses of other things, spinning fast, like on a merry-go-round. There were flashes of different worlds, and amongst the chaos he thought he could make out the shape of a man moving towards him. Like a badly edited film, the frames out of sequence, the stranger seemed to move closer and then drop back. The silhouette of the figure was an irregular shape with a spherical head, as if he was wearing a spacesuit.

Josh couldn't quite come to terms with the idea that an astronaut was walking towards him from the other side of the breach.

'Don't gaze too long into the abyss,' warned the colonel, pulling Josh away, 'lest the abyss gaze into you!'

Johansson laughed as he caught one of the monsters with his smoking mace. 'Now is really not the time for Nietzsche!' The monad's body evaporated as the censer smashed into it.

'Hey bookworm, are you seriously going to just stand there?' Johansson looked back at Josh.

Josh was finding it hard to take his eyes off the aperture. The figure was getting closer, and as it flickered in and out of view he was sure he would soon be able to see it clearly.

The protective circle was nearly completely white with diamond when one of the monads broke free of Sohguerin's deities and rushed at her. Johansson stepped between them, pushing her back and swinging the mace at its head, but he missed, and the globe shattered on the stone floor.

'Shit! Timetrap, now!' he screamed at Josh.

Josh wasn't quick enough. The monad's claws scythed off the first three fingers of Johansson's outstretched hand as Josh threw the trap.

Sohguerin was knocked sideways by the creature when it rounded for another attack on Johansson. Josh picked up the shield and forced the monster back out of the circle. The two Dreadnoughts were badly hurt, and the colonel was fighting a losing battle against a wall of horrors.

Something hit the shield with incredible force and knocked him to the floor. Stunned, Josh thought he heard the colonel shout: 'Sergeant, the bomb if you please.'

'Eighty percent my arse!' complained Johansson, using his good hand to pull a weird looking contraption out of his jacket. Josh watched him cradle it with his half-hand as he twisted the dial on top of it and threw it to the colonel.

Then the world went white.

20

ALONE

Motes of dust drifted gently down on shafts of sunlight that filtered through the shattered stained-glass window. Josh watched them for a while, his eyes slowly adjusting to the daylight.

He couldn't believe how quiet and peaceful it was. After the screeching of the monads, the total absence of sound was like waking from a terrible nightmare, until he realised it was just the ringing in his ears cancelling everything out.

Slowly, the memory of what had happened drifted back into his consciousness. Like a three-dimensional jigsaw, small pieces of the event restored themselves in random sequences. They'd been close to being overwhelmed when the colonel asked for the bomb. Someone was coming through the breach when it went off.

Josh was lying on the stone floor, with what felt like a door pressing down on his back. Lifting his head, he looked around the room for any sign of the others. The bomb seemed to have exploded away from him, blowing everything outwards: every splinter of furniture, shred of book or fibre of carpet had been piled up against the castle walls — which weren't looking particularly stable either.

Whatever type of explosive Johansson had used, it seemed to have cleansed the room of monads, breaches and the rest of his company.

Josh raised himself up on his elbows and the shield slid away. He sat up and checked himself for any obvious wounds, but there were none. He was, however, covered in a fine white dust, as if someone had thrown a bag of flour over him, which he realised was powdered diamond.

His lower back ached — someone had given him an almighty kick in the kidneys just before the bomb went off. Josh wasn't sure who, and there was no one left to ask — even the alchemist had vanished. He was annoyed that they'd left him behind — no one had hung around to check on him, but he guessed they had other business to attend to.

A light wind blew in through the blasted windows and with it came the scent of rain. It was a refreshing, cleansing smell, like the one you get after a storm. Watching the breeze brush swirls of diamond dust across the cracks in the floorboards, Josh wondered whether everything had gone back to normal now. The astronaut inside the breach was obviously trying to reach the alchemist to give him the formula — the colonel had been right about time tunnellers using the maelstrom. But the question he couldn't answer, was *why*. All he could hope now was that by stopping him, the continuum had corrected itself, and that it was the reason the present had got in such a mess.

A shout came up from outside followed by the sounds of swords clashing against shields. Josh stood up unsteadily and went to the broken window. Young squires were practising in the courtyard below; they reminded him of the ones from the picture books he'd read as a kid, all tin helmets and broadswords — and not a musket in sight.

Josh breathed a sigh of relief, their mission was a success. They had prevented the secret of gunpowder being passed to the French, though it was hard to celebrate when you had no one else to share it with.

A glass shard flew past his ear and took its place in the window. Josh span around to see a thousand more pieces flying towards him. Time within the room was reverting: pieces of furniture began to reconstruct themselves, threads of tapestries recombining into beautifully woven scenes, and the fragments of the blasted stained glass were flying back into position.

In a matter of minutes everything was back in its proper place, like nothing had ever happened.

The continuum was stabilising, Josh could feel it. As the colonel had told him he would. There was something about the way time was flowing that he just knew was intrinsically better.

All he had to figure out now was how to get back to the present.

21

RESET

Josh learned quickly that the fundamental problem with being trapped in the past without a tachyon was that he had nothing to take him forward. The tachyon's ability to record his movements through time was something he'd taken for granted — until he needed it. Even the mighty Paradox needed a sliver of a timeline to move forward through the continuum.

Josh had managed to escape from the castle once it had grown dark. The guards were too busy watching for enemies beyond the walls to be concerned with anyone trying to leave. Although, once he was out of range, he began to wonder if it wouldn't have been safer to have stayed there. The dirt road was treacherous in the darkness, and he was sure he'd heard wolves howling off in the distance.

His original plan was to search for the local Chapter House, but having no idea where to start, and with a fail in high school French, he ruled out asking the natives. Instead, he found the nearest barn and slept the night in the hayloft.

. . .

There was little in the way of technology in 11.060, and medieval was an understatement. The local peasants he encountered on his wanderings through the Normandy hills appeared to be descended from a forgotten tribe of Neanderthals — ones who'd been taught how to wear clothes. They had nothing, apart from some interesting skin diseases and a distinct lack of teeth. Josh quickly decided it was simpler to avoid any kind of contact with the locals altogether. Which led to a succession of uncomfortable nights sleeping under hedges and eating things he wouldn't wish on a vegetarian.

On the sixth night he was lying in a field with a belly full of strawberries, watching meteorites arc across the star-filled sky, when it occurred to him that he might have overlooked another way to access the continuum.

The constellations reminded him of the colonel's lifeline and how he'd been able to look forward to his end. Caitlin had told him once how the seers had the ability to look at the potential destiny of a person, and that the reavers had abused it to explore death.

Josh had never told anyone that he could do it. Seers were weird, freaks of nature and much as he liked Lyra, she was batshit crazy.

But, he supposed, if he could see the potential future of a person, perhaps he could use it to move along the timeline. At least to a point where they had electric lights and flushing toilets. The next day he found a drunk sleeping off the afternoon under an old oak tree and tested his theory.

In hindsight, he wasn't the best candidate to start with, but it worked. Josh managed to move a year forward before the man died of cirrhosis.

The next candidate he found was younger, a doe-eyed milk maid who immediately took a shine to the blonde stranger. She'd been very eager to spend the night with him in the barn, and was the first person to show him any tenderness in a while, yet he couldn't shake the hope that Caitlin was waiting for him in the present. Josh felt a small pang of guilt as he reached into the maid's timeline, until he saw her long and happy life — one that propelled him nearly sixty years into the future.

So it went on, with Josh leapfrogging through history one life at a time for nearly a thousand years. It was the strangest history lesson he'd ever had. Experiencing how civilisation had evolved over ten centuries through the lives of more than thirty generations opened his eyes to what the Order were trying to protect. It was like watching a child grow from a toddler into a teenager. The lives he 'borrowed' gave him an insight into humanity's potential for destroying itself: so many of the routes that he'd chosen ended badly, whether through disease, stupidity or war. It wasn't until he made it to the twenty-first century that Josh realised how lucky he was to have been born in that era, and he was relieved to see that everything seemed to be as it should.

Until he reached the now. The present.

Then he realised not everything had gone back to normal.

He couldn't find his mother.

Josh had gone directly to the colonel's house in Churchill Gardens and discovered it was occupied by other people — which was something of a shock for both parties as Josh came bounding in through the back door. He'd stupidly assumed that everything had reset back to the way it had been before, but as usual the continuum had other ideas. There was no sign of his mother, and as the rather flustered mum-of-two declared at the top of her voice — definitely no 'Colonel.'

He left before she called the police and made for the flat.

Mrs B. still lived on the Bevin Estate. Like some kind of universal truth or fixed point in the chaos, she sat in her front room amongst the porcelain cats and photos of her many grandchildren and poured the tea.

'I haven't seen Mrs Jones in — oh, it must be ten years now,' she said, staring into the distance. 'Not since she met that teacher. Now what was he called? Tims, I think.'

Josh inwardly shivered at the name. 'Timmins?'

'Yes. Strange man — never could look me in the eye.'

Timmins had always been odd, one of those confirmed bachelor types that had stayed too long under the influence of a domineering mother.

'Where are they living now?' he asked. It felt strange not knowing where his mother was, after he'd spent so long looking after her.

'Oh, they moved into his mother's house after she passed away. The large bungalow on Chamberlain Street, the one opposite the bus stop — with all the beautiful flowers.'

Josh knew it well; it sat in the middle of a large rose garden. Timmin's mother was a very proud woman who would open her house once a year for people to come and visit her gardens. He'd always wanted to take his mum there, but she had never been well enough.

'I heard they had a child. A boy, I think.'

Josh nearly dropped his teacup.

'What?'

'Yes. After a year or so. Margaret from downstairs bumped

into her with a pram outside Waitrose. She seemed very happy.'

Josh didn't know which was more shocking, the baby or the fact that she was shopping.

'But what about her condition?'

'What condition?'

'Her MS?'

Mrs B shook her blue-rinsed hair. 'Never heard of it. Where did you say you were from again?'

'The council. We're doing a survey.'

'Yes, the council. I think I was supposed to ask for some identity card wasn't I?' she asked, with that twinkle in her eye.

Josh stood up to leave. 'Thanks, Mrs Bateman. You've been more than helpful.'

'You're welcome, my dear. What did you say your name was again.'

'Dalton. Dalton Eckhart.'

22

MUM

Josh stood at the bus stop on Chamberlain Street trying to summon the courage to cross the road. Something was holding him back, an instinctive feeling that he wouldn't be welcome. His memory of Timmins was of a beetle-browed, older man with a stammer and bad teeth. The creep had hung around for months when they'd first moved into the flat, until his mum's MS worsened and he disappeared overnight. But it wasn't Timmins that was putting him off — it was his mother.

Josh was feeling anxious after Mrs B hadn't recognised him. He tried to reassure himself that it was because she hadn't seen him in ten years, but part of him remained unconvinced.

From the hundreds of conversations he'd sat in with the doctors he knew that her MS could have been managed better. That if she'd taken care of herself, she could have led a relatively normal life. But Josh was only eight and was hardly able to look after himself, let alone a disabled parent. To hear that she was leading such a normal life should have made him happy, and he felt guilty that it didn't.

A double-decker bus pulled up to the stop, blocking his view. He caught sight of his reflection in its windows; the unwashed, scruffy-headed bloke that stared back at him was unrecognisable. He turned away; he couldn't walk up to her front door looking like a tramp.

A mother was struggling off the bus with two kids and a pushchair full of shopping. Josh went to help her without thinking.

'Thanks,' the woman said, taking out the shopping and placing the youngest child back in the chair.

Josh hardly recognised it was his mother; she looked so young and healthy.

She smiled at him, in the way she always had, and for a moment there was a glimmer of recognition in her eyes.

'Aren't you Margaret's boy?'

'No,' Josh replied, looking down. He wanted nothing more than to hug her, but he couldn't face the rejection.

'Really? You look familiar.'

One of the kids wailed as the other one stole something from him.

'Joshua!'

'Yes.' Josh looked up, relief washing through him — only to realise she was talking to one of her kids.

He turned and walked away, tears rolling down his cheeks as he forced himself not to look back, but he could still hear her voice as she walked them across the road.

She didn't know him. Somehow in this timeline, he wasn't part of her past. A lifetime of scenes flashed through his head, each one more painful than the last: visions of her thin, fragile body in the hospital, the nights he'd spent listening to her shallow breathing, the way she shouted at the television when she got the answer before the contestant, and the way her eyes lit up whenever he walked into the room.

Josh walked for hours — wandering the streets in no particular direction, not caring where he went. His mind was too conflicted to concentrate on anything other than dealing with the emotional overload.

He tried to focus on a logical reason for what might have happened. Since he still existed, it must mean she was technically his mother, which brought him to the only likely option: she'd given him up for adoption. She was nineteen when he was born, less than two years older than he was now. It wouldn't have taken much for anyone to make that decision — she seemed all the better for it.

When he was younger, he used to scare himself with the thought of her dying. That he would be an orphan — all alone in the world. It was a recurring nightmare that had kept him awake in the cold, dark hours before dawn.

But she hadn't died, he had — or at least disappeared from her world. He wondered if she ever thought about him, her lost child. It was too painful to contemplate. He wanted to go back and ask her why, but that would cause her pain and Josh didn't want that.

He'd never been able to face the fact that he was part of the reason that she'd become so ill. All those years of sacrifice and stress he'd put her through had taken their toll.

This was the life she deserved; all he needed to do was stay out of it.

. . .

Which left him with one option: to find the Order and Caitlin. He would have to locate the Chapter House, and that, of course, would be nowhere near where it should have been.

23

CAITLIN

Caitlin snuggled further down into the leather sofa and turned the page of the large book resting on her knees. This was her favourite kind of Sunday: slouching around in the library in an old, baggy sweatshirt, leggings and big comfy socks. The fire crackled satisfyingly in the hearth, and she hugged the steaming mug of hot chocolate that Sim had made for her. He was sitting on the other sofa with Lyra, playing their own version of Scrabble — one they'd invented when they were kids.

'That's definitely a real word!' exclaimed Lyra, pointing at the board.

'No. I think you'll find "Exuderance" is most definitely not.'

Lyra flicked through the dictionary. 'Okay, it's a misspell, but you're not getting full points for that.'

'Since when did we start discounting scores for originality?' Sim protested.

Lyra pouted. 'Since now. It's a new rule — write it down in the book.'

Caitlin smiled inwardly. She loved the way the two of them

bickered: never quite a full-blown argument, but rather more of a verbal pushing match. Sim and Lyra were her closest friends and the nearest thing she had ever known to a family.

'Shh!' she berated them both, holding a finger to her lips.

They turned and mouthed their apologies before returning to the fight over the rule-book, which had been updated many times in its long career.

Her book was a thesis on the indexes of the Royal Library of Alexandria, one of the most significant institutions of the ancient world. It was a masterpiece of academic research, by one of the greatest Scriptorians that had ever served: Berinon Makepiece — her Grandfather.

He had been a kindly old man who'd taken her on countless trips to the Royal Library when she was younger. Being her only surviving relative, her grandfather had taken it upon himself to educate her on the 'civilised world', as he called anything before 10.000.

When she got older, she realised that it had been his way of distracting her, a diversionary tactic to avoid the gaping hole in her life where her parents should have been. The 'adventures' opened her eyes to the wonders of the ancient world. It was the most amazing road trip a ten-year-old could ever have imagined. They spent the best part of a year wandering around the monuments of pre-history, and when they finally came home, he'd written her a book about it — so she would never forget.

His handwriting was a beautiful, flowing copperplate that filled each page with a calligraphic beauty. The marginalia included detailed sketches and comments that brought back those days, and she could still picture him making notes as they sat amongst the papyrus scrolls. He was no ordinary bookworm, the term that the other guilds used for Scriptorians. There was a passion and art to his work, and she missed him dearly.

A polite cough broke her reverie.

'Miss Caitlin, sorry to disturb you,' said the quietly formal voice of the doorman, Arcadin, who had an annoying habit of being able to appear without making a sound. Caitlin often wondered if he took his shoes off before entering the room.

'There is a young gentleman at the front door asking after you.'

Caitlin had never had a 'young gentleman' ask after her before, and it was both exciting and annoying at the same time. She wasn't dressed to entertain guests, nor did she feel inclined to get changed as it would completely disrupt her otherwise serene Sunday. Yet, she had to admit, it was still intriguing to have a mysterious young man call for her.

'Who is he?' she asked, realising that Arcadin was waiting for some kind of reply.

'No idea, Miss. He says his name is Joshua Jones. He has the mark of the Order, and he knew the watchword, but there is no record of him in the ledger.'

Caitlin couldn't think of any reason why a Joshua Jones would want to speak to her. She looked over to Lyra and Sim for some kind of advice, but they were already pulling faces as if she had been up to no good and she didn't want to have to spend the rest of the evening playing twenty questions.

'Take him to the guest study,' she instructed, closing the book. 'I need to get changed.'

Sim winked at Lyra and pretended to preen himself, which prompted another fit of giggling that was still going as Caitlin closed the door and took the stairs to her room.

.   .   .

As Josh expected, the Chapter House was not where he last visited it. It took three attempts to discover they'd moved to a town house in Westminster. The bookshop in Charing Cross Road had closed down, and Waterstones didn't have a clue about the *London Guide* by J.R. Bartholomew. He was close to the point of giving up when he passed a second-hand book-stall on the South Bank and found a copy. It was in the hands of a man, who by the array of cameras dangling from around his neck Josh assumed was a tourist. The stallholder was trying to negotiate on the price, but the language was proving too much of a barrier.

Josh took the book from the astonished man, flicked through it until he found the 'House of the Hundred', and tore out the page.

'Damaged goods,' he muttered, handing the book back to the tourist and disappearing into thin air.

Now, waiting anxiously in the study, he wondered what was going to happen next. He'd barely managed to persuade Arcadin that he was an actual member of the Order, and only then when he mentioned Caitlin. The old doorman genuinely seemed to have no idea who he was, but then he was half-blind and had only met him once before, so Josh tried not to think the worst.

The study was an original part of the Georgian building and saturated with history. After weeks of time travel Josh's heightened senses instinctively picked up the echoes of Dick-ensian dinner parties: men in frock coats with long, grey beards; women in grand, silk dresses, and the young army offi-cers who courted them. Everything in the room was endowed with a rich and intriguing past, and he'd had more than his fair share lately.

Exhausted, he collapsed down into a large wingback chair. Josh realised he hadn't slept for two days — not since 11.953. His eyelids grew heavy watching the flickering light of the coal fire as it played along the gilded spines of the book-lined walls. The room darkened, as the exertion of the last few weeks finally caught up with him.

His eyes snapped open at the click of a lock. A secret door opened in the bookshelf, and there, framed by an arch of golden books, stood Caitlin.

'Cat?' Josh blurted, still only half-awake.

'Caitlin,' she corrected him, not moving from the door.

Josh got to his feet. 'It's me — Josh,' he added, unable to hide the desperation in his voice. Her face was half in shadow, and he searched desperately for the faintest sign of recognition.

She took a step back. 'So I've been told.'

Josh felt the last of his resolve crumbling away. This was the moment he'd rehearsed in his head so many times — the thought of seeing her again had been the only thing keeping him going. He'd imagined her rushing up to him, the feel of her arms around his neck, her lips on his, her voice whispering in his ear — telling him that everything would be okay.

The realisation froze his heart. Just like his mother, Caitlin genuinely had no idea who he was, and the last hope of friendship died — everyone he knew was gone. Josh was literally stranded in a world of strangers.

He couldn't bear the way she looked at him with a half-expectant and slightly puzzled expression. It lacked any of the subliminal signals that a face should have when looking at someone you know or love.

Physically, Caitlin seemed different too. Her face was

slightly thinner, her gorgeous auburn hair was longer and dyed to a darker brown. She'd taken out her piercings, and there were no fine Egyptian lines drawn beneath her eyes — all the small symbols of rebellion were missing.

His frustration boiled over. 'You don't know me, do you?'

Her mouth twisted. 'Not that I remember. Where did we meet?'

This was Josh's nightmare. He didn't want to start all over again, not with her — all he wanted was for everything to be back the way it was.

'The Colonel introduced us.'

She screwed her face up in that confused way she did, and Josh wanted so desperately to hold her, but he knew he couldn't, and it was the worst kind of pain.

'I'm sorry,' she shook her head, 'but I've never heard of the Colonel.'

'Not the Colonel — Westinghouse. His name was Rufius Westinghouse! Your uncle?' Josh was shouting now.

There was a movement behind her, and Arcadin appeared. Caitlin motioned to him to stand down.

'I'm sorry,' she said in a calm, neutral tone. 'I don't know anyone by that name.'

It was then that Josh understood what must have happened.

The colonel hadn't left him behind at Gisors. He'd died, or worse, he'd been pulled into the breach. The old man had sacrificed himself so that the timeline could be corrected.

It felt like the universe was playing some cruel joke on him. Josh suddenly felt overwhelmed by everything.

Uncontrollable rage rose within him. He screamed at her, at Arcadin and the others. He would take down the whole damn timeline and restart it. He was the Paradox, he knew how it should be — didn't they understand?

Something struck him across the back of the head.

As his legs gave way, Josh could hear voices, murmurs of others all talking at the same time. They sounded a lot like Sim and Lyra.

24

RECOVERY

Josh dreamed of the beach, his mother smiling at him as he devoured the largest ice cream he'd ever seen. Gulls circled overhead in the blue, cloudless sky, waiting for a chance to steal his birthday treat. The sounds of the waves rolling up the pebbled shore were like a thousand raindrops falling on a drum.

Looking along the shoreline, he recognised some of the people he'd used to move forwards from Gisors. They shuffled aimlessly around like zombies along the water's edge. The colonel was sitting in a deck chair reading the Times, while Lenin was standing up to his knees in the shallows, shooting at fish with a gun and scooping them up with a child's fishing net.

Lyra and Caitlin were sunbathing beside him, their bikinied bodies glistening with suntan lotion while they read aloud from textbooks whose pages were covered in ever-changing symbols. Lyra looked up and winked at him.

Sim walked up the beach towards him carrying something in his hands. At first Josh thought it was a fish, but as he drew closer, he saw that it was a brain in a jar.

'Hey,' he said in a soft whisper, 'I need you to drink this.'

Josh opened his eyes to find Sim sitting at the end of the bed holding a steaming cup of tea.

'It's one of Crooke's special concoctions. Earl Grey, amongst other things — helps to mask the taste of the other ingredients.'

Sim placed the cup on the bedside table.

They were in Bedlam. Josh didn't recognise the room, but the distant screams of the insane and the strong smell of carbolic were unmistakable. The bed was remarkably soft, and Josh struggled to sit up. When he moved, he noticed an array of curious metal-headed pins sticking out of his arms and neck.

Sim stopped him from pulling them out.

'This is a recovery room. You were in quite a mess,' explained Sim, pulling the fine needles out one by one. 'Lyra thinks you must have been ghosting for quite a while.'

'Ghosting?' Josh croaked, wondering if Lyra was partly responsible for the freaky dream.

'Lifejacking. The seers use it to look into a person's future — a dangerous art. Seriously frowned upon by the Protectorate of course, mainly due to the side effects.'

'What side effects?'

'In mediaeval times they would have called it possession and burned you as a witch,' Sim joked. 'Your timeline has been commingled with every other life that you touched. Nowadays they would call it Schizophrenia, or bipolar disorder. You're lucky Lyra is such a good healer.'

Sim dropped the pins into a metal tray, their fine needles leaving the tiniest pinpricks of blood on his arms. There was a pattern to it, but Josh couldn't make out what it was.

'Why the needles?'

'Acupuncture — part of the healing process. Lyra has separated over seventy different entities from your timeline. Pretty impressive collection. How far have you travelled?'

'From 11.066.'

'Wow. Nine-hundred and fifty-one years,' Sim gushed. 'Without a tachyon. That's probably a new record.'

Josh shrugged. He didn't feel very impressive. He tasted the tea and then wished he hadn't: whatever Crooke had put in it was foul.

Sim laughed at the face Josh pulled.

'No one ever dares ask what he puts into it. I find holding my nose helps.'

It was good to hear Sim laugh, there was a quality to it that reminded Josh why he liked him so much. He was always full of optimism and hope, something Josh needed more than any medicine.

'So how did you end up back there?' Sim asked, taking the last needle out of the other arm. Josh could see now that Lyra had picked out the shape of a dragon on his skin.

'Long story. Do you have anything to eat?'

Sim smiled and pulled on a small rope that hung by the side of the bed.

25

NEMESIS

A week passed before Dr Crooke would allow Josh to be moved to the Chapter House. Sim and Lyra had taken turns keeping him company, each doing their part to restore him, but there was no sign of Caitlin.

'She's not going to come,' said Lyra on the third day. She was sitting reading a book when Josh woke from yet another crazy dream. More pins had been inserted, which he guessed she must have done without waking him.

'Who?'

Lyra peered over the top of her book. She was wearing glasses which had slipped down her long aquiline nose.

'The one you keep expecting to walk through the door every time it opens.'

She closed the book and came over to sit on the bed.

'My theory is that you and Cat were lovers in another eventuality. Sim, on the other hand, believes it was to find your mother.'

Josh tried to laugh, to mask the pain, but failed.

She touched his cheek. 'Why else would anyone ghost back through a thousand years?'

'I had to.'

Lyra's eyes glistened. 'Only to find that no one knows who you are. A stranger in a strange land, as Daedalus would say.'

'Daedalus?'

Lyra frowned. 'You've never heard of Daedalus?'

Josh shook his head.

'The book of deadly names?'

Josh shrugged.

Lyra went pale, and her hand shook a little as she took one of the pins out of his arm and held it up to him. A grotesque-looking demon's head was cast in gold at the top of it. 'Who is this?' she asked.

'Beelzebub?' Josh guessed.

Her face paled even more and she put the pin down nervously. 'Have you heard of the maelstrom?'

'I've stared straight into it.'

Lyra made some kind of religious sign. It was a subtle, instinctive reaction that he'd never noticed her do before. She got up from the bed. 'I have to go.'

Josh could tell he'd failed some kind of test. 'Why?'

She didn't seem to want to answer.

'Lyra?'

'There are certain places I cannot see within your timeline. Your past is sealed. Something that has never happened to me before.' She picked up her book — the title on the cover read: 'Malefactum Maelstrom - Daedalus' — and turned to a page. 'One will come who knows not the name of the old Gods, and his past will be a closed room — on him the future will turn, for he is the Nemesis.'

26

THE MAGE

Alixia and Methuselah were their usual hospitable selves giving him a room in the 11.980's. Josh spent most of the next few days alone, watching television and bingeing on reruns of old shows like Quantum Leap and Cheers.

He slept fitfully, his mind full of echoes and partial memories, some of which he wasn't sure were even his. It felt like his old life had died, and there was nothing left but grief for everyone he ever knew.

The colonel told him that he would recognise when the continuum was flowing in the right direction, which it kind of was. Everyone else seemed perfectly happy, the timeline was nearly back to normal, and in some ways even better than before — his mother was well, and yet he couldn't stop thinking about the old man.

Being the Paradox seemed to be more of a curse than a gift, it left him to bear witness to all the changes and deviations of the timeline while carrying the guilt of knowing how it could have been.

He desperately wanted to talk to his Caitlin. She would have known the right person to go to; probably in some obscure sub-department of the Order, or hidden in a book buried in the deepest part of the library. He could picture her now, eyebrows furrowing as she concentrated on working out what to do.

The room looped on Thursday, 9th November, 11.989. The news was full of stories about the fall of the Berlin wall and with it the reunification of Germany. Josh watched as the two sides met and exchanged tokens of friendship. The screen showed an incessant stream of happy people: East Germans relieved to be free of the regime that had sealed them behind concrete and barbed wire for forty years. The East German Police stood in the background, their faces set like stone, ever-watchful eyes permanently scanning the crowd for trouble. Josh thought their uniforms looked remarkably similar to those of the Deterministry.

Josh had no idea who had interfered with the past. The memory of the astronaut still bothered him, as did the creatures that poured out of the breach. Josh shuddered as he pictured their haggard faces leering through the aperture. These were the memories that Lyra had trouble accessing — he'd looked into the abyss, and it changed him.

And it had taken the colonel and his team.

After sitting in the flat for three days with nothing but the same three channels for company he was beginning to go stir crazy. There were too many unanswered questions in this timeline and he was eager to learn more about it. So he decided to start with his birth, at least one of the few solid leads he had. He had the date and the name, and now all he needed was the place — and for that he had to find his birth certificate.

Except he didn't have one — not one that he could get to easily, but the registry office would have.

The records department was a difficult place to find in the labyrinth of corridors within the council building. It reminded Josh of an Antiquarian storehouse: long silent passageways with unassuming doors that led to rooms of unimaginable treasure — except in the case of London's municipal records department it was more likely to be cabinets full of index cards.

The clerk told him that everything was digitised and available online, or microfiche — whatever that was. Josh had preferred to see the real thing, which was an odd request for a millennial, but the clerk shrugged and gave him a note with a series of numbers and sent him up to the fourth floor.

Josh didn't get on with computers: they were incompatible on some level. On a good day, he could use one for five minutes before it would breakdown — the same was true of mobile phones, anything that a typical teenager would take for granted. It made him different, and when he found out he could use his talent for disabling car alarms it got him into a whole load of trouble.

It would have been a dangerous place for a reaver, the records of so many births and deaths kept in one place, going back hundreds of years.

And somewhere in here was the first clue to his past, his birth — his own breach into the continuum.

The numbers on the card the clerk gave him were an index. He worked down the rows of wooden drawers, checking the labels until he found a match.

Pulling open the draw, his fingers shook a little as he flicked through the records.

'Are you sure you want to do that?' asked a matronly voice.

Josh turned to find Alixia standing behind him, wearing a long, dark raincoat and carrying an umbrella. She reminded him of Mary Poppins.

'I have to start somewhere. I don't feel connected to this world — no one knows me here.'

She smiled and closed the drawer gently. 'You know that bad things can happen when you start looking into your own past. That's why it's forbidden.'

'I need to know who I am.'

She nodded. 'From what Lyra has told me about you I'm not sure it would help.'

'What do you mean?'

'She believes you're an anachronist — a remnant of another time. That you've been involved in a significant temporal event.'

He nodded.

'Which would make you rather interesting to a certain group of people.' She took a large ring of keys from her pocket. 'There is something I would like to show you — it may help shed some light on your predicament.' She selected a key and slid it into the lock of a cupboard. 'But first, you need to dress appropriately.'

Alixia opened the door to reveal a set of travelling robes.

'What the hell?' exclaimed Josh.

She smiled and held up one of the iron keys, with a date stamped into the fob. 'Displacement keys, one of my husband's little brainwaves. He's a temporal architect.'

I know, thought Josh. He'd spent enough time in the Chapter House to be familiar with Methuselah's many talents.

'Turning it clockwise returns it to normal, like so.' She closed the door and demonstrated, opening the cupboard to show it was full of arch lever files. 'Anti-clockwise activates the temporal field.'

Josh struggled into the robe while Alixia went to the office door and selected another key. She opened it onto a bustling London street of ramshackle houses and shops from the sixteenth century.

The sun streamed through the open doorway.

'Is it going to rain?' Josh asked, nodding at her umbrella.

'You'll see,' she replied with a knowing smile.

Alixia stepped out onto the dirt road carefully avoiding the piles of horse dung and rubbish that had been dumped into the street.

She put up the umbrella and waved at Josh to join her beneath it. It was a warm day, and there wasn't a cloud in the sky, but he did as he was told. She put her arm through his and nodded towards a line of shops.

'First Cole and Sons, then perhaps Dalwhinney's for lunch. No one makes instruments like Benjamin Cole.'

Josh wasn't sure the air they were breathing could be classified as fresh. The pungent fumes of the gutter were certainly clearing his senses, if not making his eyes water.

'It does take some getting used to,' she laughed, 'stay close!'

She pulled him inside the protection of the umbrella as a shower of urine cascaded down from an upstairs window.

'Seventeenth-century plumbing is still rather primitive.'

Cole's shop was located next to the Globe Tavern on Fleet Street. It was an Aladdin's cave of scientific and optical instruments: orreries, microscopes and gleaming brass telescopes were elegantly displayed on marble plinths and mahogany tables, while the shelves were stacked high with glass vials and jars of all sizes and shapes.

'My dear Mrs De Freis, how delightful to see you this fine morning!' They were welcomed by a short, stout man in a grey wig.

'Mr Cole. May I introduce my new friend, Mr Jones.'

The shopkeeper's face beamed as he shook Josh's hand. 'Delightful. Indeed, a perfectly serendipitous moment, for I have this very second finished wrapping your order.' He clicked his fingers, and a young clerk in a long apron came out with a box elegantly labelled and tied with gold ribbon.

Josh guessed Alixia expected punctuality when it came to her deliveries.

'Oh, how perfectly fortuitous!' declared Alixia, 'Now to another matter — I wish to introduce Mr Jones to the Turk.'

Cole's smile dissolved, and he wrung his hands before putting them behind his back.

'Y-Yes of course,' he stuttered. 'Please be so kind as to follow me.'

They walked through to the back of the shop, passing the engineers and technicians busily grinding large glass lenses and inspecting intricate clockwork mechanisms.

'Your husband's latest design is a most unusual challenge, as one doesn't often get requests for a mirrored array of this magnitude or configuration.'

'Indeed.' Alixia smiled politely, but Josh could see she was eager to move on, unlike Mr Cole who seemed reluctant to meet the 'Turk'. Josh wondered what on earth he was getting into.

The shopkeeper fumbled with a small ring of keys as they walked up a set of narrow stairs. The first floor was empty except for a large wooden cabinet that stood on the bare boards. Cole finally found the key he was looking for and handed it to Alixia.

'As agreed.'

'Thank you, Benjamin, you may leave us now.'

He needed little encouragement. The door slammed on his heels as he hurried out.

Alixia unbuttoned her overcoat and carefully hung it on a peg. She handed Josh the key. 'Open it please,' she asked, winding her long black hair into a bun and pinning it in place.

Josh inserted the key into the cabinet and turned it. Unseen clockwork mechanisms stirred and the cabinet doors folded back and away to reveal a metal figure dressed as an Arabian mystic. The face was jointed like a puppet with a painted enamel beard. His tin head was topped by a purple turban, and his body coated in a richly embroidered golden coat, trimmed with fur. His metal hands extended out as wooden panels slid from hidden compartments to create a felt-topped table onto which was deposited a deck of tarot cards.

Alixia took the cards and began to shuffle them. 'This is the Mechanical Turk. An automaton created by Wolfgang von Kempelen to impress an Austrian Empress. I think Mr Cole believes it to be possessed.'

She placed the cards in the open hand of the machine, and its head rotated towards her.

There was something quite eerie about the subtle movements of his mechanical eyes as they blinked and the head even tilted as if looking at the deck. With small, jerky actions the machine's other hand began to deal five cards out face down before Josh.

'You'll have to forgive the somewhat unusual nature of this

request, but I have to be sure. The Turk is the nearest thing we have to an unbiased randomisation algorithm. Please choose one card from the deck.'

Josh turned over a card. It was a picture of two people falling from a stone tower being struck by lightning.

'Tower,' Alixia noted.

The machine removed the other four cards and dealt out another five.

This time Josh chose a card with a wheel surrounded by symbols.

'Wheel of fortune — once more, if you please.'

Again the machine reset the cards, dealing out the final hand.

'Magii,' she whispered, as he showed her the image of a wizard holding a wand and staff.

'What does it mean?' Josh asked, giving her the three cards.

'Nothing and everything,' she muttered, examining each one individually. 'Lyra has an uncanny gift for seeing the true nature of a person: it's what makes her such a powerful seer. When she told me that she thought you were the Nemesis I have to say I was a little sceptical. But she's my daughter, and a mother always knows when her child is lying.'

She went to the cabinet and pulled a lever, and the cabinet doors unfolded and reclaimed their contents, drawing the automaton back inside and sealing it shut.

'These cards are part of the Major Arcana. Twenty-two cards in a deck of seventy-eight. For you to draw these specific three cards, the chances are less than one in one-hundred-and-fifty-thousand. Pretty unlikely odds wouldn't you agree?' She handed him back the Magii card.

'You're the Magician. See how his wand points to the sky

and his other hand to the ground. He's the channel between two worlds — the physical and the metaphysical.'

She held the second card. 'The wheel of fortune represents change. For better or worse, you're the change-bringer. A dangerous thing to be in terms of the continuum, especially when you associate it with the Tower,' — she held up the last card — 'which is indicative of disaster or upheaval.'

'But this doesn't mean anything, right? It's not like a science.'

'No, it is not. But despite the Copernican's many hours of statistical computation, I still believe that random systems like this can give us signals about things yet to happen.'

'Or, I could be just about to hit the big time in Vegas?'

Alixia laughed. 'Maybe the fool would be a better card for you. I can see why she's interested in you.'

'Who, Lyra?'

'No. Caitlin. She's been asking for updates every day since she's been away.'

'Away?' Josh was intrigued. Perhaps she hadn't been ignoring him after all.

'It's the anniversary of her parents' disappearance. She always spends this time at their memorial in the Moon Garden — it's a very special place.

Josh looked at the Magii. It was the name that Lilz had used. 'So, I'm the Nemesis?'

'Perhaps. For now, I would keep that to yourself. There are many who would see you as a threat. That damned book has created disharmony within the Order, between those who favour Nemesis and others who believe it is Daedalus who holds the key to our survival. The discord could prove catastrophic.' She held up the Tower card once more. 'The Copernicans will start to pick up their own signs of your arrival soon enough, and they will involve the Protectorate.'

Josh took the card from her, and noticed the girl falling from the tower had auburn hair.

'What should I do?'

Alixia put her hand on his. 'You're not alone. You're a member of the Order, so you will always be welcome in my house.'

There in his hand was a bright, shiny new tachyon.

'I think the best plan would be to lie low while I consult a few of my colleagues. Professor Eddington is a man of principle — he can be trusted. But while I do, we need to put you somewhere safe.'

Alixia put on her coat and handed him the umbrella. 'Let's discuss it over lunch. I think it's time I introduced you to Mr Dalwhinney's marvellous pies.'

27

SKULL OF DAEDALUS

[British Museum, London. Date: 11.960]

Lyra stood staring in awe at the skull sitting on a velvet cushion in the middle of the exhibit.

'Don't you find it deliciously mysterious?' she whispered to Caitlin, who had no idea why she spoke so quietly considering the museum was closed and Sim and Josh were browsing a collection of stone age weapons on the other side of the hall.

'Not really,' replied Caitlin. 'You know I think they made the whole thing up. Demons and elder gods are nothing more than stories to scare children. Daedalus is just playing on your need to believe there is something more to the universe than us.'

'But there is!' Lyra gushed. 'The maelstrom is full of ancient beings, ones that time has forgotten.'

'So he says.' Caitlin nodded towards the head.

'Just because your parents never came back doesn't mean he couldn't have.'

Lyra was the only friend brave enough to say such things and Caitlin respected her for it. Everyone else skated around the subject as if they'd died, but Lyra had a unique perspective — she saw the world differently, and Caitlin loved her honesty.

'The only thing that came back was the book,' Caitlin corrected.

'And his head.'

'Yeah, literally just his head. It's not like he actually returned whole is it?'

Lyra pouted and crossed her arms. As a seer, she was tuned to a different wavelength — as Sim would put it so delicately. Her world was full of fairies and demons, and Daedalus' revelations about the maelstrom were nothing but fuel to an already raging fire.

Caitlin watched Josh out of the corner of her eye. He intrigued her: there was something unconventional about him, nothing like the other boys in the Order. Lyra said that his timeline was incomprehensible, so damaged that she couldn't read him — which was unheard of — Lyra was one of the best seers in the Order.

'Has my mother taken you to meet her mechanical friend?' asked Sim, pretending to stare at a collection of stone jars full of bones.

'The Turk? Yes, that was weird.'

'It's one of her tests. She believes that fate can be divined from systems of chance. I'm not sure what real scientific basis she has for it. The thing is too subjective, too open to interpretation.'

Josh remembered Alixia's warning; that they would come looking for him, and he should find somewhere to lie low — at least until he understood what the threat might be. There was something ominous about being the Nemesis — this wasn't like the Paradox: this seemed to be more sinister.

'Who's Daedalus?' asked Josh, joining Lyra and Caitlin at the exhibit.

'The father of Icarus,' joked Caitlin.

'Nobody knows for certain, but there are a few theories,' corrected Lyra.

Sim joined them. 'It has to be Belsarus. The crazy old coot spent years trying to find a way into the future — he was bound to blow himself out of the continuum at some point.'

The girls both laughed while Josh just looked confused.

'Belsarus was an inventor obsessed with finding a way past the frontier. He created all these crazy machines that never worked, and usually ended with him blowing something up,' Sim explained.

'Usually the house,' Lyra added with a chuckle.

'He's related to Caitlin somehow, third uncle or something.'

'Second uncle, and no I don't think he's Daedalus, because he doesn't exist.'

Josh stepped over the velvet rope and went to take a closer look at the old skull. 'It could be anyone. How do you even know it's really him,' he said, placing his hand on the glass.

'Because the archaeologist that found it was one of ours,' whispered Sim. 'Now come out of there before one of the Daedalans shows up.'

'Daedalans aren't anyone you want to mess with,' Lyra agreed. 'They'll cut your heart out and burn it as a sacrifice to Azeroth.'

Josh laughed. 'They sound like a friendly bunch.'

'Don't be a dick,' said Caitlin. 'You'll get us all into trouble.'

Josh couldn't remember Caitlin ever being scared. They all were, there was something about the Daedalans that frightened them.

'How do they feel about the Nemesis?' he asked, stepping back over the rope.

'They believe his blood will lead them to Daedalus.'

'You mean like a bloodline?'

'No,' Lyra said quite matter-of-factly. 'They believe the Nemesis must be sacrificed to appease the gods and resurrect their master.'

28

CHAPTER HOUSE

The dining room was by far the easiest place to find in the Chapter House of an evening. No matter where it was located, there was always the scent of meat charring nicely to guide him.

Josh was relieved to find the long table lined with unfamiliar faces; all too busy chatting or eating to take any notice of him. Sim and Lyra were in their usual positions — as far away from their parents as possible and talking over each other while shovelling forkfuls of food into their mouths at the same time.

Caitlin was nowhere to be seen.

Sim stood up and waved to a seat next to him. Josh smiled. If there was one constant in this random universe, it would be the kindness of Sim. Lyra gave him a wary smile and turned back to finish her conversation with a girl next to her.

'It's Carpathian boar,' Sim said, nodding at the enormous pig that was slowly turning on the spit.

Josh had to fight back the urge to say, 'I know.'

'Dad has it brought from the tenth, says they don't taste as good since the end of the Dark Ages.'

Methuselah and Alixia both nodded demurely to Josh as he sat down. They were sitting with a group of serious looking men whose uniforms looked familiar.

'Draconian Twelfth Legion,' whispered Sim, offering Josh a large plate of steaks. 'They're here to interview Dalton.'

Josh glanced over at Dalton who was looking even more pleased with himself than usual.

'He's being considered for the trials.'

'What trials?'

'Are you kidding? The Draconian Defence Squadron. Cat's livid.'

Why would Cat be angry? thought Josh. He knew that her parents had disappeared on a Draconian mission, but he couldn't see how it would matter whether Dalton joined them or not — unless...

'Are they an item?' Josh asked, half wishing he hadn't.

Sim chuckled. 'What cave have you been living in? They've been together for years!'

Josh lost interest in the food, this timeline really was beginning to get on his nerves. He wondered whether he shouldn't just go back and start it again.

Then Caitlin walked in.

Josh could tell she was upset: her bottom lip stuck out slightly more than it should, and from the way her jaw was moving, he knew she was grinding her teeth.

'Cat!' bellowed Dalton. 'There you are! We've been wondering where you'd got to.'

She dutifully came and sat beside Dalton. He wrapped his arm around her and kissed her on the neck.

'How's the head?' he continued in his over-loud voice as if he was rehearsing for a play.

Josh didn't hear her reply, but he could tell from her body

language that she wasn't comfortable with the way Dalton treated her — like she was his possession.

'So what are these trials?' Josh asked Sim without taking his eyes off Caitlin.

'Belioc's Balls! What epoch have you been living in?' Sim jibed. 'Every twenty years the DDS are allowed to recruit from other guilds. The elite get invited to try out, while the rest of us mortals have to apply. Many fail — it's an honour even to be considered.'

Josh studied Caitlin, trying to catch her eye, but she kept her head down and focused on her food. His stomach reminded him that he hadn't eaten in a while and he helped himself to a large slice of meat.

Dalton was bragging to anyone who would listen about his invitation to the DDS. 'The trials are notoriously difficult, you know — they say you have to face a monad.'

'Really? No, surely not a monad?' Lyra teased Dalton from across the table.

'Yes, in the final trial,' Dalton replied, utterly unaware of the sarcasm.

'Well, you're awfully brave. I can't think of anything more frightening than fighting those nasty monsters,' Lyra fawned. 'Cat don't you think he's a hero? You must be so proud!' Lyra was pouring it on a little thick now, goading Caitlin into responding.

'Cat doesn't agree with my decision. Do you pumpkin?'

Pumpkin! Josh nearly choked on his food. The Caitlin he knew would have punched Dalton's teeth out for that.

'You want to go fight the maelstrom, it's your funeral,' Caitlin snapped, her cheeks flushed. 'Just don't expect me to weep at your grave. Not that there would be one — since your body will never be found.'

'Charming!' Dalton took his hand off her shoulder.

At the far end of the table, the Draconian officers stood up and bowed to their hosts. As they turned to leave, Josh thought he recognised one of them from the rescue team back in the Mesolithic cave. They all wore the same solemn expression of men who had seen too much.

'Dreadnoughts,' whispered Sim in Josh's ear, 'the elite of the Draconian Defenders.'

The entire room fell quiet as the officers walked up to Dalton, whose arrogance seemed to fade as they approached. Josh thought he looked a little pale when he stood up and obediently followed them out of the room.

29

DDS

'How do you get onto the trial?' Josh asked, climbing the stairs up to their rooms.

'To the DDS?' scoffed Sim. 'Why on earth would you want to do that? Haven't you read Daedalus? Protecting us from the maelstrom is the most dangerous job in the Order.'

Josh didn't care. The moment he'd recognised the Dreadnought officer, he knew what he needed to do. He couldn't explain to Sim about losing the colonel, but if there was even the slimmest chance that the old man was alive somewhere inside the breach — he owed it to him to try.

'I need to. I can't explain it. It's like my destiny.'

Sim frowned. 'Don't use that word.'

'Why not?'

'Er, maybe because I'm a Copernican and we don't believe in it?'

'So how do you get in? Without an invitation?'

'You needed to apply — like ten years ago,' said Sim, using a tone that meant the conversation was over.

. . .

When they walked into Sim's room, Lyra and Caitlin were waiting. Lyra was combing Caitlin's hair and singing to herself.

'Hey,' Caitlin said, and sighed without looking up from the book she was reading.

'What's up Cat? You missing him already?' Sim asked, sitting down next to her.

'Yeah right!'

'She's thinking about her parents,' answered Lyra in a sing-song voice.

'It's okay. They won't let him anywhere near a breach, not for at least two years,' said Sim, with the authority of someone who had obviously studied everything ever written on the subject of the DDS.

Caitlin shrugged. 'They can throw him through an aperture tomorrow for all I care.'

Josh wasn't entirely convinced by Caitlin's indifference. It was clear she did care, but he was glad to see that at least her stubborn streak had survived into this timeline.

'This has nothing to do with him saying that girls aren't good enough to join the Dreadnoughts?' asked Sim.

Josh tried to work out what was different about her. She wasn't anywhere near as feisty as the Caitlin he'd known, more subservient, more reserved and demure — everything the colonel wasn't. His character must have had a significant influence on her. From what she had told him, the colonel had become her tutor and guardian when her parents had disappeared. Josh had no idea who'd taken his place in this timeline, but whoever it was, they certainly hadn't taught her to stand up for herself.

'So, Joshua,' Caitlin said, changing the subject. 'Lyra tells me you came back nine-hundred and fifty-years without a tachyon?'

'I did,' admitted Josh, hoping she wasn't about to ask why.

'And how exactly did you do that?' Caitlin's eyes narrowed a little.

Josh was conscious that all of their attention was focused on him now, and as he looked into their familiar faces it was hard to accept he wasn't back in his own timeline: this one was so similar.

'I ghosted them,' he said, glancing at Lyra. 'I used their personal timelines.'

'You ghosted for nearly a millennia? Don't you know how dangerous that can be? How many people was that?'

'Seventy,' Lyra intervened. 'Took me nearly a week to separate their lines.'

Caitlin looked slightly disgusted at the idea of it.

'I didn't have a lot of choice,' Josh tried to explain.

'And how exactly did you end up in 11.066 without a tachyon in the first place?' asked Caitlin.

It was the one thing no one had bothered to ask him, pretty obvious when you thought about it, which was another thing he loved about her — she wasn't afraid to ask the hard questions.

Josh sat and told them about the polluted worlds of the Ascendancy and the Shade; the schism between Determinists and the Chaotics; the blockading of the past. But he spared them the details of the torture and Caitlin-History-Burner. As they listened wide-eyed, he described their discovery of the gunpowder formulas, how they were being passed down to the Norman alchemists through a breach which led to a thousand years of war and destruction.

It felt like a confession. Telling someone else helped to make it real, no matter how crazy it might have sounded. Josh finished with the closure of the aperture and the disappearance of the colonel and his team.

· · ·

'It wasn't a normal bomb in that sense,' said Sim. 'They call it a Hubble Enclosure or an Invertor. It's a device for ending a branch of time using Chaotic Deflation. He basically ended that timeline and reverted it. You're lucky to exist; most people who come that close to a Hubble Inverter usually end up eradicated.'

'It's not luck,' muttered Lyra, holding up the Malefactum Maelstrom.

'Lyra thinks you're the Nemesis,' Sim chuckled. 'She's read too many books about the maelstrom.'

Lyra pulled a face. 'There's more to heaven and earth than are dreamt of in your philosophy.'

'Statistics doesn't require faith — religion without science is blind,' quoted Sim.

Josh presumed Nemesis was just another word for Paradox. In this timeline, they'd apparently developed a different set of beliefs, but it seemed to be the same basic prophecy. Whatever they called it, he had no intention of being labelled again.

'You're telling me you've actually looked into an aperture?' Caitlin interrupted him, ignoring the others.

'Yes.' Josh could still see the figure coming towards him. 'It was like looking at a merry-go-round, thousands of images spinning too fast for you to make anything out clearly.'

Lyra nodded. 'That's why they call it the maelstrom.'

Caitlin stared at Josh as if he had suddenly grown a second head. 'And you think that someone was using the maelstrom to move through time?' The way she phrased the question made it sound like the craziest idea ever.

'The colonel believed it was possible.'

'What do you think happened to this colonel and his team?'

'I think they got pulled into the breach.'

She scowled. 'That's convenient, since that leaves no one to corroborate your story.'

'I saw something in there,' Josh insisted. 'A person.'

Caitlin shook her head. 'No one survives the maelstrom, everybody knows that.'

'Daedalus says...' Lyra began.

'I don't care about bloody Daedalus's fairy stories!' Caitlin snapped.

Lyra pouted and went back to reading her book.

'I need to go in and find them.'

Lyra's face lit up once more. 'You want to enter the maelstrom? The realm of the Djinn? Do you seriously think they're still alive?'

Sim raised his eyes in disbelief.

'Yeah, but first I need to find a way to join the DDS.'

'There's no way you or any of us are getting into the Dreadnoughts,' declared Sim.

'I know a way,' Caitlin said thoughtfully, 'but you have to take me with you.'

30

MOON GARDEN

[China. Date: 9.790]

Josh felt a strange kind of peace as he walked beside Caitlin through the garden. The sky was a canopy of midnight blue stretching over the horizon, and with only a half-moon to light the scene it created a solemn, tranquil place where the only sound was the night wind as it moved through the leaves of the darkened trees.

They reached an archway, heavily laden with blossom, and Caitlin stopped to watch the large silvered moths flitting from one jasmine-scented flower to the next. Josh tried not to stare at her, but the moonlight painted her skin with a pale luminous glow.

The sound of water falling over stones greeted them when they stepped into the glade. In the centre was a circular pond with a large stone fountain in the shape of a Chinese water dragon, its wings raised as if about to take flight.

'I used to come here a lot when they first disappeared,' said Caitlin with a sigh.

'It's beautiful.'

'It's the moon garden of Emperor Qin Shi Huang — the nearest thing I have to a memorial.'

'What happened to them?'

She sighed deeply. 'There was a Pharaoh back in the second dynasty who was experimenting with some kind of dark magic, trying to summon ancient gods. They were on a routine surveillance mission — the records on him were incomplete and needed updating or something. Anyway, he managed to open an aperture, a level seven breach occurred, and they were caught in the chaos that followed. They called it the "Great Breach". The whole era is cordoned off — no one can go back there.'

'And you think they went inside?'

She nodded. 'There was no sign of them, so they must have done.'

'What were they like?'

She walked around the dragon pool. 'Brave, happy, fearless. It took me a long time to stop blaming them.' She fingered the dragon pendant on her necklace. 'I go back sometimes and watch them getting prepared for that mission; my father looking so handsome in his uniform, my mother fussing over their equipment — it's all I have left.'

Josh thought about the last time he'd seen his mother and felt the sadness rising. At least she was alive and happy, he told himself. It must be so much worse to not know, and to be left to imagine the ways in which she could have suffered — that would be the worst kind of torture.

A splash drew his attention to the two large albino fish swimming around in the pool. Caitlin knelt down and dipped her fingers into the water.

'Master Derado gave me these the first time he brought me here,' she said, as the fish swam lazily over towards her. 'He said they were like two souls swimming in a pool of uncertainty. My grandfather laughed at him and called him a senti-mental old fool, but it helped at the time.'

She took her hand out of the water and watched the ripples scatter across the surface. Josh saw both of them reflected against the dark velvet sky; there were no stars — just the single silver crescent of the moon.

'Your grandfather looked after you?'

'Yes, he was the Grandmaster of the Scriptorians at the time...' Her voice trailed off a little. 'He was rather old-fash-ioned. Didn't agree with women in certain professions. He passed away a few years ago.'

'And Derado?'

'He's the Grandmaster of the Draconians, and my godfather.'

'Would he let you join the DDS?'

'He might, assuming he doesn't still agree with my grandfather.'

Josh looked up at the dragon. 'And if he does?'

'I have a Draconian birthright, I just need to persuade him to uphold it.'

'And what about me?'

'Well,' she said, standing up and drying her hand on her skirt, 'there are two possibilities: one is that as a member of the guild I could sponsor you.'

'And the other?'

She looked at him with a straight face and said: 'We get married.'

31

DRACONIAN TRIALS

[Ascension Island. Date: 11.927]

Sitting outside the Draconian Grandmaster's quarters, Josh was still contemplating which option he preferred. Caitlin had been inside for over an hour now, and from the sound of the raised voices, she hadn't completely lost her stubborn streak or her temper.

The Draconian headquarters appeared to be housed in a vast lighthouse on an island somewhere in the middle of the ocean. The view through the long narrow windows showed nothing but sea in every direction.

Caitlin used the dragon sculpture to transport them directly to the headquarters from the Moon Garden. It was a way-marker linked to their base, which doubled up as the Dreadnought garrison. The moment they appeared they'd been immediately surrounded by a detachment of heavily armoured guards. Josh was convinced they would've been killed if it hadn't been for Caitlin knowing the watchword and demanding to be taken to the Grandmaster's office.

. . .

Josh was instructed to wait outside. He spent a while wandering around, admiring the old ceremonial uniforms of the previous Grandmasters which were displayed in cases around the curved outer wall. The names of the masters were beautifully etched into the glass, and there was a quirky mix of styles — reflecting their personalities and the times they lived in. Some of them looked like they could stop a bullet: heavily armoured chest-plates emerged from courtly robes, while others would have looked at home on the set of Batman, Assassin's Creed or at the court of King Arthur. Then there were simple academic robes — less superhero, more stately. The Draconians definitely had a fascinating history if their past-masters' uniforms were anything to go by.

An hour later Caitlin came storming out after another tirade of shouting, traces of tears still streaking her face. Josh wanted to comfort her, but he could see from the steely glint in her eyes that she didn't want his pity. She strode down the hall without waiting for him; he guessed that was his cue to follow.

'So we're getting married?' Josh joked, trying to lighten the mood.

'No,' she growled through clenched teeth. 'My godfather has forbidden it.'

'Didn't he let you in?'

She wheeled around on her heels and shouted loud enough for Derado to hear through the still open door. 'No. Apparently GIRLS AREN'T SUITABLE FOR THE DEFENCE SQUADRON! It's like we're trapped back IN THE DARK AGES!'

Josh flinched at the power of her voice as it echoed off the walls.

She turned and stormed out. He thought about going in to

see Master Derado himself, but he decided it was wiser to stick with Caitlin.

He caught up with her. 'So what do we do now?'

Caitlin's temper was cooling. 'My parents had many friends within the Guild, and not everyone is so backward. Uncle Temperus will do anything for me.'

'Won't the master block him now he knows you want to join?'

'Aren't you forgetting something?' She pulled out her tachyon. 'This conversation never happened,' she said with a half-smile, grabbing his hand as the corridor began to vibrate and then disappeared.

32

INDUCTION

[Bavaria. Date: 11.457]

Vassili Temperus was more than happy to welcome Caitlin onto the trials — evidently he was one of her grandfather's closest friends. By the time he had stopped crying and hugging her, there was no question of refusal. However, he did insist on giving her a pseudonym: Lisichka, which, he explained in his thick Slavic accent, meant 'Little Fox' in Russian — just in case her godfather happened to browse the names of the latest recruits. If she graduated, Derado would have no choice but to accept her under Draconian law.

He reminded Josh a lot of the colonel, a larger-than-life character who bore all the scars, both physical and mental, of an experienced soldier. Vassili had been the drill sergeant for the Draconians for as long as anyone could remember, Caitlin explained on their way to the academy, and was responsible for all training and evaluation, but was happiest teaching combat on the proving ground.

. . .

The Draconian Academy was located in a Bavarian Castle somewhere in the fifteenth-century. It was an austere, turreted fortress set deep in a pine forest between two mountains. The dormitory wing housed a hundred and forty-four candidates, grouped into teams of twelve. They would eat, sleep and fight together for the next twelve weeks. Josh wasn't sure what the significance of the number was, and was just happy to be on the same team as Caitlin — Aries226.

The other members of Aries were a mixed bunch. As they argued over who got which bunk in the dormitory, Josh could tell they were going to be difficult. It reminded him of the first day on community service. There were the alpha's — the ones who immediately tried to take control, who had an innate ability to pick out the weaker kids and own them. One larger, awkward-looking boy with bright red hair was getting the treatment from a tall, dark-haired lad who was determined to take the top bunk.

'Sorry, red, I don't think they're built to take your weight.'

Some of the others laughed. The ginger boy's face flushed.

'Think you better get off there before you break it!'

Josh hated bullies, and he'd spent most of his life trying to rid himself of one. As far back as he could remember, Lenin had always told him what to do. Ever since junior school he'd been there bossing him around. Josh had spent years trying to figure what it was that had let him be so dominated, what flaw in his character allowed someone like Lenin to take control. "Some people are natural leaders, others were born to follow," was one of his favourite sayings.

Red was struggling to get off the bunk. The dark-haired kid was still taunting him, and a couple of others had joined in:

'OFF, OFF, OFF!'

Caitlin glared at Josh as if to say: 'don't get involved,' but

Josh couldn't help himself. He moved between the bunk and the small crowd.

'And who do we have here?' said the dark-haired boy squaring up to Josh. They were virtually the same height and build.

'Leave the kid alone,' Josh said, looking straight into the boy's eyes.

The boy held his ground, his eyes flickering between Josh and the ginger kid as he tried to assess his next move.

'And who the hell are you? Yet another Blue Falcon I bet.' He laughed, and the small gang that had gathered behind him joined in.

Josh had been challenged like this many times, it was always about resolving the pecking order. He knew from bitter experience that the quickest way to address it was to take the alpha down; go in fast and hard before he had time to work out what had happened. He felt his fists clench and his heart beat a little quicker as he prepared himself.

'There will be no Blue Falcons in my troop,' declared a woman's voice from the back of the room.

She was a tall, pale-skinned woman, with white hair and purple eyes. The name on the front of her uniform spelt 'VEDRIS', and the insignia on her shoulders marked her as an officer.

Everyone looked mystified as to how she came to be standing where no one had been a moment before.

'My name is Corporal Vedris. You will refer to me as your Majesty, or Ma'am, for short. I am your training instructor, dorm officer and general ass-kicker for the next twelve weeks.'

Her voice carried strong undertones of command, and unspoken threats lingered beneath her words.

'Now line up. I want to see what a miserable bunch of rejects you truly are.'

It wasn't an order she had to give twice.

They formed an awkward line, shuffling and elbowing each other until they had got into a semblance of a straight line.

The red-haired boy insisted on being next to Josh, forcing Caitlin to take a step back and stand one place removed.

Corporal Vedris took her time studying each of them. She held a clipboard with their names and details floating around in complex equations on the page. There were candidates from every guild: Scriptorians, Antiquarians, even a seer — a pale-looking boy with scruffy hair called Michaelmas.

When Vedris came to Caitlin, she paused and checked her notes twice. Josh held his breath, wondering if somehow Master Derado had already vetoed the application.

'Li-sich-ka?' Vedris read out slowly. 'Unusual name?'

'Russian,' Caitlin replied.

The corporal scrutinised Caitlin's face, twisting her head slightly as though looking for something. 'You remind me of someone. Do you have other family members in the guild?'

'No, Ma'am. I will be the first,' Caitlin lied.

Vedris looked unconvinced but moved on all the same.

Red, whose real name was Bentley, came next. It turned out he was the son of a famous Antiquarian engineer that Josh had never heard of. His dad had apparently developed a material called 'Voltaic Flux,' which meant nothing either, but the Corporal seemed genuinely impressed.

'Jones,' she said, with the all-too-familiar overtones of a headmaster calling him into his office. 'You appear to be something of an enigma, Jones,' she remarked, studying his chart. 'When exactly do you hail from?'

'The present,' Josh replied.

There were a few sharp intakes of breath. Apparently, there weren't many who'd come from that close to the frontier. He didn't want to go into too much detail, and especially wanted to avoid all the superstitious crap about being the Paradox or Nemesis — he wanted to be normal, like everyone else.

'Interesting,' Vedris noted thoughtfully, studying him closely with her indigo eyes. 'You've stated here that you're a journeyman of the watch — who were you training under?'

Josh caught himself before he mentioned the colonel, picking the next name he could think of.

'Methuselah. Methuselah De Freis.'

Vedris' eyes narrowed slightly. 'How goes Alixia's restoration of the extinct?'

Josh couldn't tell if this was just a polite query or a test. 'Her Dodo, Maximillian, has this crazy thing for fish.'

Vedris held his gaze for what seemed an uncomfortably long time before moving on.

The bully that Josh squared up to turned out to be called Darkling, the son of a Draconian Commander. Vedris treated him with the same level of contempt she showed to the others — she wanted to make it clear that no one was going to get an easy ride under her command.

'Right,' she barked loudly after completing her inspection. 'You've each been designated a locker,' — she pointed over to a wall of tall wooden cabinets — 'in which you will find your training fatigues. I expect you to be changed and on the quad in five.'

With that Corporal Vedris turned and disappeared into thin air.

. . .

The changing of their clothes made for an interesting diversion. There was no privacy in the dorm room, so Caitlin turned her back to Josh, trying her best to maintain some dignity. Most of the boys, however, stripped down without a second thought. Josh — trying not to stare at Caitlin's peach of a bottom — watched Darkling as he pulled on his uniform. The guy was ripped, and would've been quite a handful if they had actually got into a fight.

There were two other boys that had already gravitated into Darkling's circle. Both had newly shaved heads and keen, steely eyes. They were obviously brothers, twins by the look of them, and were taking this induction very seriously.

Bentley started getting changed next to Josh, who tried not to stare at the folds of white fat that wobbled as the overweight boy struggled to get into his uniform. It didn't go well, as Bentley rushed to pull on his trousers he lost his balance, fell against Josh and ended up on the floor with his arse sticking out like two white balloons. The laughter from the others made every one of Bentley's cheeks burn.

Josh helped him up.

'Thanks.'

'Take your time, this stuff doesn't want to be worn,' Josh said, pulling the last strap tight on his jacket.

A set of doors opened in the far wall. Josh couldn't be sure that they'd even been there five minutes ago. A long corridor stretched out before them and they could see other squads already hurrying down it.

'Hurry up, fatty,' said Darkling, jogging out of the room. 'Don't want to be the Blue Falcon do we?'

The other's followed, and Josh caught Caitlin's eye as he waited for Bentley to get his last boot on. She looked quite cute in her uniform. As she tied her hair back, she reminded him slightly of the more severe version he had met in the ministry.

'What the hell is a Blue Falcon anyway?' he asked.

Caitlin smiled. 'It's code, Bravo Foxtrot, someone who lets the team down — A Buddy Failure.'

Josh was sure the 'F' stood for something cruder, and that the old Caitlin would have used it.

Marching behind the others, Josh's training fatigues felt stiff and itchy. They were made from a waxed canvas material that felt indestructible and refused to bend to the needs of his joints.

'They take a few days to wear in,' Caitlin warned. 'My father used to say it was best to sleep in new fatigues.'

They walked out into the central courtyard of the castle. The sound of a hundred and forty-four excited candidates all talking at once was deafening. Their voices were amplified by the stone walls which stretched high up into a bright blue sky. Josh thought he caught a scent of the sea and the breeze that swept eddies of dust across the training ground was warm.

'Did we shift,' he asked Caitlin. 'I didn't feel it.'

She was studying the sky. 'Draconian engineering is subtle. We've definitely moved geographically. Smells more equatorial to me.'

In the centre of the courtyard was a raised stone dais that looked like it had once been a well which had a wooden platform built over it. Drill Sergeant Vassili was standing on it watching the last of the new recruits filter into the back of the crowd with a look of pure disdain.

'Silence,' he shouted, his voice echoing across the square.

Josh noticed that Vassili leaned heavily on his staff. There was a subtle shift of weight onto his other leg when he brought the end of the stick down onto the wooden stage, and a resounding boom echoed from the well chamber beneath his feet.

Everyone stopped talking, all heads and ears craning to hear what he had to say.

'My name is Vassili Temperus. I am the master of instruction for the Worshipful Company of Draconii. You will refer to me as Master Vassili.'

He lifted the staff slowly, rotating on his good leg to point at the upturned faces around him. 'Today is the last day of your life. Who you were and what you knew is of no consequence to me — you are nought but clay. I will unmake you, discover your hidden truths and deepest fears until I find the steel within.' As he uttered the word 'steel,' he twisted the staff and it transformed into a long shining broadsword.

'Most of you will fail. A Draconian does not go lightly into the breach, as ours is the fate of the damned — we cannot falter.'

Josh had heard more than his fair share of this kind of speech, old men trying to tell him how they were going to make him a better person, or worse, how it had been so much harder in their day. He looked sideways to Caitlin, but he couldn't catch her attention. He thought she was too absorbed in Vassili's sermon, until he followed her gaze and found that it wasn't Vassili she was fascinated by, but the dark, scowling face of Dalton staring directly towards them from the other side of the yard.

'Over the next twelve weeks we will test your ardour,

stamina and most importantly your mettle. In the first quarter you will be judged as a team, and at the end of this the lowest scoring two will be cut.' Vassili sliced the air with his sword.

'So it will continue over the next two quarters as the missions become more challenging. Finally, in the last quartile we will judge each of you on your individual merits — only twelve of you will be selected.'

Josh looked around the training ground. One-in-twelve weren't the worst odds he'd ever had, but they were pretty close.

'Now, to the first test.' Vassili's tone changed as he brought the sword back down and it became a staff once more. 'As the more astute of you will have noticed we're no longer in Germany. We are currently standing in the Alcazaba of Málaga, a Spanish sea fort on the southern borders of Castile. Each team has been given a key — your first vestige. There are ten secrets within this castle and they lead you to the location of the Crown of Castile — there are extra merits for the team who return with four or more artefacts.' He held up four fingers, and his index finger was shorter than the other three. 'I won't necessarily be in the same timeframe as you, so you may have to improvise. This is an essential quality for a Draconian.'

With that Vassili shimmered and disappeared.

As the teams grouped together, Josh watched Dalton closely. He was part of a strong team and they were already looking to him for leadership. Caitlin turned towards Josh and produced the key from her pocket.

She turned the old iron object over in her hand. 'Looks like I'm the Keymaster.'

33

CASTILLIAN QUEEN

Darkling took the key out of Caitlin's hands and inspected it carefully. She tried to get it back, but he held it just out of her reach. While he was showing off, the other teams were quickly disappearing.

'We're losing time you twat!' Caitlin shouted at him.

His face was a picture of idiotic indifference, as if he didn't seem to care. Josh wanted to punch that ridiculous grin right off his face. Others in the team were complaining, pointing out that they were now going to be the last to leave. The courtyard was entirely deserted before he relinquished the key.

Caitlin opened up the timeline, and her eyes grew wide. 'No way.'

'What?' Josh asked while the others gathered around.

Caitlin laughed and looked directly at Darkling — who still had that smug, all-knowing grin plastered on his face. She started walking towards one of the iron-barred doors.

'What?' repeated Josh.

'It's a trick. We're already in the right timeframe,' Caitlin said without looking back.

'Yup,' agreed Darkling.

'You read that fast?' Bentley said in astonishment.

'Believe it, fatboy.'

'Stop calling him that, his name's Bentley,' said a girl called Nin, who'd stepped in. She had a hard edge about her, and held herself like a warrior. Bentley blushed a little at her coming to his defence, but the warning seemed to have the desired effect on Darkling.

Caitlin used the key in the door, and it opened with a satisfying click. Darkling and the twins congratulated each other as they barged their way past her to be first through the portal.

The others followed them into the cool of a marbled antechamber; an impressive stateroom of one of the legendary Kings of Spain, designed to receive foreign ambassadors. Golden latticed windows spanned the entire length of the opposite wall, framing the view of a glittering turquoise sea. The room was a reflection of status, where every piece of decoration had been carefully selected to impress, from the golden serving spoons to the hand-woven tapestry that hung behind the plush throne — which was currently being occupied by Darkling. He had instantly gravitated to the royal seat and began ordering the others to search through the rest of the room.

Josh and Caitlin were examining the silverware that had been elegantly arranged along a highly polished mahogany sideboard. 'What was the trick with the key?' Josh asked.

'Sympathetic misdirection,' she said, picking up a silver goblet engraved with hunting scenes. 'The key had been imbued with all the traits of a much earlier version.'

She took a grape from the impressive fruit sculpture, placed it under the goblet and pushed it away from them. 'But it had been planted, taken back and dropped off a few centuries ago. It wasn't that easy to detect, but it was there. Darkling may be an arse, but he certainly knows how to read a vestige.' She slid a different goblet forward and lifted it up to reveal a grape, which she picked up and ate.

Josh wasn't quite sure that explained anything, other than she knew a few magic tricks. He was about to ask how she did it when the arrogant arse barked another set of orders at the other members of their team. A line formed as they began to bring him objects to check.

'What exactly are we looking for?' Josh asked under his breath.

Caitlin tutted. 'The next clue of course. This is a treasure hunt. Something in this room is out-of-place — masquerading as if it belongs.'

The other members of the unit were running out of artefacts to examine. Darkling had vacated his throne and was busy rifling through the pages of an old book. Behind him the wall was painted to look as if there were more windows looking out on other parts of the bay, an optical illusion that made the room feel as though they were in a tower high above the sea. Mermaids and sea dragons swam in the cool azure waters and in the distance was an island with a white palace standing on it.

Josh went to the real windows and compared the view. Out toward the shimmering horizon he could vaguely make out an island — it was too far to see any details. A brass telescope stood on a wooden tripod by one of the windows, and when he looked through it, he smiled.

'Everybody stop!'

They all turned to look at Josh.

'You're looking in the wrong place. It's not here.'

'Why's that, genius?' demanded Darkling, sounding like Josh's superior.

'It's the view. Look down. There are twelve boats in the bay. Does that sound like a bit of a coincidence?'

They all peered out of the windows. The bay was empty, and Darkling laughed. 'No, there aren't!'

Caitlin put her eye to the lens. 'There are, just not in this time.' She stepped back. 'The telescope is a lensing device. We need to get down to the beach.'

Darkling and the others all took turns in looking through the spyglass until they were satisfied, and then one of them found the door in the outer wall and they filed out down the narrow steps towards the bay.

'Nice work,' said Caitlin.

And there it was, the smile in her eyes, the one he had walked a thousand years to see once more.

34

BEACH

The sea was calm when they reached the beach, crystal blue waves gently washing over the white sands. White gulls swooped across the bay, soaring along the line of cliffs on unseen thermal currents. Josh imagined what this place would be like in four-hundred years, no longer a smugglers cove, probably, but a holiday resort full of sunburned twenty-somethings sleeping off their hangovers.

Darkling spread the team out along the shoreline looking for clues, or any remnant of a ship that could be used to locate them.

The descent down the cliff path had not been easy for Bentley, and he'd struggled to keep up with the others — his face was flushed pink by the time he caught up with them.

'When are the boats?' he asked, panting heavily.

Caitlin looked up at the position of the sun. 'Pretty recent: they probably left on the morning tide.'

'Bet you never thought you'd say that,' Bentley said, smirking.

A shout went up from further down the beach, where one of the twins was holding an empty bottle and pretending to drink out of it.

The group gathered around Darkling, who held the bottle in one hand while waving the other one around. His eyes were closed, and Josh thought he looked like one of those daytime TV psychics hamming it up for his audience.

'Crew of three, no four, came in yesterday — spent the night on the beach and left at dawn. They came from some island out over there.' He pointed out in the general direction of where Josh guessed it would be — beyond the horizon.

'We need to get to the island,' Josh announced. 'The crown is on the island.'

'And how would you know that?' snapped one of the twins, as if no one had given Josh the right to speak.

'The mural on the wall was a kind of map, and there were sea dragons swimming towards the island,' he replied, getting more than a few nods of appreciation from other members of the squad.

Darkling was clearly annoyed at missing that clue. 'So, Einstein, since you have all the answers, what do you suggest we do next?'

Caitlin winked at Josh. Darkling was trying to reassert his authority.

'Get to a boat,' Josh said, taking the bottle out of his hand, its timeline unravelling the moment he touched it.

He wove back through its recent past, to yesterday evening, and a warm fire on the beach and the feel of many hands passing the rum around as the crew each drank their share. He moved back further, finding it sat wrapped in hessian in the hold of the ship, then further still to a storehouse of a Portuguese brewery. Josh chose the cargo hold.

'We wait in the hold until they come ashore and steal the boat,' Josh said, holding the bottle out for everyone to touch.

'Sound like a good plan?' Caitlin asked the group, placing her hand on top of Josh's. Darkling shrugged and grabbed the other end.

35

BOAT

The hold of the boat was cramped and reeked of rotting fish and bilge water. Between the wooden bulkheads, the members of Aries226 crouched silently, listening to the heavy tread of the crew's footsteps as they went back and forth across the deck. They spoke in a deep, guttural language that Josh couldn't understand, but from the tone of their voices he could tell they weren't happy.

The hold was full of supplies: salted fish, bottles of rum and hessian sacks stuffed with dates. Darkling took a bottle out of the straw and pulled the cork out with his teeth.

'Dutch courage,' he whispered, taking a drink.

They passed it around, each taking a swig and trying not to cough as the harsh liquor scourged the back of their throats. The warmth of the rum helped to ease the cold, damp feeling that was creeping into their bones, but after they opened the second bottle, they all began to feel rather brave.

After a long muscle-cramping hour, they heard the stones of the shore grate along the underside of the hull, followed by the sound of chains as the anchor was cast down. Everyone sighed with relief — Caitlin had to stifle a giggle when Bentley farted.

They waited another ten minutes until the sounds of the men faded into the waves. Darkling slowly opened the hatch and sent the twins out to check the coast was clear.

The boat was theirs. They followed Darkling's silent signals, moving into positions across the deck. The drunken shouts from the crew's camp on the beach reminded them to stay low and keep below the gunwhale.

It took three of them nearly half an hour to work out how to ditch the anchor. The chain slipped silently into the water, and the boat drifted out on the ebbing tide.

As the beach receded into darkness, Josh watched the fires and the other boats carefully. He guessed it wouldn't take long for Dalton to work out the trick, and as he strained his eyes into the night he saw a fight break out on the shore — silhouettes wrestled in front of the flames. One team had gone for a more direct approach while another boat slipped silently away from its moorings.

'Does anyone actually have any experience of sailing one of these?' Bentley asked once the fires were nothing more than pins of light. The rest of the group sat around on the deck, marvelling at the star-filled sky.

'Or navigate at night?' Caitlin added, admiring the view.

Darkling stood at the wheel, attempting to look like he knew what he was doing. Without any sail, the currents were determining their direction.

'I do,' said a younger boy whose name tag read ARAMAND. 'The star navigation thing I mean. I have no idea about sailing.'

'Great!' Darkling sneered, turning to look at Josh. 'So, what's the next part of this brilliant plan?'

Josh had always been good with maps — his mind had a

way with directions. Instinctively, he knew they were off-course and that the island was east of their heading. There was a light breeze that would put them back on track if they could get some sail up.

Caitlin inspected the ropes of the rigging with an intensity that Josh knew only too well — she was weaving, studying the history of the equipment, exploring how past sailors had handled the boat and learning how it was used.

'You got it?' he asked.

'Nearly, just running through it one more time.' Her voice was distant, dream-like. She stared through him, her eyes unfocused, glazed, looking at something that wasn't there.

Her skin was bewitching in the silver light of the moon. Josh found himself moving the hair away from her face where the wind caught it.

'Okay?' she said, shrinking away from his touch.

'Yeah. You had something in your hair,' Josh lied, hoping his blushes were hidden by the night.

'Darkling, bring Tweedledee and Tweedledum over here. I need to explain this, and I'd rather only do it once,' shouted Caitlin to the boys at the other end of the boat.

36

THE ISLAND OF THE DAY BEFORE

The palace was a shimmering white edifice that glittered like a pearl in the dawn light. As the boat sliced effortlessly through the water towards the island, it reminded Josh of his auntie's wedding cake, built in columned tiers, the white marble glistening like icing sugar — that cake had lasted nearly as long as her marriage.

Josh took over the wheel before dawn after Darkling threw up for the second time. It seemed that Josh wasn't the only one who didn't get on with the sea. Although, in his case, steering the ship actually seemed to calm the motion sickness, and Josh was actually beginning to enjoy himself as he watched the morning break over the horizon.

The others were either sleeping or talking amongst themselves, hunkered down in the bow and out of the cool breeze.

Slowly, the rest of the island appeared out of the sea mist. Josh shook Aramand, who had fallen asleep against the wheel housing. The boy grinned at the sight of the palace. Josh nodded his appreciation, and Aramand took it as a signal to stand down and join the others.

Caitlin walked over to Josh with a sleepy look in her eyes. She was eating dates and offered him one.

Josh shook his head.

'It's the only thing I could find to eat that doesn't smell rank. They're really good,' she insisted, shoving a small hessian bag under his nose.

Josh had never really been into exotic food, and wasn't particularly interested in any kind of fruit beyond the odd apple. Grapes reminded him too much of hospitals, and there was something about the texture of bananas that made him want to gag. The truth was that they had never really been able to afford such luxuries — he'd certainly never tasted a date.

'Go on. You haven't eaten for eight hours. You need to have something.'

As he went to protest again, she popped one into his mouth. The taste of the sun-ripened fruit exploded across his tongue. He'd never eaten anything quite like it — it was delicious.

Caitlin turned to the island, and sighed. 'It's so beautiful, and sad. Don't you think?'

'Why sad?' Josh asked, taking another date.

'It's an Alcazar, a Muslim fortress. The King had it converted to a mausoleum for his Queen, Isabella. She was supposed to have been the most beautiful woman in all of Spain — she died in childbirth.'

'How do you know all this?'

'Books can be used for more than just holding a door open.'

'Sorry?'

'Nothing, it's just something my grandfather used to say.'

. . .

Through the clearing mists, Josh could make out the ivy-covered avenues of the lower terraces. Overgrown, unkempt gardens, whose attendants had long since died, had spread unhindered over the clean white marble, the vines slowly claiming the stone. It was a haunted place, a memorial to a forgotten time — the only living things left were the birds that circled the domed spires.

'What do you think the next clue will be?' asked Josh, turning the wheel towards the quay.

'No idea,' she said with a shrug, 'but it looks like we're not the first.'

There was already another boat moored on the dock. Someone had hung a makeshift flag from its mast, and on it was the insignia for Gemini.

'Bloody Dalton,' Caitlin cursed under her breath.

Inside, the building was cold — really cold, the kind that chilled you to the bone. Shafts of sunlight made feeble attempts to shine through the broken roof, but the marble and stone kept the temperature down at the point of involuntary shivering — like being outside on a frosty winter's morning without a coat.

Now back on solid ground, Darkling had recovered enough to take his usual place at the head of the party. They followed him into the wide open space of the entrance hall.

High above, a flock of exotically coloured birds wheeled, flying in formation below the painted angels of the domed ceilings. The floor was slick with years of accumulated droppings, and the smell was overpowering.

Bentley began to cough and wheeze as he slipped and slid on the dirty tiles.

'What's wrong now?' snapped Darkling.

'Birds — I'm allergic.' Bentley coughed, pulling out a small glass vial and shoving the narrow end up his nose.

Darkling just rolled his eyes and walked off.

'Bentley, why exactly do you want to be a Dreadnought?' Josh asked.

'Because everyone said I couldn't do it,' Bentley declared between fits of coughing. 'I wanted to prove them wrong.'

Josh patted Bentley on the back. He could relate to that. He'd always hated it when someone told him he couldn't do something.

They reached the atrium. It was a grand open space like a cathedral, and towering over them was a tall, golden effigy of Queen Isabella. The words "Quos valde ámas numquam vere moriuntur" were carved into its base. The team spread out around the statue, each inspecting a part of it for clues.

'Anyone know what that means?' Darkling pointed at the Latin.

Fey was staring at the words. 'It's something along the lines of: "Those whom you deeply love never truly die," but there's a misspelling on the word "love", an accent where there shouldn't be one.'

Josh examined the carved letters. He touched the cold stone of the accented letter and felt it shift slightly under his hand. 'I think it's a button or a catch.' It moved inwards as he increased the pressure.

There were grinding noises from below the floor, a rumbling that could be felt through their boots as the statue's base rotated through ninety degrees to expose a secret entrance beneath and a staircase that descended into darkness.

'Guess we found the crypt,' said Bentley.

37

TOMBWALK

The stairs spiralled deep into the rock, ending in a network of natural catacombs far below the palace. The old king had them carved into a baroque labyrinth of tombs and vaults.

'The graveyard of Kings,' whispered Caitlin, passing a wall of stone tombs. 'The island has been used as a burial ground by generations of Castilian monarchy. There's more than one Queen buried down here, but Isabella is by far the most interesting.'

'How come you know so much about her?'

Caitlin gave him one of her quirky smiles. 'Because Isabella was awesome. She re-unified her country, brought down the national debt, created a police force and even financed Christopher Columbus to find the new world.'

An idea struck Josh. 'So how many Queens are buried down here?'

'I would guess ten, maybe more.'

'More than twelve?' he asked as he brushed the dirt off of a nameplate on one of the vaults.

'Careful,' warned Caitlin, pulling his hand away from the

stone. There was a moment when her fingers touched him that Josh felt something pass between them. A memory from before, like a dream that awoke in both of them.

'What?'

She let go of his hand, her eyes full of questions. 'Ossuaries, they're —' She shook her head dismissively. 'They're not the kind of vestiges that you want to weave with.'

Josh smiled. 'Are you afraid of ghosts?'

Caitlin shook her head. 'They're not ghosts, more like bad memories. Echoes of old lives.'

'So they're harmless.'

'No, not exactly. Reavers believe that they're a way to open a door to the other side. They call it Tombing.'

The catacombs opened up into a chapel of rest, the cave walls carved with the ornate reliefs of the crest of Castile and scenes from the bible. Darkling was standing irreverently on top of the tomb of Queen Isabella.

'So, as far as I can tell we're the first to make it down here. I'm guessing the next clue has something to do with this Lady.' He squatted down and looked at the white porcelain effigy that lay serenely on top of the coffin. 'I assume they don't intend for us to dig her up, so there must be something else. Everybody spread out and search for a clue.'

The others broke off into groups of twos or threes, exploring the room and the tunnels that led away from it.

'Do you think we should tell him about the Queens?' Josh whispered as Caitlin inspected an alcove full of skulls.

Caitlin stepped back, winding an old cloth around the end of a piece of bone. 'No, I would rather try and figure it out first. I don't want him to end up blaming us for a dead end.'

Darkling sat on the end of the sarcophagi, swinging his

feet and drinking from one of the bottles he'd taken from the ship. It was apparent he wasn't about to get his hands dirty. One by one, the teams disappeared into the catacombs. At first, Josh could hear their voices echoing back along the tunnels — but then everything went silent.

Caitlin lit the end of her home-made torch and walked off into a dark passage.

'What's with all the heads?' Josh whispered as they walked along the tunnel. The walls were stacked with the pale, eyeless remains of thousands of skulls.

Caitlin was unusually quiet, and Josh could tell that something was bothering her.

They came to a T-junction, where a small shrine had been carved into the rock ahead of them. Caitlin pushed the torch into the alcove, and the guttering flames lit up the yellowing bone of a skull covered in runes and glyphs. A rictus grin leered out of the darkness, its jaws displayed an array of gold and be-jewelled teeth.

'Skull cults were popular in the fifteenth,' Caitlin mused, studying the symbols. 'They believed that the souls of the beheaded were trapped in purgatory, and that they could use them to communicate with the other side.'

'Can you read what it says?'

She whispered something under her breath. A word that Josh couldn't quite hear.

'Cat?'

Wind caught the torch, creating wild shadows across the surface of the rock wall.

'Shit!' Caitlin cursed.

Josh felt a cold chill in the air, his breath suddenly visible in the weak light of the torch.

Josh reached out to touch her shoulder. 'What is it?'

'Don't touch me!' she screamed, turning to face him. 'Why didn't I see it. Shit! Dalton you bastard!'

As she moved out of the way, Josh saw that the skull was changing, the bone slowly regaining its flesh — it was decay in reverse.

'What?'

'We've failed. It's a trap. Dalton's been here and left us a harbinger.'

'What the hell is a harbinger?'

'It's a type of snare. You trigger it when your mind deconstructs the sigils.' She pointed to the nearly human head that sat on the shrine. 'The symbols on the skull are Akkadian — it's an archaic language, one that his father decrypted years ago. He bloody knew I'd read it. We're time-bound now — locked into this stupid head's timeline until they come and let us out.'

'But I can't read it.'

'You got dragged in the moment you touched me.'

'So, how do we get out?

'We wait,' she said, sitting down on the floor. 'Dalton will probably tell Vassili once he's won. I would assume that every one of team Aries is currently trapped in some side pocket of time.'

'Except Darkling.'

'Yes,' she said with a smirk. 'I'd noticed our self-appointed leader doesn't like to get his hands dirty.'

'Do you know him?' Josh asked, sitting down next to her.

She shrugged. 'A Dalton clone as far as I can work out.'

Josh wanted to ask what it was that made her go for Dalton, but couldn't find the right words.

'I know what you're thinking,' she added.

'What?'

'How did I end up with Dalton? Lyra told me you were asking about him and me.'

Josh felt the warmth rise in his cheeks. Lyra already guessed about their relationship from when she'd been inside his head.

'It's just — well, it was just different before.'

'In your time?'

'Yeah, you and Dalton were — '

'Don't tell me!' she screamed, sticking her fingers in her ears. 'Nemesis preserve us! Don't you know how unlucky it is to share an alternate outcome with a nescient?'

Josh laughed. 'You were never this superstitious before!'

'Stop it!' she said, trying not to laugh herself. 'I'm serious!'

'What's all this voodoo? Who is this Nemesis? Lyra seems totally obsessed with him.' He looked up at the now fully human face on the shrine — the man's eyes stared directly at Josh, and he had to look away.

Caitlin frowned. 'You're telling me you have never heard of the Nemesis? The change bringer? They're a kind of fairy story except with demons — the type you get told when you're a kid. He keeps the night creatures at bay. He knows the names of the Djinn. Blah, blah, blah.'

'And who are the Djinn?'

She took a long, deep breath. 'The ancients, the gods of chaos, those that live beyond time in the maelstrom. It's all a load of nonsense, really.'

Lyra had mentioned something about a book before, but Josh couldn't remember the title. 'The ones in the book — that Daedalus wrote.'

'The Malefactum Maelstromo, or Reaver's Bible, first ever account of the world beyond time. It's supposed to be one of our oldest manuscripts. Personally, I think it's a fake, but many amongst the Order have become true believers.'

Josh realised then that the book had to be part of the change in this timeline. No one had spoken of a Reavers Bible before, and certainly not created a religion out of it.

'Who was this Daedalus?'

'The bravest Scriptorian that ever lived,' Caitlin quoted rather sarcastically. 'The only man to ever cross into the maelstrom and return. No one knows his true name — they discovered the book under Herculaneum, after Vesuvius, conveniently.'

'Why conveniently?'

'No way to trace back, as the volcano wiped out any useful artefacts.'

'So, you're saying he made the whole thing up?'

She laughed. 'Yes, but don't tell Dalton. He'll have you burned for heresy!'

Josh was shocked. 'Wait, Dalton believes in all this?'

'Why do you think he was so keen to join up? Dalton is obsessed with finding Daedalus' second manuscript — the so-called Book of Deadly Names.'

'Why?'

Caitlin pointed up to the severed head. 'Because Daedalus wrote in the Malefactum: "it holds the key to an ancient power, one not limited by time," and "to know a name of a thing is to hold dominion over it".'

'And this second book is lost?'

She nodded. 'Daedalus mentions it, but never revealed it's whereabouts. Dalton is determined to find it.'

38

HAAST EAGLES

Dalton was unbearable that evening — team Gemini paraded him around the refectory on their shoulders at dinner. He held Isabella's Crown over his head like a victorious football captain who'd just won the world cup. Caitlin had walked out halfway through their first lap of the canteen. Josh wasn't sure what was going on between them, but he knew better than to interfere.

Three of the teams had been caught out by Gemini's tricks. It had been a hard first lesson, as there weren't any rules during the trials and cheating seemed to be positively encouraged — Vassili called it 'Ingenuity.'

First blood went to Dalton. Josh's heart sank as the points went up onto the leaderboard. Aries were last — and they had less than two weeks to make the cut.

Josh found Caitlin sitting on the roof of the castle, watching birds of prey as they hunted across the valley. He followed their effortless flight, gliding on unseen winds as they soared over the dark canopy of pines — he'd never seen something quite so deadly and yet so beautiful.

'Did you know the Lord of this castle had the last breeding pair of Haast Eagles?' Her tone was despondent, subdued as if she'd been sitting up here all this time contemplating throwing herself off.

He sat down beside her, careful not to get too close. The flat roof felt hot from the sun and the warm evening winds fluttered the banners that hung from the turrets. There was a calm up here that even the distant screech of the hunting birds calling to each other couldn't disrupt.

Her fingers toyed with the dragon pendant. 'Do you ever feel like you want to go back and start again?'

'Every day,' Josh said with a chuckle.

'Dalton's asked me to join Gemini. I want to tell him to stick it!'

'So what's stopping you?'

She sighed, letting go of her necklace and dabbing at her eyes with her sleeve. 'What was I like? The me that you knew before.'

'You told me not to tell you.'

'Do you always do as you're told?'

When she spoke that way, it was hard not to think of the old Caitlin — the grief almost overwhelmed him. 'What do you want to know?'

'Was I different?' She turned to face him, trace lines of mascara still wet on her cheeks.

'Yes.'

'How?'

Josh didn't think she was in the right emotional state to have this kind of conversation.

'You weren't with Dalton. You thought he was a dick.'

She nodded, as if Josh had spoken some incontrovertible truth. 'He always has been.'

'Then why put up with him?'

'His family took me in when my grandfather couldn't. They were very good to me.'

Josh couldn't imagine what it would have been like to live with the Eckharts. Ravana, Dalton's mother, was a terrifying woman and hardly someone you'd want to leave children with, let alone bring them up.

'I thought your grandfather raised you?'

She shook her head. 'He tried, but he had to manage an entire guild, and that didn't leave a lot of time for family. Although he always took me away every summer — Dalton used to call him the fairweather grandfather.'

'What's Dalton going to do now he knows you're here? Won't he try to get you kicked out?' It was a question Josh had been worrying about since they arrived.

'Oh, no. I know too many of his dirty little secrets.' Her face grimaced as she thought of them. 'Tell me something else.'

Josh was trying to imagine what Dalton's guilty secrets might be and wasn't concentrating when he replied. 'Well, you still lost your parents when you were ten.'

Her lips stretched into a thin white line. 'I was hoping for something more positive.' She glared at him with eyes full of fire.

There were so many memories to choose from, moments that he'd wanted to tell her about and yet couldn't bring himself to share; they belonged to another time, and just like the photos of his childhood that kept under his bed, they were precious.

'I once watched you take out the most hideous bunch of strzyga, single-handed, in under ten seconds.'

Her eyes widened. 'How many?'

'Like fifteen, or maybe twenty,' he said, exaggerating.

'So I could kick ass?' she asked, relishing the idea.

'Oh yeah.'

'It's weird to think that you know things about me. Yet I don't know anything about you at all!'

Josh shrugged. 'Not sure how much I can tell you. We were friends, you taught me a lot about the Order — saved my life more than once.'

'I need you to do something for me.'

'What?'

'Share the memory,' she demanded, putting her hands on his temples. 'I want to feel what it was like to be that girl.'

39

DAEDALANS

Bentley couldn't shake the feeling that someone was following him. He'd tried several times to change direction, taking random diversions down different passages and stairs into the bowels of the castle.

The echoes of his footsteps on the flagstones made it impossible to be sure, but when he stood still, listening to his breath, there was a shuffling sound in the shadows behind him.

It wasn't the first time he'd felt watched since he'd found the old stock room. He'd spent every night down there, converting it into a workshop. But in the last week, he started to get that creepy sensation down the back of his neck.

The storeroom was full of discarded equipment and tools, either too old or broken to be useful. Bentley was in his element, and having always wanted to be an artificer like his dad, he liked nothing better than trying to fix things, and there were some amazing toys in there to play with.

It took him less than a week to exhaust the supplies in the first room, which is when he started to explore the lower levels and began to hear things. He'd tried to tell himself he imagined it, that it was just an old castle and full of antiquated plumbing, but he couldn't shake the thought that he wasn't alone.

A figure stepped out of the shadows, blocking the passage.

'Who walks within the darkness?'

He couldn't see the face because the man was wearing a cowled robe, but the voice seemed familiar. The question sounded like a kind of password challenge.

'Who's that?' Bentley stammered.

'None of your damned business. This is off limits,' the man growled, moving towards him.

Bentley caught a glimpse of a metal mask beneath the hood and knew immediately he was in trouble.

'Daedalans,' he hissed under his breath.

There was a rush of footsteps behind him and hands grabbed his arms roughly, pushing him to the floor.

'He's spying on us!' said the other voice, who sounded younger than the first.

'He's too stupid to be a spy,' said the first man. 'What are you doing down here, fatty?'

Bentley's head was pulled back so that he was made to stare directly into the demonic mask. He tried hard not to look scared.

'I was just looking for e-e-equipment,' Bentley stammered, 'for my a-a-artificer exam.'

'Aaartificer?' Mocked their leader. 'You'll be lucky to make the next cut — Vedris must have really screwed up to end up with such a bunch of rejects.' He leaned in close so that Bentley could see his piercing blue eyes through the golden mask.

'You tell Caitlin she's picked the wrong team,' he hissed, then raising his fist, he smashed it down into Bentley's face.

Bentley was knocked to the ground, his nose pouring with blood.

The man leaned over him, grabbed his hair and pulled him up.

'Next time I see you snooping around I'll use this.' He pulled out a curved copper sickle and turned it so it glinted in the light. 'And Nemesis himself won't be able to protect you.'

40

LESSONS

The weeks of the first quarter were spent drilling the candidates in the essential skills that a Dreadnought was expected to master: survival, combat, engineering, mapping, navigation and a hundred other things. Unlike all those tedious hours he had spent in school, Josh was relieved to learn that most of their training was centred around practical exercises.

Every day Corporal Vedris would wake them at six. They slept in their clothes since the castle was not heated and no one had figured out how to keep the fire going all night. They were expected to be at breakfast by quarter past.

Josh had still not managed to master the internal layout of the academy. Every morning seemed to require them to take a different route to the 'Trough,' as the canteen was more affectionately known. It was decorated in the style of a Bavarian drinking hall, complete with massive wooden barrels, heavy oak beams and lederhosened staff. There were tables and benches to accommodate twice as many candidates as the current intake, and enough food to feed twice as many again.

The training regime made them ravenous, and breakfast was a seemingly never-ending supply of eggs, bacon, toast and a wide variety of sausages that the chef had obviously taken a great deal of pride in creating.

Caitlin always went for porridge.

The teams would sit apart from each other, the rivalry between them growing more intense with each day and spurred on by the leaderboard that hung over them like an ominous reminder. A small team of grumpy attendants would grudgingly climb up rickety ladders during meals to update points and positions as the candidates earned merits from their training.

Dalton's team, Gemini226, were permanently close to the top spot, while the middle of the table was in a constant state of flux. No one really cared because everyone was concentrating on the simple red line and the two teams that sat below it. Aries226 had slipped beneath it more than once, and they were currently only two points above it now.

It was Friday morning of the third week, and Josh sat opposite Caitlin — or rather Lisichka, as he had to keep reminding himself.

They had just spent three days learning how to survive in the wilds of pre-colonised America. Josh never wanted to see another nut, berry or uncooked piece of fish ever again — not to mention the constant threat of grizzly bears and timber wolves. He devoured the first serving in total silence while Caitlin sat and slowly stirred her bowl of oats.

'Have you thought about becoming a vegetarian?' she asked as Josh sat back down with his second plate of sausages and eggs.

'Nope.'

'It's just that meat won't always be that easy to come by.'

'All the more reason to enjoy it when you can.' He smiled and forked in a mouthful of scrambled egg.

Bentley shuffled into the seat next to Caitlin with a small bowl of sliced fruit and a glass of orange juice.

'Seriously?' Josh exclaimed between mouthfuls.

'Ignore him.' Caitlin put her spoon down. 'He's having a caveman moment.'

Bentley smiled in a way that said: 'It's okay, I'm used to it.'

'Why do they bother teaching us all this survival stuff?' Josh asked, forking a sausage and biting off one end.

'Because some of us will be staying?' Bentley shrugged, pushing the fruit around the bowl as if looking for a hidden sausage.

'No. I mean why not just intuit everything we need to know?'

Caitlin glared at Josh.

Bentley leaned forward and whispered: 'Because intuiting is like cheating! You're using someone else's knowledge. Being a Dreadnought is about thinking on your feet, using your own instincts — not the previous experiences of someone better than you.'

'Plus we'll get thrown out of the academy,' Caitlin added. Josh could feel the heat in her cheeks from the other side of the table.

'Okay. I just thought it would be quicker, that was all.'

'Quick can get you dead,' chanted Bentley, imitating Corporal Vedris.

'Well, we need all the help we can get right now.' Josh nodded to the leaderboard. Aries were only just above the red line. 'Two days to go.'

'We'll be fine,' Bentley said confidently. 'Darkling's got a plan.'

'Let's hope it's better than the last one,' Caitlin grumbled.

'So it's weapons training today, right?' Josh said, squashing a sausage between two pieces of toast.

Bentley stared longingly at the last morsels of Josh's breakfast. 'Or herbal remedies with Voynich — it's a split option.'

'He's a good teacher,' Caitlin remarked, trying to sound convincing, but they all knew it was an excuse. She had avoided every single combat lesson in the last three weeks. Josh had begun to wonder whether the memories he'd shared with her hadn't worked. She'd disappeared after dinner every night and Josh assumed it was to practice the techniques he'd shown her from the fight with the strzyga, but he daren't ask. Like a friend after a drunken one-night stand, there was an uncomfortable awkwardness between them ever since she'd taken the memory.

'Do you have a problem with personal space?' Josh pushed his plate away, clearing the table between them.

Caitlin looked up from her bowl. 'What?'

Bentley quickly finished the last of his fruit and decided it was a good time to leave the conversation.

'Well, I know combat training involves getting physical, and I wondered if you don't like getting too close to people?'

'What kind of question is that? I'm just not into fighting.' Her cheeks were beginning to burn.

'So, what happened to being that girl?'

'I'm not ready.'

'I bet you are. I tell you what. How about I go veggie for a whole week if you come to fight club. You can even have the first shot.' He stuck his chin out.

She pushed her spoon around her bowl, pretending to gather up the last of the porridge.

'You won't pass basic training if you haven't been through

combat,' he added. 'Do you want to prove all those who said that girls couldn't cut it were right?'

'No.'

'Come on! You know we need every point we can get!' he added, pointing at the leaderboard with his knife.

'Alright! I'll come. But don't make a big thing about it.'

41

VORPAL COMBAT

Corporal Vedris looked formidable in her skin-tight, black combat gear: part ninja, part SWAT officer, with a long black staff tucked under one arm. Her hair was pulled back into a tight ponytail, accentuating her sharp cheekbones — she struck an imposing figure in the middle of the training floor.

The room was borrowed from an Austrian military college. Sabres and regimental banners hung from the oak-panelled walls, and the portraits of generations of fencing champions looked down on them with the arrogance of a forgotten Prussian aristocracy.

The wooden floor was sprung, like a gymnasium, its varnished boards deeply etched with decades of duelling scars. Running down the centre of the room was a fourteen metre strip of tightly stretched canvas, 'the piste', as Vedris called it. Laid out on the floor around it were rows of well-used leather mats, some of which looked stained with blood.

Vedris went through a series of fluid acrobatic moves that brought her closer to the group. She was so fast, so strong, and looked as if she could snap your neck with one finger.

'Today you will learn the basics of self-defence. There will be times when your body may be the only weapon you have to work with.'

Josh groaned inwardly. He was more interested in weapons. The previous lessons had covered guns, bows and swords — all of which he found he was quite good at. It seemed a little mundane to go back to kung-fu.

The nine members of Aries226 who had chosen combat over herbal remedies were ordered to line up on both sides of the fencing strip. Darkling made sure he was standing opposite Josh. He grinned at him like a heavyweight boxer trying to psych-out his opponent before a fight.

'We will begin with the basic defence moves. You will each pair up with the person to your left and follow my lead. Lisichka, you will be my partner today,' Vedris ordered, throwing the staff to Caitlin.

Caitlin caught it one-handed and glowered at Josh as she stepped onto the canvas. This was obviously his fault, and she was going to make him pay for it later.

Bentley moved into Caitlin's place beside Josh, who couldn't help but smile at the look of disappointment on Darkling's face.

They all paired off and moved to the nearest floor mat. Bentley picked up the wooden pole that was lying on it and span it around his arm clumsily, more of a danger to himself than anyone else. Josh wondered if it wouldn't have been better to have paired off with Darkling instead.

Vedris assumed a defensive stance. 'Okay. Now Lisichka, I want you to try and knock me off my feet.'

Josh watched Caitlin carefully, looking for any sign of the skills he'd shared with her: in the way she gripped the staff or how she shifted her feet to lower her centre of gravity, but there was nothing. The other male team members were too busy studying Vedris' taut body.

Caitlin made a half-hearted thrust, and Vedris blocked it, effortlessly swiping the staff away and knocking it out of her hands.

Everyone tried to copy the move and failed. Bentley accidentally managed to strike Josh in the balls. There were a few stifled laughs from their neighbours as Josh got back to his feet.

'Sorry,' Bentley mouthed.

Vedris picked up the staff and threw it back to Caitlin. 'Concentrate! The art of deflection is based on using your opponent's force against them. Again!'

Josh watched Caitlin as she crouched lower, her cheeks flushed red, her fingers whitening around the staff. Her eyes narrowed as she focused and he knew she was trying desperately to summon the moves.

This time Vedris swept her legs from under her with one kick and Caitlin fell heavily onto the floor.

'Your opponent's balance as they strike can also be a weakness. Study their stance — the body is only as stable as the feet.'

Caitlin got up slowly from the floor.

Josh only caught a glimpse of her scowl as Bentley came at him again. This time Josh managed to dodge his thrust, and his opponent went down like a sack of potatoes.

Vedris circled Caitlin on the balls of her feet, like a panther stalking prey, her hands performing slow, circular motions as if she were folding invisible sheets. Caitlin, on the other hand, seemed to relax, loosen her stance and roll her head on her neck.

Nobody expected what she did next — except for Josh.

One moment she was there, the next she appeared behind Vedris knocking away her legs.

Everyone gasped at once.

Josh smiled — there was the old Caitlin that he knew.

42

RETURN OF THE CAT

'What exactly was that?' asked Bentley for the second time, walking back to the dorm. Corporal Vedris had required a medic after Caitlin's surprise attack, and the lesson had to be abandoned.

'It's called a Vorpal move,' Josh informed him.

'Never heard of it.'

'You won't have. It's a temporal fighting technique that graduates are only taught after initiation,' Caitlin explained with the air of someone that would rather not discuss it.

'And you know it because...' Bentley continued, clearly intrigued and ignoring her reluctance.

Caitlin glanced covertly at Josh. 'Because my parents taught it to me when I was a kid. Now can we please change the subject?' Her lips tightened, and she flashed her eyes at him.

Darkling caught up with them, his whole demeanour towards Caitlin changed. There was a note of respect in his voice. 'Well, Lisichka you can certainly kick ass. Vedris is going to be off her feet for a week.'

'I doubt it,' said Bentley. 'Draconian healers are some of the best in the Order.'

'Better hope we don't get marked down for that little stunt though,' Darkling added, pushing past Bentley. 'We need all the points we can get.'

'So?' Bentley persisted after Darkling was out of earshot.

'So what?' Caitlin hissed.

'Will you teach me?'

Caitlin frowned at Josh. 'Do I have a choice?'

Josh smiled. 'Not if you want any peace.'

43

PREPARATIONS

The next day Vedris was there, as usual, to wake them. She seemed distracted, agitated, and Josh wondered if it was because of the injury, though there was no sign of a limp. However, she was a little more cautious around Caitlin.

In a tight, strained voice, Vedris reminded them that today was the day of the first reckoning; when the two lowest performing teams would be eliminated. Her tone changed as she announced that they were also going to be honoured with a special visit — the Grandmaster of their guild, Derado, was to make a rare appearance. All candidates would be expected on the parade ground in dress uniform, their boots polished and their dorms spotless.

Over the next few hours, Vedris grew more anxious. She fretted over the smallest things, making them repeat mundane tasks like cleaning the floor, the toilets, anything that kept them busy. Several times Vedris left unexpectedly, reappearing minutes later with new instructions as if she had jumped into the future to see how the inspection had gone.

'What's up with her?' Josh whispered under his breath. 'She's acting crazy.'

Caitlin grimaced as she extracted a glutinous mass of hair out of the shower plughole. 'I believe she's worked out who I am.'

'Or her application for active duty's been turned down again.'

With only an hour to go, Vedris disappeared once more. Caitlin took a knife and went into the toilets with one of the other girls. Ten minutes later she came back with a drastically shorter haircut.

Josh considered it wiser not to comment. She looked remarkably similar to the alternate version — the one he'd left back in the Ministry.

'Do you think that will fool your godfather?'

'He's short-sighted and vain, so he won't wear his glasses. If I stand behind you, he may not even see me.'

They both knew it was a terrible plan, but neither wanted to think about the alternatives.

Vedris reappeared, her eyes red-rimmed.

'Get dressed,' she ordered.

Twenty minutes of fussing over buttons and collars, and the summoning bell finally rang. Aries226 trooped out onto the parade ground in low spirits.

44

DERADO

Grandmaster Derado was a tall, thin man with short dark hair and piercing blue eyes. Josh could see by his bearing he was a military man. He had that kind of lean, muscular way of carrying himself that came from constantly being on his guard. The same could be said of every one of the detachment of Dreadnoughts that accompanied him. They were twelve of the meanest-looking soldiers Josh had ever seen. Like time knights, their temporal armour was so black that light didn't seem to reflect off its surface. Josh saw the tachyon dials embedded into their gauntlets as well as the legendary gunsabres hidden beneath their dark cloaks — weapons that only they were allowed to carry. Bentley was nearly hysterical; these were the closest things to superheroes for him.

The Dreadnoughts moved in unison, surrounding the Grandmaster at all times, while he inspected the ranks of candidates with Vassili.

The training master was wearing an old, faded uniform, his hair combed down and oiled in an attempt to tame it. He'd greeted the Grandmaster like an old friend, reaching up to the taller man and kissing his cheeks. Derado smiled and slapped his old friend on the shoulder.

Their entourage moved slowly along the lines of teams until it reached Aries. Vedris stepped forward to greet the Grandmaster and introduced each member of the team in turn. Caitlin stood beside Josh, and he felt the apprehension emanating from her without needing to turn around.

'And this is Jones,' she announced as they stopped in front of Josh.

The Grandmaster extended his hand. 'Jones. Pleased to meet you.'

Vassili's eye twitched as he stood behind Derado. Josh wasn't sure if he was concerned about Josh or what was about to happen when the Grandmaster recognised his goddaughter.

Except she wasn't there.

'Something the matter, Jones?' coughed Vedris. 'Lost your manners?'

'No. Sorry sir,' he stuttered, shaking the Grandmaster's hand.

Then the world stopped turning.

Everything froze. The banners that hung from the balconies stiffened in the stillness, and birds hung motionless in the blue skies above them.

Time had stopped.

'You can come out now Kitkat, or should I say Lisichka,' Derado declared, looking at the space next to Josh. 'I see you've learned a new trick.'

Caitlin reappeared out of thin air.

'Nice hair. Practical, but perhaps a little too severe?'

Caitlin stepped towards her godfather and kissed him lightly on the cheek.

'Hello, Godfather. This is a little unexpected.'

'Is it? I suspect you're being slightly disingenuous, aren't you? Vedris here' — he nodded at the statue-like Corporal — 'reported your prowess in Vorpal combat yesterday. You broke both her legs, apparently.'

Caitlin tried to look mortified, but she wasn't really pulling it off.

'Well, if I had told you I was joining you would have forbidden it.'

'Not I, my dear. I am simply following your Grandfather's orders. May he rest in peace.'

'Grampy was a dinosaur who thought women were for babies and sewing robes!'

Josh could sense a repeat of the argument he had overheard in the master's lighthouse.

'He had good reasons, but that's beside the point. I haven't come here to dissuade you.'

'You haven't?'

'No. I come with news. The skull of Daedalus has been stolen. The Copernicans suspect your friend here had something to do with it. They've been petitioning me for days.'

Josh found he couldn't speak or move, and although he was conscious it was as if he'd been paralysed entirely.

'My spies tell me that this young man is causing something of a stir amongst the Daedalans. They wish to question him.' Derado leaned in close to Josh's face. 'They're stirring up discord within the Order. They suspect he's an anachronist, a counterfact — the so-called Nemesis.'

'Really — but that's just a myth?'

'Indeed.'

'And they seriously believe it?'

'This religious hysteria could lead to no end of trouble.'

Josh felt the master's grip tighten.

'You see, I'm more of a pragmatist, Mr Jones. I say what I see, and it strikes me that you are either a threat or an advantage. For the moment I'm going to err on the latter — until I have more data. Just know that you're being closely watched.' The veiled threat made Josh's blood run cold.

The Grandmaster turned to Caitlin.

'You shall be my eyes and ears, goddaughter. Observe him and report back on anything you deem noteworthy. For the moment you're safe within the academy — even the Protectorate wouldn't dare enter these walls.'

Caitlin winced at the mention of the secret police. 'Why would the Protectorate get involved?'

'Because of the damned book! The Copernicans will go whispering in the founder's ear. Grandmaster Xaromord is always looking for a way to discredit us, and Ravana will be itching to interrogate this boy.'

Derado took out an ornate watch from inside his robes and flipped open the cover.

'I would estimate we have two, maybe three weeks before they'll have enough of a case to open an investigation. I will do my best to contest it of course.'

He closed the lid with his thumb and handed it to Caitlin. 'Keep this. It was your grandfather's. He estimated an eighty-four percent probability of you following your parents. I think he would want you to have it now.'

Caitlin took the watch and hugged Derado for a long time.

'It appears your team was to be cut today,' he said, stepping back. 'That would be a mistake. Corporal Vedris deducted several points for your use of Vorpal. I believe she was driven by personal motives — somehow you have managed to get into her bad books. I've sent someone back to have it corrected.'

Derado released Josh's hand, and suddenly it was over, the world snapped back into motion. There was still a glint in his eye as his gaze left Josh's and moved on to the next in line.

'This is Lisichka,' Vedris continued, 'not one of our most promising candidates.'

The Grandmaster nodded sternly to Caitlin and moved on down the line without a word. Vassili looked visibly relieved.

Josh let out a long, slow breath, the first in what seemed like an hour. Caitlin nudged him with her elbow and nodded towards the leaderboard: Aries were no longer below the line. Capricorn and Libra were now in the dead zone and looking very unhappy about it.

45

TRIAL II

The next trial came out of the blue — a week after the visit from the Grandmaster. They'd just completed a punishing five-day route march through fifteen centuries using shadow paths — untraceable routes, or 'backdoors', as Vedris called them.

Everyone completed their tasks successfully, and they were ecstatic about the forty merits they earned. The team was exhausted, collapsing wearily onto their bunks and comparing tactics as they kicked off their muddy boots.

'So, you found the path from the Barbary Coast to Liverpool in the bottom of a cask?' Darkling exclaimed, his voice rising above the others. 'Why didn't you use the chart?'

Aries were split into four groups of three, and each started from a different waypoint.

'What chart?' asked Michaelmas, the scrawny seer who always looked like he'd been pulled through a hedge backwards.

De'Angelo unrolled a large map and held it up for everyone to see. 'You mean this one?'

They all laughed as Michaelmas chased De'Angelo out of the dorm.

Josh never grew tired of Caitlin's laugh; it was as beautiful and warm as before. He lay back on his bed and listened to her chuckle, thinking about what Derado said on the parade ground. She didn't know that he'd overheard their conversation, although she'd been acting weird around him ever since.

There wasn't time to discuss what her godfather had said during their march. Bentley — and a girl that everyone called Fey, even though her real name was Wendell — hadn't left their side throughout the entire five days. At one point, he had to chase Bentley off when he followed Josh into the bushes to take a dump.

Corporal Vedris appeared out of thin air just as Michaelmas and his team walked back in carrying a limp De'Angelo.

'Ran into a wall,' insisted Michaelmas.

She ignored them, cleared her throat and held up a mirror.

'Does anyone want to tell me what this is? And before you answer, Darkling, this is not a mirror.'

The room fell deathly quiet — no one had a clue. Vedris had that anxious expression that Josh's teachers always used to get when surveying a room full of blank faces — one that searched for a vague glimmer of hope: that just once their pupils would reward the years of sacrifice with an intelligent response.

'The future?' Bentley wondered aloud, just as everyone else realised that the mirror's reflection showed an empty room.

Vedris was impressed. 'Not bad, Bentley. Your father would be proud. For those that don't know, it's called a Lensing Plate — a form of temporal prism which allows us to look at other eventualities, other potential paths within the continuum. One of the specialisms you can opt for, should you graduate, is Lensman — a highly honourable position with the guild.'

A brass stand appeared from out of nowhere, followed by a table on which sat a curious looking helmet with an array of lenses over the eyes.

'Bentley, please step forward and sit down.' She motioned to a chair that conjured itself into existence.

He did as he was ordered and Vedris strapped the helmet contraption to his head.

'Now tell the others what you see,' she instructed, adjusting the straps under his chin.

They all tried and failed to stifle their giggles — Bentley looked ridiculous, but he wasn't listening to them. His jaw had dropped, and his hands were tracing imaginary lines in the air.

'There are so-so many,' he stammered, 'like ghosts.' He stood up and looked around, nearly tripping over the chair.

'What private Bentley is trying to vocalise are the multiple timelines he is observing through the binocular lensing. He's experiencing upwards of sixteen simultaneous alternatives. Something that,' — she produced a large metal bucket and handed to Bentley as he went deathly pale — is known to induce nausea in the uninitiated.'

Bentley threw up.

They took turns to wear the helmet. Everyone reacted differently, which meant the bucket was required more than once. Darkling, much to his chagrin, found that he couldn't stand more than a few seconds inside the multiverse, before barfing all over his trousers.

Then it was Josh's turn.

He kept his eyes closed as Caitlin help strap it to his head, praying to at least beat Darkling's record by a few seconds. Nervously, he opened them, only to find he was staring at the same scene as before. At first he thought that the device must be broken; he blinked and swivelled his head to see if he could induce some kind of second or third image — but nothing happened.

'Hey, I think they're busted. I'm not seeing anything differently.'

Which was not strictly true. The mirrored arrays were set up to reflect a one-hundred and eighty degree view — so he was effectively looking at a slightly distorted panoramic of the room.

Caitlin helped him take the lenses off and tried them on herself. 'Nope, nothing wrong with that,' she said, removing them quickly and giving them back to Josh.

'Is there a problem?' Vedris came over to them.

'It doesn't work on Josh,' Bentley chipped in. The other members of the team gathered around.

'What makes him so special?' Darkling moaned, sitting on his bunk and holding his head between his knees. Fey applied a cold compress to the back of his neck, confirming what everyone else had guessed — that they were an item.

Vedris strapped the helmet back onto Josh's head and spoke quietly.

'Tell me what you see?'

'Easy. The room, you standing in front of me. Darkling getting pawed by Fey.' Some of the others laughed. 'Everything is normal.'

'Now look closer at my face.'

As Josh focused his attention on her, she seemed to blur. It was a weird sensation: she literally split into two, three, then four — each one doing something different. The multiples were ghost-like and transparent, but one image was clearer than the others, reaching for a knife, and he knew instinctively that she would bury it in Caitlin's chest if he didn't try to stop her.

Reflexively, his hand flashed out and caught hers — stopping the blade an inch from Caitlin's breast.

'Very good, Jones.' Vedris put the knife away. 'Aries, I think we have found ourselves a natural.'

Josh took off the helmet to find everyone looking at him in amazement, including Caitlin, who was still stunned about being the target.

'To be a good Lensman, you must have a keen sense of the most likely eventuality,' Vedris explained. 'This is not something that can be learned. It is an inherent quality, and it's very rare.'

Josh was beginning to feel uncomfortable with all the attention.

'But this next mission will require more than a Lensman... you will need to work together in ways you never imagined.'

46

KAFFA

[London. Date: 11.664]

The abandoned church loomed over them, shrouded by a sombre grey sky. Ravens perched on the roof, cawing at the uninvited guests. They stood in the cold, cloying mud watching the rain turn the gravestones slick and black, and in the dim light of pre-dawn they looked like rows of broken teeth.

The graveyard was somewhere near London in 11.664. It had taken them two days of dead-ends and false starts to find it, and when they did, they all wished they hadn't.

Signs of plague were everywhere. Inverted white crosses had been painted on all the houses they'd passed. The stench of disease permeated everything, and nothing could stop the smell, not even the ridiculous bird masks they wore — whose beaks were stuffed full of herbs.

'Yersinia pestis: the Black Death,' cursed Darkling, sitting down on a nearby grave and pulling off his mask. 'Only Draconians could have sent us on a mission into the worst bloody pandemic in history! Do we know how many died in this time?'

'Fifty million,' Josh answered, unstrapping his mask. His mother's TV game show addiction was nothing if not educational.

Caitlin pulled her own plague mask off and took a long slow breath. 'I'm impressed. I never had you down as a historian.'

Josh winced as the wind picked up, blowing a smokey miasma of funeral pyres in their direction. It smelled just as bad as Kaffa — the city they had just escaped from 11.347.

Two days ago, they'd found themselves in the middle of a siege. The Golden Horde was trying to conquer an Italian trading city on the Crimean peninsula known as Kaffa. Caitlin, as usual, gave them all a quick history lesson on the place: The Horde was the Northwestern arm of the Mongol Empire and sold the city to the Genoese in the late thirteenth century. The city flourished under the Italian administration, becoming a powerful trading port, and controlling access to the Black Sea while prospering off the back of the slave trade.

At some point, the Mongols decided they'd made a terrible mistake and tried to take the city back. The ensuing siege was a long and protracted affair, not helped by a terrible disease that was withering their army.

'It was the first ever use of biological warfare,' Caitlin explained as they watched another body fly over the outer wall and disappear into the city.

Another, less successful shot, rebounded off the high stone parapet they were standing on and landed in the street below them. 'They're using their dead?'

'Not just dead — infected. The horde is riddled with the bubonic plague.'

Everyone stopped talking and followed the next body as it arced across the blue sky and exploded against a stone tower.

'Shouldn't we be taking precautions?' Bentley asked in Italian — they'd all been allowed to intuit the basic dialect.

'Don't you know anything, Red?' Darkling scoffed, 'The moment you're contaminated the medics pull you out. One of the benefits of non-linear medicine. I'll give three-to-one it will be you.' He turned to the twins who shook on the wager.

The city was well fortified. A series of concentric stone walls with tall, thin buildings wedged in between — each one trying to reach beyond the shadow of its neighbour. The streets were narrow, dark and full of the dying. Open sewers flowed along the main avenue where rats swarmed in large groups attacking anything that didn't have the strength to fight back.

The siege was in its second year, and there was a look of the damned in the eyes of those they passed. Josh tried not to stare, but their haunted faces disturbed him — they had the same look as the Shade.

'Where are we going exactly?' he asked Caitlin as the team turned down another gloomy alley.

'The administrative quarter.' She nodded towards a tall group of towers at the heart of the city. 'We need to get to the safe zone as soon as possible.'

As they neared the inner defences, the packs of roaming infected increased. Josh had to use the Lensing helm to avoid them while navigating through the maze of alleyways. It was hard work, and focusing on sixteen different possibilities — each of which nearly always ended with one or more of the squad being contaminated — was exhausting. His head was pounding by the time they reached the gates.

They were closed. A heavy iron portcullis barred the entrance.

Steel helmets glinted off the battlements high above. It was a fortress within a city. Guards and archers watched for anyone who came within range. The ground between them and the gate was strewn with bodies bristling with arrows, making it abundantly clear there was no negotiation when it came to the enforcing of their quarantine laws.

Darkling took the twins off on a scouting mission while the others waited out of sight in an abandoned shop.

After they had checked for occupants, the team made themselves comfortable and cracked open the rations.

Josh took first watch at the window, which was made of small panes of randomly coloured glass held in with lead strips. The glass was old and distorted the image of the plaza like something from the hall of mirrors at the seaside.

Caitlin came and sat opposite him on a packing case, holding a glass tube with what looked like a bone inside it.

'What's that?'

'One of the many fingers of John the Baptist,' she laughed, giving him the tube. 'There are about fifty of them back there.'

Josh held it up to the light. 'Why would anyone want this?'

'Holy relics were a massive tourist attraction in these times. People would travel for hundreds of miles to visit relics that had performed miracles. Towns would even steal the bones of saints from churches just to boost their economy.'

'Fascinating.' Josh stared at the whitened bone. 'I'm sure the Grandmaster will be very interested to read about that.' He was angry and tired, and the conversation with her godfather was gnawing at him like a mosquito bite he couldn't scratch.

Caitlin's eyebrows knitted into a frown. 'Why would I tell him about it?'

'When you write up your report about this mission — after all, you're his eyes and ears, KitKat.'

'You heard that?' She looked genuinely stunned.

Josh wondered if admitting to overhearing their conversation had just confirmed everything that the Copernicans suspected.

'Every word.'

Her cheeks flushed. 'Well, I'm not going to tell him anything he doesn't already know. Vedris will have already reported your aptitude with the Lens. It's not like it makes you some kind of superstar.'

'You're still going to spy for him though?'

'Is that why you've been so weird lately? Would you prefer he asked someone else? Better me than Darkling or Dalton, don't you think?'

She had a point; if anyone were going to shadow him, he would rather it be her. But it created an uneasy friction between them — he didn't know if he could trust her.

'I don't want anyone spying on me! I don't want to be different.'

That wasn't strictly true. When his mother had been ill the first time, he was so desperate to cure her that he'd wished every night for some kind of superpower. He had promised whatever gods were listening a whole list of good deeds, but they'd been too late — even now when he had one, it couldn't make her better.

Caitlin's eyes softened, and she put her hand on his shoulder.

'If Lyra is right, you may not have any choice about that.'

'About being the Nemesis? What's so bloody important about him anyway?'

'Well, if you believe Daedalus — he can travel outside of time, that he's not bound by the laws of the continuum.'

'Go into the future?'

'Yes.'

Josh sighed deeply; he'd been here before. This was the Paradox all over again.

'I never wanted this.'

'It's just a prophecy — a bunch of stories someone wrote in a book. It doesn't make it true. My grandfather used to say that you made your own fate. Others may write about it afterwards, but you're the master of your own destiny.'

'If I tell you something, do you think you could keep it a secret, at least for a while?'

So, while they sat watching the birds pick at the bodies in the square, Josh told her about his mother and the life he had before.

A half-dead man shuffled out of a nearby alley and into the sunlight, moaned at the brightness and lifted his hand towards the light. They watched in silence as the shaft of the first arrow skewered him through the chest. He didn't appear to notice, lurching zombie-like towards the gates. There were shouts from battlements as the threat escalated and more arrows flew.

Josh counted every one of the fourteen hits it took to put him down.

'So, I guess a frontal assault is out of the question?' Caitlin groaned.

The scouting party returned a few minutes later.

'There are only two gates: North and South.' Darkling

drew a line across the table with his knife. 'Both are equally well guarded. Basically, they're in lockdown. Our only chance is if Jones can get a vector on the last time the gates were open and hope we can get inside without too much fuss.'

'Who is it we're trying to reach exactly?' Josh asked, putting the headgear back on. He winced as Caitlin buckled up the strap, his neck rubbed raw from the chaffing of the leather.

'A merchant navigator by the name of Nicoloso da Recco,' Fey replied, showing him a page from her almanac with an engraving of Da Recco. 'He's been in there for at least three months — along with the rest of the merchant princes. He should have a map of all their trade routes.'

'So they shut themselves in and just left the peasants to the Mongols and their plague?' Michaelmas said, picking up a large crucifix and hefting it from one hand to the other. 'Seems like it's time for a revolution.'

Josh had never taken him for a political type, but the skinny, scruffy seer seemed to be genuinely upset.

'It's standard quarantine procedure — you'd have done the same in their position. The epidemic spreads because they have no idea they're infected and jump onto their ships the minute they get the chance.' Fey had been a Scriptorian before joining the trials, and her historical knowledge was nearly as vast as Caitlin's. She rearranged the symbols on the page until it displayed a miniature map of Europe — and then drew a timeline down the margin, black ink spots bloomed and shrank over the continent.

Bentley took the book and studied the map. 'They're the ones who took it all over Europe?'

'Yes. This is ground zero. I think we're here to find out exactly who and where. The records are patchy between 11,354 and 11,666 — hem-stitched.'

'Hem-stitched?' Josh asked.

'You know, in and out, like a thread through a hem?' She snaked her hand through the air.

'Or a Wyrrm,' one of the others muttered, but Josh couldn't tell who as Caitlin was still adjusting the lenses.

'So, how are you planning to get in?' Darkling asked as Josh went towards the door.

'Frontal assault, of course.' Josh nodded towards the gate.

47

ARROWS

The paths of the arrows left vapour trails in the air around Josh as he walked towards the gates. The moment the bowmen took aim, the Lens allowed him to trace the projected trajectory of each of their steel-tipped shafts — he avoided every single one. It was a weird sensation, watching the predictions of his death with every step. Beads of sweat ran down into his eyes as multiple shots were loosed towards him — time slowed, allowing him to move easily between them.

Dodging their shots, Josh picked his way carefully across the corpse-littered square. The dead were everywhere, and over a hundred bodies lay between him and the gate, making his approach even more treacherous. As he stepped over them Josh noticed there was something unusual about their life-lines; the Lens couldn't find anything about them, and everybody was just an empty shell, their pasts all drained.

Strzyga, thought Josh, remembering the creatures that had attacked the colonel. They could hollow out a life, take every memory and leave nothing behind. He wondered if they came at night, reaping the pasts of the dead when the guards were too tired to care.

By the time he reached the gates, the soldiers had resorted to throwing rocks and were struggling with a large bucket of boiling pitch. Josh fell, exhausted, against the hard metal of the gate as they began to pour. He could smell the tar as he reached up to touch the gate.

The portcullis was iron, forged in the heart of a distant city. He sensed every blow of the hammers that beat it into shape, every sinew of the heavy-muscled arms of the slaves that had cast it. Josh wove through its timeline to the day they raised it into place and jumped before the black pitch reached him.

[<<]

Removing the helm, Josh walked nonchalantly through the open gateway, nodding to the Captain of the Guard who was proudly inspecting his new defences — the man had no idea that one day it would be used against his own people.

Kaffa was a bustling city in the early years of the Genoa stewardship, a busy trading port with a colourful mix of cultures and creeds, but all with one common goal — making money.

Josh walked into the flesh market where the slavers paraded their latest stock on wooden stages, calling out for bids from the well-dressed merchants that passed by. Men and women stood stoically in chains, some not much older than children. It sickened Josh to see them manacled like animals, prodded and poked by passers-by, but he knew there was nothing he could do about it — slavery would be around for at least another three hundred years.

Leaving the market, he came to a square full of stalls selling exotic birds: peacocks in wooden cages hung next to hooded birds of prey and half-tied swans. There were shelves of eggs in all shades of blue and purple, each one stolen from the nest of some soon-to-be-endangered species. Josh half expected to see Alixia shopping for her next extinction project — she would have hated the way these beautiful creatures were being bought and sold for nothing more than the colour of a feather or a Duke's breakfast.

Josh understood why Michaelmas was so angry; the rich squandered while the poor starved. Kaffa taught him more about inequality in five minutes than two years of Ms Field-house's history lessons. He turned away from the square and found a shady doorway to hide in, reminding himself that all he had to do was move forward to 11.347 and find this merchant navigator, Da Recco, and his map.

He took out his tachyon. It was the first time he'd used one since he lost Caitlin, and it made him a little nervous. As the timeline opened and the alley began to shimmer, he noticed something unusual at the edge of his vision — like a smudge on a lens, there was something that avoided his gaze.

[>>]

The administration quarter was a very different place when he reappeared. Beyond the high walls, he could hear the cries of the dying and the far off beat of the Mongol drums.

Merchant's buildings formed the four sides of the square. Built out of an eclectic mix of Italian Renaissance and Persian architecture, each occupying ruler having tried to surpass their predecessor. The wealthy merchants weren't shy in flaunting their wealth, and the towering minarets that rose up around him made Josh smile — size obviously mattered a great deal to these people.

It was nearing midday, and the sun was beating down on the tiled plaza. Waves of heat shimmered off the white marble, and Josh began to swelter in the heavy robes that Vedris had insisted he wear. Beneath his padded doublet was a leather jerkin, and on top of everything was a cloak. It felt like wearing all his clothes at once, and the lack of deodorant was beginning to make itself very apparent.

He shucked off his cloak and unlaced the front of his doublet to let some air circulate. The water from a nearby fountain looked cool and clear, and he cupped a handful onto the back of his neck and felt the droplets trickle down his back.

Josh was about to immerse his head when he heard a noise, a click, as if a door were opening ever so slightly; the creak of a hinge, perhaps. He pretended not to notice, but moved one hand to the pommel of his knife as he took another handful of the cold water and rubbed it into his neck once more.

Again the click, and moving his hand away he felt the point of a blade hovering close to the back of his head.

'Please be so good as to drop your weapon,' a polite voice requested in Italian.

48

DA RECCO

'He's a Venetian spy!'

'If he is, he's not a very good one.'

'How do you know he's not infected?'

'I don't. That's why he's in the barrel.'

'You're crazier than a codfish, Da Recco. I would've run him through where he stood.'

'And he would've fallen into the only fresh water source we have.'

The voices sounded like they were at the far end of a tunnel. Josh's ears were ringing, and his body was numb. He had no idea where he was, but it felt like he was underwater.

'You still believe that bathing can cure them of the disease?'

'Prevent, not cure — it is a subtle difference, I admit.'

'Benvolo told me last week that he had seen a cloud of flies in the shape of the devil.' The man spat a curse. 'Fra Gerolamo is to hold a special mass to bless the guard and anyone else with concerns.'

'Anyone with a scudo, you mean! If the devil is truly walking among us, the rich should be very afraid.'

'Well, I still think you're crazy. Wait until the Consul finds out. He will throw you off the wall himself. The edict was pretty clear — no one in or out.'

'So how did this young one get in, eh? Wouldn't it be wiser to find that out before we send him to his maker? I'm sure the Consul would be interested to find out there's a weak point in our defences, no?'

'Whatever. I have a meeting — it's on your head, Da Recco. I was never here.'

Josh heard the other man leave and opened his eyes. He was in a basement, like a wine cellar, surrounded by ancient oak barrels. The room was dimly lit by a single lantern sitting on a table next to a middle-aged man dressed in a flamboyant doublet of dark red. He was picking the mould out of his bread with a stiletto blade. Josh's helmet lay in pieces next to the food.

'At last, my prisoner awakes,' Da Recco exclaimed, driving the knife into the table and picking up the lantern.

It was only as the Italian walked towards him that Josh realised he was floating in a barrel of what smelled like brandy and that he wasn't wearing any clothes.

'You are fortunate that it was I that found you,' he continued. 'I'm one of the few men in this madhouse who wouldn't have killed you where you stood. The others are all stir-crazy, looking for demons and devils in dark corners,' he added, flamboyantly gesturing with his free hand and creating strange shadows on the walls.

Josh tested the bindings that held his arms behind his back, but the ropes had swollen with the brandy.

'So why didn't you?'

'Because of the colour of your skin, your hair.' He pointed at Josh's head. 'You came a long way to break into our city. I've studied natural philosophy, I understand these things. You are not Italian... more Norse perhaps?'

'English.'

'No! The English are stupid, ugly oafs! I think your mother met a Norseman when your father was tending to the pigs, no? Who can say?' He shrugged, putting down the lantern. 'Your Italian, however, is nearly perfect. A little too Florentine for my ear, but still very good!'

'Thanks. What is this?' Josh nodded to the liquid that surrounded him.

'A little concoction of my own devising. Some of the finest brandies, plus some Salt of Tartar, Hartshorn, Vitriol and of course the basic ascorbics — it should cleanse you of the scourge.'

Josh had no idea what the others were, but the name Vitriol came back to him from one of his mother's shows; it was Sulphuric Acid.

'Get me out of here now!' he ordered, jumping around in the dark liquid.

'But my experiment must run its course!'

'Screw your experiment! Get me out now, and I'll tell you all about the scourge and how to protect yourself from it. I'm sure there are plenty who'll pay for that!'

Da Recco considered the idea for a few moments before nodding. 'Fine. But I burned those ugly clothes you were wearing so you will have to wear some of mine.'

That's the least of my problems, thought Josh, as the Italian picked up a hammer and smashed open the barrel.

. . .

'So these bacteria live within the flea?' Da Recco asked with a hint of disbelief, 'and you can only see it with a lens?'

'A microscope,' Josh corrected, pulling on the second boot. The clothes the navigator had given him were similar to their travelling robes: a long black cloak draped over a green velvet suit.

'So by burning the clothes and submerging the patient —'

'You drowned the carriers, although it wouldn't have cured them.'

Da Recco's mouth widened into a smug grin. 'No, but I was close.'

Not close enough, thought Josh, wondering what it must be like to live in an age where they had no idea what made you ill. Da Recco was clearly a clever man, if not a little crazy.

'How do you know all this? The English are not revered for their sciences? Perhaps you studied under the great Suleman of Araby?'

Josh realised he'd already given too much away; bacteria was something that wasn't supposed to be discovered for another couple of hundred years — Caitlin was going to kill him.

'My father was an alchemist and a lens maker.' Josh pointed at the Lensing helmet. 'He made that for me.'

'Ah, yes. I was wondering about that. Not like any helm I've ever seen. I doubt it would stop a sword.'

'Oh, you'd be surprised.'

'Not much surprises me. I've seen many things on my travels, and I doubt there is much that would — except perhaps the appearance of an Englishman in the middle of a Mongol siege. What exactly are you doing here?'

'I need safe passage to England. I was told that your city had the best ships.'

'Indeed we do, and the best navigators. Unfortunately, the two are rather unacquainted at the moment.'

'You can't leave?'

Da Recco shook his head. 'There is a dispute between the ship owners and the guild of navigation. Neither can agree on a price. Crazy I know,' — he waved his hands in the air — 'when you consider the spectre of death that awaits beyond those walls, but this is business. All of our charts have been confiscated by the Consul. Without maps we are blind, and there is also the small matter of leaving this sanctuary to reach the ships.'

Josh wondered what would have happened if their ships had never left port. Perhaps the spread of the black death would have been stopped in its tracks.

He could save millions of lives just by walking away right now and leaving these arrogant idiots to starve to death behind their walls.

49

DIVERSION

'So you didn't tell him everything?' asked Caitlin, trying not to sound too concerned, but unable to mask the underlying disappointment from her voice.

'Not completely,' Josh lied, desperately trying to figure out how to stop this conversation from ending badly.

They were following Da Recco in single file through a tunnel as he guided them back underneath the administration district.

Caitlin slowed down so the others wouldn't hear.

'How much?'

'Enough to get his co-operation. Just about the bacteria, and the fleas — basic stuff.'

'Basic for the twenty-first century maybe,' she snapped, raising her eyes. 'Bacteria won't be discovered by Leeuwenhoek for another three hundred years. I can't think of anything more stupid that you could have possibly done — other than walking through a barrage of arrows of course.'

'And he kind of knows we're not from this time.'

She stopped in her tracks.

'You told him about the Order?'

'Not exactly. He took one look at the tachyon and guessed. He'd already taken the lensing helmet apart — he's a very inquisitive dude.'

Josh could see the scream gathering in her chest, watching it rise like a red wave up her neck and into her cheeks.

'And how exactly did he get hold of your tachyon?' she snarled through tight lips.

The tail end of the group had stopped, and were all looking back at the pair of them.

'No, don't tell me! It's probably better if I don't know when the Protectorate interrogate me,' she shouted, storming off.

The tunnels were carved out of rock, the ceilings low, and Josh had to hunch over to stop from hitting his head. Da Recco's lantern was growing faint as he tried to catch up with her.

'He's the only one who knows where the maps are kept.'

She didn't respond, marching on towards the dull glow.

Bentley fell back to walk beside Josh as they caught up with the end of the group. 'She's been worried about you ever since you left. That trick with the arrows nearly gave her a heart attack, but it was so cool — Darkling hasn't stopped talking about it.'

Josh tried not to show how pleased he was with the news.

'How many times did you see yourself die?'

'Too many,' Josh muttered. He was still enjoying the idea of Caitlin worrying about him.

'You were awesome.'

Josh shrugged off the compliment. It hadn't been that hard.

'What's a Wyrrm?' he asked, changing the subject.

Bentley drew a sharp breath through his teeth, the way Josh's mum used to do whenever he asked her for money. 'It's not something we talk about. They're a bit of a myth, like the bogeyman I guess. Stuff your parents would scare you with if you didn't do as you're told.'

'Like the Djinn?'

Bentley shook his head. His red hair was now matched by a fine beard which made him look older, and the chubby cheeks were gone too — the training regime was beginning to agree with him. 'No, these actually existed. They're supposed to have been huge, some said to have spanned hundreds of years.'

'You mean hundreds of metres?'

'No, Years. Wyrrm's are supposed to live on the edge of the continuum. Their bodies span decades as they grow.'

'Nice. So what have they got to do with the plague?'

'The stories tell of how they are able to burrow through weak points in the chronosphere. When they do, death and disease follow — it's like a signature, a pattern through history, but no one has seen one for ages. They probably don't exist anymore.'

Josh thought Bentley didn't sound too convinced, but he could see the team waiting impatiently at the tunnel exit. Caitlin was ignoring him, and he knew that she wasn't going to be in the mood to discuss another fairytale.

'So, here we are,' — Da Recco's voice echoed down the smooth stone walls of the tunnel — 'below the Counsel chambers. Above us reside some of the most powerful men in Kaffa: including the Pope's representative, Fra Gerolamo, who has the Papal Guard, Pontificia Cohors, protecting him and his treasure.'

De'Angelo's attention was piqued at the mention of treasure.

'You'll need to find the navigation charts. They will be

stored in the vault two floors above us. Joshua tells me you can reach them without bloodshed — which I have serious doubts about, but I try to keep an open mind while ensuring I have a backup plan.'

He drew out a metal ball, with a fuse sticking out of the top. 'This is something I like to call "La Bollente", because it has something of a temper. It will cause enough of an explosion to make them look the other way.'

'Where exactly are you going to set that off?' asked Darkling.

Da Recco shrugged. 'Maybe by the South Gate. Give them something to keep them really busy.'

'You're going to blow a gate?'

'They've been sitting comfortably on their fat backsides for too long. Someone needs to give them a bit of a kick. Yes?'

Michaelmas grinned at the idea and immediately volunteered to go with him.

As he and Da Recco ran back down the tunnel, the Italian turned and his voice echoed along it. 'I'll see you at the map room!'

50

THE MAPS

They waited for the detonation. In hindsight, it would have probably been easier to have gone back in time and entered the building in a more peaceful period, and then jumped forward. Yet there was something exciting about living in the moment, like a linear — having to deal with the world in real-time.

The team members were nervous as they huddled in the dark tunnel. Josh could tell from their rapid breathing they were scared. He remembered the first time he'd stolen a car. His hands shook so much he couldn't get the thing into first gear. It was a feeling that never left you — fear was a potent drug, and he loved the way it turned to elation when he overcame it.

Caitlin's hand brushed against his and closed around his fingers. It was a small, child-like gesture that invoked protection and reassurance. Somewhere deep within him, something unlocked, a memory he'd sealed away — the time he'd woken in the Mesolithic cave, her arms wrapped around him, her body pressed against his.

'Sorry,' she whispered, so close that he felt her lips brush his ear.

He squeezed her hand in the way of a reply.

The explosion rocked the foundations of the buildings, raining dust down onto them — whatever Da Recco had concocted packed one hell of a punch.

Their ears were still ringing when they climbed the narrow staircase. Darkling took the lead, as usual, followed by the twins. By the time Josh and Caitlin made it up to the ground floor any guards that hadn't abandoned their posts had been dealt with.

The next two floors were in chaos: confused servants and merchants were running around like frightened children, trying to understand what had happened.

Someone screamed, 'They're at the south gate!' and a group of soldiers charged down the stairs, completely ignoring the dusty members of Aries226 as they headed for the door. The more level-headed members of the nobility were trying to persuade the remaining guards to bar the doors, but their orders fell on deaf ears.

Da Recco's face appeared amongst the crowd, closely followed by the beaming smile of Michaelmas. The Italian motioned to come with him, and they went unnoticed through the empty corridors until they reached the Consul chambers.

They watched in awe as De'Angelo took less than a minute to unlock the metal studded doors.

Inside, the chamber was an obscene display of wealth: gilded candelabras hung from the painted ceiling and portraits of fat, rich merchants presided over the long mahogany table which stretched down the centre of the room, flanked by golden chairs.

The table was laid out for a lavish dinner. Roast suckling pig and guinea fowl steamed on silver platters amongst the fruit and wine. It was as if the meal had just been served when the bomb went off. Suddenly everyone realised they hadn't eaten for over twenty-four hours.

'Not now!' Darkling ordered, as they moved eagerly towards the food. 'Find the treasure room first.'

While the rest of the team was spreading out, Josh went onto the balcony to assess the damage Da Recco had done.

It was carnage, the street was now full of people climbing over each other to get away from the smoke rising from the southern gate. Through the haze Josh could make out the outline of shapes slowly groping their way over the debris — the infected were inside.

'Hey, Jones, are you going to help or what?' Darkling demanded.

The maps were easy to find, and there were so many latent memories tied to the objects in the room that it took mere minutes to locate the vault. A large painting was slid aside to reveal a hidden, metal-plated door. The lock proved no problem for De'Angelo, and there was a collective gasp at the sight that greeted them when the door opened to the treasure within.

'This is definitely something the Antiquarians are going to want to get their hands on,' Bentley said, as they began to open the chests. There were artefacts collected from all corners of the globe. Not just gold and jewels, but sacred objects from civilisations that none of them had ever seen.

Caitlin had found the charts in a wooden plans chest, and spread them out on the table. Josh studied them. It was weird to see the world according to the fourteenth century: the misshapen outlines of continents and the illustrations of sea beasts and dragons to hide the mapmaker's lack of knowledge.

'I can't believe they can find anything with these!' Josh pointed at a particularly crude rendering of Africa that just petered out towards the South.

The maps fell into two categories. Some cartographers had tried to draw the world: 'Mappa Mundi,' Caitlin called them, and they were so badly drawn that Josh wondered if they still believed the earth was flat. Others were less ambitious, creating detailed charts of Europe and the Mediterranean; these were covered in notes and nautical markings.

'Ah. Come to papa, my beauties,' murmured Da Recco, picking out four of the more detailed ones. He discarded one and rolled the others up carefully.

'Are we seriously going to let him leave?' Darkling asked, walking over with an ossuary of a ringed hand which rattled around inside the glass case. Da Recco had gone into the treasure room and was wrestling a map case from one of the twins.

'It's what was meant to happen.' Fey opened her almanac and pointed at the relevant page. 'You can't argue with the Copernicans.'

'Well, you could...' Darkling began.

'Why don't we see where it would take us next?' Caitlin suggested, intercepting Da Recco as he left the vault. She touched the case of maps and went rigid, the colour draining from her face. Da Recco looked thoroughly confused.

Josh knew instantly that something was wrong. 'What is it?'

Caitlin didn't reply, her eyes glazing as she was caught up in the weave of the timeline the maps were invoking.

She gasped.

The stench of decay was overpowering as a fibrous black tentacle materialised in the air above her. A grotesque, ulcerated limb that thrashed blindly around the room like a root in search of water.

'Get down!' shouted Darkling as the grim tendril swept over their heads.

Ducking under the long table, Josh saw the seeping, open sores puckering across its surface. 'Let go!' he screamed at Caitlin, wildly searching for something to knock the map out of her hands.

Da Recco stared blankly into space, oblivious to the Wyrrm's spectral limb as it coiled around both of them. Coming out from under the table, Josh saw that the ceiling had transformed into a festering underbelly of tentacles, like a giant millipede. He ducked and rolled across the floor as another twisting feeler reached for him, crashing into Darkling who was pulling a pair of swords off the wall.

'We need to get her away from the map!' Josh shouted over the raucous screeching of a thousand insects.

Darkling nodded and handed Josh one of the weapons. 'Whatever you do, don't let it touch you.'

Josh felt the weight of the blade, swinging it around as the tentacle came back for a second attack.

The metal slid through the ethereal fibres of the limb as if they were smoke, causing no damage at all.

'Not like that!' barked Darkling. 'Reinforce it with a temporal strike.'

Josh thought back to his training. Vedris had shown them how to find a previous attack in the timeline of a weapon and use it to multiply the damage on a target. With practice, you could harness more than one event to increase the power even further.

He reached into the sword and found a duel: two men carving the air with the deft strokes of master swordsman. It was enough, and he brought the force of their moves into his next swing, feeling the past intersect as the edge cut into the coils around Caitlin. The tremor travelled down his arm as the blade connected with solid matter, and a screech from some-where above told him that it felt pain.

More tentacles dropped down from the ceiling, blindly searching for him. Caitlin was looking deathly pale, and Josh knew he had one chance to put it right. He dodged the flailing tendrils and brought the flat of the blade down hard on her hand. The blow brought her back to reality with a jolt, her face screwing up with agony as she released her grip on the map case, instinctively cradling her injured fingers.

The writhing mass of tentacles above them melted away like black ice.

'Wyrrm,' was all Caitlin managed to utter before she fainted.

51

1664

Darkling entered the church, first as always. The others trailed behind in dribs and drabs, no one too eager to find out what was inside.

After they had left Kaffa, ensuring that Da Recco and his uninfected crew were clear of the port, the team had followed the trail of the Wyrrm through the next two centuries, sometimes manifesting itself as a small outbreak of plague in an isolated village like Eyam, other times wiping out half a country.

By the time they reached 11.664, their elapsed time on the mission was nearing two weeks. Everyone was tired, and tempers were beginning to fray. Caitlin and Fey kept records of every instance, plotting their next jump as they tried to anticipate the trail of the creature.

'I think we're close to the head,' whispered Caitlin, consulting her notes.

Josh was past the point of caring. He was sick of the smell of death, the lack of decent food and the constant moaning from other members of the team. They blamed him for losing the lensing helmet and for passing Da Recco forbidden information. Fey checked into his records and discovered Da Recco had gone back to Italy and tried to convince the Pope and his council that the plague originated from a bug they couldn't see. They rejected his theory, upholding the belief that it was the work of the Devil — to which Da Recco pointed out that was also an unprovable theory and was summarily executed for heresy.

Josh had liked Da Recco, a man before his time, and it pained him to think that he may have inadvertently caused his death.

There was no one inside the church.

Like a well-drilled crew, Darkling, Michaelmas and the twins swept the transepts while Caitlin, Fey, Bentley and De'Angelo set up a base and discussed the options.

'We should call this in,' suggested Bentley, for what felt like the ninth time. 'This is way too dangerous.'

'And fail another test? No way!' objected Fey. 'The whole point of this trial is to prove we can deal with an unexpected situation.'

'But a Wyrrm?'

De'Angelo, who had been mulling over the situation, suddenly snapped his fingers. 'We could try to spike it.'

'Do you know how to do that?' Fey asked.

'I'm okay on the theory, but I'll need Bentley to build it.' De'Angelo nodded at him.

'What's a spike?' asked Josh.

'A fixed point in time, when you create a closed time loop and bind the target with some kind of lure. The Xenos use it for trapping monads,' De'Angelo explained.

'But the Wyrrm is nearly a thousand-years-long,' said Josh, stretching his arms out.

De'Angelo smiled. 'We only need to nail the head.'

Josh turned to Bentley. 'Can you build it?'

Bentley looked around the nave. 'It's basically a Hubble Invertor. I need a conductor like copper, and the oldest arte-fact you can find, plus something from one of the infected. A head would be best, but a limb will do.'

'Really? You're asking us to touch one of them?' Fey complained so loudly it reverberated off every wall.

'I'll do it,' offered Darkling, walking back up the aisle.

They all turned towards him.

'Are you sure?' asked Caitlin. 'The Wyrrm will come after you the moment it senses you.'

'It's not that quick.' He winked at her. 'And besides, I'm faster than any of you.'

Josh had to give Darkling his due, he was always the one that went in first, and whether you called it bravery or stupid-ity, there was something endearing about his lack of fear.

'Good luck.' Josh held out his hand.

Darkling gripped it tight and smiled. 'Like you wouldn't have done the same.' He leaned in closer. 'Do me a favour and keep hold of this.' He handed Josh his locker key. 'If for some reason I don't make it, you may be the only one who can stop him.' Then walked off to consult with the twins.

'Can't we just kill it? Josh asked Caitlin while the others were busy finding the components for Bentley.

'No.' She shook her head. 'They are a perdurant species — Wyrrms are not based in one single timestream, and as a rule we try not to kill things. It causes too much of a disturbance in the continuum. We do get to name it though.'

Josh was not impressed. 'How come no one found this one before?'

'They're rare creatures, and most people don't even want to admit they exist. If we can spike it here the Xenos will be able to study it. This is quite a significant find.' She smiled a little. 'Dalton's going to hate it. The Order will be talking about this for years.'

'About Darkling you mean,' Josh muttered, watching him explaining his plans to the twins. The locker key was cold in Josh's hand. He wasn't sure what Darkling was asking him to do with it, so he slipped it into his pocket and duly forgot about it.

Darkling and his crew were gone for over an hour. In the meantime, the others busied themselves with the details of the trap. De'Angelo was enjoying the role of project manager, directing Bentley on the various component parts of a spiking.

Josh watched them work together; there was a seamless ease in the way they moved around each other, intuitively knowing what their partner would do next — they had finally bonded into a team. The challenges of this mission had forced them to come to terms with their differences, had made them overcome their prejudices. There was trust between them now, and Josh realised that was the primary goal of the mission.

Then Darkling walked through the door and collapsed.

'Don't touch him,' Caitlin ordered. 'Everybody stay back.'

Black tendrils of smoke coiled in and out of Darkling's body. His eyes were glazed, and boils bubbled under the skin as the virus ravaged his body.

Everyone drew back as Darkling tried to stand, but he

wasn't in control — he moved like a marionette, suspended on invisible strings.

Caitlin looked to De'Angelo and Josh saw something pass between them.

De'Angelo and Bentley gathered their equipment and began to lay it out a few metres ahead of the lurching step of Darkling's twisted feet.

'Are you going to save him?' asked one of the twins, coming through the door behind him.

'No.' De'Angelo's face was solemn. 'He's beyond that.'

'Where are the medics?' the other twin shouted. 'Aren't they supposed to rescue us!'

'No one's coming,' Josh growled. 'We're on our own.'

Darkling's body was nearing the first of Bentley's contraptions. A stream of saliva and pus dribbled down his chin as his head twisted at an unnatural angle and his mouth gaped open.

'Doo ittt noowww!' was all they could make out as De'Angelo activated the first device.

There were a series of static charges, as though Darkling had stood on a live wire. The air around him shimmered and suddenly the church was filled with the vast carapace head of an insect-like creature, its mandibles holding up Darkling's body like a doll. He was lifted into the air, twisting back and forth like a man on the end of a hangman's noose.

'Finnnisshhh!' Darkling managed to utter as a spectral claw opened his throat.

A tentacle caught De'Angelo around his ankle and dragged him away from the second trap. The others were all too stunned to move as he was pulled down the aisle of the church towards the vast head. Josh grabbed for him but missed. De'Angelo was screaming, desperately clawing at the passing pews as he tried to stop himself.

'The spike!' Bentley shouted, pointing at the detonator.

. . .

Josh jumped over the rail and up onto the altar. Tentacles flew out from every direction, the walls of the church blackening as dark, root-like veins spread through the plaster. Josh slammed his hand down on the makeshift switch, detonating the second trap and creating a sphere of energy that enshrouded Darkling and the creature's head, freezing them in place.

De'Angelo was released as the stasis field shimmered and stabilised.

Thirty seconds later, the Dreadnoughts arrived and everything went from bad to worse.

But nobody cared.

52

AFTER

Darkling's death was an unspoken curse that filled the silences of the next few days. The Dreadnoughts brought the rest of team Aries back to the academy via a short visit to the medics. No one else was seriously injured, although Michaelmas had to be quarantined after it was found he'd been infected with typhus.

The outcome of their second trial was still under investigation. Although four points had been awarded to Fey for her documentation of the outbreaks, it was small comfort considering their loss. They spent time apart from the others, wandering the grounds or being interviewed by various members of the Xenobiology department.

Everyone voted unanimously to name it after Darkling when the Xenobiologysts asked at the final debriefing.

'Death is an unwelcome visitor. Harder on those who are left behind than those that pass — you will learn to endure the loss as we all do. One day you will remember these events and appreciate the sacrifice that we must all make for the Order. Ours is the fate of the damned — we cannot falter.'

'We cannot falter,' the congregation repeated, the sentiment like a prayer.

Vassili was speaking at Darkling's memorial. Following Dreadnought tradition it was held in Notre-Dame Cathedral in 11.345, the year he was born. There wasn't a casket; the Xenos couldn't extricate the body from the spike without releasing the Wyrrm. The old training master looked tired and genuinely moved by his death — no one had perished at the Academy for over a century, and Vassili was taking it hard. Every member of the Draconian High Command had interviewed him; there was even a rumour that the Protectorate had paid him a visit.

'Why didn't they rescue him?' Bentley muttered to himself as they left the chapel and re-entered the parade ground of the academy.

'Because the Wyrrm disrupted the timeline, and they had no idea it was coming,' Caitlin said, putting her arm around Bentley. 'It's not your fault. Darkling knew what he was doing.'

Bentley looked like he was about to burst into tears and shrugged off her arm. 'They're going to have to retire us now we're two men down, and his death will have been for nothing!'

Caitlin was about to say something else, but she bit her lip. Josh saw the conflict on her face as Bentley stormed off.

'He's going to leave,' she said, watching him go.

'No, he won't. He's not a quitter.'

'But he's right. With a team of ten we're not going to earn enough points to make the cut. Gemini is going to thrash us.'

Dalton's team had discovered a new path from the Minaret

of Firuzkuh in Afghanistan and succeeded in locating a forgotten Tajik civilisation — which on any other day would have been seen as a great result if it hadn't been overshadowed by the discovery of the Wyrrm. Josh inadvertently caught Dalton's eye as he was talking with one of his lieutenants, a boy called Jarius. The arrogant twat turned and came straight towards them.

'Sorry about Darkling.' He looked genuinely upset. 'He was a good man.'

Caitlin and Josh were dumbfounded, 'thanks,' was all Caitlin could manage.

'So I guess this is goodbye, pumpkin,' Dalton added, stepping closer to Caitlin. 'With your best man gone you haven't got a hope. Shame you didn't take my offer when you had the chance. See you at home in a couple of weeks?'

He leaned forward to kiss her, but she leaned back and kicked him hard between the legs.

'Piss off, Dalton,' she growled. 'Yes, Darkling was good, but stupid too. He reminded me a lot of you, but with more spine. You can take your condolences and stick them where the sun never shines!'

Dalton lay crumpled on to the floor, holding his crotch as she turned and marched off.

53

THE SECOND CUT

In keeping with tradition, the team's points had been removed from the leaderboard; the final scores from the last three weeks of training were a closely guarded secret. Aries was more than fifteen points behind their nearest competitor when the board had been cleared, and no one had bothered to keep score since.

The mood in the refectory was sombre, the usual banter between the teams tempered by Darkling's death — his name was gleaming brightly on the wall of honour next to the other fallen Draconians.

Josh scanned through the names of the lost, their golden letters growing more tarnished with age as his eyes scanned up the list. He paused when he came to the entry for Caitlin's parents:

JULIANA & THOMAS MAKEPIECE, EGYPT 7.320 (M.I.A.)

. . .

He wondered what it would have been like to die in the maelstrom, or whether it was even possible. Sim had told him that they couldn't age because time didn't exist in there, that nobody really knew what effects it would have on the human body. Someone could come out a thousand years later and still be the same age as when they went in — he called it 'temporal dilation'.

Vassili stepped up onto a table and slammed his staff down so hard the plates jumped. He looked like a man who hadn't slept for a week. His eyes were red-rimmed, and there was a hoarseness to his voice when he spoke.

'There have been some,' — he stared directly at Dalton's team — 'that have lobbied for team Aries to be disqualified in light of the losses suffered by their team.' A chorus of objections rippled around the room. Vassili raised his hand to quiet them. 'We have consulted the regulations on this and can confirm that there is no issue with their continuation.' Everyone apart from Gemini showed their appreciation by banging their cups on the table. The old training master continued. 'Also, having consulted with the Xenobiology department, we have decided that they should be awarded a special dispensation for their contribution to science and the prevention of further pandemic infestation.'

While the other members of the team looked at each other in astonishment and relief, Josh watched Caitlin — they'd got the recognition they deserved, but she didn't seem too happy about it.

'Based on this new development, it's my duty to declare that the teams who will be leaving today are — Cancer and Sagittarius.'

Both teams rose to their feet at the announcement and began to protest. Vassili slammed the end of his staff down impatiently.

'Your scores are some of the lowest ever recorded for a second quartile, so please have the good grace to leave my academy with what's left of your dignity and never darken my doors again!'

He stepped off the table and disappeared, leaving the other tutors to deal with the disgruntled team members.

'So we p-passed?' Bentley stuttered in disbelief.

'It appears so.' Caitlin was glaring at Dalton, who was celebrating Gemini's first place as the scores were updated on the leaderboard.

'Don't really feel like partying,' mused De'Angelo.

'Bullshit! Darkling would've wanted to go out and get totally wasted!' declared one of the twins, surprising everyone, as no one could remember him ever speaking before.

'Yeah, like that time we got trapped in the hold under the boat,' Bentley agreed.

'That time you farted you mean?' De'Angelo waved his hand in front of his face.

Everyone laughed and began recounting their own stories about Darkling.

Caitlin went to console Fey, who looked like she was going to burst into tears again. She'd taken Darkling's death harder than the others, for obvious reasons.

Josh was very, very drunk. Not so far gone that he couldn't see straight, but far enough to blur the edges of the last few days.

After the cut, everyone received a twenty-four-hour pass. Some of the other teams came over to invite Aries to join them but were politely declined. Dalton, who was keeping a wide berth from Caitlin, was rumoured to be hosting an impromptu party for Gemini back in his family's eleventh-century castle — no one bothered to gatecrash.

Aries hadn't wanted to spend the evening with the others. They'd decided, unanimously, to spend the night together in one of Darkling's favourite clubs — the Hellfire, in 11.751.

Located in the ruins of an abbey, the Hellfire was the favourite hangout of the Bohemian and avant-garde of the eighteenth century. The religious surroundings may have explained why the hosts had decided to dress as monks while dispensing generous amounts of a bright green liquid called 'Absinthe' into champagne glasses.

The guests were an odd assortment of eighteenth-century high society, with prostitutes and a very exotic collection of dangerous animals leashed to equally ferocious looking circus performers.

'What do you guys want to do next?' Josh asked, watching a leopard as it prowled past, chained to a half-naked, heavily tattooed woman.

'Drink ourselves stupid,' chimed the twins in unison.

'No, dance! I want to go dancing!' Fey got up and dragged Bentley and De'Angelo through a door that was marked: *Pacha, Ibiza 11.973.*

The Hellfire was run by a retired Draconian artificer who'd ingeniously linked all the most iconic nightclubs together into one of the most unusual venues Josh had ever experienced. There were rooms that led to Woodstock, The Viper room, Hacienda and even The Cavern Club.

Caitlin was sitting opposite Josh on a velvet chaise-longue, absent-mindedly playing with her dragon pendant and sipping a dark liquor the colour of blood. She was wearing a sheer, black dress with a corset pulled tight into her waist, and her short hair accentuated the swan-like curve of her neck. Her eyes were darkly shaded, with Egyptian-style lines drawn into the corners — just like the way she used to.

When the others drifted off with Fey, she came over and sat beside him. 'Do you think they'd be so happy if they knew the real reason we made the first cut?'

'Because of your godfather?'

'Godfather. Shh! It's supposed to be a secret, remember?'

'Yeah, sorry, *Lisichka*.'

She took another drink from a passing monk. 'Lisichka. It's quite liberating pretending to be someone else — have you ever thought about it?'

'No, not really,' Josh lied. He'd spent his life wishing he could've been someone else, at least until he met the colonel.

'I didn't — until I met you.' She waggled her finger at him. 'The way you look at me, it's weird, like you're seeing someone else.'

Josh thought of all the other Caitlins, each one changed by circumstance.

'I don't know, you're pretty much the same person in every version I've met. Except maybe the dominatrix — you were seriously mean in that one!' He smiled at the thought of her in the tight leather uniform.

'Really? Are you sure you didn't prefer her?' she asked, narrowing her eyes.

Josh shook his head. 'No, she was too extreme. You're way more normal than her.'

Caitlin pouted. 'Normal? You mean boring.'

'Not at all,' he replied, realising he was on dangerous ground. 'Just, you know — more like the first version I met.'

'So, this version of me isn't quite the same?'

Josh was struggling to find an answer that didn't dig him deeper into the hole. She'd warned him before about starting this conversation, but it was something that they'd never fully resolved since that evening on the roof.

'Am I still the girl you'd walk back through nine centuries to find?'

'It's not the same. You can't expect —'

'Answer the bloody question!' she interrupted.

Josh was aware other guests were beginning to watch them. She was close now, he could feel her breath on his neck and her breasts were nearly bursting out of the dress.

'You're different. It's hard to explain. You had more attitude — it's still there, under the surface. You always knew what you wanted, and no one could force you to do something you didn't want to do.'

'You mean like this?' she said, wrapping her hands around his neck and pulling him towards her.

The kiss seemed to last for hours, as their lips parted and while her tongue explored his mouth, her hands rifled through his hair. He just let it happen, too drunk and too happy to care if it was real or not. This Caitlin wanted him, even if she wasn't quite the same one he'd fallen for. It wasn't like he was cheating on her: the waves of pleasure confirmed that. He slipped his arms around her and they fell back into the sofa.

'Yo!' Bentley nudged Josh awake.

'What?' Josh complained as Caitlin lifted her head off his chest.

'Much as I'm glad you two have finally got together, I'm sorry to report we have a slight issue.'

'What time is it?' Caitlin groaned as she adjusted her dress.

'We're t-minus two hours from the end of our pass and the twins have gone missing.'

'They'll be in the bar.'

'Checked that, and all the other places that a pair of meat-heads might end up — did you know they have a bear pit downstairs?'

'Shit,' said Josh. 'Where are the others?'

'Behind you,' came a chorus of voices.

'Okay. So everybody knows,' groaned Caitlin, trying not to sound too embarrassed.

'Everyone knew weeks ago,' said Fey. 'We're just relieved you got it over with.'

54

WITCH-HUNT

The third quarter was when things got serious. The lessons were more intense and focused on core skills. They were divided into smaller groups, and rotated through the specialisations: navigation, defence, engineering and evasion.

Josh and Caitlin spent every spare minute together. They were hardly ever in the same classes, but made up for it each evening, sneaking off to random parts of the castle where they wouldn't be disturbed. It became a running joke within the team that there would soon be a new member of Aries — even if they would have to wait nine months for it to arrive.

Caitlin spent a lot of time in the library, which had been borrowed from the Bodleian. Duke Humphrey's Library was a beautiful old reading room full of rare books stacked into carved wooden alcoves on ornate balconies. She was in her element, her nose stuck in a book, a stack of old manuscripts piled beside her. Josh would basically act as her gopher as she sent him off for one ancient text after another. He was beginning to wonder if she wouldn't have been happier staying in the Scriptorians.

'What exactly are you looking for?' he asked, struggling to find space on the table for a stack of bestiaries.

'I'm researching the Wyrrm. I can't bear the idea of Darkling being stuck in there forever.'

Josh remembered Darkling's key, and still had no idea what he was supposed to do with it.

'Surely the Xeno's would have already done that?'

'There is no greater fool than an expert — as my grandfather used to say.' Caitlin took out the watch that Derado had given her. It was an old pocket-watch, the casing inscribed with a series of intricate circles, like the orbits of planets around a star symbol.

'I've been meaning to ask you how you disappeared that day,' he said, remembering the moment on the parade ground.

Caitlin looked up from the watch, then smiled and disappeared.

'I wasn't asking for a repeat performance,' he muttered.

She reappeared behind him and covered his eyes.

'Boo!'

He turned around and caught her waist, kissing her. 'So?'

'It's not easy to explain... you kind of stop time. Like setting your tachyon to loop on the same moment.'

'Like you do in vorpal combat?'

She shook her head. 'This is different, as you don't need a tachyon. It's kind of like holding your breath — you move sideways in time.'

'Can you teach me?'

She disappeared again, reappearing back in her seat behind the desk. 'If you're good,' she said, smiling wickedly.

Caitlin opened her almanac.

'Shit! Sim says Alixia has been arrested!'

'What? Why?'

'Hold on. He's still writing.' She spread the book open so that Josh could read the text too.

Sim's handwriting was a fluid copperplate that swept across the paper as they watched. Caitlin read it aloud.

'Protectorate are holding her on suspicion of consorting with a fugitive and fatecasting — no details. Father's gone to petition the founder. Lyra is in pieces. Phileas is furious, believes it's some kind of Nemesis witch hunt — won't stop ranting on about the bloody Daedalans.'

Josh thought about the Tarot reading that Alixia had made him go through. He still had the cards in his locker.

'What the hell do they think she's done?' wondered Caitlin aloud.

'It's me, isn't it?' Josh sighed. 'Like Derado said, they're coming after me.'

'You're hardly a fugitive. You haven't done anything wrong.'

Josh remembered all those nights he'd spent in police custody; at first, his mother or the social worker would come and pick him up. Then as he got older, they left him there overnight — probably hoping to teach him a lesson, but the food was better, and he got a decent night's sleep, so he didn't see it as a punishment. He guessed that detention by the Protectorate probably wasn't as cosy.

What do you want us to do? Caitlin wrote beneath Sim's message.

Stay put. Sim replied. *Not safe here.*

The words were already beginning to disappear as they read them.

Josh sat on his bed staring at the Tarot cards and thinking about what to do for Alixia. She'd been kind to him — in every timeline they had met. It wasn't fair that such a good woman should be treated so badly. He'd thought about going back to Cole's shop and warning her, but something about Sim's words — *Not safe here* — had stopped him. Derado said they wouldn't dare come into the academy, which meant for now he was beyond their reach, but he had no idea for how long.

Putting the cards back into his locker, he remembered Darkling's key. He'd forgotten about it when things had heated up with Caitlin.

He studied it, but as with all academy equipment, there was no timeline to weave — nothing here had a past. Josh assumed it was some kind of anti-cheating system, to ensure that no one could jump back and crib notes off previous candidates. Whatever reason Darkling had for giving him the key, Josh wasn't really looking forward to finding out why. No one came to collect his stuff, which everyone thought a little weird considering that his dad was supposed to be some high-ranking Draconian officer.

The wooden lockers were all the same, except for the name card that sat in the brass frame on the door. Josh slid the key into Darkling's lock and pulled the door open.

At first, he saw nothing unusual: a set of spare combats, his dress boots, wash kit and all the usual crap that blokes dump without thinking. Josh flicked through some of the dodgy magazines — he could never imagine Darkling having a private porn collection, it didn't fit with his self-righteous hero image. Then, Josh remembered Alixia's displacement key and closed the locker, turning the key the opposite way to open the door.

This time, the inside of the cabinet looked entirely different. There were ritual robes, a ceremonial dagger, and behind it Josh found a mask pushed right to the back. Made of beaten metal and shaped to look like a snarling demon, it reminded

Josh of the faceplate the warrior had worn at the Battle of Boju.

He pressed the mask to his face, looking through the eyes as Darkling would have done, and as the metal touched his skin, he felt its history unfold.

The room was lit by candles, located somewhere deep inside the castle that Josh had never seen. A windowless space, the walls covered in archaic symbols and demonic images.

He wasn't alone: others knelt around him, each with a mask of their own. They wore long, hooded robes like monks, all black except for one in red at the front, kneeling before a stone altar, his hands held high above his head as he led the chant.

'O you who guard the gates, you who keep the gates of Osiris,

O you who guard them and who report the affairs of the two worlds to Osiris;

I will know you and I will know your names.'

There were at least thirty of them, a secret sect within the academy worshipping something unholy, though Josh couldn't quite make out what it was, the priest obscuring his view of the altar piece.

And Darkling had been a part of it.

The minister stood and turned towards his congregation. His mask was shaped like a skull, the silvered metal covering his head and eyes but leaving his mouth free to speak. And when he did Josh knew immediately who it was.

Dalton.

'He who knows their true names knows the way,' he intoned.

The others repeated in unison.

'By the ancient ones shall we find the path through the

storm,' he recited, drawing a blade and carving runes into his skin, the blood flowing freely down his arm and turning his hand red.

Again they echoed his words.

Dalton turned towards the altar and picked something up with his bloody hand. Josh saw then that it was a skull, covered in sigils like the harbinger that had trapped Caitlin.

'Lead us to the Nemesis. O prophet of darkness,' implored Dalton. 'So that we may end him and set you free.'

Something happened to the yellowing old relic as Dalton began to recite the mantra. It seemed to absorb his blood, feeding on his energy — a ghostly outline of a face materialised around the bone. Dalton was turning back time, summoning the spirit of the owner back to his body. Josh knew he was a powerful seer, but this was impressive even for him.

As the face solidified, Josh saw the mouth was moving silently, as words formed and fell away from its lips unheard.

Josh pulled the mask away from his face. He was breathing hard, and there were beads of sweat rolling down his cheeks. He was having trouble processing what he had just witnessed.

The face had taken a while to recognise without the beard, but it was him — Josh was sure.

Dalton was holding the head of the colonel.

55

ZENOSCOPE

The Protectorate inquisitors were arresting more people every day. The mood in the academy darkened as others received news of family members who'd been taken in for questioning. Rumours began to circulate that whoever had stolen Daedalus' skull had summoned the Nemesis, releasing him to execute the unworthy. Everyone knew it was only a matter of time before the inquisition came knocking on the doors of the Academy.

Aries226 were speculating on some of the wilder theories at lunch when Bentley arrived looking rather pleased with himself.

'I've built a zenoscope,' he whispered, sliding in next to Josh.

'A what?' Josh asked, pushing his tray aside to let Bentley put his down. The usual salad had been replaced by a massive bowl of pasta — Bentley was obviously celebrating.

'Temporal observation device. It's supposed to allow you to look into the maelstrom,' Caitlin explained, scowling at Bentley, 'and totally illegal — unless you're a Dreadnought.'

It transpired that every evening, while Josh and Caitlin

were 'busy', Bentley had been secretly working in a lab he'd built for himself in one of the castle's abandoned cellars.

'It's only a prototype... it's not like I'm going to create an aperture.'

Caitlin frowned. 'You're not seriously thinking of using it?'

Bentley looked a little guilty. 'I already have.'

Josh ignored Caitlin's indignation. 'You've looked into the maelstrom?'

Bentley beamed. 'Yup.'

'And?'

'Well, it's mostly chaos, but I did manage to see other things.'

'Did you see any Djinn?' Caitlin asked sarcastically.

Bentley shook his head.

'What is it with this demon thing?' asked Josh.

'Daedalus wrote that the Djinn are the most powerful beings, ancient entities that can literally control time,' explained Bentley.

Josh turned to Caitlin. 'And you don't believe they exist?'

She pulled a face. 'They're just stories to scare children.'

'But what about the Book of Deadly Names?' protested Bentley.

'By their true names shall you own them,' Caitlin said with air quotes, ' — it's a load of bullshit.'

'Not to the Daedalans,' Bentley interrupted, 'they take it very seriously.'

Caitlin sighed and sat back in her chair. 'My grandfather spent his whole life trying to convince everyone that it was all a fake. He used to say there was nothing more dangerous than a man with an obsession.'

'Anyway, I wasn't looking for the Djinn,' Bentley protested. 'I was trying to find out what Dalton was up to.'

Caitlin looked intrigued. 'You've been spying on Dalton? For how long?'

Bentley blushed a little. 'Since his stupid cult beat me up.'

Josh was stunned, but Caitlin didn't seem shocked at all.

'So you know,' she sighed as if a heavy burden had lifted off her shoulders. 'Did you see who the others were?'

Bentley shrugged. 'Some of them. Darkling was one.'

'Obviously.'

'What cult?' Josh feigned ignorance. He wasn't sure if he wanted to admit what he'd seen through Darkling's mask.

'We shouldn't discuss this here,' warned Caitlin, standing up. 'Take me to it, right now.'

Bentley pushed his food tray away. 'That may be more difficult than you imagine.'

Bentley's zenoscope was a crude device, cobbled together from spare parts scavenged out of old storerooms. It consisted of a large mirror wired into a series of clock parts and Van De Graph generators. The whole thing was nearly three metres tall.

'I kind of started it as a personal project,' he said, tweaking one of the many dials with no effect. 'Vassili gives extra merits for artificers who can prototype.'

'Not exactly mobile is it?' said Caitlin, inspecting the device.

'Not yet,' Bentley said defensively, 'but this is the Mark I. She's going to be beautiful when I've made some refinements.'

'She got a name?' Josh joked.

Bentley blushed. 'I call her NORA. Non-Linear Observable Randomisation Array.'

No one wanted to point out that spelt 'NLORA'.

'So why did they beat you up?' asked Josh.

'I was exploring the lower levels when I bumped into them. They were all wearing masks. Then they accused me of spying on them.' Bentley explained, touching his cheek, a faint yellow bruise just visible below his eye.

'How did you know it was Dalton?'

'He called you Caitlin.'

Her eyes narrowed. 'And how do you know that's my name?'

'I heard Josh call you it once when he thought no one was listening.'

'What did Dalton say exactly?' Caitlin glared at Josh, who smiled weakly as if trying to say sorry.

'That you were playing for the wrong team.'

Bentley managed to get the machine operational with the flick of a few switches and the light tap of a hammer. The mirror's surface shimmered as power fluxed along its edges. He made some final adjustments to the controls and the reflection resolved into a picture of swirling chaos.

Josh stood in front of the mirror, staring directly into the maelstrom. It was just as he'd remembered; a spinning montage of scenes from random times and places, and looking at it for too long made you feel dizzy.

'Wow!' exclaimed Caitlin. 'I can see why they call it the maelstrom.'

'So, this is where I started.' Bentley shifted a handle, and the hum of the voltaic flux condensers changed.

The view through the zenotrope was of Vedris, sitting in her office. There wasn't any sound, but Josh could see she was upset, Dalton stood on the other side of her desk shouting at her.

Bentley, Caitlin and Josh all watched as Dalton took something from his pocket and held it up — it was a photograph of a woman — a Dreadnought officer.

'Dalton's blackmailing her?'

Bentley nodded. 'He found out about an affair she was having with another officer. I think he wanted to make sure we failed.'

'That explains a lot,' Josh said, reaching out to touch the surface of the mirror, but Caitlin grabbed his hand and pulled it back.

'Not a good idea.'

'Time burn, nasty things — itches for days,' Bentley warned, subconsciously rubbing his arm.

'I think you'll find this more interesting.' He moved another set of controls, and the image swam for a moment before refocusing on Dalton, Darkling and a bunch of masked acolytes breaking into an exhibit in the British Museum. The skull was still in pride of place its case.

'They stole the skull?' declared Caitlin, nearly touching the mirror herself.

'Yup.'

'What's so important about the skull?' Josh asked, wondering how much longer he could keep up the pretence.

'The Daedalans believe that it's the key, that it can show them a path through the maelstrom — one that leads to Daedalus and the second book.'

'Dalton wants to go into the maelstrom?'

'He will do anything to get his hands on the book,' answered Caitlin. 'He's obsessed with the idea of the Djinn and their powers of eternity.'

'If they exist,' Josh joked.

'This is no joke,' Caitlin snapped, staring into the mirror. 'Vassili and my grandfather spent most of their lives fighting this kind of fanaticism. They hated the hysteria that surrounded the books of Daedalus. If Dalton's got the skull, then it means he's about to do something dangerous and people are going to get hurt.'

The image wavered in the mirror as the power failed.

Caitlin turned to Bentley. 'Can you get it back? We need to find out what they're planning to do.'

'I'm trying,' Bentley grunted, frantically adjusting the equipment.

'I know some of them,' said Josh.

'How?'

'Darkling left me his mask.'

Caitlin looked confused. 'Why would he do that?'

'He was trying to tell me something. I think he knew I was in danger.'

'When exactly did all this happen?'

'Just before the Wyrrm got him.'

'And you were going to tell me...'

Josh shifted uncomfortably under her stern gaze. 'I could never seem to find the right moment.'

Caitlin turned back to Bentley who was still struggling with the controls. 'Do you know where they've taken the skull?'

Bentley's face turned pale, and he nodded.

56

SKULL OF DAEDALUS

Bentley led them down to the temple. It was just as Josh had seen through Darkling's mask: the obsidian altar, the walls rendered with archaic symbols, the gory remains of sacrifice staining the floors. There was something unnatural about the room; the air was deathly cold, like an ancient tomb full of the ghosts of long-dead ancestors.

The temple was well hidden, and it took them over an hour to navigate the labyrinth of passageways below the castle. Josh noticed that they had crossed at least one time border as they descended. Bentley refused to go into the chamber, making some excuse about forgetting to switch off his machine and disappeared quickly back up the stairs.

The skull was kept inside an ornate golden case that sat on the altar. It lay inside the felt-lined box covered in runes. Caitlin warned Josh not to try and decipher them, which was pointless since he had no idea what language they were written in anyway.

'I think,' Caitlin began, taking the skull carefully out of the box and placing it on the altar, 'we need to get this back to the museum.'

Josh stepped past Caitlin and up to the altar. Staring into the hollow sockets of the skull, he tried not to think of how the colonel had come to this. Ever since he'd saved the old man from the strzyga, there was a part of his timeline that had always haunted Josh, a dark void filled with malevolence which he'd always assumed was his death.

He picked up the skull. 'Hey old man.'

Josh felt the timelines unwind at his touch. Hundreds of fragmented events exploded in his mind, a million-piece puzzle of the colonel's life with no sense of linearity or order.

Yet it was still him. Josh could sense his essence — like the first notes of a favourite song. Somewhere in this chaos was his friend and the truth about what had happened to him. Josh weaved through the random flux, catching flashes of strange worlds and fearsome creatures.

Josh tried to turn away, but the connection held him. Caught inside a nonsensical showreel of the colonel's life, flying through scene after random scene: a girl running towards him down a hill, a battle on a bridge, a room full of maps, each one twisting around him like fireflies on a dark night.

Waves of sound broke over him: the screams of lost souls on a sinking ship, the grinding squeals of a train crashing, explosions, cannon fire and a thousand voices talking at once in a hundred different languages. He wanted to scream, to find a way to make it stop. His eyes streamed with tears as he tried desperately to let go of the skull, but it held him.

Frantically, he searched for some familiar thread, a place he could hide from the tirade, and like a drowning man Josh flailed around for anything that he could latch onto.

Then he remembered what Lyra had said about the Nemesis: 'He will not know the names of the elder gods.'

But he knew the true name of Daedalus, and he focused his mind on it, using the intuit method.

WESTINGHOUSE? RUFIUS WESTINGHOUSE?

Instantly, the chaos calmed, and there was the old man, sitting at his desk in some elaborate observatory, the walls covered in drawings and notes.

'RUFIUS?' Josh called out, but the old man ignored him.

'No time,' he muttered to himself as he bound the pages into a leather book. 'Never enough time.'

Josh tried to hold on to the memory, but it slipped away.

Suddenly, the world twisted and Josh was standing in the middle of a Saharan desert. Ahead of him, across the dusty plain, the colonel stood before an army of the Djinn, each one towering over him like a thirty-story skyscraper. He was reading from a book, calling out their names and conjuring weapons from the air to throw at them. Chains flew from his hands as he chanted the strange and archaic names of the demons. As the Djinn came closer, the colonel began to walk backwards, still reciting the words from the book — like a preacher on a Sunday school outing. The ground beneath his feet began to crack and split, and huge rents appeared in the sand as the rock parted. More terrible creatures crawled out of the abyss, and Josh knew the colonel didn't stand a chance. He seemed to realise this too and turned as if to run, but something caught him by the ankle and dragged him into a dark pit.

· · ·

'Josh!' screamed Caitlin, from somewhere far away. She was in danger — he could hear the fear in her voice.

The overwhelming urge to protect her was enough to break the connection, and he felt the smooth surface of the bone under his fingers grow cold.

'Nemesis!' hissed Vassili.

The skull hit the stone floor and broke into pieces. Sinking to his knees, Josh heard someone curse as they hurried to gather up the scattered fragments. He turned towards Caitlin and saw that she was surrounded by a gang of masked figures — all except one.

Dalton was holding a crescent-shaped dagger against her neck. 'Well, isn't this all rather cosy?' he said, pushing the blade harder against her skin.

'Ruined!' moaned Vassili, his face was ashen as he held up the pieces of the skull. 'All the years of planning and it's ruined!'

'It doesn't matter now that we have him!' Dalton shouted, pointing at Josh.

Caitlin stared open-mouthed as the old man carefully placed the parts back into the case. 'How long have you been a Daedalan?'

'Since the beginning,' Vassili said, closing the box and turning back towards her. He motioned to Dalton to release her.

'You're not going to try and deny it?' she snarled, rubbing her neck. Josh could see there were red lines where the dagger's edge had been.

Vassili shrugged. 'Why should I? I'm far too old to change now.'

'All that time, when grandfather was trying to have the book banned.'

'I was recruited because I was close to him.' Vassili smiled.

'He was a brilliant man. I couldn't have asked for a more interesting mission.'

Her face flushed with rage. 'You're a spy? All those years and you were observing him?' Her hands clenched into tight fists.

'I was his friend too. Not everything was so black and white in those days. I knew him better than your damned tight-ass godfather — who I'm surprised you haven't told already.'

'He trusted you,' Caitlin growled.

'He was supposed to,' Vassili said, folding his arms over his chest. 'So what exactly were you hoping to gain by taking the skull?'

'I know who it is,' said Josh.

Vassili's eyes went wide. 'The prophecy unfolds.'

The others repeated his words.

'We should go — we have everything we need now,' Dalton reminded Vassili.

Caitlin crossed her arms defiantly. 'You know I can have the grandmaster here in a heartbeat.'

The old training master walked towards Caitlin without the aid of his staff, his limp seemingly gone.

'Your grandfather was always so quick to dismiss the stories of the ancients. He closed his mind to other possibilities. Daedalus showed us that this is not the only way.' His eyes were glistening as he placed his hand on her shoulder. 'My dear Lisichka, you remind me so much of him. You've always been like a granddaughter to me. Let us see if we cannot convince you of the power of the Djinn.'

Josh tried to get to his feet, but Dalton brought the handle of the sickle down on the back of his head and the world went black.

57

MISSING

When Bentley walked back into the dorm the next morning, he'd visibly aged overnight. His face was haggard, and there were dark shadows under his eyes.

'Where the hell have you been?' asked Fey, 'and what have you done with love's young dream?'

Bentley slumped onto his bunk. 'They're not back yet?'

She blushed. 'No one's seen them since yesterday afternoon — we assumed they were... busy.'

Bentley closed his eyes. 'I was with them until —' He stopped himself. 'I mean, I left them about four. They were going to see the training master,' he lied. He'd spent the whole night creeping around the lower levels trying to find his way out of the maze while avoiding the Daedalan's — they must have caught Josh and Caitlin red-handed.

Someone screamed, and De'Angelo chased Iolanda out from the showers. They were half-naked and flicking towels at each other.

Fey looked at Bentley's hands; the long nights of work on the zenoscope had left them blistered and raw with temporal field burns. 'I have something for that,' she said, walking off to her locker.

'So, where do you think they've gone?'

'No idea,' muttered Bentley, wincing as Fey applied the salve to his blistered palms. The cream smelled of lavender and tea tree, and he relaxed as the pain eased. 'Herbal remedies?'

She grinned. 'I rewound and did both classes. How exactly did you get these?'

'Messing around with Hubble enclosures, they're fiddly little buggers.' Lying had never come easily to Bentley, his cheeks always flushed when he tried to hide the truth.

Fey studied the burns. Her hands were soft and delicate compared to his fat, calloused fingers. She'd become quite introverted since Darkling's death. Bentley wanted to say that he was sorry, but part of him wasn't that sad to see him go.

She pursed her lips, squinting at the patterns that extended up his arm. 'These look like temporal lesions.'

'I... I've been working on a project. It was supposed to help, but I think I have made things a lot worse —'

He realised he was going to cry if he didn't stop talking.

Fey gently rubbed more cream into his arm, her dark eyes widening as she smiled. 'Start from the beginning.'

Bentley took a deep breath and told her everything: about the zenoscope, Dalton and the Daedalus cult and who Lisichka really was. As he spoke, De'Angelo and the others came and sat wide-eyed, listening intently to his story.

When he was finished, there were many, many questions. Bentley was relieved, by sharing the burden it had given him a new sense of purpose. He'd never really had a good group of friends, and looking at what was left of Aries226, he realised how close they had all become.

'I think they're in a lot of trouble — we need to help them.'

Everyone nodded, all eyes on him, and he realised they were looking to him for leadership. He had no idea what to do next, but the decision was taken out of his hands by the sudden arrival of Dalton's cronies.

There was a manic quality to Jarius' expression, his eyes wide and staring, an arrogant smirk plastered across his face. It made Bentley want to punch him very hard. He was like a kid with a secret he was dying to tell.

'What do you want?' demanded Bentley, striding over to him in a very un-Bentley-like way.

Jarius produced a scroll and handed it to him. 'Emergency orders; every available Draconian is being called-up.'

As he unrolled the parchment, Bentley's lips began to move, trying to decipher the hieroglyphs.

'Ren-nebum' he read slowly. 'Golden calf?'

'Nynetjer,' Jarius corrected. 'Egyptian Pharaoh, second dynasty.'

'What kind of emergency?' asked Fey.

'Breach, a bad one by all accounts.'

'Shouldn't Vedris be delivering this?' Bentley asked suspiciously.

'She's with the masters working on the plan. Gemini has been tasked with rounding up the rest of the teams. Although you're rather low on members,' Jarius sneered, looking around the dorm. 'Maybe you should volunteer to help the medics.'

Fey was glaring at Jarius so hard there should have been a smoking hole in the middle of his forehead. Her hands were balled into fists — the knuckles turned white.

Jarius turned to leave. 'See you at the Pyramids!'

'That's fourth dynasty, you twat!' Fey shouted, as the rest of Gemini trailed out behind him.

'You okay?' Bentley asked Fey, knowing it was possibly the stupidest question ever.

'This is serious. Bentley's right — Josh and Caitlin are in serious trouble,' Fey told the others.

'Why?' asked Michaelmas.

'The second dynasty has been off-limits since the Great Breach. If the Daedalan's are trying to get into the maelstrom, Dalton could use Caitlin's timeline to get close to the event, her parents would lead him straight to it'

'And Josh?'

'If they believe he's the Nemesis... he's a dead man.'

58

***

BRIEFING

'From what we know so far this is a level-seven breach. Aries has been assigned to recon the period ten years prior to the death of this mysterious Pharaoh. The Dreadnoughts want causation data; anything that can explain why his reign would have been redacted from Egyptian records.'

Corporal Vedris was in her element; this was everything she'd trained for. Whatever reason they had to keep her out of active service was forgotten. This was her chance to shine, and she was relishing every minute of it.

Team Aries, on the other hand, was struggling with the basic task of getting into their Dreadnought armour.

'Closest most of you are ever going to get,' Vedris observed while they were admiring themselves. Each uniform seemed to fit perfectly, as if tailored for them. 'Prescient,' was all that the corporal would say when they asked about the material. No one was quite sure what she meant by that.

'The Copernicans are divided on where the centre of power was during the second dynasty. Our objectives are located around Memphis and Saqqara, as three of the previous kings were buried there.' She pointed to a map of the area that was pinned to the wall. Lines and notes were changing on it constantly. 'Does anyone have any idea where Jones and Lisichka have got to?' She tapped her clipboard with her pen. The silence was deafening.

'Since our numbers are depleted, we'll be paired with another squad, and the other teams will be designated to Thinis and Abydos respectively.'

'Who?' asked De'Angelo.

Vedris consulted her notes. 'Gemini.'

Everyone groaned.

'This is serious, we're not playing some game here. There's only ever been one other category seven breach in the history of the Order — a lot of good officers died that day.'

59

CAIRO STONE

[Museum of Antiquity, Egypt. Date: 11.882]

'Little is known of this period.' Commander Brïghtfyr stood beside a carved stone stele. 'Nynetjer's forty-five year reign appears to have been expunged from their records.' He pointed to a series of blank spaces on the grey slab.

'This is the Cairo Stone, created during the last eight years of his life. I know it's hard to weave with organics but we don't have a lot of choice.'

The teams were crammed into one of the storage vaults beneath the museum. They were all wearing Dreadnought battlesuits and had been issued with the legendary GunSabre. Part rifle, part sword, the weapon made them realise that this was no test.

Brïghtfyr flicked a switch on a small metal box and a four-dimensional holographic sphere of timelines expanded out from it. There was a collective gasp from the room as they all realised it was a type of holo-lantern.

He moved his hand through the model, and it rotated to show a faint red line encircling a clustered node of events.

'The Twelfth Legion has already been deployed to contain the situation. You will be working on the periphery of the event; no one from the academy is allowed to enter the ten-year exclusion zone.'

A team of Draconian doctors appeared with cases full of medicines. 'Synchronise your tachyons to return to this location. I don't want any of you getting lost back there. There's also a high risk of contamination from pathogenic fungi so we're immunising as a matter of precaution.'

'I hate needles,' said De'Angelo as they filed past the medics.

'You'd hate Tuberculosis a lot more,' said one of the technicians, injecting Bentley.

'Or the parasitic flatworms ,' Fey grumbled, rubbing her arm. 'Don't drink the water.'

One by one the teams touched the Cairo Stone and disappeared. Bentley looked around the rapidly thinning crowd. 'Where's Vassili?'

Fey nodded towards Jarius and the rest of team Gemini. 'No sign of Dalton either.'

60

THE OLD KINGDOM

[Egypt. Date: 7.320]

'Damn. Stone is so bloody hard to navigate,' coughed Bentley, getting off his knees.

De'Angelo was helping Fey to her feet, and the rest of Aries were in various states of recovery.

They'd arrived in a temple. Lamps of burning oil hung down from the high ceilings, their flames illuminating the stone sculptures of evil demons carved into the walls.

Fey was frantically checking her almanac and comparing it with her tachyon. 'Shit!'

'What?' asked De'Angelo.

'We're off course.'

'Not possible,' replied Michaelmas. 'Not all of us at the same time.'

Fey, who they all agreed was their best nautonnier, was holding up the book and pointing at the symbols that were redrawing themselves across the page.

'Eight, maybe nine years south of where we should be.'

'We're inside the exclusion zone!' exclaimed Bentley.

'Shh! I'm trying to think,' she snapped, and began to talk to herself, making calculations in the margins of her journal.

De'Angelo took Iolanda, Nin and the twins and established a perimeter. They soon discovered that the temple was in the middle of a vast interconnecting labyrinth of chambers deep below ground. Following standard procedure, they scoured each room for reference objects, but found nothing but grave goods and sarcophagi — it was as if they were in a vast Egyptian mortuary.

'What the hell is this place?' asked one of the twins, coming out of a room of Coptic jars full of body parts.

'I was beginning to ask myself the same question,' said De'Angelo.

'The house of the dead.' Iolanda translated the hiero-glyphs on one wall. 'It's the same in every room.'

'Not a house I'd want to hang around in,' De'Angelo joked nervously.

'Shh!' hushed Iolanda, listening intently.

When they first arrived the place had been ominously quiet, and like a tomb the walls seemed to swallow sound. She'd assumed it was the rock and sand that had muffled their voices and footsteps, but now there was a distant murmur, a low rhythmic hum of voices chanting something over and over again.

'Monks?' asked the twins in unison.

De'Angelo shrugged.

'I think we should go back,' suggested Iolanda.

Bentley left Fey to her calculations and wandered around the temple. He was fascinated by the effigies of their strange gods.

They weren't the usual Egyptian deities, but more like the creatures of nightmares, with tentacled heads and grotesquely twisted bodies. Between them were painted scenes of battles, with the Pharaoh leading lines of mounted cavalry and chariots against an army of terrible monsters. The hieroglyphs roughly translated as the 'End of Days'. He'd only just managed to intuit a few basic lessons in hieroglyphics before they jumped, and the memories were still embedding.

'There's been some kind of temporal deviation,' muttered Fey, 'a bifurcation.'

'Someone's been screwing around with time,' Michaelmas translated for the others.

De'Angelo's team ran into the room. They were breathless and scared, and looking back over their shoulders as if something was chasing them.

'We think we should abort,' De'Angelo said defiantly.

'No,' growled Fey, 'not again. We're going to sort this.'

'But protocol states —'

'Bugger protocol,' Fey interjected. 'I think Josh and Caitlin are in here somewhere.' She held up her almanac for all to see. 'I just need to work out where.'

De'Angelo and Iolanda exchanged a knowing look. 'We think we know where they might be.'

61

SACRIFICE

J osh opened his eyes slowly, blinking until they grew used to the lights of the temple. He couldn't tell where he was exactly, but the ceiling above him was covered in some kind of ancient star map, and the Egyptian gods that looked down at him were a dead giveaway.

His arms and legs were bound tightly with linen bandages, like a mummy, and placed upright in a wooden coffin — which smelled of cedar and almonds. The inside was painted with hieroglyphs which spoke of the afterlife and the journey of the deceased through the Duat, the underworld.

At the far end of the temple, an Egyptian priest was standing over Caitlin, his bald head glistening in the light of the oil lamps. He hadn't noticed that Josh had woken — he was too busy reciting prayers and painting glyphs onto her naked body.

Josh tried to move, straining against his bindings, but the more he flexed his muscles the tighter the bandages became.

'You've got to hand it to the Egyptians,' Dalton's voice began from out of Josh's eye-line. 'They really know how to hold a funeral.' He walked into view, resplendent in the robes of a jackal-headed god. 'Osiris. God of the Dead. Quite appropriate don't you think?'

He drew a copper sickle from its ceremonial sheaf and let the blade catch the light — it was razor sharp. 'I thought it only right that I should use Darkling's blade for this.'

Dalton took off the mask and leaned in close to Josh's face. 'I have to admit I'm going to enjoy this. Not just because you've been screwing my girlfriend, but if Vassili is right and you are the Nemesis — you're my ticket to eternity.' His pupils were wide, like he was on drugs, and there was a manic quality to his voice. 'There's a poetic justice in that... some would even go so far as to say, fate.'

He chuckled to himself as he walked slowly towards Caitlin, who was still unconscious.

'She, on the other hand, has a less auspicious future. Our host, Pharaoh Nynetjer, is a master of dark arts. He's estimated to have sacrificed over a thousand subjects in his attempts to commune with the elder gods. Quite mad, of course, but useful with the right guidance.'

Dalton stroked the symbols on her thigh. 'Such artistry — a literal book of the dead.' He sighed, as his hand lingered. 'She never really knew what happened to her parents. My poor lost girl, it was as if a part of her was missing.'

Nynetjer stopped what he was doing and spoke in harsh Egyptian to Dalton.

'Indeed, my dear Pharaoh, the time is coming,' Dalton agreed, putting the jackal head back on.

Vassili arrived with an entourage of Daedalans, each one of them wearing a twisted, demonic mask of a Djinn.

They knelt before the altar. Nynetjer took the sickle from Dalton and used it to gently open Caitlin's mouth, chanting over her body in a language that was crude, guttural, not so much speech but modified cries of anguish and pain.

For a moment, Josh was sure that he was going to slit her throat, then the pharaoh's eyes fixed on him and motioned for his guards to bring him forward.

They lifted Josh out of the coffin and carried him towards the altar.

Caitlin looked beautiful in the flickering lamplight, her naked body inscribed with ancient texts and hieroglyphs. Josh couldn't help but linger on the curves of her thighs, her hips and breasts. It was impossible, no matter how hard he tried, not to desire her — even knowing this was probably the last time he would ever see her.

They forced him down to his knees on the altar steps. Dalton and Vassili joined Nynetjer, and they began to chant as one.

Josh desperately searched the grotesque masks of those around him for any sign of help, but found none. As he watched, Vassili opened the golden case, and Dalton brought out the broken skull of Daedalus and held it over his head. The fervour of the chanting heightened. Dalton passed the skull to Nynetjer. With an insane grin on his face, the crazed pharaoh stepped down towards Josh. The Daedalans were chanting — 'the blood of the Nemesis' — over and over again as Nynetjer's eyes darkened to two black orbs.

Josh felt a hot searing pain as the copper sickle cut through the linen and into his skin. Blood flowed from the wound as Nynetjer drew the blade slowly across his chest. His heart was racing, blood hammered in his ears, each breath was like a knife in his ribs and his vision began to darken.

Then everything slowed.

The pharaoh's face froze into a contorted mask of insanity.

Dalton and Vassili stood behind, leering at the spectacle like posed marionettes.

Waves of temporal energy flowed from the blade, slowly weaving into the figure of Darkling.

'Darkling?' Josh gasped through clenched teeth.

'We remember that name.'

Josh heard his voice, even though his lips weren't moving. Darkling's eyes appeared to be full of stars.

'You're Wyrrm?'

'We have been called many things.'

'What are you doing here?'

'Your timeline attracts us — it is quite unique.'

'Can you get me out of this?' Josh asked, straining against the bindings.

Darkling looked thoughtfully at where the sickle had cut into Josh's skin.

'It is not fatal — you will survive.'

'And Caitlin. Can you save Caitlin?'

Darkling-Wyrrm seemed to phase in and out of existence for a moment.

'Her only chance lies within the maelstrom. We will guide her to a safe place.'

'What?'

Again the figure faded for a second.

'Tell Daedalus you're from page two-eight-five.'

Darkling disappeared and time returned to normal.

Nynetjer handed the sickle to one of his acolytes, smeared the skull in Josh's blood and turned back towards the altar. Josh looked down at the blood-soaked bandages and felt them give a little where he'd been cut.

62

THE GREAT BREACH

T he air was stale and full of dust that caught in the back of the throat. De'Angelo led the team silently through the maze of passages, the scent of decay increasing as the sound of the chanting grew steadily louder. They had no idea where they were going as the passages twisted back and forth — only the noise of the ritual gave them any sense of direction.

Finally, they reached the entrance to the temple.

'Nobody's on watch,' De'Angelo whispered, pressing himself flat against the wall out of sight.

From their voices, it was difficult to estimate how many people were inside. No one was keen to go in and find out. Bentley wondered if they were all secretly hoping the Twelfth Legion would arrive, but they were nowhere to be seen.

'Can you see what they're doing?' Fey asked.

'How do we do that without being seen ourselves?' De'Angelo hissed. 'I say we wait until the cavalry arrive.'

Bentley wasn't listening to their conversation, he was focused on the chanting.

'Shhh!' he said, raising his hand. 'They're using some

really ancient dialect. Not Coptic. Something about: "Blood of the Nemesis".' He pushed away from the wall and crept along the shadows towards the temple entrance.

'Are you mental? You're going to get us all killed?' hissed De'Angelo, starting to walk after him.

Fey held him back. 'Wait.'

'We can't just let him go in there alone!'

'I've worked out what this is — I think it's the Great Breach.'

'You mean the one that killed all those Dreadnoughts?'

She nodded gravely. 'We're in a closed time loop.'

'Shit, where the hell is the Twelfth when you need them?' said De'Angelo going after Bentley.

63

TWELFTH LEGION

Nynetjer held the skull above Caitlin's chest, and Josh watched the drops of blood fall onto her skin. The priest's voice deepened as he began to recite the words of summoning and the faint outline of the colonel's head manifested over the bone.

Caitlin groaned, her body tensing as the symbols on her skin began to glow with an iridescent blue. The pharaoh placed one hand on her head, and his arm was instantly covered in the fractal pattern of temporal energy weaving out of her body.

Josh was growing weak and light-headed from the loss of blood. He watched through blurred eyes as dark shapes formed from the energy leaching out of Caitlin. Dalton had to hold her down as she began to thrash around, and Josh realised that whatever they were doing to her was going to kill her.

The skull attracted the dark energy like eels to a corpse. It coalesced around the pale bone until there was no sign of the colonel, the eyes sockets glowing red as a hideous creature took form.

. . .

'Djinn,' De'Angelo whispered in awe, staring at the tentacle-headed monster with glowing eyes that was floating above Caitlin. Dalton and Vassili had all fallen to their knees. The rest of the congregation was bent over, touching their heads to the floor.

Behind the creature, a sphere was forming, distorting space like a molten bubble as it blistered and grew.

'Aperture,' added Bentley, flicking the safety off his gunsabre.

Distorted black figures appeared inside the breach.

'Monads!' Bentley moaned as they clawed their way out of the maelstrom. The grotesque creatures fell on the congregation, tearing through the still-kneeling assembly with a brutality that froze the members of Aries to the spot. The despair that emanated from them was overwhelming, and no one thought to run — there was no point: they would all be taken.

The aperture widened until it spread across the entire wall, and only those closest to the priest, who's skin was now covered with sigils, were spared by the spawn that flooded out of the swirling rift in time.

'Stand aside,' ordered a heavily armoured Dreadnought, pushing past Bentley, a Hubble enclosure already primed in one hand and a gunsabre in the other.

The Twelfth Legion swarmed into the temple.

Time slowed as Josh struggled to his feet. He felt the gravitational waves of the aperture flow through him as it dilated, the event horizon reaching out to envelop them.

The tentacles of the red-eyed Djinn curled around Vassili.

The old training master tried to scream as the demon invaded his body, the sound dying in his throat as darkness poured into his mouth.

Dalton was in some kind of trance, standing directly behind Caitlin with his hands on each side of her head. Josh guessed he was trying to control the creature, but something was wrong. Nynetjer was gibbering like a lunatic, spitting and frothing at the mouth while still holding the skull aloft.

'NO!' Bentley screamed, watching the graceful arc of the Hubble enclosure as a Dreadnought threw it into the mass of monads spewing out of the expanding aperture.

Josh summoned what was left of his strength and ripped off the linen bindings.

He hit Dalton as hard as he could, knocking him back and out beyond the range of the Djinn. Caitlin and the pharaoh were still too close to the creature. The empty husk of what was left of Vassili crumbled into dust on the floor and the Djinn turned its attention towards them.

Caitlin's eyes opened. She smiled when she saw Josh standing over her, but it dissolved as the monster loomed up behind him. 'Djinn!' she cried.

Josh grabbed the sickle from the acolyte and sliced through the ties on her arms. 'I know.' He helped her to sit up and held her face in his hands. 'I don't have time to explain, and this isn't going to make a lot of sense yet, but I will find you.'

Her eyes widened slightly as she realised what was about to happen. Words formed on her lips but were stolen away by the time-vortices that washed over them.

. . .

Bentley watched helplessly as Josh, Caitlin, the pharaoh, and lastly the Djinn, all disappeared into the aperture. Chaos surrounded him as more Dreadnoughts arrived and tried to stem the flow of evil that was pouring out of the breach. The stone walls of the temple cracked and columns crumbled as the aperture disrupted their atomic structure. Large blocks of stone crashed to the floor, crushing monads and men alike.

He spotted De'Angelo and Fey trying to fight off a monstrous looking creature with a Hibbert Lance. Bentley shouldered his gunsabre and fired three shots into its bloated head. The recoil from the gun bruised his arm, but he ignored the pain — his anger giving him a singular focus, and he was already targeting the next monster as his friends ran back to help him.

The Twelfth moved amongst the bodies scattered all over the temple. Displaced and disjointed, parts of them had shifted, and others remained. Limbs were fused into the floor and walls as if they had been caught in some volcanic lava flow.

Dalton was found alive and escorted out of the room under heavy guard. Commander Brïghtfyr began to issue orders to his artificers, who were unpacking heavy pieces of containment equipment.

All the members of Aries were rounded up and brought before him.

He looked at each one of them in turn with cold eyes. 'Today, you have witnessed first-hand what it is to be a Dreadnought. I expect some of you may be regretting your choices. For those that don't, I welcome you to the Twelfth.'

A few seconds later the Protectorate arrived, one of their

senior officers walked over to Fey and saluted her before handing over a sealed document.

Her face seemed to change as she read the report. Bentley had no idea what was going on, and when she looked up, he tried to catch her eye, but she ignored him and gave a rapid series of orders to the officers, she turned and walked out of the chamber.

'Shit,' Bentley cursed under his breath. 'I hope you know what you're doing, Jonesy.'

64

SINGULARITY

[California. Date: Present day]

Fermi studied the complex three-dimensional models that rotated slowly on his screens, each one plotting lines of probability — branching and bifurcating in real time.

He was exhausted. The last few weeks had been stressful, and the times when he had managed to get some sleep were disturbed by caffeine and a nagging headache that painkillers couldn't seem to shift.

But it had been worth it: the numbers were good. After thousands of simulations Fermi knew he was close, and yet something escaped him. According to all his calculations, the technology he developed should have shown at least a ten-fold improvement after the last adjustment.

He'd tried adding more computing power: more GPUs and data centres with thousands of networked machines, all trying to recreate what the watch could do effortlessly.

For the last two years, the military had sponsored him without question. They'd been more than happy with the advanced medical technology that his company developed.

Their lack of interest in the science behind the rapid healing devices had made it a profitable business — one that could fund his secret obsession... his research into time travel.

The lower levels of his headquarters were equipped with the most expensive quantum computing available, yet still it wasn't enough.

He had sent many things into the future, starting with simple inorganic objects like metal bolts, paper clips and any other random items from his desk. But nothing larger than a postage stamp, and no more than a few seconds forward.

All of them had failed to materialise.

Each time he tried, the power required would have kept the lights on in a city for a month.

Until, in his attempts to boost the displacement fields, he overloaded the circuit and took out half of the state. The incident brought his facility to the attention of the NSA, and the next day a whole fleet of 'spooks' arrived, parking their Chrysler vans all over the campus lawn.

No one was that interested in his ideas about time travel. Fermi knew it would be professional suicide to tell them what he was really trying to achieve. So he fed them a half-truth, something to explain away the millions of dollars of equipment that was humming away in his nuclear bunker of a basement.

'Singularity?' Deputy Director Sanderson said incredulously, staring at the endless racks of servers.

'Artificial Intelligence. Battlefield AI and strategy modelling,' said Fermi, using terms that the military were extremely interested in.

Some of it was relevant. He was using machine learning to help process the mass of data required to instigate a quantum divergence — that would be a good enough defence if he needed it later on.

Sanderson wasn't wholly convinced. It was obvious he was thinking about revoking Fermi's green card.

'It's a defence project, top-secret,' Fermi added.

'We know. Although no one will tell us exactly which department you're working for.'

Fermi shrugged.

'Damn skunkworks,' Sanderson added as he turned to leave.

Three weeks had passed since the NSA visit, in which time all of his military contracts had been frozen. Tomorrow they were coming to see him — he needed to show them something.

65

MAELSTROM

There was a silence, or rather an absence of sound, within the breach. Like flying through the middle of a snowstorm at night. Icy cold sensations brushed against her skin leaving the faintest trace of cold which lasted no longer than a breath.

She had no sense of up or down. To Caitlin, it was as if she were standing still and everything was moving around her — like a child standing in the middle of a carousel, one that was spinning at a thousand miles-per-hour.

The time fields strained to hold her as she approached the outer layers of the chronosphere. Then she experienced a singular moment of dislocation as her lifeline was cast off like the mooring lines of a ship, and she knew she was no longer connected to the continuum.

Segments of disjointed time collided with her as she entered the maelstrom. It was like being inside a tornado of disconnected events: random sequences of forgotten moments caught and held her for a few seconds before being replaced.

Instinctively, her mind tried to make sense of the chaos, searching for a pattern or meaning, but there was none. A door in a nineteenth-century Viennese hotel opened onto a street in an ancient, deserted Saharan city. A cry of a child became the screech of brakes on a train, the walls of an abandoned house dissolved into a tomb of a long-forgotten king.

She closed her eyes and tried to calm herself. *Focus on the problem*, she told herself, *assess the situation*. She was alone, thanks to Josh, with no idea what the hell he was planning to do. The only book that existed about this place had been written by a so-called mystic who ranted on about primeval gods and demons.

If he hadn't just made it up, she thought.

For Caitlin this wasn't a fabled netherworld full of magical beings, it was where her parents had died. When she was a child, she'd tried to convince herself it was like heaven, but her mind would never quite accept it. 'Time's graveyard,' her grandfather used to call it.

In the infinite number of seconds since she had entered, something her internal clock was having trouble estimating, there were only a few certainties: the first was that she wasn't dead, so that was a bonus. The second was that there weren't any signs of threats. And finally, there were parts of linear time here — if she could stay in one for long enough she might be able to get her bearings and maybe some clothes.

'Improvise. Adapt. Overcome.' The words of her father came back to her. She'd always cherished those idyllic summers spent in the Mesolithic and Pliocene: making camps, living off the land, shadowing the nomadic tribes of early man as they fought for survival. He'd taught her how to keep herself alive in some of the bleakest epochs that had ever existed.

Back then she had been obsessed with breaches. The idea that monsters lived outside of the continuum, threatening to burst through at any point, had given her nightmares. Her favourite memories of him were the stories he would tell by the campfire to calm her terrors.

'There are so many things in this world to scare you,' he would say to her, 'and you choose the ones that live in another dimension.'

'Tell me about them, the ones you killed,' she would insist in the way that only six-year-olds could. Knowing her father could defeat them made the world safer. She would fall asleep listening to his stories of monads and strzyga — imagining how he drove them all back into the maelstrom.

'Caitlin?'

For a second, she mistook the voice for her father, but her eyes snapped open to find that floating before her, unaffected by the chaos, was Darkling.

'How?' she said, wondering whether to try to cover her modesty and then giving up. Her body was painted entirely in hieroglyphs, like wearing a second skin.

His eyes were like glowing pools of starlight. 'I am Wyrrm,' he said, staring at her body.

'Do you mind?'

He continued to read the runes. 'These are the names of the ancients, powerful ones.' As he read them, the symbols peeled off her skin, floating towards his hand like a murmuration of starlings until only one remained on the palm of her hand.

'And the nearest thing I had to clothes.'

'I do not perceive you as a physical being.'

She glared at him.

He closed his eyes, and suddenly she was dressed in leggings and her favourite baggy jumper.

'Er. Maybe something more practical?'

The clothes were replaced with a standard set of travelling robes.

'Why are you here?' she asked, rolling back the sleeves.

'I promised the Nemesis.'

'Josh asked you to save me?'

'It was the only outcome that guaranteed your survival.'

Caitlin wasn't entirely sure how this was much better than death. Entering the maelstrom was something that she'd dreamt of doing her whole life, but never dared to try. Since Josh had appeared with those memories of her other life, it was as though something had been awoken inside her.

'Where is he?'

Darkling appeared to shrug. 'Elsewhere.'

Great, she thought, staring out into the chaos. *I'm stuck in a timeless nowhere with a cryptic, chronologically ambiguous super-being.*

The rapidly fluctuating timescape was slowing, as though Darkling's presence was creating a gravitational field, stabilising the storm. Sim had a word for this kind of behaviour: he called them strange attractors; fixed points in an otherwise chaotic universe.

A jumbled city gathered around them. Caitlin found herself standing on a street built from the architecture of a hundred different ages. Renaissance and baroque merged seamlessly into post-modernist concrete skyscrapers and Victorian hovels. It was the work of an insane architect, a graveyard of redundant and forgotten buildings.

When she turned back, Darkling had disappeared.

66

JOSH

It seemed to Josh, as he stood amongst the teetering towers of junk that were stacked all around him, that he'd landed in the middle of the universe's lost property department. Everything, from broken old cars to steam engines, aeroplanes to furniture and clothes, had been randomly dumped here by some kleptomaniac dragon with no sense of order.

Caitlin was nowhere to be seen. The pharaoh however, lay on the floor a few metres away. He was manically whispering in an archaic language and clawing at his chest as if something was trapped inside his body. Josh saw the outline of tentacles under his skin and realised the Djinn had possessed him.

Nynetjer's eyes opened as Josh approached — they were burning red, like hot coals.

'Oh, shit.'

There was a noise from behind one of the stacks, and Josh turned towards it. He had the strangest sensation that they were being watched. Picking up the copper sickle, he pointed it at Nynetjer.

'Where is she?'

Clumsily, the Egyptian got to his feet. He was like a broken marionette, his arms and legs moving independently of each other, sticking out at obtuse angles as the Djinn struggled to gain control of his body.

'With the ancient ones,' rasped the demon through the Pharaoh's slack mouth. 'They will devour her!' He walked awkwardly towards Josh, strings of black bile dripping from the corners of his lips.

Josh caught the flicker of something moving behind a pile of stuffed animals to his right. He stepped backwards and felt the edges of metal tracks press into his back. His way was blocked by a tank from World War Two. There was nowhere to go and the possessed pharaoh was rapidly mastering the art of walking.

'Come on then!' Josh shouted, his fists tightening around the handle of the sickle, wishing he'd paid more attention in combat training.

Nynetjer's mouth twisted into a grotesque grin, his hand reaching out with claw-like fingers. Before Josh could take a swing, the handle of a walking stick hooked around the pharaoh's legs and pulled them from under him.

'I wouldn't let him do that if I were you,' said a familiar voice.

It was the colonel.

67

DAEDALUS

It took all his willpower not to hug the old man on the spot. Josh was a mass of conflicting emotions, all running simultaneously through his head. It was like coming home after a long trip, or putting on your favourite pair of trainers. There was a sense of relief and disbelief that somehow, after all the shit he'd gone through over the last few months, it had actually been worth it.

He wanted to tell the mad old bugger how much he'd missed him, and all the other things that had gone wrong since he'd blown himself out of existence. Yet there was something holding Josh back: not some macho reservation about hiding emotions, but the colonel's expression, the way his good eye studied him. He wasn't quite either version of the man he remembered; it might have been the lack of recognition in his face or the slightly eccentric way he was dressed: he was wearing a long trench coat, leather aviator hat, goggles, and a kilt.

'He's possessed,' observed the colonel, putting his foot on the chest of the pharaoh to hold him down.

'Djinn,' Josh agreed.

'Hmm. Pentachion to be precise.' The colonel took out a long pair of leather gloves. 'Did it touch you?' he asked, pointing at the cut on Josh's chest.

Josh shook his head.

'Then I suggest you stand aside. Pentachions tend to be a little unpredictable.'

Josh shuffled along the side of the tank while the colonel twisted open the top of his cane and pulled out a long silver blade. In one swift move, he drove the point of the sword through the chest of the pharaoh, pinning him to the floor. Nynetjer's mouth yawned wide and dark tendrils writhed out of from it. The colonel studied the creature as though it were an insect under a lens, then took out a piece of chalk and drew a circle around the body of the writhing man.

Finishing the circle he walked around it, taking things out of his pockets and positioning them at key points along its circumference. Next to each object he wrote a series of numbers, and then stood back and uttered a phrase that Josh couldn't quite hear. The white chalk line began to glow like a lit fuse. An orange, effervescent fire coursed along it and the floor fell away. The Djinn, still struggling to free itself from the pharaoh's body, fell, screaming arcane curses into the darkness beneath.

Josh carefully stepped up to the edge of the hole and looked down into the swirling mass of chaos — the body was gone. In the roiling clouds below he thought he could see the outlines of terrible creatures.

There was a click from behind him, the unmistakable sound of the cocking of a pistol.

'What's to stop me throwing you in there?' growled the colonel.

Josh felt the end of the barrel on the back of his head. Instinctively, he raised his arms and dropped the sickle. He'd no idea what was going on. He was light-headed from the blood loss and wasn't sure what to say to the old man. Then Darkling's words came back to him: 'I'm from page two-eight-five.'

The barrel retreated, and there was a shuffling and mumbling from behind him as he heard the pages of a book being turned.

'Ah, two-eight-five. Yes, of course, that explains it.'

Josh relaxed and put his hands down.

'Stand back, boy! TikTok front and centre,' ordered the colonel, placing the copper sickle into a small shopping bag and shaking off his gloves. A bizarre-looking clockwork monkey appeared out of the fuselage of a partly restored Lancaster bomber and scuttled over to them. It clicked and whirred for a few seconds before beginning to repair the hole with an assortment of old doors, socks, bus tickets and broken umbrellas.

'He tried to invoke an elder? What kind of fool does that?' the colonel said, chuckling to himself as they walked through the cavernous junkyard. Josh got the impression that the old man hadn't had much in the way of company. A couple of times he thought the colonel had forgotten that he was even there.

'He took Caitlin,' Josh said defeatedly. The initial relief of finding his old friend was quickly replaced by concern as he realised the state of the colonel's mind.

The old man didn't seem to hear him. 'Many have tried, but they should know better. The Djinn have long since forgotten we exist, and waking them up is homicidal or worse.'

'I'VE LOST HER! AGAIN!' Josh shouted.

The colonel span round and bellowed. 'I HEARD YOU THE FIRST TIME!'

The old man was staring directly at him with a glazed expression, looking straight through him.

'This is the place of the lost things. If she were here I would know. TikTok would've told me,' he said, pointing back towards the clockwork monkey. 'She isn't here.'

'So how do I find her?'

'Now that's a very interesting question — stuff generally tends to find me, and I can't remember the last time I actually had to look for something.'

Other than your marbles, thought Josh. 'You don't remember me do you?'

'Would it be rude of me to say no?' the colonel replied. 'There's something familiar about your face, but this place has a way of making you forget. Memories have a tendency to slip away — I used to keep them in tins, but even then I began to forget where I put them.'

They came to a wall of keys, each one hung on its own numbered metal hook. In the middle of it was a small wooden door.

'What I do know is that sometimes it helps to get a different perspective on the situation. Let me show you my observatory,' he said, selecting a specific key and putting it in the lock.

They stepped into an American-style elevator, it was like something straight out of the nineteen-twenties. The colonel pulled a series of brass levers, and it shuddered into life and began to grind its way upwards — at least that was how it seemed to Josh.

The view through the metal cage changed as they

ascended, scenes from different times and places sliding past as though they were climbing through floors of random scenes from history.

'The maelstrom is not quite as chaotic as it first appears,' the colonel explained like a tour guide.

A gas-lit Victorian street swept by only to be replaced by an ancient woodland.

'For the most part, it's entirely empty, but there are clusters of reality here and there; small junctures of time that have been excised from the continuum. Lost moments set adrift, repeating their few precious minutes over and over again. It has taken a considerable amount of study, but I have noticed that their movements are not entirely random. There are forces at work even here. I believe that without the restrictions of time, the universe still tends towards some kind of order. This is my theory of chaos, as I like to call it.'

The woodland was replaced by the inside of an aeroplane, then a picturesque beach somewhere in the South Seas. Each flashed by before Josh could really focus on it.

'So how long have you been here?'

The colonel's expression soured. 'Twenty hours. Four hundred years — it's all the same. You'll realise when you've been here a while that time is irrelevant. You don't age; it's hard to accept at first, but you get used to it. I've taken up a hobby,' he said, tapping the bomber command badge that was badly sewn onto his coat. 'Restoring the old Lancasters keeps me sane.'

'And the Djinn? Where will they have taken Caitlin?'

'That's what we're about to find out.'

The elevator slowed to a stop, and the colonel pulled back the metal grille.

'Welcome to Vienna,' he said, stepping out into a cobbled street.

68

OBSERVATORY

The roof of the observatory reminded Josh of Alixia's palm house; an enormous dome constructed entirely from glass and iron. Beneath it, on a raised rotating platform, sat a massive brass telescope and a threadbare armchair surrounded by piles of notebooks.

'This is one of my favourite places. I discovered it, or rather it revealed itself to me, whilst I was looking for my name — not a simple thing to lose, by the way.'

'And did it help?'

'Not in the slightest, but it's shown me many other things. One in particular that I might be inclined to show you — if you help me.'

'What can you see?' asked Josh, climbing up onto the platform. The dark, chaotic storm outside the dome was punctuated by intermittent flashes of lightning.

'This is a Huygens.' The colonel patted the metal cylinder tenderly. 'Although, I have made some modifications: added an achromatic lens along with a Foucault parabola. It's been very helpful with my research. I'm making a lengthy study of the maelstrom, from the darkest recesses of the primordial all the way to the mordant realms.' He swept his arm theatrically across the arc of the dome. 'You can even follow the continuum back to its origin if you know where to look,' he added with a wink. 'I've been making a map.'

'Mordant realms?'

'Clusters, like this one, where drifts of time have gathered like flotsam on the ocean.'

'And you think she's in one of those?'

'That would be my guess. Now let's find you some clothes, and I should probably have a look at that cut.'

Josh sat in the armchair and looked into the eyepiece. When his eye touched the cold metal rim, there was an instantaneous connection with the device, drawing his mind into the void. The overwhelming emptiness of the chaos engulfed him, as if he was a pinprick of light in a world of night.

Hopelessly, he wondered where in all this Caitlin might be, and whether Darkling had managed to protect her. He tried not to linger on the look of fear on her face as the breach took her.

The telescope shifted suddenly, sweeping around to focus on a sinuous ribbon of light that weaved through the darkness. The lenses clicked as they adjusted automatically, increasing the magnification until Josh recognised the continuum in all its glory.

'Ah,' said the colonel, pushing Josh back into the seat with his cane and breaking contact with the telescope. 'Probably best if you leave the searching to me — until you get your sealegs, as it were.'

Disorientated, Josh struggled up out of the chair, and the old man took his place. The colonel produced a monocle from his pocket and polished it on his shirt sleeve. 'Lensing glass helps,' he explained, placing it onto his good eye and leaning into the device.

'Pentachion?' the colonel said after ten minutes of tutting, huffing and twiddling of various dials and levers. 'That's at least a nineteenth-level Djinn, which should put her somewhere in the third quadrant of the lower realms.' He cranked a lever on the side of the telescope and the platform rotated so quickly that Josh nearly fell off.

'Do you have anything of hers? Something we can use to track her.'

Josh considered telling the colonel about Darkling, but wasn't quite sure how to explain what had happened with the Wyrrm.

'No.'

'Never mind. TikTok, bring me the blade of that ridiculous priest... he was headed in the same general direction.'

The clockwork monkey appeared from nowhere and took the bloodstained sickle out of the colonel's shopping bag and scuttled across the floor to his master.

'Well, she's not there either,' the colonel said, sighing, and taking out the monocle then rubbing his tired eye.

'But I saw her, I followed her in.'

The colonel sighed again. 'That was a courageous thing to do my boy, but as far as I can tell she's not with the Djinn. Which should give you some hope. Although finding her in this place is nigh impossible without a tracer.'

'Where else could she be?'

'If my theory is correct,' — he pointed at the circular wall that were covered in thousands of notes — 'she should begin to influence the chaos, attracting and altering the pattern, and if we wait long enough her presence will reveal itself.' He looked up into the dark swirling clouds above them. 'Assuming that she can keep herself safe.'

'Safe?'

'Oh yes, there are all manner of unmentionables out there. This is not a place to be wandering around alone.'

69

LOST

Caitlin had only just begun to explore the unusual city when she noticed the first spectre. It was the name she'd given it to try and make it less frightening; she had considered 'Harvey', or 'wraith', but settled on spectre when she caught sight of the second one.

They were pale, ghost-like creatures that drifted through the streets fading in and out of existence. She kept a safe distance, studying them from a suitably secure hiding place.

Once she'd got over the initial shock, and realising they didn't seem to pose a threat, she was fascinated. They were shadows of people just going about their daily lives: walking the dog, taking the kids to school, meeting friends. It was groundhog day, an echo of their routine caught in an endless loop.

Caitlin discovered hundreds over the next few hours. The more she looked, the more her eyes became accustomed to finding them, as though tuning in to a different visual frequency. They made her feel less alone, even though she wouldn't dare approach one. It was reassuring to know that there were other beings stranded in this place.

She caught herself looking for Josh amongst the faces. Although she hadn't seen him follow her into the maelstrom, she knew that he wouldn't abandon her. He would be here somewhere — although she'd no idea what his plan was.

Her instincts told her that this wasn't the kind of place to hang around and wait for some kind of rescue. No one came back from the maelstrom — except maybe for Daedalus, and even his return was something of a mystery. All she could do was find a safe place to hole up and start working out how she was going to survive.

The buildings around her shifted; some disappeared and were replaced by others, as if someone were playing a gigantic game of chess with them. The street was becoming more unstable since Darkling left, so she would have to find a more reliable region, one where she could start to build a base.

A grinding sound pre-empted the sudden disappearance of the wall that Caitlin had been hiding behind, and she found herself standing before the spectre of a middle-aged Victorian governess pushing a pram. The ghost turned towards her, its pale eyes scanning in Caitlin's general direction as if sensing a presence but unable to see her.

Caitlin stood perfectly still, holding her breath. The apparition left the pram and wandered over towards her. The air around them prickled with static as the woman came closer; the hairs on Caitlin's neck stood on end as its aura brushed against her skin. She could hear voices too — like children whispering in another room, all talking at once.

The woman reached out with long, bony fingers, snatching at the air in front of Caitlin as if she were trying to catch a fly.

Caitlin carefully moved back from the spectre, unsure of what it was trying to do, but instinctively knowing that making physical contact with it wasn't going to end well.

Her heel caught on a step that hadn't been there a moment ago, and she fell backwards onto a flight of stone stairs.

The governess was so close now that Caitlin could smell the faint scent of her perfume, her grasping fingers raking at the air where Caitlin had stood, chasing her shadow.

Before she could get to her feet, there came a terrible sound from the other end of the street; a low, guttural howl that resonated through her bones. The governess seemed to hear it too and turned towards the noise, her body flinching when the howl came again, and forgetting Caitlin, she turned and ran back to her child.

All of the spectres were running from the noise, fleeing into side streets, disappearing through doors into houses that collapsed seconds later. Caitlin didn't wait to see what they were running from. She picked herself up and, ignoring the pain in her back, ran up the stairs into the grand building that had appeared at the top.

Legions of monads swept along the street. Using the roofs of the buildings, they leapt from the chimneys, weaved in and out of attic windows and skittered over tiles towards her. She watched them from an upper floor of the government building as they hunted.

There were too many to count. They were like a pack of wolves, working together to single out their prey; the spectres too slow or too stupid to escape were taken mercilessly, their essence turning to dust as the monads devoured them.

They howled as they stalked their targets, a strange, haunting shriek like a detuned scream of despair.

Caitlin watched, horrified, as the last of the stragglers were caught and dispatched. She sighed with relief when she realised the governess had escaped, even though she wasn't sure if she had meant her any harm, she wouldn't wish a monad on her worst enemy.

The horde gathered at the foot of the stone stairs, their bodies shrouded in skeins of smoke and dust, the remnants of the lives they'd taken — wearing them as trophies.

At their centre stood a larger, more powerful creature, not something that Caitlin had ever seen before. It wasn't the usual monad — something that had once been human. The thing stood nearly twice the height of a man, and it was wearing armour that had a mirrored metallic quality as though it were made from mercury. It wore an oval helmet with a symbol of two F's back-to-back etched onto the side.

The monads gathered around it, each jostling for attention while the creature collected their essences like a beekeeper drawing honey. They glowed a little as it attended to them, their decrepit bodies replenished by its touch.

The analytical part of her was intrigued by this interaction — no one knew that the monads hunted in packs, let alone that they were organised by a higher being — an alpha. Caitlin looked round the room for something to make notes on. She was in some kind of Russian records office, full of boxes and filing cabinets, with a long table covered in old personnel files sitting in the middle. Paper was not a problem, but no matter how hard she searched she couldn't find a pen or pencil.

While Caitlin was trying to lever open a locked drawer with a letter opener, a scream went up from outside, and she ran back to the window.

The scene was the same, except for a small figure that had been dragged into the centre of their circle. Caitlin had to strain her eyes to see what the monads were screeching about, but then she recognised the figure of the governess and her heart sank.

The alpha held the thin woman up like a doll and studied her, twisting her limp body one way then the other before parading it in front of its minions. They sniffed at her, like hounds getting a scent.

Tossing aside the lifeless shell, the creature turned directly to the building that Caitlin was hiding in and raised an arm. There was no mistaking the instruction — she turned and ran, the sound of its shrill command still ringing in her ears.

The building was immense, with long corridors that led off in all directions. Her first instinct was to find somewhere to hide, but she knew that they wouldn't stop until they found her, and there were too many to fight. As she ran through the building, making random changes in direction, she tried to think what could possibly throw a monad off the scent. She'd need something with a stronger attraction than her, or move so far out of their range that they'd lose her trace.

A monad appeared at the far end of the corridor, and Caitlin instinctively bolted through the nearest unmarked door.

She stepped out onto the platform of an abandoned tube station. A stale wind from the tunnel shuffled the old newspapers and discarded coffee cups in endless circles. The distant rumble of trains echoed from somewhere further down the line. There were three exits, two of which were barred by iron shutters, so she made for the third, a small maintenance door on the other side of the track whose security warnings flapped uselessly in the breeze.

Caitlin jumped down without a second thought and grabbed the handle of the door. The sound of monads echoed along the tunnel as she wrenched it open and jumped inside.

The interior was dark and smelled of damp and decaying

things. It was some kind of sewer or service tunnel. She walked as quickly as she dared, trying to avoid the random pipes and obstructions that threatened to take lumps out of her head.

A hundred metres of painfully slow progress, and Caitlin came to a ladder, a ring of daylight bleeding through the edges of the hatch at the top of it, and she took the rungs two at a time.

Climbing through the manhole she found herself in the middle of a bombed-out city: buildings were broken open like dollhouses, their contents blasted to pieces and spread over the street. Bodies were trapped under cascades of bricks — pale, dusty limbs protruded through the debris, still clutching the treasured possessions they had tried to save as they ran for cover.

She was losing precious time, and there was no room for sentiment — a wail echoed up from the sewer, reminding her they were only a few seconds behind.

Across the street an old door stood defiantly in its frame, surrounded by the remnants of a wall that had once contained it. Caitlin scrabbled over the piles of broken bricks to land on it, knocking it down flat in the process.

Hauling the heavy door open she dropped through the gap.

The water was freezing; she felt her fingers numbing as she pulled herself up towards the glittering surface. It seemed to take forever to reach the air, and gasping lungfuls of it, she found herself in the pool of some ancient subterranean city.

She didn't recognise any of the silent, statuesque idols that stood guard over the pool; Gods of a forgotten age, their blank eyes and eroded features lost to thousands of years of water damage — a forgotten civilisation whose only proof of existence was recorded in the old, crumbling limestone rocks.

Pulling herself out of the water she became aware of a malevolent presence; a disturbing feeling of disorientation, as if she was being drained by something truly evil.

Ahead of her, beyond a plateau of dark stagnant pools and grim statues, stood a vast ziggurat, a stepped pyramid carved with reliefs of ancient demons and symbols of power. It emanated a malignant, baleful aura that was a thousand times worse than anything she had ever encountered from any monad. Something was pulling her towards it, drawing her in likc a moth to a flame, even though she knew that terrible things were waiting for her inside.

Her bare feet felt the smooth sandstone floor give way to hard granite flagstones as she entered the heart of the ziggurat. There had been no sign of her pursuers, and she guessed that even the monads were too scared to follow her into this place. For some reason, she found this comforting — although she had no idea why. Perhaps, it was just a relief to have a break in the chase, or the finality of knowing that there was no escaping her fate. Whatever was waiting for her in the depths of this old temple had been there for aeons, and no matter which route she'd taken through the maelstrom, she knew it would always have led to here.

The glyph on her hand began to glow. She had no idea why Darkling had left the final symbol, but it was reacting to the malevolence around her — trying to warn her of something.

As she descended a set of worn stairs into the depths of the tomb, Caitlin knew that her chances of escape were shrinking with every step she took. Wherever Josh was, it was too late, this was her end, and if nothing else at least she would get to meet the most ancient beings in the universe.

It was just a shame she would never live long enough to tell anyone about it.

70

TWENTY HOURS

By Josh's reckoning, they'd spent nearly an entire day in the observatory. It was difficult to keep track of time with no clocks or natural light to go by. The colonel had spent most of it staring through the telescope, calling Josh over every now and then to show him some cluster or other, but nothing had brought them any closer to finding Caitlin — the maelstrom was infinitely vast, and they had nothing to go on.

There were thousands of notes pinned to the walls of the circular room. Josh had spent most of the time reading random snippets; they were like the unconnected ramblings of a lunatic — at least that was how it seemed at first.

Half-finished sketches of Djinn were scratched on pieces of paper torn from old books, newspapers and the backs of cereal boxes. There were memos, to-do lists and references to places and times — some of which Josh recognised. The word 'Nemesis' came up more than once, and sometimes symbols were given a number and charted on a grid against others.

Beneath the paper, Josh found lines of temporal formulae, time-coordinates and symbols scratched in charcoal around the walls, as though the colonel had tried to protect the room with some form of magic runes.

The most interesting notes were the descriptions of the Djinn. The colonel had identified many different kinds of demon, like a Victorian butterfly collector, giving them names like Beliaoc, Mapheal, Asazeal. Each one looked more demonic and primeval than the last. If he hadn't seen the Pentachion for himself, he would have thought he was looking at the work of a deeply disturbed man.

'What do you think?' the colonel asked, walking down to join Josh. 'I've been working on a new catalogue. Discovered over seventy of the ugly buggers so far.'

'They're like something out of a nightmare.'

'Indeed, I believe our basic concept of evil may be derived from a genetic memory of these horrors. Their influence may still continue to pervade our subconscious.'

Josh shivered as he remembered the terrors that had lived in the dark places of his bedroom. The imaginary monsters that had kept him awake as a kid; perhaps his fear of the dark wasn't so daft after all.

'Have you written many books?' Josh asked.

'Only completed one. A kind of journal, about my observations within the maelstrom. This second book is shaping up to be more of a bestiary.'

'And it's all about the Djinn?'

The colonel smiled. 'Yes. Everything I've learned about them. They're fascinating creatures, and their true names are based on an archaic mathematical system.'

Josh realised then that he was looking at the Book of Deadly Names — or at least the research behind it.

'So, have you got anywhere?' Josh asked, pointing at the telescope. 'I can't just sit around and wait for her to turn up.'

'I might have one potential solution, but it's risky.' The

colonel's eyes creased slightly. He studied Josh intently as if deciding whether to tell him. Then a clock chimed somewhere and his expression grew more concerned. 'Time, TikTok? Time?'

The monkey whirred back to life, small metal-jointed fingers opening a panel in its chest to reveal the dial of a clock. A single hand was rotating anti-clockwise as a set of numbers in the centre counted down towards zero.

'Where does it go? Dammit! Listen carefully boy, I haven't got long to explain — I'm caught in a time loop. TikTok's clock here will reset and so will my mind, and my memory of the last twenty hours will be erased — TikTok knows what to do, but it will be quicker if you remind me of what has occurred.' He handed Josh a tattered old book that had the words 'Read me' scrawled on the cover.

There was a chime from inside the monkey's casing, and everything stopped for a moment — it was a chilling silence, the kind that made you hold your breath. The colonel's eyes seemed to glaze over for a second, staring through Josh as if he wasn't there. It reminded him of the way his grandfather had looked at him the last time his mother took him into the hospital. The final stroke had robbed him of his memories, seventy-three years of life wiped out in less than two minutes.

The automaton whirred back into action, the numbers in the clock reading: '1.2.0.0.'

The colonel's eyes focused once on the book and then on Josh. 'Who are you?'

Taking a deep breath, Josh turned the book to page two-eight-five. It was headed: 'The Nemesis coefficient.'

71

BAD EXPERIMENT

The generals were lined up along the viewing window, every one of them with their arms crossed and a well-practised look of disappointment on their face.

Fermi had tried to explain the basic principles of his experiment, but time travel was a hard concept to put into words that a group of simpletons could understand — it was like Einstein trying to explain relativity to a class of five-year-olds.

What made things worse was that the damned experiment was failing.

Lenin stood silently beside the console, his white coat stained with the blood of the rat they had just watched explode in the field generator.

'Are we to understand you're asking for another two billion dollars to fund this fiasco?' came a tinny voice through the intercom.

'This is cutting edge research, General MacIntyre. The ability to weaponise time could lead to a major leap forward in stealth warfare. Imagine being able to remove a dictator before he was born? To stop his very existence — to do reconnaissance into the future to determine the best strategies for victory.'

'Tell that to the rat,' the General said, turning to leave as others followed him.

'I just need a more powerful system! The NSA's quantum array...' Fermi shouted, staggering as he lost his balance. 'An AI that is capable of assimilating all of the variables!' He reached out for Lenin.

'You okay boss?' asked Lenin.

'No,' gasped Fermi. 'These imbeciles, they can't see the potential — we could change the world with this technology!'

'You just need more time,' Lenin agreed.

Fermi felt the pain in his head grow worse. His hands were shaking, and then he collapsed.

72

GODS & MONSTERS

Caitlin could feel their twisted minds probing hers. Cruel, primordial entities whose memory of what they once were had long since shrivelled and died — replaced with the madness of the void.

The Djinn were insane. Made mad by their hatred of the temporal plane, it had consumed them until nothing remained but a hollow shell of self-loathing.

Caitlin had felt their hostility ever since she'd arrived in the maelstrom. This was their realm, and she was an unwelcome visitor — or more accurately, prey. There was a certain inevitability about what was going to happen next.

'The gods of eternity waste no tears on the fate of mortals.'

For all his faults, Daedalus had a knack for putting things in perspective.

Caitlin wondered if this was how it had ended for her parents. Had they managed to survive longer than her? They were undoubtedly more prepared, and they had each other. When she was younger, she'd made up stories about how they were hiding somewhere in the void, fighting demons and trying to find ways to escape.

Those fantasies had faded away years ago. Now she'd experienced it for herself, Caitlin knew there was no way they could have survived for eight years. This place belonged to the dispossessed and the forsaken; there was too much despair here for anyone to stay sane.

Like walking down into hell, the stairs wound down into a vast chasm with deep fissures falling away on either side. The steep walls that towered over her were covered with the fossilised bones of terrifying creatures.

Above her, floating high in the inky darkness, she could make out the outlines of massive bloated bodies; a haunting collection of nightmares watching her in silence. She studied them in breathless wonder as they drifted in and out of sight, wishing she had a way to capture the scene — Lyra would've been so pleased to know they actually existed.

Finally she reached the bottom of the stairs. A circular stone floor, its flagstones carved with archaic symbols from a forgotten language, had been created out of a series of ever-decreasing concentric circles.

Caitlin walked slowly into the centre.

She shivered as the first probing touch of spectral tentacles brushed against her face. The smell of corruption and desiccated flesh assaulted her nostrils, and her stomach lurched. Like circling sharks, they probed her defences, a little more with every pass. She had nothing left to fight with, nor any clue as to how — she'd apparently skipped the class on how to fight a Djinn. Exhausted, she sank to her knees, wondering if it wouldn't have been wiser to let the monads take her; somehow their hunger was more honest — their desires less complicated.

The gigantic, tentacled head of a grotesque beast loomed out of the darkness, red eyes glowing fiercely as it closed in. Its touch was colder than ice, leeching the heat from her body — she felt her energy draining away. The Djinn were nothing more than giant parasites, feeding on the life-force of others.

Collapsing onto the floor, she wished she could have seen her parents one last time. She'd ever dreamed of getting into the maelstrom for so long and to have finally got here and failed was the cruelest of jokes. She wanted to blame Josh, but she couldn't. There was something in the way he looked at her that made her feel capable of anything. He believed in her, and for all his faults he'd made her realise there was more to her life than she'd dared to imagine. In another time they would have grown old together, which gave her some comfort, but it still felt wrong not to see him one last time before she died.

As her vision dimmed and the world around her turned grey, she closed her eyes, feeling the cold stone under her cheek. The sharp-edged grooves of a symbol cut into her skin and Caitlin lifted her head weakly to look at it. Her eyes focused on the archaic glyph, realising that it was the same as the one on the palm of her hand, the one Darkling had left her with. Trembling, she placed her hand over the symbol and collapsed once more.

The Djinn seemed to retreat a little as she felt a slight tremor in the rock, a grinding sound that resonated through her bones — a tiny earthquake which rumbled from some-where deep below.

Weakly, she opened her eyes to watch the conning tower of a submarine surfacing through the stone floor, and then, finally, she lost consciousness.

73

TIME LOOP

'So your loop is exactly twelve-hundred minutes?'

'According to this, yes.' The colonel flicked through the book that Josh had given him. The pages were a pastiche of printed cards and old labels covered in scribbled notes. Obviously blank paper was something of a scarce resource in the maelstrom.

'Twenty hours isn't a lot to work with,' Josh observed.

'Not when you have to spend most of it reading this damn book,' the colonel agreed, 'but it adds up over the years.'

Josh could tell from the condition of the pages that it had been read many times. TikTok had done its best to repair the worn out binding.

They were sitting in an abandoned roadside diner in the middle of some mid-western desert. Josh had assumed it was all part of the ritual reboot; the monkey led them through a series of doors into the air-cooled sanctuary of the restaurant and went off to make coffee.

'So what do we do now?' Josh asked, wiping the dust off the window to get a better view. Outside was nothing but a heat-baked plain of dry sand and tumbleweeds. A rusting, bullet-riddled sign rattled in the wind. Josh could just make out the words: 'TUCSON: 55 miles.'

'You say we've already tried the observatory?' asked the colonel, showing Josh a page entitled 'things to do first'. It was a list that had been rewritten and corrected many times — the observatory was heavily underlined in red crayon.

'Yeah. You spent over half your time on that.'

'Hmm. What was the last thing I said to you?'

'Something about a risky option?'

'That was it?'

TikTok brought over two steaming cups of black coffee and a plate of pancakes covered in syrup.

Josh shrugged as he helped himself to the food. 'Should be in the almanac, shouldn't it?' he added, pointing at the colonel's book.

The colonel stiffened, as though Josh had just used a sacred word.

'A what?' he whispered.

'Almanac — your notebook.' Josh tapped on the front cover with a fork.

'I recognise that word, though for the life of me I can't say why,' he said, staring off into the distance. 'Say something else.'

'Copernican?' Josh obliged.

The colonel nodded, waving his hand eagerly for Josh to continue.

'Draconian. Scriptorian. Tachyon.'

The old man closed his eyes and took a long, deep breath.

'Watchman,' he sighed. 'I was a Watchman,'

'Yes.' Josh thumped the table with his fist. 'And a good one. You taught me about the Order, remember?'

The colonel nodded. 'I met you... in a park?'

'Churchill gardens,' Josh said, laughing. 'I broke into your house — do you remember?'

Something was happening to the colonel's other eye: it seemed to be clearing as he spoke. 'You stole — a medal?'

'And changed the outcome of the World War Two,' Josh said, relieved the colonel remembered that timeline. He'd begun to think he was the only survivor, the last witness of his reality.

The colonel wasn't really paying attention, too caught up in his thoughts. 'We were looking for the ones who gave the secret of gunpowder to the Normans.'

The old man's mind was having trouble merging the two timestreams. Josh didn't want to dwell on those events; he still felt responsible for what had happened, but didn't dare ask where Sohguerin and Johansson had got to.

'We kind of did. At least you sealed the breach and stopped them coming through.'

'Did I?'

'Yes, and landed yourself in here in the process.'

Then the old man smiled. 'I think I know what the risky thing was now.'

'What?'

'You had to remind me who I was. You had to break the loop.'

'Okay...'

The colonel got up from the table with fire in his eyes. 'I KNOW MY NAME!' he shouted at the empty cafe.

Josh shrank back in the seat a little.

'Rufius Vainglorious Westinghouse!' There were tears in his eyes as he threw away the tattered book. TikTok went scuttling after it and tenderly checked it for damage. The clock in its chest had reset to '0.0.0.0.'

'So how exactly is that risky?' Josh asked cautiously.

'Because I remember who you are and what happens next,' said the colonel, clicking his fingers. The walls of the diner melted away, leaving them standing in the middle of the hot desert.

'We're going to need a more defensible position,' he added with a wave of his hand, and the walls of a vast medieval castle rose out of the sand around them.

'Great! You can control buildings, but what has that got to do with what happens next?'

'Not just buildings. The very fabric of the maelstrom.'

The colonel walked out through the main gate, whirls of sand catching hold of his coat — a wind was gathering. 'There,' he shouted, pointing towards a swathe of dark storm clouds that had formed across the horizon. 'The Djinn are gathering — drawn to the presence of the Nemesis.'

'They're coming for me?'

'Your presence was more disruptive than I predicted, it seems.'

'But I don't know how to —'

'Fear not!' the colonel winked, and a large leather book appeared in his hand. 'It appears I have been preparing for just such a scenario.'

'How exactly are you going to fight them with a book?'

'Taxonomy — knowing the name of a thing creates order, and in a chaotic system, that has incredible power.' He squinted into the distance and started to thumb through the Book of Deadly Names.

Josh wasn't convinced. 'Any chance I could have a weapon? Like a sword, or a gun maybe?'

The colonel shrugged. 'Ask, and ye shall receive.'

Josh felt the leather of a handle form in his palm, and a scimitar shimmered into existence. The sudden weight pulled his arm down, and he struggled to hold it.

'Are you sure you're alright with that? I can summon something smaller if it helps.'

74

NAUTILUS

Caitlin woke from a dreamless sleep to the muted sounds of people talking in another room. They sounded remarkably like her mother and father, and she wondered for a moment if perhaps she was a child again. It was nothing more than a cherished memory from her past. The gods were being cruel, or the maelstrom was up to its usual tricks — she didn't really care which; it was a comforting place to be, and she snuggled down into the bed and drifted off listening to their voices.

'Cat?'

A familiar voice whispered to her from somewhere beneath the darkness.

'Caitlin Makepiece, wake up, you lay-a-bed!' Her mother's voice pierced through the shroud of sleep.

She could smell the Earl Grey tea, the strawberry jam melting on hot, buttered toast, and her stomach growled at the thought of it. Caitlin couldn't remember when she had last eaten: the adrenaline rush of the maelstrom had overridden her appetite.

At first, she thought it was another dream until she moved and her aching body reminded her of the welts from the Djinn attacks, and her eyes snapped open.

'Mum?' she said, looking into the radiant face of her mother.

Gathering Caitlin up in her arms, she whispered. 'Hello darling.'

Her hair smelled of lavender and engine oil, and a whole bunch of other things Caitlin had almost forgotten. Holding her close, Caitlin could feel the gentle sobbing in her chest as her mother cried and repeated: 'I'm sorry. I'm so sorry.'

There were too many emotions, and her mind short-circuited trying to process what was going on; disbelief and anger competed with elation and joy.

'You're alive? Dad's —'

'I'm here too pickle,' came the deep voice of her father.

Caitlin lifted her head from her mother's shoulder and saw through bleary eyes the unmistakable shape of her dad.

They were exactly as she remembered on that day, all those years ago.

'You haven't changed?' she snivelled.

'That's the time dilation effect of the maelstrom, my dear,' explained her mother, letting her go and wiping the tears away. 'You, on the other hand, have blossomed!'

Her father beamed as he came in for the best hug she'd had in a very long time, and then they were all crying and laughing, holding hands and kissing. They were like a dream come true, the hundreds of hours she had spent wondering where they were, the countless sleepless nights crying into her pillow all forgotten in an instant. It was like having all those missed Christmases at once, or the best wish you could ever hope to be granted.

Her parents were alive.

'How did you find me?'

'Your mother picked up the sigil,' her father said, pointing at the faint mark on her palm. 'Quite ingenious of you to use the Nynetjer cartouche.'

Caitlin offered up a silent thank you to Darkling, wherever he was.

'Are we on a submarine?' she asked, in-between mouthfuls of toast and tea.

'The Nautilus?' her father said, tapping his knuckle against the metal wall. 'Best timeship in the maelstrom.'

'The only timeship,' her mother corrected. 'Your father and I built her from scratch. Not a bad little craft; it has got us out of more than a few scrapes.'

'Nautilus, like twenty-thousand leagues?' asked Caitlin.

'Straight from Jules Verne. Your father is not the most original namer of things.'

'I like it.' Caitlin touched the metal wall. 'What is it? Brass?'

'Mostly. Brass and copper seem to be the most prevalent metals. There's a lot of Victorian tech in here, and it turns out your mother is one hell of a riveter when she puts her mind to it.'

'So, is that what you've been doing? Building a timeship and exploring the maelstrom?'

Her parents looked at each other as if trying to decide what to say next.

'Not quite,' her mother replied.

'We need to talk properly. When you've recovered,' her father added.

'Yes, you should rest,' her mother agreed, pulling up the blanket. 'Get some more sleep, and we can talk later.'

Caitlin did feel very tired. The soporific effect of the tea and the warming food in her belly were pulling her back under the covers.

'But I have so many questions,' she pleaded sleepily.

'They can wait, honey. We've all the time in the world.'

'So you left me?'

'Not exactly,' her mother said, sitting opposite her in the galley. The metal table was etched with routes and notes scratched into the bronze patina.

'But I was a child. What kind of parent leaves their kid?'

Caitlin's father grimaced at the accusation. 'We had no choice: bringing you wasn't an option.'

Caitlin scowled, like a petulant ten-year-old. 'Staying wasn't an option? Watching me growing up wasn't an option?'

Her mother stood up, her face flushed. 'You're angry, and you've good reason to be. It wasn't a decision we took lightly, but you need to hear all of the facts before you judge us.'

'Fine. Let's hear it.' Caitlin crossed her arms defiantly.

Her mother turned to her father. 'Maybe it would be better if you explained.'

He stood up and pulled a map down like a roller blind from the low ceiling. Caitlin recognised it immediately — it was a horograph, a map of time, or more specifically, a personal timeline; her name was written in cursive across the top of the chart.

'This was given to us on your tenth birthday,' her father said gravely. 'My brother, Marcus, created the primary calculations, but your mother should take the credit for the quadratic probabilities.'

'And beyond the technical execution and artistry,' prompted her mother.

'We didn't believe him at first. Marcus convinced us this was the best chance we could hope for. We tried every possibility, but —'

'It always ended badly,' Caitlin interrupted, studying the branching set of fine lines that flowed across the surface of the chart. There were hundreds of tiny formulae and annotations scribbled across the map where they had tried every eventuality.

Her father sighed. 'No, but the best option was the worst you could ask a parent to consider.'

'I don't understand. Why would leaving me — protect me?'

Her mother had tears running down her cheeks. 'It's complicated. You're the reason we're in here. We had to be here for you — Marcus predicted you would come.'

'He predicted it?' she asked, not quite able to believe what she was hearing. 'He knew I was going to be part of that?'

'The probability was too high to ignore,' said her father, tapping a nexus point on the chart. 'He estimated there was an eighty-seven per cent chance you would end up in here once you coalesced with the Paradox. It wasn't an easy thing to hear.'

'The Paradox?' Caitlin exclaimed.

'Change agent, the strange attractor.'

Caitlin's forehead creased. 'You mean the Nemesis — Josh?'

'Is that his name? We never had any detail, just a symbolic reference.'

'So what's he like?' asked her mother, in a way that only she could.

'He's the idiot who put me in here,' she growled.

'Ha!' Her father clapped his hands. 'I was right!'

Her mother rolled her eyes. 'As if it really matters now.'

Caitlin stared at the lines that made up her life, the branching tree of alternative paths it could have taken, the many ways in which she never ended up here.

'I spent a long time trying to imagine where you were and what you were doing. I never believed you were dead. I don't know why. Maybe because grandfather always talked about you as if you were off on some great adventure.'

Her father stood next to her and put his arm around her.

'Well, we kind of were. It's been hard — we've waited an eternity for this day.'

'But at least you knew!' she shouted, shirking off his arm. 'You had a plan. All I had were memories, and pain — grief is a bitch when there are no answers, nothing to mourn. I was only ten, and you abandoned me!'

'That's not fair!' Caitlin's mother complained.

'No shit!' scoffed Caitlin, storming out of the room.

'Well, that went better than expected,' her father said, sitting down.

'What are we going to do, Tom? She has to understand the bigger picture, and soon.'

He smiled. 'She's just like you darling; she needs time to come to terms with the situation and then work out how to fix it.'

A frown formed on her forehead. 'Are you saying I sulk?'

'No, no.' He held up his hands defensively. 'You just like to contemplate your options in private seclusion — with choco-late. It's not a criticism.'

'Hmm...'

. . .

Caitlin hated herself for the way she'd reacted. She had rehearsed their reunion so many times, only to go and spoil it by losing her temper.

She'd always known they would never merely walk back through the front door. There had been a secret, childish dream in which she would meet them again, a glimmer of hope that had waited quietly in the back of her mind while she'd got on with her life.

To find out that they had left her intentionally wasn't something she'd prepared for. She'd spent years imagining many different and more extreme ways in which they had been taken: from being carried off by hordes of monads, absorbed by strzyga, to being devoured by the Djinn. Caitlin had thought of everything — except betrayal. It had never occurred to her that they would leave her on purpose, even if they felt they had a good reason.

She walked along the bulkheads, not caring where she was heading. The *Nautilus* was a beautiful ship; she could see the detail and care that they had put into building her. Not one pipe or valve was out-of-place; it was a piece of engineering perfection, and she felt an overwhelming desire to destroy it. She looked around for some kind of weapon but found nothing useful.

She went up to a clock-like face of a dial and kicked it hard, shattering the glass into a thousand pieces. It was a deeply satisfying feeling, and she pivoted on her heel looking for another target. There was a whole row of them waiting for her, but as she rounded on the next one, she stopped and watched the shards of glass reverse back into place.

'What the —'

'Chronologically locked,' commented her father. 'Everything in this ship has been temporally safeguarded against failure. You know your mother is a control freak.'

She collapsed into his arms and cried for what seemed like an hour until the rage abated, slowly replaced by relief and love. She wanted nothing more than to be held by him and told everything was going to be okay. The small spark of hope rekindled and flared as he hugged her tight and whispered: 'We've missed you so much, KitKat, you're all we ever wanted.'

'Why did you leave?' was all she could manage through the sobs.

'Because we found out something else, bigger than you or I. Something that we need to show you.'

Caitlin stood back and wiped her eyes. 'What?'

'Best if we do this somewhere more comfortable ...'

75

ESCHATON

'You've been out of the maelstrom!' exclaimed Caitlin.

Her father looked down nervously, avoiding eye contact. 'Once or twice.'

'How?'

'The *Nautilus* is fitted with a breacher. We can enter the time stream for a few minutes. Of course, when we do, it causes no end of trouble — monads follow us everywhere,' her mother explained.

They were sitting in the 'bridge' of the ship, decorated with an eclectic mix of antique furniture and brass control systems. A large segmented glass window looked out onto the void ahead of them.

Her mother was at the controls, pulling levers and tweaking dials as they appeared to move through the maelstrom. Caitlin knew that in reality, it was the other way around — that the chaos was flowing past them, but it was pretty much the same thing.

She wanted to ask why they hadn't come to see her, but it just came out as: 'Why?'

Her father walked over to the window. It looked like it had

been salvaged from some giant clock. He sat down in one of the tattered leather viewing couches and patted the empty seat next to him. 'There are things that you learn once you leave the continuum that make you question the Order's motives, especially those of the Copernicans.'

Caitlin came over and sat beside him. The view through the window was incredible, but her eyes were focused on him.

'We've discovered routes within the maelstrom that appear to have a purpose. Like ancient roads, they lead to some strange places, whole branches of time that seemed to have been isolated, hidden from the continuum.'

'Hidden by the Copernicans?'

'Or the Augurs,' grumbled her mother.

'What for?'

'We've caught glimpses of other travellers in here, and we think there's some kind of secret test going on — there is evidence that someone is preparing for an Eschaton Cascade.'

'A what?'

'It's a theory — a statistical prediction, which forecasts there will be a temporal collapse caused by a series of events that will deflate the entire continuum — something catastrophic in the future travelling backwards through time.'

'Oh. You mean the end of times — like the final battle with the Djinn.'

Her father looked confused. 'The what?'

'That's what Daedalus called them — the Elder Gods.'

'And who exactly is Daedalus?'

Caitlin realised the Maelstrom Malefactum was only discovered after her parents had disappeared.

'He wrote a book about this place. Hundreds of years ago. It was discovered when I was twelve.'

Her father looked puzzled. 'And this book, it talks about the elders — the Djinn?'

'It's become quite a cult, and there are hundreds of believers within the Order.'

Her father grabbed her hand. 'What exactly do they believe in?'

Caitlin was a little disturbed by the way he was acting. 'That the Djinn have extraordinary powers and will one day break into the continuum and end time. Only the Nemesis can change the outcome. No one really knows what exactly is supposed to happen, and when Josh showed up things got a little weird. They actually tried to sacrifice us to create a breach. Josh saved me — kind of. They did manage to summon a Djinn.'

'It's worse than we thought.'

'Do we know who this Daedalus was?' her mother asked calmly.

Her father let go of her hand. 'What does it matter! They've already progressed through the first two precursors of the crisis.'

'Don't forget the Paradox,' her mother reminded him, executing a rapid series of course corrections. 'Damn Heisenberg rudder is failing again! Back in a sec!' She jumped out of the pilot seat, grabbed a tool belt and disappeared down a spiral staircase.

Her father stood up and began to pace around the bridge. 'Alright, so let's talk about the Paradox, the "Nemesis", as you call him.'

Caitlin remembered the day she'd found him in the study; Josh had looked like he had been dragged through a hedge backwards, but still, there had been something very cute about the way he had smiled at her.

'He literally walked out of another time.'

'Did he know you?'

She blushed. 'Yes'

'Did he talk about the future?'

'He said he'd seen an accelerated version of the present. We all thought he was a bit crazy.'

Her father went to the window, his arms folded and stared out into the void.

There was a strange whining sound from below, like a generator powering down, and then the lights flickered and went out. Caitlin could hear her mother hitting something metallic and cursing at the top of her voice.

The emergency lights kicked in with a soft amber incandescence, like candlelight, and Caitlin went to stand next to her father.

'There have been outcomes where the Paradox was seen as a messiah, a prophet of sorts — like your Nemesis. We think that some branches of the continuum were abandoned just because of the Order's obsession with his existence. He has a dangerous effect on the timeline. So much so, it was decided that a secret department of statistical theorists should be formed to study the consequences. The founder didn't want any unnecessary hysteria and division amongst the wider membership.'

'These are the Augurs?'

'Yes.'

'And they were created to stop the Paradox?'

'To understand the effect.'

'And did they?'

'I don't think even an Augur could've predicted that someone would create a religion based on the elders, but it does align with one of the precursors that lead to the end of times.'

'Exactly how many are there?'

'There were at least twelve if I remember correctly. My old

Copernican tutor would fuss over the equations for hours, trying to isolate the statistical inference.'

Caitlin laughed. 'You were a Copernican?'

'I was training to be one when I met your mother,' he said, smiling wistfully. 'She can be very persuasive.'

'And the precursors?' she asked, quickly changing the subject.

He held up one hand and started to count off on his fingers. 'It starts with Prophecy — belief in a paradox leading to factional division within the Order and either dissolution or insurgency. Then there are a whole number of other factors like fluctuations in Standard Random, chronospheric anomalies such as perdurant activity —'

'Perdurant — like a Wyrrm?' Caitlin interrupted.

He lowered his fingers. 'Jörmungandr? The Midgard Serpent? That's just an old Norse myth.'

'I've seen one — it killed one of my friends.'

'That's not good. Not good at all!' her father said, shaking his head.

'So, Josh really is this Paradox? He can travel into the future?'

'That's never been proven. I always favoured the theory that his father is from the future. The Copernicans had enough trouble dealing with the known variables, let alone adding in a wildcard from a future scenario. It would cause no end of rewriting of the algorithm — easier to deny his existence: less admin.'

'But how would it happen? I mean, assuming that someone actually came back from the future and you know –'

'Impregnated his mum?' her mother interrupted, climbing back up through the hatch, her frizzy red hair held back by a pair of welding goggles.

'Ah, now that's number eleven!' her father declared as the lights came back on. 'Someone would have had to invent a time machine.'

'You mean a linear? A non-member could move back through time?'

'Not through time as such,' her mother answered.

'No, more like outside.' Her father nodded at the glass window.

'Through the maelstrom?'

'Yes.'

76

BATTLE

T hunderous clouds rolled across the plain towards them. A chill wind drove waves of sand before the storm, and on it came the stench of decay and death.

'There are some things that are universal,' said the colonel, coughing and covering his nose with his hand, 'and the smell of corruption is one of them.'

Josh gagged but managed to hold down the rising bile. He felt overwhelmed by despair as the demons approached. Random images of his mother, frail and sallow, lying in some miserable hospital bed flooded his mind; followed by Gossy's body broken and limp in the front seat of the wrecked car, his grandfather staring blankly at him as the nurse told his mother he was going to die.

'They will use your pain and grief against you,' warned the colonel over the noise of the gale. 'You must stay focused on something positive.'

It was truly the stuff of nightmares. Red eyes smouldered as they approached through the darkening clouds. Their forms took shape and Josh could make out many-headed giants chained to smaller, paler beings whose thin, distorted bodies glowed as if lit from within. Tentacle-headed serpents larger than skyscrapers weaved through the air like Chinese dragon kites, while grotesquely bloated corpses marched below. As the sound of a million wings reached him, Josh realised the dark clouds were made entirely of flies.

The colonel was busy drawing circles in the sand with his cane. Lines of energy filled the groove as he carved, whispering in a language that Josh couldn't recognise.

'What exactly is the plan?' Josh shouted over the howling winds.

'Taxonomies — classifications. The naming of things — the Djinn have secret names, old ones that haven't been spoken in a thousand millennia.' He stood inside the first circle and shouted: 'Astaroth!' while tearing out a page from his book. It had a mathematical symbol on it that instantly burst into blue flames. A tall black creature with long spindly limbs and a horned crab-shell head fell to the floor, iron chains binding it to the ground.

The Djinn army screamed and pressed forward. The colonel stepped into the next circle. 'Haagenti!' he boomed, holding another sigil in the air, and a serpent creature twisted as spikes pierced through the entire length of its body.

The other demons slowed as the colonel jumped into the third circle and cried: 'Malphas!' A B52 bomber appeared above the many-headed beast and dropped its payload over the horde.

'Boom!' Josh punched the air as they watched the firestorm engulf the swarm.

Something caught Josh's eye. 'Six o'clock!' he shouted, pointing in the opposite direction.

The colonel turned towards the second wave.

There were literally hundreds of them, a horde, surging towards them.

'Okay. I think we're going to need a better plan!' Josh added, as the world grew dark.

A huge tornado of flies surrounded them, dying as they tried to cross the boundary of the colonel's last circle. They fell from the sky like black snow. Beyond them, the Djinn circled, hundreds of grotesque silhouettes edging ever closer, looking for an opportunity to strike.

The colonel and Josh were pressed back-to-back watching the swirling darkness as they slowly rotated around each other. Josh lashed out with his sword at anything that came too close, but it was pointless.

'So, you don't know all of their names?'

The colonel closed the book sheepishly. 'Not all of them, no.'

'How exactly was this going to help us find Caitlin?'

'Well, to be honest, I was actually hoping she would find us.'

A tentacle shot out of the dark wall and struck the colonel across the side of the head. Josh sliced it in half and grabbed the old man before he fell. A gnarled hand stretched out and snatched the scimitar away from Josh.

'Shit!'

The colonel was too stunned to conjure another weapon.

The creatures seemed to sense the weakness and surged forward. Josh tried to reach the colonel's book, but it had fallen too far from them to get it safely.

'Can you stand?' Josh tried to pull the old man up, but he was too heavy.

'Her name, use her name,' he moaned.

Josh could feel them on his skin as he screamed Caitlin's name.

The first creature that touched him froze, its putrid flesh turning to crystal. A connection instantly formed between them. Josh could feel its timeline unravel, and his mind instinctively reached into it.

The other Djinn stood back in fear, watching one of their own crystallise at his touch.

Gossamer thin lines of the past wove out before him like spider threads. He teased them apart, following their path back into the distant past; millennia of bleak void stretched back into obscurity. Josh experienced the terrible, empty yearning of aeons of solitude. Whatever the creature had once been was lost, the traces of its origins a shadow in a dark room. But Josh couldn't let go — he pursued the path into its forgotten history.

As he travelled further into the darkness, Josh remembered the void that he'd seen at the end of the colonel's timeline. This had the same threat of unseen dangers, although it felt like he was on the other side and being drawn towards something secret. He forgot about everything except for the path and the promise of hidden truths. In the distance, Josh could sense a nexus of activity — a cluster of nodes that he instinctively knew would hold the key to everything.

'Josh?' said a familiar voice — one that reminded him of someone, of a girl he'd once known. He ignored it, focusing on the nexus.

'JOSH!'

Her voice was like a nagging fly buzzing around inside his head.

'You have to let go! Now!'

There was a strange flickering glow inside the cluster, as if it were lit by a thousand fireflies. Josh strained to reach it, but somehow it stayed out of range.

There was a blinding light, and the connection died.

77

GRIMOIRE

'Are you okay?' Caitlin asked, sitting beside him on the bunk.

Josh had a splitting headache and the weirdest metallic taste in his mouth. 'No,' he said, rubbing his head. 'Feels like someone hit me.'

'Sorry, that was me,' Caitlin confessed. 'I had to do something as you wouldn't let go.'

'What happened?' Josh propped himself up on the bed. 'Where are we?'

'On my parent's timeship. We rescued you and some crazy old man from the middle of a massive swarm of Djinn. My father says he's never seen anything like it.'

'You have the colonel?'

'That's the colonel? I never imagined he'd look like that.'

'He's probably a bit confused.'

'I don't think so. He's on the bridge with my father discussing tactics.'

'Your dad's alive?' Josh exclaimed, realising what she'd said.

Caitlin nodded. 'Mum too. It's a long story. I'm not really sure I understand it fully either.'

Josh swung his legs down off the bunk, and the world shifted uneasily.

'What did you hit me with? A brick?'

'Close,' she said holding up the colonel's old leather book. 'It's a Grimoire. *The* Grimoire in fact — the Book of Deadly Names. I don't know how he came to have it.'

'Because the colonel is Daedalus.'

'What?'

'He's been studying the Djinn for years, he has an observatory full of research.'

Caitlin looked at the book thoughtfully. 'I've never thought of him as a real person. I thought the Daedalans made him up.'

Josh rubbed the back of his head. 'Well, it bloody hurt considering it wasn't supposed to exist!'

She kissed his head. 'Serves you right for throwing me into the maelstrom.'

'So, this is the Nemesis we've been hearing so much about,' her mother declared as Josh followed Caitlin up onto the bridge.

'Josh,' he replied, shaking her hand.

'Nice to meet you, Josh.' Her father handed him a mug of steaming tea. 'Caitlin's been telling us all about you.'

Josh smiled awkwardly, wondering exactly how much detail she had gone into — he wasn't really the kind of boy that girls took home to meet their parents.

Caitlin winked at him. 'Don't worry, nothing bad.'

'So back to the business in hand?' interrupted the colonel brusquely.

'Yes, of course. We've been discussing the Eschaton projections.' Caitlin's father pointed to a complicated time chart that was spread across the table.

'It confirms what I'd suspected.' The colonel leant over and traced one of the hundreds of lines back to a nexus point. 'These convergence curves are unmistakable. They point to an intentional deviation in the continuum. Someone is manipulating the past — as predicted in your father's Eschaton hypothesis.'

Caitlin's father blushed while her mother rolled her eyes.

'To cause the end of time? What would be the point of that?' Josh asked.

'That may not be their end goal,' answered her father. 'The Eschaton theory is a complex sequence of events. Whatever they're trying to achieve may have much more selfish motives.'

'Like Dalton wanting the Book of Deadly Names?' Caitlin suggested.

'Exactly. These events are not coordinated.' He tapped along the central line of points. 'Each one is a product of the last, or in some cases, a trigger for the next.'

Josh stared at the thousands of interconnected points on the map, fine spidery lines weaving between them and across the paper. 'So where do we begin?'

The colonel tapped on the chart. 'I think we have to start with the inciting incident.'

Josh focused on the spot beneath the colonel's finger; it was surrounded by a collection of handwritten notes and symbols that spread out into a web of new threads.

There was a word underlined in red ink: "1. Prophecy."

'A powerful tool, in the right hands,' the colonel began. 'The Order has always considered itself agnostic. The internal factions that developed as we expanded have always been treated as healthy, rational, and in no way a threat to the higher purpose. But,' the colonel traced a line to the next node, which read: "2. Division", 'if we introduce prophecy in the form of a messiah-figure, the Order becomes divided, radicalised, and resentment ensues.'

Two major lines split out from the division node; one leading towards: "3a. Insurgency", the other to: "3b. Disbelief".

'As you can see, by the third iteration we're looking at the internal collapse of the Order.'

'And chaos,' added Caitlin's father.

'They've started arresting people like Alixia, just for helping me,' said Josh.

Caitlin took his hand. 'That's not your fault.'

Josh turned to the colonel. 'If you hadn't gone into the maelstrom, you'd never have written the book. They wouldn't have learned about the Djinn or Nemesis.'

'This book,' Caitlin's father interrupted. 'How did it get back into the continuum?'

Everyone looked at Caitlin.

'It was found in Herculaneum in 11.738, but no one knows how it got there.'

Her father put a pin in the timeline at the appropriate point and scribbled a note next to it.

'Who discovered it?'

'An Antiquarian by the name of Johansson.'

Josh's eyes narrowed. 'Are you sure he wasn't a Dreadnought?'

Caitlin looked confused. 'Why?'

'Johansson was an artificer, one of the team that disappeared when we closed the breach.' He looked to the colonel for some kind of confirmation. 'It's too much of a coincidence. Do you remember him?'

The old man nodded. 'He's the one that made TikTok.'

78

THE BOOK

[Herculaneum. Date: 11.738]

Johansson was exhausted. It had taken three weeks of hard graft to clear through the outer rooms and reach the inner chamber. Ash and rubble from the ruined palace above them had choked every passageway he'd tried to enter, making the schematic that Alcubierre had sold him worse than useless. The internal layout of the lower levels had been rearranged by the seismic activity from Vesuvius and left most of the old tunnels impassable or in a state of total collapse.

There was no doubt that the breach had caused the eruption. The gravitational shift that accompanied the opening of an aperture would have stressed the underlying mantle and initiated a pyroclastic surge, sealing Herculaneum and the book under hundreds of tonnes of rubble and ash.

It was the perfect time vault. No way to reach it before the event without dying in the process and no easy way to get into it afterwards. Sohguerin could be a complete pain-in-the-ass when she put her mind to it; a genius, but a pain nonetheless.

Johansson was working for a Spanish engineer called

Rocque Joaquin de Alcubierre, who had been commissioned to excavate the tunnels by the King of Two Sicilies. They were extending a deep well that had been dug thirty years before, one that had unearthed a cache of Roman statues. The site had been abandoned when Pompeii proved easier to excavate, having only four metres of volcanic ash to dig through rather than Herculaneum's twenty.

They were close now. The Villa of Papyri, as it would come to be known, was only a few metres away. Once owned by Julius Caesar's father-in-law, Lucius Calpurnius Piso Caesoninus, the villa had a vast library stretching over four levels and that according to later records was totally intact. Thousands of scrolls were trapped beneath the lava flow, but Johansson was only concerned with one book, a small journal that would make him rich — if his stubborn, bitch of a wife hadn't buried it under twenty metres of rock.

It had taken them months to find each other in the maelstrom, or to be more accurate, for her to locate him. Sohguerin was always the self-sufficient one. Johansson was in a pretty bad way when she found him. Although he'd managed to avoid the monad hunting parties and find shelter in a stable cluster — a train journey between London and Edinburgh in 11.890 — the loss of his fingers affected him severely. Unable to use his hand to make anything useful, he'd spent most of his time drinking in the buffet car, a kind of drunken groundhog day, repeating the same nine-hour journey.

She broke him out of the loop and helped heal the hand with what was left in her med kit. Then they got to work on an escape plan.

Neither of them was looking for the colonel when they found him. The maelstrom had an unusual capacity for random coincidence. The old man was stuck, living the same twenty hours over and over again. He was obsessed with remembering everything, writing it all down in 'the book' — which he said was full of secrets, things he'd seen and subsequently forgotten.

Sohguerin tried everything, but nothing worked. Every time the twenty hours was up, they would have to hand him the book and get him to reread it — at least the first three chapters. Once he reached page fifty, he would usually begin to flick to the end or other random pages.

There were a few seconds as the loop reset when Johansson had the book to himself. It was full of illustrations and notes on the most incredible parts of the maelstrom. While he'd repeatedly been getting wasted on the Flying Scotsman, the old man had been travelling across thousands of different worlds.

Once, when Johansson tried to hide the book, the old man became so agitated and inconsolable that Sohguerin had to force him to give it back — as if the colonel was somehow missing it without knowing it existed.

They discovered that he had accumulated a vast collection of random objects, a scrapyard of a thousand years of discarded and forgotten machinery. For fun Johansson built him a clockwork automaton, a monkey with a timer in his chest — so they all could keep track of the loop. He added a few basic routines so that it would warn him when the time was nearly up and hand the book back after the reset. At some point, the robot became possessed by the ghost of some low-level entity and quickly became the old man's personal assistant.

As time passed, or rather didn't, Johansson began to spend longer periods alone amongst the scrap. During meals, Sohguerin would complain that he was shirking his duties when it came to caring for the colonel, but he refused to tell her what he was doing. His scavenging had found most of the parts for a breacher, and its construction became his obsession. Weeks passed in twenty-hour segments until he stopped appearing for meals altogether.

Sohguerin came to find him on the last day. She was concerned that the old man, who would disappear for hours at a time, was losing what was left of his mind. She told Johansson how she'd seen the colonel tearing specific pages from his book, ranting about a 'Nemesis' and something called the 'Djinn.'

Johansson tried to tell her about his escape plan, but she didn't seem to care about leaving anymore. In fact, she seemed to have thrived since they'd been stranded. Her love of the spiritual and ethereal found the whole thing deeply interesting. More than once he'd caught her communing with the 'ghosts' — the non-corporeal remnants of previous residents — all of which he found a bit creepy.

He showed her how the breacher was fully functional and tried desperately to persuade her to leave, but she wouldn't — not without the colonel, and Johansson had no intention of taking the crazy old dude back with them. He didn't tell her, however, that he planned to steal the book, because he knew she wasn't about to let him do that. When the loop reset and he tried to take it, they got into an argument which turned into a fight, and she fell through the open aperture. It took him another five loops to get the machine working again, by which time he'd lost any hope of following her.

Finally, after three weeks of excavation, he found her body still clutching the book, both encased in a cocoon of ash.

79

EXHIBIT

[British Museum, London. Date: 11.954]

'So why can't we just go back and take the book from Johansson?'

'Too many unknowns. It would take an entire division of Copernicans a year to even work out the first tier of consequences, let alone the butterfly effect,' whispered Caitlin.

'And the skull doesn't?'

She folded back the set of doors on the cabinet. 'Dad thinks it was the catalyst. Without it, Dalton and his cronies would have been powerless to open the breach.'

'Can't imagine how they got hold of my head,' the colonel said, rubbing his neck and staring at his skull as it sat on a velvet cushion.

Josh remembered the dark pit that he'd watched the colonel being pulled into and wondered if that had ended as badly as he imagined. The colonel would have no memory of it after the time loop reset, but somehow his skull had ended up in the continuum.

They were standing in the British Museum, in front of an

exhibit called 'Earliest Hominid', which was a collection of ancient skeletons supposedly collected in the Sterkfontein caves, in the Gauteng province of South Africa, dating back over a million years.

'How did they find it?'

'One of the discoverers — John T. Robinson was an Antiquarian — picked up the skull and got the shock of his life; what he saw drove him mad,' Caitlin said, putting on a pair of leather gloves.

Josh looked confused. 'And it's a million-years-old?'

'According to the Antiquarians, yes — the Copernicans refuse to acknowledge it of course.'

'Why?'

'The maelstrom knows no limits. Therefore time is immaterial,' intoned the colonel.

Caitlin stared at him for a moment, she was still having difficulty coming to terms with the fact that he was Daedalus. She carefully picked the skull out of the case and held it up in the light. 'I don't think you should touch it,' she warned the colonel. 'The last thing we need is a closed loop.'

The colonel nodded and went back through the aperture and into the Nautilus.

Caitlin placed the skull into a simple wooden box and took out a replacement.

She inspected the fake and placed it in the cabinet. 'Don't want them thinking it's missing do we?'

'But won't Dalton notice?'

'It won't matter, and better his plan fails now. Hopefully, his followers will see the failure as a sign and forget about the whole thing.'

'I doubt that,' said Fey, stepping out of the shadows.

'What on earth are you doing here?' Caitlin said, closing the box quickly.

'When Bentley told me who had stolen the skull. I simply followed it back to the most logical intercession — I've been waiting for you.'

'We didn't steal it, that was Dalton — at least the first time,' said Josh, 'we're trying to stop him — like Darkling asked me to.'

Fey pulled out a pistol. 'There's a thirty-two-point-three per cent probability that this constitutes an Eschaton precursor. Keep your hands where I can see them.'

Caitlin raised her hands. 'I don't remember Scriptorians carrying weapons.'

'Augurs have privileges,' she said, smiling. 'Especially ones assigned to eschaton-three-alpha.'

'You're an Augur?' Josh said in amazement.

Fey nodded. 'Darkling and I were assigned to you.'

'So you know we're trying to avoid an event,' Caitlin pleaded.

She cocked the gun and held it up to Josh's face.

'What was eschaton-three-alpha again?' Josh asked Caitlin flippantly, trying to buy them some time while he tried to think of a way out.

Fey waved the gun for them to move away from the cabinet. 'Insurgency — which is what I'm arresting you for, under the Eschaton Confinement Act.'

Four more Augurs appeared around them, each one holding an antique gun.

80

ILLNESS

The MRI scan had shown no sign of a tumour, but did reveal a network of small dark patches that were called 'Amyloid Plaques' — a sign of early-onset Alzheimers.

Fermi wasn't listening as the doctor babbled on about BACE inhibitors and anti-amyloid drugs; he was too busy processing the death sentence. Alzheimer's was a degenerative neurological disorder; his brain was slowly decaying as plaques stole his memory and the ability to control his body.

There was only one question that mattered.

'How long?'

'Two, maybe three years. If you stick to the medication maybe a little longer.'

The doctor seemed a little taken aback by Fermi's reaction. They had known each other for years, and the man was genuinely upset by the diagnosis, but Fermi didn't have time for sentimentality. His research had been his life for the last two years, and he was so close — now he had a deadline.

There was no one in his life to console him, no wife or children to hold his hand and cry at his bedside while he forgot their names. It would be a simple death, uncomplicated by emotion, but he needed to postpone it as long as possible — long enough to complete the job.

While he'd been hospitalised, Fermi had a lot of time to think. He'd been inspired by something that Lenin said just before the blackout — about needing more time. He was so focused on trying to move things into the future, so frustrated by the limitations of the technology, that it hadn't occurred to him that he go back and improve the past.

The complexity of calculating the future was proving too much for the equipment, but historical data was a known set of parameters, at least the more recent periods. It would require significantly less processing to calculate a temporal trajectory into the past, and if he was successful, he could accelerate the technology exponentially — shift the digital revolution back thirty years, and by Moore's law his current CPUs would be over thirty-thousand times more powerful.

That kind of computing power could model new break-throughs in drug therapy — find a cure for his condition before he was even diagnosed.

81

FOUNDER

'Bloody Fey. I should have known!' Caitlin paced around her cell like a big cat trapped in a cage.

Josh sat on the bench in the cell next to hers, thick iron bars between them — which was not such a terrible thing at that precise moment. He'd experienced this kind of mood before, and it was safer to have a few inches of metal between them.

'How could you know?'

'Her abilities with timelines. I was so busy being annoyed with Dalton that I missed it.'

She grabbed hold of the bars with two hands and shook them.

'But the Wyrrm — he took that one for the team.' Josh put his hands over hers.

'He was just doing his duty; trying to stop a perdurant, one of the precursors of an Eschaton cascade.'

'You don't know that for sure.'

Caitlin bit her lip. 'They were watching the skull — tailing Dalton probably.'

'Waiting for him to steal it?'

She nodded. 'Waiting for someone to try.'

She sat back down on her bunk and put her head in her hands. 'This was supposed to fix the problem. Now we've made it even worse! We changed the continuum.'

'How?'

'Think about it. Dalton's not going to use the skull to open the breach, that's never going to happen now. But he knows you're the Nemesis and they've initiated some kind of Eschaton emergency plan. It couldn't have gone much worse.'

Josh didn't know what to say. He had no idea where the colonel and her parents were; they would be stuck in the maelstrom waiting for a signal — which was never going to come: Fey's team had confiscated all of their equipment.

'Can't we just tell them what we know — what's the worst that can happen?'

'Well, they might redact us for starters. I don't know about you, but I quite like my memory the way it is.'

A steel door opened at the end of the corridor, and they heard the heavy tread of army-issue boots.

'Jones, Makepiece, the founder requires your presence,' declared an officious civil servant surrounded by a squad of guards.

Lord Dee sat in an old leather chair in the middle of his private library. The pages of the book that rested in his lap were handwritten, and as he closed it, Josh thought he recognised the cover, even though it was aged and worn with use.

'Do you know what this is?' he asked, holding up the book to them.

'The original Malefactum?' Caitlin replied.

If the founder was impressed, he didn't show it.

'The first book of the Djinn,' he said, putting it on the table and standing up. 'It has taken over a thousand years of meticulous research, and yet we still don't completely understand what goes on within the maelstrom — nor who wrote that damned book. Daedalus remains a mystery.'

Josh shared a knowing look with Caitlin.

Dee walked over to the tall arched window and stared out at the blue sky. It felt like the first time Josh had seen it in weeks.

'The Augurs tell me that you were inciting a level three Eschaton event. The Copernicans are demanding an excision or a redaction as a minimum sentence.'

Josh went to speak, but the founder held up a hand to quiet him.

'I've never been completely convinced by the theory of the Eschaton Cascade. I remember when your uncle Marcus first presented it before the council — it was ridiculed. Fortunately, the Copernicans persuaded me to commission the creation of the Augurs. Which, it seems, was somewhat prescient based on recent events. They say they have overwhelming evidence that you will bring about the end of time.' He pointed a finger at Josh. 'They've convinced the council to invoke an emergency confinement order.'

'How did my uncle propose to avert it?' asked Caitlin.

'He didn't, and his presentation was never concluded.' Dee said with a sigh. 'He was lost in the Great Breach — along with your parents.'

'Couldn't Josh and I go back and find him?'

'The Protectorate inquisition has already confiscated all of his work, and they're refusing to release it to me.'

'They can't refuse your orders!'

'Oh they can,' he said grimly. 'Because under the confinement act we're effectively in a state of martial law — In fact, I believe they are about to relieve me of my office.'

'This sounds like they're fulfilling the Eschaton predictions!' Caitlin exclaimed.

The founder grimaced. 'The Daedalans have powerful allies — including none other than the Chief Inquisitor Eckhart herself. Ravana has been looking for a way to depose me for some time now — she's already created an Eschaton division within the Protectorate and put her son at the head of it.'

He turned to Josh. 'I created this Order to protect the future of humanity, not to serve the ambitions of its leaders. They have forgotten our prime directive, and I believe you may be the only one who can restore it — assuming you're able to escape from this particular predicament of course.'

'How?'

'Find out who your father was. This paradox begins with him.'

There was a knock at the door.

'That will be your escort,' the founder observed.

'At least they knocked,' added Caitlin.

The doors opened, and Dalton walked in with a group of Protectorate officers. They were all wearing black armour, but there was something different about Dalton's — instead of the usual Protectorate insignia of a shield, his uniform had a silver skull — like a Nazi death's head.

'Jones. You're to be held until further notice under section two of the Eschaton Confinement Act.'

Two officers positioned themselves either side of Josh, hands resting on their holstered sidearms.

'Caitlin Makepiece, I am arresting you on suspicion of

collusion with entities unknown for the purpose of disrupting the continuum.'

Again, two officers flanked Caitlin.

'Sir.' Dalton addressed Lord Dee with disdain. 'By order of the High Council, I hereby relieve you of your command and all duties and powers associated therewith.'

The founder waved a hand as if to say he couldn't care less, opened the book once more and continued reading.

Dalton was unmoved. He turned to the rest of his detail and walked out, and they followed behind, taking Josh and Caitlin along with them.

82

BEDLAM

B edlam was not a place that most people made a habit of visiting more than once. This was Josh's third time, and it wasn't getting any more hospitable. The seers sanctum was nothing more than a fancy name for a lunatic asylum, and Dalton had obviously taken great pleasure in picking out the worst cell he could find for Josh — Caitlin had been moved somewhere else.

He'd thought the cold showers and the lice powder had been bad enough until they shaved his head and threw him into a dank cell.

Josh overheard the guards talking about some kind of purge. Apparently, there was going to be a massive round up of the unbelievers. He couldn't quite understand the details, but it sounded like they were preparing to do exactly what had happened in the Determinist reality.

There was little in the way of daylight or comfort in his tiny cell; the bed was stuffed with damp, mouldy straw, and rats and cockroaches skittered back and forth across the wet flagstones — Josh was glad it was too dark to see. When he stretched his arms out, he could touch both walls.

The door was oak, bound with a metal that seemed to have no past. His gaolers had been quite meticulous when they'd built the prison. The history of every component, every bolt and screw, had been redacted so that it couldn't be used as a path of escape.

Hours passed with nothing more than the cries of the insane to keep him awake. Josh shivered as the temperature dropped and the tiny shaft of daylight faded away. He knew this wasn't the punishment, just a bit of morale-breaking psycho-bullshit while they prepared something even more terrible for him.

He tried to shut out the screams and the wailing by drifting back into his memories, ones that he used to keep for the really horrible nights when his mother would squeeze his hand so tightly while moaning with the pain.

It was his tenth birthday, and Josh could picture his mother dancing around the table to her favourite song: *The way you make me feel*, by Michael Jackson. She had some crazy moves, her hands waving above her head, laughing and singing like she didn't have a care in the world.

It was a good memory — a keeper. It reminded him that they'd been happy once, in his timeline. He wondered what she was doing now: sitting in Churchill park with her boys, playing hide and seek in the rose garden or cooking their tea. Tears rolled down his cheeks as he thought about what it would've been like to grow up in this world, with her so healthy. Anger welled up in him as he thought about all the hardships he'd endured over the years. Fate had knocked him down more than once, but it had made him stronger, and he wasn't about to give up now.

The founder had said it started with his father, which

meant going back into his past, but Josh had no idea where to start. His mother would never speak about him — ever. The nearest he'd got to an answer was a bunch of old photos of her when she was at University before she'd had to leave to have her baby.

The idea of going back to that time disturbed him.

83

CAITLIN

'You could save yourself,' said Dalton, staring at Caitlin through the bars of her cell.

She sat on the bed of straw weaving the sheaves together. 'My mother taught me to do this.' She held up the straw man. 'It's one of my earliest memories of her.'

'Are you listening to me?' he snapped. 'They're going to crucify you. There's talk of using you and him as breach fodder.'

'I think I've spent long enough following your orders.'

'You didn't use to mind. Why the sudden change of heart?'

'Because I know who I'm supposed to be now.'

His mouth stretched into a sardonic grin. 'Really? Did Jones show you the light?' There was something disgusting about the way he thrust his hips against the cage.

Caitlin put the straw doll down and walked over to the bars. 'I was thirteen when grandfather died, and you were supposed to take care of me. Not use me as some kind of slave.'

'Poor KitKat, did life give you a hard time?' He pretended

to wipe a tear from his eye. 'Fate's a bitch. Don't come mewling to me when the monads are chewing your face off.'

He turned to leave.

'I used to pity you after the beatings,' Caitlin began. 'I saw what your father used to do and I felt sorry for you. Whatever you inflicted on me was nothing compared to the damage he's done to you. You're a pussy compared to him — a real disappointment.'

Dalton looked back, his eyes like dark coals, and she knew she'd hit the mark.

'I was going to make you a proposition,' Dalton said through clenched teeth. 'For the sake of our friendship.'

Caitlin looked unconvinced. 'Really? I doubt that.'

'What if I told you I know where your parents are,' he said slyly.

'Where they've always been,' she replied.

He looked mildly amused. 'I mean where they really are.' There was something about the way he phrased the question that bothered her.

'Exploring the maelstrom in a timeship?'

'That's where they were,' he grinned, 'before we caught them trying to steal the infinity engine.'

Now it was Caitlin's turn to look bemused. The plan had been to borrow it, effectively blinding the Copernicans and allowing her father to use it to accurately calculate the best strategy for avoiding the Eschaton Cascade.

Dalton relished the look of concern that flashed across her face.

'Ah, were you waiting for mummy to come and rescue you?' he asked as she picked up the straw figure. 'Hard luck.'

'Are they here?' she shouted as he walked away. 'In Bedlam?'

He shrugged his shoulders.

'Dalton, come back!'

He continued down the passageway.

'Come back, you arrogant dick!' She rattled the door of the cell. It wasn't the best she could come up with, but the insult simply bounced off him.

84

TORTURE

J osh was strapped to some kind of medieval rack; his arms and legs were bound to the wooden frame and stretched to the point that was just beyond uncomfortable.

Dalton paced around the room, while his minions laid out an array of sharp metal objects on the table in front of Josh.

'That will be all,' he ordered, inspecting the tools.

Dalton waited until they left, then took off his leather gloves. 'This may seem like a bit of an inquisition, but I don't have the luxury of time; quite ironic when you think about it. The Order is now under martial law, which allows me the liberty to exercise any means necessary to ensure its security.'

'Really? Are you sure you're not just doing it for kicks?' Josh joked. 'Caitlin told me you were a bit of a sadist.'

Dalton smiled. 'Did she? It's good to know I made such a big impression on her.'

'Yeah — I've seen the scars.'

Dalton ignored the remark and picked up one of the small knives from the table. 'I don't suppose you've ever heard of the Talons of Torquemada?' he asked, holding up the weapon in front of Josh's eyes. It was a thin blade with the head of a dragon on the pommel.

'Can't say that I have.'

'They are a fascinating form of punishment, crafted to inflict nerve pain by degrees. There are fifteen of them, and when used correctly by a Castillian painmaster they are supposed to inflict the torment of every one of their previous victims — loosening the tongue of the most stubborn heretics.'

Dalton took the razor-sharp blade and pushed it slowly into Josh's shoulder. A hot pain lanced through his arm, making him wince involuntarily — it was like being stabbed with a six-inch needle.

'Damn,' he seethed through clenched teeth. 'I take it you're not a master then?'

'Not in the slightest, but the talons have enough latent knowledge for me to acquire. They're quite literally telling me where to put them.' Dalton chuckled.

The next one went into Josh's leg, just above the knee, and felt like someone had set fire to his foot.

'So are you going to ask me a question?' Josh spat through clenched teeth, as the third spike was inserted into his wrist.

'Not yet,' Dalton said, smiling. 'I think this one has a special place,' he said, holding up the strange gargoyle on the end of the handle. 'Homunculus.'

The pain was flooding into Josh's brain from every nerve until Dalton put the Homunculus into the back of his neck; and then everything stopped.

Josh took a deep breath.

'Neurological block. A thing of beauty, and without doubt the most masterful stroke of genius. With this one blade, I can relieve you of all of your pain.'

He placed two more talons into Josh's other hand and leg then removed the Homunculus.

Waves of new and excruciating pain wracked his body, and he felt the world fade away for a moment as if someone had turned down the lights.

'So, you see, now I have your full attention,' Dalton whispered into his ear as he placed the blade back into Josh's neck.

And the pain was gone.

'So, tell me, Jones, what else has the lovely Caitlin told you about me.'

'Don't you want to know about the skull?'

'In time, but first I want to know what that scheming bitch has told you.'

Josh's head was heavy, the strain on his neck becoming too much, and he let it fall forward. He tried to think of the best way to play this. Dalton was obviously obsessed with what people thought of him, and Josh could use that.

'She said you were a bully, that your father beat you — so you take it out on others.'

'That's public knowledge,' Dalton said, sneering. 'You need to try harder than that.' He played with the end of the talon in Josh's neck.

Josh thought back to the times they'd been alone. She hadn't told him much — Dalton wasn't something that she wanted to spend much time discussing. There'd been one thing after they had made love for the first time. Caitlin had told him that Dalton didn't like sex, or more specifically, his penis — that he'd thought about cutting it off.

'She told me you hate your dick.'

Dalton smiled as if Josh had just given him the best Christmas present ever. 'Thank you. Now we're telling it how it is, we can begin.'

. . .

Dalton hit Josh across the face. 'You expect me to believe you're the Nemesis? That you've actually been into the maelstrom?'

Josh spat blood and raised his head to look him in the eye. 'I am, and I have — it wasn't pretty.'

'You do realise this is heresy? I can have you excised just for speaking those words.'

'Somehow, I don't think you're going to.'

Dalton wiped the blood off his hands. 'And what, out of interest, did you see in there?'

'Random bits of time, a whole bunch of lost things, and the Djinn, of course, nasty bastards — then there was a crazy old man, Daedalus I think he called himself,' Josh added with feigned ignorance.

Dalton's eyes widened. 'Did this old man have a book?'

'Yes,' Josh said, nodding. 'He called it his Book of Deadly Names.'

'Liar!' shouted Dalton. 'Caitlin told you to say that!' He struck him so hard that it shook the Homonculus pin out of his neck and Josh passed out from the pain.

'If you're the Nemesis,' Dalton continued once Josh had regained consciousness, 'then you're supposed to be from the future.'

'Cat warned me not to discuss other eventualities.'

'Indulge me,' he said, playing with another blade. 'What lies beyond the frontier?'

'Pollution, fear, poverty, elitist overlords and of course, flying cars — someone had seriously accelerated the technology, not that it seemed to have done much good.'

Dalton tutted and inserted another talon into Josh's arm.

'Anyone could've dreamt up that.' He went to pull the nerve-block out again.

'Wait! This timeline had been in a constant state of war since the Middle-Ages. The cities were built on the ruins of more than one nuclear strike.'

Dalton paused. 'Who did it?'

'Politicians with too much firepower I guess?'

'No, I meant who advanced the tech.'

'I don't know. Someone was messing with the continuum. I thought it might've been you — but you were running the Government.'

Dalton's eyes narrowed. 'Was I now? What was I like?'

Josh knew this subject would interest him even more than the missing book.

'You were leading the Order, and you'd become very powerful.' He watched Dalton's face as the facts sunk in. This was the future he craved, and Josh could see the raw ambition in his eyes. 'It was terrible.'

'Why?'

'The world was dying, and the Order was at war with itself; you really screwed it up.'

Dalton reached out and pulled the Homunculus out of Josh's neck.

'You're a heretic. Do you really think anyone cares whether you live or die?'

Josh couldn't speak. His teeth bit through his lip, blood poured into his mouth, and the pain was so great he passed out again.

'Wake up!' Dalton slapped him across the face.

Josh could taste the iron tang of blood in his mouth,

though the pain had stopped and the stinging of his cheek was nothing in comparison.

Something stopped him from opening his eyes; the faint touch of a familiar timeline. He let his mind drift into the metal of the blade in his neck. The iron was centuries-old, and he felt hundreds of lines weaving out into the past, each one of them connected to a previous victim.

Josh gently probed the other blades. They all had their own tales to tell; so many gruesome, horrible ways to die, and yet one of them was familiar.

'Wake up, weaver!' Dalton growled, striking him again.

'I'm awake!' snarled Josh.

'Good, now tell me more about my future.'

So Josh did exactly that. He told him about the Ministry and the bombs, the schism between the factions of the Order, and as he recounted the story, he quietly explored the timelines of the tortured.

Dalton's face was transfixed by the details of the world he had come to lead. Josh could see a religious zeal in the man's eyes as he hung off of every word.

'So, what caused this technological advance?' Dalton asked when Josh had finished.

'Something from inside the maelstrom.'

'A Djinn?'

'No, more like a man in some kind of weird spacesuit.'

Dalton was deep in thought, processing all the new information. Josh had told him what could be and how to get it; all he needed now was for his ego to kick in.

In the meantime, Josh finally located the timeline that felt so familiar. It was Da Recco's, the crazy Italian navigator he'd met in Kaffa, 11.347. The Vatican had obviously been using the blades on its heretics long before Torquemada got hold of them.

Josh didn't waste another second; he found the safest moment and shifted inside it.

85

DA RECCO

[Palais des Papes, Avignon. Date:11.364]

D a Recco looked half-dead. His head hung down while the rest of his limp body was bound to the rack. Josh wasn't feeling that much better himself; the blades were gone, but the memory of the pain was still too real, too vivid.

'Da Recco?' Josh whispered.

There was no response.

Josh counted fourteen talons. He pulled them out in sequence, making sure he left the Homunculus in the neck until last.

He knew he wouldn't have long. Dalton would be hot on his tail as soon as he got a bearing on the timeline Josh had used. It would be a few minutes at most.

'Joshua?' Da Recco whispered weakly. 'Is it you? What are you doing here?'

'Da Recco, do you think you can walk? We need to leave now!'

The navigator shook his head. 'Tired. Too tired.'

Josh untied the knots at his feet, and then his wrists, and Da Recco collapsed into his arms.

'Inquisitors; they never believed me — said I was working with El Diablo.'

He was heavy and smelled really bad. What was left of his clothes were stained and soiled — it took all of his remaining strength for Josh to keep from dropping him.

'Where are we?' Josh asked, looking around the dark stone basement.

'Avignon, Papal Palace — not somewhere I would recommend for its hospitality.' He held up his hands; the nails were ragged and missing, and two fingers were broken.

'I need something old,' said Josh, lowering the navigator into a chair. 'Preferably man-made.'

'Well, there are many tools to choose from.' Da Recco nodded to a wall covered with instruments of torture.

'I was thinking more like a watch or a compass — something that hasn't been involved in killing things.'

'Or a coin?' said a familiar voice, as a small metal disk bounced across the bloodstained floor.

Josh turned to find the colonel standing in a breach in the middle of a stone wall.

'How?'

'No time. Bring your friend. Eckhart and his cronies are less than ninety-seconds away.'

'I thought the Inquisition might have caught you too,' Josh said, putting Da Recco into one of the timeship's bunks. He'd passed out from the pain of being moved.

The colonel was busying himself with an odd-looking first aid kit. The old man mixed a series of exotic looking ingredients together and poured them into a copper syringe.

'I tried to talk Caitlin's parents out of their madcap scheme, but they left me to guard the ship.'

He injected Da Recco, watching as the concoction entered his bloodstream and his body relaxed.

'Milk of the Poppy — never fails.' The colonel patted Da Recco. 'But he really needs a healer.'

The colonel took a large bottle of whisky out of one of the steerage compartments and poured them each a large glass. They sat down on either side of the chart table and took a drink.

'You look like you've been through a Russian prison camp.' He pointed at Josh's shaved head.

Josh instinctively lifted his hand to his scalp and rubbed it. He hadn't dared to look in a mirror.

'Dalton likes his men bald, what can I say?'

'That boy has been an evil little sadist since birth, and his father was just as bad.'

'Was?'

The colonel knocked back the rest of his glass. 'From what I remember he was killed in a hunting accident. Dalton was the only witness.'

'We need to go back — he's got Caitlin.'

'I know,' the colonel said, pouring another drink.

86

DALTON

Dalton stood in the centre of the Papal torture chamber while the Protectorate carried out a full sweep. He knew it was pointless: Jones was long gone.

He studied the tools of the Inquisition, impressed by the Church's wide selection of persuasive instruments. The room was a master class in physical interrogation.

One of the officers returned and stood to attention.

'Nothing to report, sir,' he reported, his voice altered by the mask.

Dalton waved him away with a casual flick of his hand. He was intrigued by the location, and what might have brought him all the way back here. His gaze fell on the talons that were scattered across the floor. As Dalton gathered each one, he explored their histories, searching for a connection between their latest victim and Jones.

When he found that the prisoner had been an Italian navigator who was no more than a privateer, a mercenary for hire, Dalton felt no closer to an answer. Why the inquisition had decided to interrogate him was a mystery, and he didn't have time to dig any deeper.

Then he saw the coin.

It was sitting wedged in the clogged cracks of the flag-stones, an untarnished golden disc in an otherwise grim setting.

He dug it out with the point of his blade. 'Captain!' he barked, reading the inscription. 'Recall your men.'

Dalton held it up to the light to be sure. The latin around the edge of the coin read:

'FUTURUM NONDUM SCRIPTUM'

'The future is not written,' he translated.

87

ARMAGEDDON

Caitlin whiled away the last few hours studying her cell. Every spare inch of stone was covered in the ruminations of the previous occupants. They'd each scratched their own theory of Armageddon into the rough brick: complex temporal coordinates, pictograms of vengeful gods and indecipherable symbols were scrawled across the floor, walls and ceiling.

She touched some of them and felt the insanity ebb through the fine grooves of granite.

'You all saw it,' she whispered to herself. 'In your own way.'

It made her sad to see all of their interpretations, that they had lost their minds trying to calculate the end of times, not knowing that the Eschaton Cascade was being studied by a secret department all along. She wanted to add her own contribution, but had nothing except her fingernails to work with — and she wasn't crazy enough to sacrifice those yet.

The prison door creaked as it opened, inciting howls of contempt from the other inmates — the gaolers had returned.

Caitlin tried to control her breathing, to still the beating of her heart — no matter what happened next she mustn't show any sign of fear. She knew that her parents had been the only chance of rescue and that if Josh wasn't cooperating, Dalton would use her to persuade him.

'Could do with a break about now,' she muttered to the wall.

Dalton walked casually past the cells, tapping his cane on the bars like a child along school railings. The prisoners shrank away as he approached, hiding in the shadows and muttering curses — they knew better than to provoke him; he needed little excuse to punish them.

He held the coin tightly in his gloved fist, the words of the inscription rolling around in his mind as he tried to decide which of his many questions he should ask Caitlin first.

Dalton was convinced that Jones was the Nemesis, that he knew how to reach Daedalus and the Djinn. He may have escaped, but Dalton still had one important piece of the puzzle — his beloved Caitlin. She would know who was helping him, although it would take a particular kind of persuasion to get her to tell the truth. But he knew her well — he knew her nightmares.

It would begin with something kind. Caitlin hadn't eaten anything since they'd captured her, so he'd ordered her favourite: freshly baked croissants, blackcurrant jam and tea. He was still a gentleman after all, and no matter what happened after that he would make sure she was well fed. The conversation would begin pleasantly, and if he felt she was withholding he would take a more physical approach. It wouldn't be the first time she'd felt the sting of his hand.

· · ·

As they turned the corner they met the guard, a squat little man with a blank expression that matched his intellect.

'All's well?' Dalton asked as the man snapped to attention.

'Aye, sir.'

It was then Dalton first noticed that the howling had ceased. It was a sound he'd learned to ignore over the last few days, but now, in its absence, there was an eerie silence. He felt the eyes of the inmates on him.

'What's wrong with the prisoners?'

'No idea, sir. Been like that for the last ten minutes, off and on.'

Dalton's step quickened as he made for Caitlin's cell.

It was too late.

She was gone.

88

PLAN

'You don't look so good?' Caitlin murmured into Josh's ear as she wrapped her arms around him.

'Been worse,' he lied. 'What did he do to you?'

'Nothing,' she said, and sighed. 'But I think he was planning to.'

'I'm going to — '

'No, you're not,' she interrupted, sniffing back a tear. The relief of seeing him appear through the cell wall had been so great that she couldn't help but cry — and she hated crying.

'You two finished saying hello yet?' her mother's voice echoed through the speaking tube.

'Coming,' Caitlin responded. 'Thanks for saving them.'

'Least I could do. Was mostly the colonel's idea... he seems to think they might be useful.'

She bit his ear.

'Ow!'

'So what happens now?' Josh asked, walking back into the mess.

'Rufius has some interesting ideas,' Caitlin's father replied.

'Harebrained more like,' her mother added.

'No more harebrained than trying to steal an Infinity Engine,' the colonel retorted.

'The founder told us to look into Josh's father,' said Caitlin.

The colonel stared at the map of the Eschaton Cascade laid out across the table, and scratched his beard.

'We have two options: go back to the beginning, or try and head off the next event.' He tapped on the fourth node on the chart.

'I vote we deal with the Daedalan effect,' said her father. 'If we remove the knowledge about the elders and the maelstrom we reduce the likelihood of a division and the insurgency.'

Josh shook his head. 'I've seen a reality where they knew nothing about Daedalus but they still believed in the prophecy — they called it the Paradox.'

'Which is how we remember it too,' Caitlin's mother agreed.

'In that one, someone had screwed around with technology and nearly destroyed the planet.'

'Because someone intervened from the future,' Caitlin said, tapping on the seventh symbol.

Josh nodded. 'Someone's using the maelstrom to move about through time. You called them "Sappers" once,' he said, turning to the colonel.

'Time miners,' the old man agreed. 'Never actually caught one in the act, mind you. Just a theory.'

'I've seen one,' said Josh. 'Just before you closed the breach at Gisors. He had some kind of space suit.'

'Was it mirrored? With this symbol on it?' Caitlin drew a logo of two F's back-to-back.

Josh shook his head. 'Didn't get that close.'

She bit her lip. 'Something was organising the monads

when I was in the maelstrom. It seemed to be controlling them.'

'We've seen it too,' admitted her mother. 'We assumed they were Augurs.'

'I don't think they're anything to do with the Order,' declared the colonel, shaking his head. 'I think the founder was right, that it's something to do with you Joshua — we need to go back and find out who this mysterious father of yours was.'

89

2000

[Cambridge, UK. Date: 12.000]

T he university grounds were shrouded in darkness. The night sky was clear, and the music from the ball drifted over the lawns and into the bushes where Caitlin and Josh were hiding.

Josh had only ever seen a couple of photos of his mother when she was younger — before he was born. They were faded old polaroids: one of her with a group of her friends, all dressed in party clothes in some kind of club, and the other standing on a boat on the Thames in the middle of winter.

It was weird to think that at this point in time she was only two years older than him.

The colonel appeared from behind a stand of trees using the light from his tachyon as a torch. He took out his almanac and flipped through a few pages, as if reacquainting himself with an old friend.

'Still feels peculiar being back in the linear.'

'Nowhere near as weird as being in there,' Caitlin muttered, looking back to the aperture that was flickering in the wall of the porter's lodge. Her mother and father were waving from the other side of the shimmering portal as it slowly shrank to nothing.

'I'm still not quite sure why they insisted we dress up,' Josh said, pulling at his starched shirt collar for a little more breathing space. He felt like an overdressed waiter in the evening suit they'd made him wear.

'I think they're making up for all the times they didn't get to,' Caitlin replied. She looked stunning, wearing a long ball-gown of midnight blue that accentuated all her curves. Her mother had woven silver threads into her hair, which glinted in the moonlight. Josh wondered if this was what it was like to go to a prom, like one of those kids that actually graduated.

'Must be weird having them back.'

She put her arm through his. 'Not as weird as witnessing your own conception.'

'Trying not to think about that.'

'Where are we?' Josh squinted at the turreted towers of the university.

'Girton College, Cambridge, 12.000. Your mother's in her second year of a history degree,' recited the colonel without looking up from the pages of his book.

'You never told me she went to Cambridge!' Caitlin sounded impressed.

'I didn't know. She never talked about it.'

Josh thought back to all the arguments they'd had about him finishing his education. His mother had been so keen to get him into university — the life that she'd given up — but he was adamant that he didn't want to go.

He knew that she'd left because of him, that she'd given up everything to care for her baby. A combination of dyslexia and

ADHD had made it impossible for Josh to get the grades he needed and gradually they'd come to an unspoken under-standing that he was never going to make it in academia — what he hadn't realised was how brilliant she must have been.

'This is one of the best colleges in the country. The profes-sors are among the elite, and four of them are in the Order,' the colonel said smugly, tucking his almanac inside his tuxedo. He looked like something from a seventies lounge band — maroon velvet with black collars and a ruffled shirt. 'Now, who would care for a drink?'

It was a beautiful summer's evening. The darkening sky was slowly matching the colour of Caitlin's dress, and the gardens around the college were full of sweetly scented roses. It was like a country house from one of his mum's period dramas.

Josh was pleasantly surprised to find the ball was actually more like a rave than something from 'Strictly Come Danc-ing'. A long white marquee had been pitched on the college lawns; the roof was an ever-changing light show of lasers and disco ball rainbows pulsing to a nineties club classic. They navigated their way around numerous couples in ball gowns and tuxedos in various states of undress, while others wandered drunkenly off into the grounds.

'There's something odd about this,' commented the colonel, who was staring intently into a lensing sphere. 'You two mingle and see if you can locate her. I need to check on something.'

He marched off into the dark, holding the lens ahead of him like a crazy, myopic wizard, but no one paid him any attention.

They reached the marquee as the Prodigy's *Firestarter* kicked off. Josh and Caitlin looked into a seething mass of bodies jumping around in time to the beat. It was impossible to make anyone out in the strobing light — especially a woman who he had only seen in a faded photo.

He turned back to find Caitlin trying to contain her excitement. She was nodding her head in time with the bass, and there was a wild look in her eye. There she was again — his Caitlin, just like the time in the pub when she'd made him stay for the gig — sassy and confident.

'No!' shouted Josh over the music. 'No dancing! We're on a mission.'

A wide grin spread across her face. 'Undercover!' she shouted back, taking Josh's hand and pulling him into the tent.

When they reached the centre, the music switched to *Beautiful Stranger,* by Madonna. The bodies around them were hot and glistening with sweat. Caitlin writhed to the music, pushing her body against his as the beats pulsed through their bones.

For a moment he forgot everything: the sea of bodies around them, the horrors he had witnessed in the maelstrom, the search for his mother.

There was nothing but the sound and the sensation of her against him.

She danced around him like a cat, sinuous and seductive, an enchanting display that was attracting the attention of the crowd. Josh grabbed her around the waist and pulled her in tight.

'You're getting noticed,' he whispered.

She wrapped her arms around his neck and bit his ear. 'You're not jealous are you?'

Two guys in starched tuxedoes were making their way through the crowds towards them.

'Time to mingle,' Josh said, leading her away from the dance floor.

The song was coming to an end, and the next track was a badly misjudged tempo change by the DJ. Everyone began to separate and move off, creating a sudden obstacle for the bouncers and giving them time to disappear into the masses.

They slipped in and out of the jostling crowd until they reached the bar. Josh instantly recognised it from the polaroid; this was the right place, but there was no sign of his mother.

'Right place, wrong time.' Caitlin shrugged as she helped herself to the punch. 'Guess we'll have to mingle a bit more,' she added, downing the glass of bright red liquid in one go.

The music grew louder as the next track got faster and people began to drift back onto the floor. Josh watched the procession of drunken dancers, looking for any sign of the younger version of his mother, but there were too many.

Then a thought struck him. 'Wait here,' he said, and walked off towards the DJ.

There was one song that had dominated his early childhood, something that had been seared into his memory by the countless number of times he'd had to listen to it. A song that she used to play over and over again.

When he returned, Caitlin was sipping champagne and chatting to a couple of very tall guys who looked like they were captains of the rugby team or something equally sporty. They were the bouncers Josh had been trying to avoid — Caitlin seemed to have them wrapped around her little finger.

'Josh, meet the Davreau twins.' She introduced them with a convincing upper-class accent.

They shook hands cordially.

'I was just explaining how you were looking for your sister,' she added with a wink.

'Yeah, Martha. Martha Jones.'

The slightly taller of the twins looked like he was deciding whether to kick them out or make a move on Caitlin when the unmistakable beat of Josh's request kicked in — *The way you make me feel*, by Michael Jackson.

'Sorry guys, this is our song.' Josh grabbed Caitlin and pulled her towards the crowd.

'No, it isn't,' protested Caitlin, shrugging off his hand.

'No, it's hers,' Josh explained. 'She called it my birthday song, used to play it every year,' *until she forgot what day it was,* he thought to himself.

'Ah, good idea,' Caitlin admitted with a drunken smirk.

It was a popular track, and the entire ball seemed to have gravitated to the dance floor. Josh and Caitlin worked their way into the middle of the crowd and danced casually as they scanned opposite sides of the room.

There were so many different people it was hard to focus on any one face for more than a few seconds before they disappeared back into the throng.

Caitlin leaned in. 'Can you see her?'

Josh shook his head.

The lights were pulsing to the music, creating flashes of light and dark moments, the scene changing with every beat.

Josh used the music, reaching back into his memories to all those times his mother had danced around him when he was small. The same silly dance around the kitchen table as he tried to blow out his candles. Swaying her hips with hands raised high above her head as it rocked from side-to-side like some kind of mental patient. Not something that the debutantes in this place would ever have the lack of grace to do.

He stopped looking at their faces, studying the way they moved instead. It took no more than a minute to find her, less than two metres away — the same distinctive moves, two hands waving around in the air.

He smiled at Caitlin and nodded in the direction of his mother, who was surrounded by a group of girls that matched the ones in the polaroid.

She was so happy rocking out to her favourite tune that Josh held back; he couldn't bring himself to spoil the moment. She was full of life, having a good time with her friends as they copied her ridiculous dance moves. This was not the woman he had known — this was another life, one that she'd given up to have him. He felt a pang of guilt as he considered what was to come and was having trouble coming to terms with the idea that someone in this tent was probably his father. This would be the closest Josh had ever been to knowing who he was, and now he wasn't sure if he wanted to. All those years of dreaming about what he looked like, studying his own face in the mirror, trying to separate her features from his. Then later, the gradual realisation that he would never know, and hating her for not telling him, not keeping him.

So many conflicting emotions surrounded this mysterious nobody, and they had haunted him his entire life, yet as Josh studied the men around her searching for some hint of paternal bonding — he felt nothing.

They shadowed her for the rest of the evening. It was fortunate that she was so drunk because they were terrible spies. As the evening wound down and the revellers slowly drifted away, his mother's group grabbed the last of the champagne and their shoes, then wandered out into the cool night air. Josh took Caitlin by the hand and followed close behind.

The colonel was loitering outside like some kind of embarrassing dad at a school disco. 'Where have you been?'

'Mingling,' Caitlin said with a giggle and waving her shoes in the air. She'd been rather over-indulgent with the free drinks, and Josh could tell the colonel wasn't impressed. But he guessed that finding out your parents were still alive after eight years of grieving was a good enough reason.

'So I see,' growled the old man.

'We found her.' Josh nodded to the group of women zig-zagging slowly towards their halls singing: *The way you make me feel* at the tops of their voices. 'Any sign of the sperm donor?'

'I don't think he's arrived yet.' The colonel tapped his almanac. 'We stay with your mother and wait.' He strode off in pursuit.

'What are we going to do when he does appear?' Josh asked Caitlin, who was walking unsteadily beside him. Her hand slipped around his waist, more for balance than affection.

'Since we don't have a seer, I guess we tag him. Get something we can trace. There's never really been a case of a future intervention before, so we don't have a precedent. Oh shit!'

He moved away from her. 'Are you going to throw up?'

'No, you arse! Do you know what this means? You really are the Nemesis!'

'Paradox.'

'Whatever. I never thought about it before, but this is epic — I mean really off-the-scale huge. Do you know how many people want to believe you exist?'

Josh felt like he'd had this conversation before. 'Believe me, this isn't the first time you've asked me that.'

'That freaks me out too! All the things you know about me.

Did you and I — you know, hook up before? You came a hell of a long way to find me.'

For some reason, Josh felt slightly embarrassed by the question. He'd come to think of her as the same person, not realising that she would think of herself differently, and it was true there were subtle differences, probably because of the way she had been brought up. Without the colonel's influence, she was less feisty, and maybe a little more reserved — he loved her no less for it.

'It's complicated, and you've had too much to drink for it to make any sense.'

'Ah, you're blushing — we did, didn't we! I knew it!'

She was getting louder, and the colonel looked back with a fierce glare that silenced both of them.

The lights of the common room glowed warmly through the leaded windows. Josh watched his mother and her friends finishing off the last of the champagne. There was no sign of any men, and he was beginning to wonder how exactly this was going to play out.

The colonel was staring intensely into the lens, pacing around the garden like a water diviner.

Caitlin was sat on a bench watching the old man. 'I still can't believe he's Daedalus. He's not how I imagined.'

'The book was his memory,' Josh replied casually, distracted by the vision of his beautiful, vibrant mother having such a good time with her friends — it was so different to the memories he had of her.

'Have you ever tried to travel into the future?'

'Not really.' He came and sat beside her on the bench, feeling her shiver as he put his arm around her. 'But I have seen what it might look like.'

'And?'

'It was different — you were all on some kind of power trip. The world had been totally messed up by constant wars, and even the Order were fighting with each other. Everyone was scared.'

'Of me?'

'Of you, of everything. They were living in a permanent state of fear. They were all slaves to their tech, and it was killing them. It was as if they had lost something.'

'But you changed it.'

Josh thought about the figure he'd seen in the aperture just before Johansson had detonated the bomb.

'Do you think someone could create a suit that would work like your parent's ship?'

She laughed. 'Did you see how much power that thing needed? Most of the ship was a field generator. I can't see how you could miniaturise that kind of technology into anything small enough to run in a car, let alone a suit.'

The colonel came crashing out of the bushes.

'I'm picking up a convergence half a mile east of here. Whatever it is, it's creating a huge temporal distortion in the chronosphere.'

Caitlin jumped up. 'Time to meet the father-in-law!' she said with a smile.

Josh didn't know which was scarier, her last comment or the fact that he was about to meet the dad he'd never known.

90

DAD

They followed the incandescent glow of the colonel's tachyon into the night. He moved quickly and quietly towards the 'waypoint,' as he called it.

Josh could feel the air charge with static as they approached. Ahead of them, he could see there was a strong magnetic field changing the nature of the space around it.

'Stay back!' ordered the colonel, going closer.

Ripples of energy coursed through the ground, the trees and plants, distorting everything until their structure seemed to collapse and break down into atoms. Through the centre of the swirling morass of molecules stepped a figure in a mirror suit, his face obscured by an elliptical helmet with two F's on the side.

'Timesuit,' was all Caitlin could manage before the stranger fired a weapon at the old man.

Josh pulled her behind a tree and clamped his hand over her mouth.

They could hear the hiss of the night air as it condensed on the superheated surface of the suit. An eerie calm descended as the stranger waited for the portal to collapse and the atomic structures of the surrounding fauna to stabilise. Josh watched them recombine into twisted caricatures of what they'd been before.

There was a series of clicks and whirrs from the servos on the suit before Josh heard footsteps moving away from the site. He counted to ten before looking out from behind the tree, and saw a dark silhouette of a man running across the lawns. The suit was still steaming, standing empty over the body of the colonel.

Josh let go of Caitlin and ran over to the colonel. He checked the old man's pulse, then took the lens out of his hand.

'Look after the old bugger,' he said, kissing her gently. 'And don't follow me. Okay?'

She nodded and knelt down beside the colonel.

Josh slowed when he reached the lights of the college. There was no sign of the stranger. He'd tried to keep him in view, but the guy was fast, and once he'd cleared the lawns it was impossible to see where he went.

Keeping one eye on the lens Josh walked into the entrance hall, allowing the alternate worlds to overlay his vision. There weren't as many as he'd expected. The stranger had gone straight up the stairs and onto the second floor in most of them. In one, where Josh had rushed ahead, the guy had waited for him to make the first-floor landing and taken him down. Not one of the scenarios showed Josh who the man was, and there was a part of him that wondered if it would be better not to know.

He followed the path that kept him safe. The lens showed

him the man entering his mother's room, and he could feel the rage building as he tried not to imagine what was about to happen next.

This was not going to be some casual one-night-stand.

The vision was blurred, a ghost-like trace, but he could see that his mother was comatose, lying on top of the bed still in her party clothes, the stranger standing over her with what looked like a knife.

Josh stood outside the bedroom, his heart hammering in his chest, one hand on the door. This was the moment he'd dreaded: to know what happened was hard enough, but knowing that if he did something about it — it could mean the end of him.

If he didn't allow this to happen, then he would never have existed, and maybe his mother would never have gotten ill. He put the lens away. Whatever was going to happen next, he didn't want to know what the other options could have been.

Josh took a deep breath then kicked the door open.

In the semi-darkness he could just make out the man on top of her. Something flashed in his hand as Josh entered, and then they were fighting.

He grabbed the stranger and slammed him against the wall. Blind rage took over, and he smashed his fists into the man's body. Surprise had given him the advantage, but his opponent was unusually strong and Josh found himself struggling to hold him.

And then he saw his face.

It was a much older version of his friend Lenin.

There was something wrong with his eyes, and in the moment that Josh hesitated Lenin knocked him off his feet and across the floor.

Lenin took out a gun and pointed it straight at Josh. There

were sounds, like a scanner, and Lenin scowled as he rechecked the settings on the device.

Josh leapt to his feet and took him out at the waist, knocking the weapon out of his hand.

The two crashed against the bookshelves and onto the floor, his mother's mementoes tumbling down on top of them as they grappled with each other.

Josh struggled to keep Lenin down, his punches seeming to have little effect on him. The cold look in his eyes showed no sign of recognition, no emotion, and he was like a machine, an immensely powerful robot.

Lenin got his hand around Josh's throat and pushed him back off his chest until he could stand, then in one swift motion he threw him across the room onto his mother's desk, which collapsed on impact.

In the few seconds that it took Josh to come to his senses, Lenin went over to the bed and picked up the blade he'd dropped. Josh watched in a daze as Lenin pulled up his mother's clothes and drove the steel into her stomach.

'No!' screamed Josh, grabbing Lenin's gun and pointing it at him.

'Josh?' Caitlin called from the corridor.

'In here!'

As Caitlin came through the door, Lenin jumped off the bed and crashed out through the window.

Josh went to follow him, but Caitlin held him back.

'Don't,' she said, holding his arm. 'We aren't supposed to interact.'

'He stabbed her!' Josh yelled, waving the gun at his mother's limp body.

Caitlin looked concerned and went over to check her.

'She's unconscious, but still breathing, and her pulse is fine.'

Josh came over and examined where he'd seen Lenin drive the blade into her. There was no blood, no sign of any kind of wound.

'I saw him,' he said in disbelief.

'What did it look like?'

'I don't know, like a knife — I guess.'

There were noises from down the hall as the students came out of their rooms to see what the commotion was.

'We have to go,' Caitlin pleaded. 'In a minute there are going to be too many questions to answer.'

She went over to the window and looked down.

'It's only one floor down onto the lawns... think you can make that?'

Josh looked at the comatose body of his mother.

'Come on, she'll be fine.'

No, she won't, thought Josh, following her out of the broken window.

'Where's the old man?' Josh asked when they got back to the clearing. The timesuit was gone, and so was the colonel.

'With my folks. They turned up after you left. My mother took some photos of the suit and then sent me to stop you from killing yourself.'

'I had to do something,' he said, and sighed. 'I thought he was going to kill her.'

Caitlin smiled and put her hand on his cheek. 'No, quite the opposite in fact.'

'But he didn't.' Josh found it hard to say the words. 'He didn't rape her... there wasn't time.' The idea that Lenin could have been his father sickened him.

'Yet you're still here.'

'So?'

'I think the knife was some kind of injector. I think he was inseminating your mother artificially.'

'What does that mean? I'm some kind of test-tube baby?'

Caitlin frowned. 'I don't know. Show me the gun.' She held out her hand.

Josh handed over the weapon. It looked like an old-fashioned pistol that had been heavily modified. There were additional buttons and dials fused along the wooden stock, as well as a small glass screen where the gunsight should have been.

'It's dead,' Josh told her. 'I tried to shoot him, but nothing happened.'

'Probably locked to his palm print.' She pointed at the handle. 'There's some crazy tech going on in this. It's built on antiques to survive the transition, but the way its put together is definitely from the future. Same with the suit — very steampunk.'

'So, someone sent him back to inject my mother?'

'Yeah, I'm pretty sure he wasn't your actual father.'

Josh looked relieved. 'Then we need to find out who is.'

'My parents thought you might say that.'

'Did they have any better ideas?' Josh asked, taking back the gun.

Caitlin looked nervously at the weapon. 'You're going to use that?'

'It's our only lead. We have to follow it.'

'But it's in the future. No one has ever travelled beyond the frontier.'

The lines of energy were unravelling as Josh felt the weapon's timeline open. He could see paths that led beyond the present: they glowed with a different light, a pale effervescent blue that wove out into the maelstrom.

'Do you trust me?' he asked, holding out his hand.

'Yes,' she said, smirking. 'You are the Paradox, after all.'

'So, let's find out what that means.'

He opened the furthest node and took them both into it.

To be continued...

ESCHATON

The adventure continues in book three...

Other books in the Infinity Engines universe.

The Infinity Engines

1. Anachronist

2. Maelstrom

3. Eschaton

4. Aeons

5. Tesseract

6. Contagion

Infinity Engines Origins

Chimæra

Changeling

Infinity Engines Missions

1776

1888

You can download 1776 for FREE plus get updates and news by subscribing to my mailing list (simply scan the QR code below).

ACKNOWLEDGMENTS

Thanks to my lovely family, as always I am so grateful for all your support and understanding.

To all those who helped this along the way: Aaron, Jez, Andrew, Mark and the many others who have put up with my witterings - I owe you all a beer or two.

During the writing of this book I lost my father. Not something I expected ever to have to write, and to be honest I still don't quite believe it's happened. He was a good dad, and a wonderful grandfather — he is still very much part of our lives and a lot of him is in these books.

Just a shame he never got to read them.

I miss you every day dad.

A.x

ABOUT THE AUTHOR

For more information about Andy and The Infinity Engines series please visit: www.infinityengines.com

Please don't forget to leave a review!

Thank you!

- facebook.com/infinityengines
- x.com/infinityengines
- instagram.com/infinityengines

Made in the USA
Las Vegas, NV
28 March 2024

87847062R00245